BATTLESAURUS

Rampage at Waterloo

BRIAN FALKNER

BATTLE

SAURUS

Rampage at Waterloo

Farrar Straus Giroux
New York

Farrar Straus Giroux Books for Young Readers
175 Fifth Avenue, New York 10010

Copyright © 2015 by Brian Falkner
All rights reserved
Printed in the United States of America
Designed by Andrew Arnold
First edition, 2015
1 3 5 7 9 10 8 6 4 2

macteenbooks.com

Library of Congress Cataloging-in-Publication Data
Falkner, Brian.
    Battlesaurus : rampage at Waterloo / Brian Falkner.
        pages cm
    Summary: In this alternate history, Napoleon wins at Waterloo by
unleashing a secret battlefield weapon—a legion of giant, carnivorous
dinosaurs imported from the wilds of the Americas—and only
fifteen-year-old Willem Verheyen stands in the way of the emperor's
plan for world domination.
    ISBN 978-0-374-30075-3 (hardback)
    ISBN 978-0-374-30076-0 (e-book)
    [1. War—Fiction. 2. Magicians—Fiction. 3. Dinosaurs—Fiction.
4. Napoleon I, Emperor of the French, 1769–1821—Fiction. 5. France—
History—Consulate and First Empire, 1799–1815—Fiction. 6. Science
fiction.] I. Title.

PZ7.F1947Bat 2015
[Fic]—dc23

2014040677

Farrar Straus Giroux Books for Young Readers may be purchased for business or
promotional use. For information on bulk purchases please contact Macmillan
Corporate and Premium Sales Department at (800) 221-7945 x5442 or by email at
specialmarkets@macmillan.com.

*For Kathleen, a wonderful lady and
a very special friend*

PROLOGUE
February 17, 1815

THE PRISONER
OF ELBA

The letter arrives by boat.

It arrives at night on a small schooner that should not be traveling these waters in the darkness, but the urgency of the situation has been pressed on the captain and he has reluctantly agreed.

The letter arrives in a canvas sack with other mail, for other residents of the island, and is handed ashore by a ten-year-old ship's boy who knows nothing of the contents. The sack is passed to a shorehand, roused from sleep just a few minutes earlier and still bleary-eyed from the aftereffects of a half bottle of nut liquor. He likewise has no idea that simply by taking the letter, he is striking a flint that will set the world on fire.

Indeed the only person on the island with any idea of the contents of the letter stepped ashore from the schooner just moments earlier. A major of the Imperial Guard, Marc Thibault is a veteran of more than seventy campaigns, with an earring of gold and handsome sideburns. He is armed with a short saber and a flintlock pistol, and is an expert with both.

Few documents would warrant such an escort, and furthermore the major is not alone, but is accompanied by two trustworthy grenadiers, with matching earrings and sideburns, sound of heart, keen of eye, and well hardened in battle.

The ship has brought other provisions, perhaps to disguise the real purpose of its trip, and the three soldiers wait under the lamplights as these are loaded, along with the mail sack, into the back of the goods cart.

A rough-edged sign on the front of the harbormaster's office declares the name of the town: Cavo. In reality it is little more than a collection of ramshackle huts and trading posts, centered on a series of long wooden jetties. The jetties are old and sagging as if melted by the heat of the island's summers, although the true culprit is rot and decay. By day, dogs fight over scraps and old fishermen snore under awnings. Even the winter sun is fierce on Elba.

There are bigger, more modern wharves at the island's capital, Portoferraio, but the arrival of the schooner there, at this time of night, might have attracted the eyes of the king's men.

Once loaded, the goods cart sets off for the residence of the island's reluctant ruler. The three soldiers follow on mounts that the harbormaster has scrambled to provide.

The escape of the prisoner of Elba has begun.

The world is about to burst into flames.

Book One

THE COMING OF THE BEASTS

March 3–April 4, 1815

THE BOY WHO BRINGS THE BREAD

The boy who brings the bread is Willem Verheyen.

This is not true.

His name is Pieter Geerts, but neither he, nor his mother, nor anyone in the world has used that name in so long that it is just a distant reflection of a life that once was.

Willem was born on the first day of the first month of the new century. When he was just seven years old, he saved the life of a village girl from a bloodthirsty raptor.

There are many dangerous animals in the forests of Europe, wolves, bears, and boars among them. But these animals have learned to fear man and do not attack unless threatened. Only raptors—large, meat-eating saurs—regard man as prey. Of all the raptors, the largest and most terrifying is the firebird: a huge, vicious beast, feathered like a bird. When stretched to full height, it is almost as tall as a man. Few people have faced a firebird and survived. It can kill with its teeth, its talons, or the terrible claws on its strong hind legs. But seven-year-old Willem, alone, faced such a creature to save the girl's life. That is a secret he keeps to himself.

Today, eight years later, Willem will again face a firebird, but he does not know that yet.

Willem quietly opens the gate to the house of the village healer, Madame Gertruda.

The girl he saved, Héloïse, is sleeping in the garden. She uncoils herself at the base of a tree and hisses at Willem as he shuts the gate behind him. She is a scrawny thing with wild brambles of hair, wearing just a plain woolen smock despite the chill of the early spring air.

He steps warily. She once launched herself at him without provocation, scratching and biting, spilling his breads in the herb garden.

Héloïse does not attack. She crouches in the garden as he knocks on the door of the cottage. He waits. Madame Gertruda is old and slow.

It is his second-to-last delivery. Only the schoolmaster's house remains, then Willem will be free to go and practice his act for the fête.

The basket is mostly empty and so is his purse. Those who cannot afford their morning baguette get one anyway. Those who can pay will do so when they have money. Those who cannot are still human beings, according to his mother.

A cat emerges from the side of the house and curls around his legs, rubbing its face on his shins. Two nervous microsaurus skitter among the herbs of the garden. Madame Gertruda is a magnet for sick and homeless animals.

Shuffling footsteps sound behind the door. The moment it opens, Héloïse picks up the cat and slips past him, past the healer, into the house.

Madame Gertruda is old, far older than any other person he knows. Her face is ridged as if worms have nested under her skin. Her hair is thin and white.

She glares and spits at him as she opens the door. Madame Gertruda has good days and bad days. This is clearly a bad day. Last night was no better, if Héloïse was sleeping in the garden.

Madame Gertruda is Flemish, like Willem, a minority in the

village. But her position in the village is secure. The villagers cannot live without their healer.

She offers no coin for the bread. She never does. But nor did she demand payment when Willem's mother brought him to her, blue in the face and gushing green phlegm. She asks for nothing, and wants for nothing.

He hands the healer a baguette.

"I do not want your filthy crust," she says, in French. Some days she remembers that he speaks Flemish, but most days she forgets.

"Good morning, madame, and good morning also to the mademoiselle," Willem replies.

Héloïse's face appears in a wisp of morning twilight dancing in the shadows inside the house. She snarls at him like a dog.

Madame Gertruda snatches the bread out of his hands and slams the door in his face.

Today is definitely a bad day.

Willem passes the church on his way to the schoolmaster's house, across the road from the schoolhouse in the far corner of the village.

The village is old. It is small, just a strip of stone cottages alongside the river with some newer, larger houses around a communal square. It is surrounded, to the south and east, by fields of rye, oats, and barley, from which the village derives most of its income. To the north and west march the tall, dense trees of the vast Sonian Forest.

The saur-fence that protects the village is also old, and in need of repair: a series of high wooden poles, crossbraced by diagonal supports with sharpened ends that protrude through the fence to discourage nosy or hungry raptors. In more than one place the fence sags where the supports have cracked or rotted and have not been replaced.

Outside the saur-fence, in the narrow strip that runs between the fence and the river, are long patches of lavender that, on humid spring days, waft a heady scent over the entire village.

Some say that lavender keeps saurs away, and that might be true, because there have been no raptor attacks in the village itself. But that might also be due to the fact that there are very few dangerous saurs left in Wallonia.

Jean and François are waiting by the gate of the schoolmaster's house. Cousins who look like brothers, with thick necks and arms from countless hours of cutting wood (François) or hammering in his father's smithy (Jean). Jean is the younger but larger of the two.

François looks as though he is ready for work, with a heavy ax across his shoulders, hooked with both arms. Jean carries a crossbow in a sling on his back. He made the crossbow himself, hammering the tempered steel of the spring on his father's anvil.

"You march to war?" Willem asks.

Jean laughs. "Of a sort."

"We're hunting eggs for the fête," François says.

"Saur eggs?"

"No, hens' eggs," Jean says, placing his hand on the stock of his crossbow. "But we are ready lest we encounter any angry chickens."

Willem laughs.

"Come with us," François says.

"Pierre says there is a raptor nest by the waterfall," Jean says.

"Maybe even a firebird," François adds, with a gleam to his eye.

"A firebird!" Willem says.

"You sound scared," François says.

"You should be," Willem says.

"Scared? We have ax and bow," Jean says.

"And that is what scares me the most," Willem says. "And I need to practice my act for the fête."

"Ah, the soon-to-be-famous magician." Jean laughs.

"The festival is a week away. Perhaps it is courage that you need to practice," François says.

"Come with us, Willem. You can practice on the way," Jean says.

"This is my last delivery," Willem says. "Let me think on it."

He pushes open the gate. The door of the schoolmaster's house opens and Angélique Delvaux emerges—seventeen, bleary-eyed, tumble-haired, still in her sleeping frock. She comes down the steps with her arms wrapped around herself against the chill and presses a coin into his hand as she takes the last baguette.

She smiles through sleepy, blinky eyes, and the touch of her fingers lingers. It is no accident, but nor does it signify anything deeper. Angélique simply knows, and enjoys, the effect she has on men, on him.

She turns back at the top of the stairs and waves.

Jean and François wave back in unison, gawking, a pair of fairground clowns.

The door closes, but Angélique appears a moment later at the window, opening the shutters to let in the morning sun.

"It seems only a few months ago that she was but a skinny sapling, all branches and twigs," François says.

"Now the trunk is full and well formed," Willem says.

Angélique shivers and wraps her arms around herself again. The action presses her breasts against the fabric of her thin frock.

"And the fruit is ripe," Jean says.

Willem laughs but François says, "Take care of your tongue, cousin, lest it catch the ear of God."

"I am sure He has more pressing concerns," Jean says.

"Still"—François claps his cousin on the shoulder—"you would not want to reach the afterlife to find there is no place for you in His kingdom."

"A god that would punish me eternally for a few words in jest is no god of mine," Jean says.

François laughs, but Willem sees him make the sign of the cross behind his cousin's back.

They cut across the school yard, back toward Willem's house.

"So come hunting with us," Jean says.

"Have no fear, we will protect you from any dangerous saurs," François says.

"Or any chickens," Jean says.

"I will meet you at the river bridge," Willem says, making up his mind. "If you two fools do find a firebird, someone will have to protect you."

The cousins laugh loudest of all at that. Willem laughs along with them. But his words are not spoken in jest.

Jean and François are big, strong, and well armed. But that will not be enough. Not against a raptor.

If they find one, they will need Willem.

ASCENSION

In 1807, on the eve of the feast of Ascension, Willem, just seven years old, wandered alone in the forest, his eyes red with tears that he wanted to hide from the boys who had waylaid him outside the church. His face bore the marks of their fists.

He had with him one of his father's illusions, and his mood was dark.

They say that saurs cannot be trained. They are too stupid, too smart, too primal, too evil. But Willem's father, the Great Geerts, the most famous magician of his day, had found a way.

Geerts had discovered that a saur could be mesmerized, like a lizard, and in that spellbound state, it could be taught simple tricks. After years of refining his techniques, he had been able to include a trained microsaurus as part of his act, enthralling the audience with a new kind of magic. When Willem was old enough to learn, his father had taught him the techniques. Willem had used the knowledge on several occasions, making friends with the small saurs of the forest—at times his only friends.

He only ever used the skills for amusement.

But now he would find a saur. Nothing too dangerous, a microraptor or a groundhawk. He would mesmerize and train the saur. Then he would set it loose on his assailants.

He found no saurs. Not even a dragonrat. But a saur found him. The largest and most dangerous of all the known saurs.

Some inner sense, or maybe an odd sound, warned him, and he had just enough time to climb high into a tree, his heart pounding, a rush of blood thrumming in his ears, before the raptor bounded out from a patch of bush, its neck quivering, the air filled with a deep screeching sound.

A large, lizard-like creature, taller than Willem, with a long, rounded snout and small, pointed teeth like rows of thorns: a firebird. A sheaf of long feathers extended from each arm as if God had intended it to be a bird but had changed His mind. From each of its great feet protruded a terrible hooked claw. Plumage covered the body of the beast, in flame-like bands of red, yellow, and orange. A comb of spiky, rust-colored feathers jutted back from its head.

It may have just been the imagination of a young boy, but the eyes of the creature seemed to radiate evil. Bright yellow with pure black pupils, those eyes watched him as he scrabbled for a perch in the slender, high branches of the tree. It twitched its head from side to side like a bird, staring at him. But unlike a bird, it was unable to fly, or even climb the tree to get at him.

Willem dared not try to mesmerize this beast. To do that he would have to climb down from the tree and the firebird would have him before his feet touched the ground. There was nothing he could do but wait.

For hours he was trapped in the tree, the firebird circling below.

Around him the forest was silent, as if the usual birds and small creatures that roamed the area were aware of the predator and had moved to safety.

Then the firebird cocked its head, hearing something that Willem could not. It stood on one leg for a moment, then, perhaps seeking easier prey than the boy, it moved slowly away, blending with the brush of the forest.

Willem's first thought was one of relief. While the raptor was distracted he might be able to slip away unnoticed. But then he heard voices. It was not a deer or a boar that approached. It was people. Even so he was saved. While the raptor attacked them he would be able to escape.

Even as this thought passed through his mind he felt a deep shame, revulsion at his own cowardice. He opened his mouth to warn the approaching people of the terror that lay in wait for them. But he had hesitated a moment too long. He watched with horror from his high vantage point as a mother and daughter came strolling along the path. The mother held a basket, perhaps gathering flowers or berries for the next day's feast.

Now he found his voice, but it was already too late.

With two quick steps the firebird emerged from the bush and blocked the path.

The mother was Madame Libert, the wife of a farmer.

The daughter was Héloïse, then a puff-cheeked six-year-old, her hair yet to lose its baby blondness.

Again came the deep screeching sound.

The mother stopped, her eyes filled with terror that quickly turned into a haunted resignation. There was no way to fight, and no way to flee. On this day, at this time, she had taken a path that led only to a catastrophe, for both herself and her daughter.

There was no hope, and yet with a mother's instincts she pushed the girl behind her.

"Run," she whispered, and when the little girl did not move, she shouted, "Run!"

Héloïse turned and took a couple of stumbling steps down the path. Willem watched her run. He saw the mother swing the basket at the raptor as it approached, and how easily the beast dodged it, with rapid, darting movements. He watched Héloïse freeze in

15

horror as she looked back to see the body of her mother jerking on the ground, her throat in the jaws of the meat-eater.

Not content with the mother, the raptor released her, dying but not yet dead.

Lying on the path, looking up at the trees, her throat torn out, Madame Libert's eyes met Willem's.

The firebird was distracted, and it had other prey to chase. Willem could have escaped.

But her eyes would not allow him to.

Now Héloïse turned and tried again to run, but her legs were small; she was young and slow. The firebird was quick and vicious. It would be a bloody, violent death.

Until a shaking, terrified, seven-year-old boy jumped from his tree between the raptor and the girl. The raptor slewed to a halt, surprised at this sudden appearance.

Neither Willem nor his father had ever attempted to mesmerize a meat-eater of this size. They were simply too dangerous.

Nevertheless, on this most terrible day of days, Willem stepped into the path of the firebird armed with nothing more than a simple conjuring trick.

He expected only to die, and hoped he was spending his life wisely, buying time for the girl, to allow her to escape. To survive.

But God must have been watching this place, at this time, for He gave the firebird pause, and in those few heartbeats, face-to-face with the creature, Willem was able to produce the illusion, the mesmerizing technique. And in a strange kind of miracle, it worked.

With the beast motionless on the path in front of him, Willem stepped even closer, doing nothing to rouse it from its trance-like state.

Close enough to touch the thorny teeth, he took a small pouch from around his neck. A pouch his father had insisted he always wear in the forest.

He emptied it into his palm and, leaning even closer to the snout of the creature, he blew sharply.

A cloud of fine pepper enveloped the beast's head and Willem leaped backward as a thousand tiny grains stung the delicate membranes of the creature's evil, yellow eyes.

It bellowed in agony, thrashing its head around, trying to shake away the pain, wiping at its eyes with claw-like hands.

Blinded and enraged it lunged once, twice, three times at Willem, but its jaws only snapped shut on air where Willem had been.

It turned and ran, stumbling from the path. It disappeared into the forest, careering from tree to tree in blinded rage.

Amazed that he was still alive, Willem took off after the girl.

He couldn't find her.

Afterward he returned and held the hand of Madame Libert as the light faded from her eyes. It was the light of gratitude and unbearable debt. He told her the truth as she was dying. That he could have saved them both. If he had not been selfish. If he had been braver. She must not have understood him, because there was no anger, nor condemnation in her eyes. So he told her again, tearfully apologizing for the cost of her life.

Still the light of gratitude shone.

A few days later the firebird was seen near Brussels, on the other side of the forest, and killed by a hunting party.

Héloïse was not seen for almost six years, and it was assumed that she had died, alone in the forest. But one morning she had returned, standing silently at the saur-gate, dressed only in rags, almost unrecognizable. Her father had left the village by then, and no one knew where he had gone, or how to find him. Madame Gertruda, the healer, had taken Héloïse in, but she was not the same girl she had been. At twelve, she was more like a wild creature of the forest than a girl from the village. Snarling, scratching, biting, untamable, like the saurs.

She spoke little at first, but slowly, with the healer's patient help, her language returned. When asked about the missing years, she was silent. Question her further and she would revert to the wild form, hissing and baring her teeth.

Some said she had lived among the animals.

Some said she had been found by residents of a neighboring village and kept as a slave.

Some said she had lived underground, in vast secret caves that were thought to underlie the forest.

Only Héloïse knew.

MAGICIAN

The mayor of the village is working in the kitchen when Willem arrives home. Willem sees him through the window and girds himself to be polite and respectful. The mayor is a friend of his mother.

Monsieur Claude often comes around when Willem is at school, or picking up supplies in Waterloo. Sometimes the mayor helps Willem's mother with heavy chores, but too often he comes around when there is no work that needs doing.

Monsieur Claude is a handsome, gray-haired gentleman in his fifties. He is married and owns nearly half the village. He is well liked and generous to those who cannot afford their rent. He is also, from what Willem can see, a capable mayor, a position that involves being postmaster, banker, justice of the peace, and village administrator.

Willem feels that he understands why his mother is "friends" with Monsieur Claude. She is still in her thirties, and her husband—Willem's father—has been dead for more than three years. She cannot wear a mourning coat for the rest of her life.

But of all the men in the village to be friends with, he wishes she had picked anyone other than Monsieur Claude. There is something in his mother's eyes that he doesn't like, after Monsieur Claude has visited. A certain look on her face. It is as though she has just scratched an insect bite and it has stopped itching, but has started to bleed.

Whenever Willem delivers bread to the mayor's house, the mayor's wife, Madame Claude, a stout, stern woman who smells strongly of rosewater, narrows her eyes, raises her nose in the air, and overpays for the bread. It is her way of showing her superiority.

Willem always accepts the coins graciously, but he thinks his mother is worth more than being the mayor's mistress.

Monsieur Claude smiles at him through the window as he walks past the kitchen. Willem returns the smile but stones are gathering in his stomach. Having the mayor in the house complicates things. His mother will not approve of Willem, or the cousins, venturing into the forest to seek a raptor's nest. Even if they do not find a raptor, it will be dangerous. There are wolves, bears, and snakes in the forest. Willem and his mother will argue, which will be difficult enough without having the audience of an outsider.

Monsieur Claude is alone in the kitchen.

"She is upstairs," he says. He is mixing dough in a large bowl with a wooden paddle. That is usually Willem's job, and although it is hard, physical work that he hates, he resents Monsieur Claude for doing it in his place.

Willem throws the bread basket in the corner as his pet microsaurus, Pieter, darts out from beneath a chair and chatters under his feet. The creature is about the size of a ferret or a large rat. His front legs are smaller than his rear, and he uses them as arms, only walking on them if he is foraging. His snout is short and beak-like, and his skin is banded with brown and green.

Willem bounds up the stairs two at a time and goes straight to his mother's bedroom, but she is not there. With a sinking feeling he creeps toward his own room, the microsaurus underfoot. His mother is sitting on his bed, unmoving and unspeaking, but he can sense her anger from the rigid way she holds her head. Then he sees the open door to his closet.

Willem's mother is a French-speaking Walloon, from Wallonia in the Southern Netherlands. His father was from Flanders, to the north. He was a magician, a conjurer of some reputation, who performed in the royal courts of Europe and was a favorite of Napoléon Bonaparte, the French emperor. But during one engagement at the Tuileries Palace in Paris, he did something to incur the emperor's displeasure. What it was, Willem does not know. It was never discussed. But such was the nature of the emperor that his displeasure quickly turned to wrath and Willem's father fled Paris. His disappearance from the palace and escape to Wallonia was perhaps his greatest conjuring trick of all.

It is said that Napoléon smashed crystal goblets and hurled crockery through palace windows when he heard of the magician's flight.

The family was forced into hiding. Willem's mother was the daughter of a baker and that had lent them their disguise. His father shaved off his beard, grew his hair in the Walloon style, and under his wife's tutelage the Great Geerts became Monsieur Verheyen, the baker.

The costumes and equipment and other magic trickery were sealed into chests and never spoken of, lest someone in the village should discover the true identity of the simple baker and his well-spoken but humble wife.

For a Flemish family, hiding in Wallonia was a masterpiece of misdirection. For years the emperor's men scoured Flanders, never suspecting that their quarry was hiding in French-speaking Wallonia, almost within sight of the French border.

The choice of village was clever for other reasons too. It lay on the edge of the Sonian Forest, and on the other side of the forest was the city of Brussels. Should they ever be discovered, they could steal away through the trees of the forest and lose themselves again in the bustling streets of the city.

It was a brilliant deception from a master magician.

For six years they lived peacefully in the village, hoping that the time would come when the shadow of the emperor no longer hovered over them.

And that day drew closer. Slowly Napoléon's empire crumbled. Then came his final defeat and exile to the island of Elba.

But Willem's father did not live to see that. Not even a master magician was a match for the dangerous beasts that roamed the Sonian Forest. At the funeral, his coffin had to be weighted with river stones. Willem was told there was barely enough left of the body to fill a hatbox.

Although hidden from the world, his father's chests were a constant source of mystery and wonderment to young Willem.

Many times he sat and stared at them, his mind hardly daring to imagine what magic and treasures lay inside. After the death of his father, he opened them often, dressing himself in cloaks that were far too large for him, wondering at the secrets of the hats and the pouches. Then he found the letter. It had fallen down inside one of the chests and only a corner of the paper protruded from behind a sack of potions. Perhaps it had originally been placed on top.

To my son.

It was a letter written in case the father was no longer around when the boy was grown to a man.

The letter outlined the boy's inheritance. The magic contained in the boxes. Willem read it with breathless excitement. It was many pages long and detailed the ways of the magician: the Glorpy, the French Drop, and even the Guillotine. It explained the powders and the potions, how to use them, how to make them. And the secrets of the grand illusions.

Willem kept the letter from his mother. She would not approve. But in quiet times, when she was out, or asleep, he taught himself the secrets of the chests. He learned the ways of the magician. But the tricks he performed were only for himself.

"Willem."

"Mother."

"What is this?"

"My illusions. I will perform them at the fête."

The apparatuses and powders for those tricks now lie on the floor in front of him, removed from his closet, where he had hidden them.

"You will not," she says. She unwinds her fingers from the silver chain at her neck and places her hands flat on the bed beside her.

"It is the spring festival, Mother!"

"Your father forbade it."

"Monsieur Claude promised he would not tell you of this," Willem says with a contemptuous glance down toward the kitchen.

"Monsieur Claude knew of this?" His mother's eyes narrow to slits.

So the mayor has at least kept Willem's secret.

"Then how . . . ?" Willem asks.

"Jean's mother told me you were to perform at the fête," his mother says. "You do not sing, you do not dance, you do not pipe or fiddle, and you said nothing of this to me. It was not difficult to deduce what your performance would be."

Willem shrugs.

"She said you are to be the final act," she says.

"Jean's mouth works harder than his brain," Willem says.

"Have you forgotten your father's rules?" his mother asks. Her voice rises. "Have you so soon forgotten your father?"

Willem takes a deep breath.

"I have not forgotten him, Mother, nor will I ever. But he is no longer here to make such rules. I am fifteen. I am old enough to make rules for myself."

"If you really were old enough, you would understand the need for prudence."

He reaches out and touches a finger to her lips. "You speak of prudence, so hush, lest your voice carry to the man in our kitchen."

The mention of the mayor makes her angrier. She shakes his finger away, and her voice rises further.

"A child must obey his mother," she says.

Willem keeps his tone and his volume low and even. "This is true. But I am no longer a child. You are my mother, and I love and respect you. But in return, you must respect that I am now grown. I no longer wish to cower and hide like a rat in a hedgerow."

She looks away, and after a moment her voice softens.

"You cannot bring him back by becoming him," she says.

It hurts him that she would say this. That she would even think that is the reason for his actions.

"I am not a fool," he says.

"Then don't act like one," she says. "The rules are to protect you, not to punish you."

"I am a man. I can protect myself."

There is a moment of silence, but it is a calm before a storm.

She stands and raises her hands in the air. "A man? You are a barely formed boy, and you have no comprehension of the powers that will array against you. You would undo us both with your childish desire for attention."

Pieter, the microsaurus, now runs behind Willem, alarmed at the outburst. He peers at her from between Willem's legs.

"We hide from the little emperor, but where is he now?" Willem asks. "A prisoner on a remote island."

"The man yet lives. When he no longer draws breath, then we may emerge from our hole in the world."

"I am grateful for your advice, Mother, but I will make my own decisions," Willem says, folding his arms.

"I forbid it," she says.

"That is no longer your right," he says. "I am grown." He shuts his eyes and takes a deep breath. "But more than that, I am a magician. It is in my blood and my blood burns for it. I will put on a show at the fête, and you shall say no more about it."

She looks strangely at him, shocked by this sudden display of will. Perhaps, he thinks, she sees his father in him.

She begins to cry, a woman's trick to get her way when reason and logic have prevailed. Even so it softens him, and he is on the verge of relenting.

But a steely resolution comes over him. This is his fate, his future. Will he remain a simple baker all his life? No! Fate has great things in store for him, he knows it, and they do not involve hauling sacks of flour and delivering baguettes.

He will not be swayed by the tears of a woman.

He collects a leather satchel from the floor and lifts a silk pouch off the headboard of his bed. "Come, Pieter," he says, and the tiny saur jumps up onto the bed, then scampers up his arm onto his shoulder.

"Where are you going?" she asks.

"I go where I want and do as I wish," he says. "And I will be back when I am ready."

He leaves her crying and goes calmly down the stairs, taking a baguette from the warming tray and walking out of the house without a word to his mother's lover.

It only occurs to him much later that maybe he has misunderstood the tears.

THE HUNT

Pieter goes rigid, raising himself up to his full height and balancing by placing his front feet on the side of Willem's head. His tail curls around Willem's neck. He makes a low clacking sound and his head flicks from side to side.

"Hush!" Willem says.

Jean and François stop and look back at him.

"Pieter's heard something," Willem says.

The little microsaurus perched on Willem's shoulder is very sensitive to sounds, smells, even vibrations on the forest floor. He is a good harbinger of danger.

Pieter repeats the clacking sound and goes very still.

François lifts his ax off his shoulders and holds it in front of him. Jean unslings his crossbow and loads it. The bolt glints in a sharp rod of sunlight stabbing through a gap in the tree canopy.

Willem does nothing. Pieter is just listening and sniffing the air. If there is danger, it is not yet close by.

The forest soars around them, giant oaks, firs, and beeches. Birds swoop and dart. Great winged saurs glide high above them. A breeze tiptoes through the upper branches, and the leaves whisper secrets of the trees that only Pieter can understand.

They set out from the river bridge over an hour ago and are now deep within the forest. For part of the trip they followed a stream. At a mighty oak, wider than Willem is tall, they veered off up a steep slope and along a ridgeline where new, slender trunks are evidence of a recent fire. Rain, or the geography of the forest, must have limited the fire to the ridgeline, and this section of the trail is hard going. The regrowth has brought with it dense underbrush that scratches and snaps at their legs as they push through it. Each footstep brings up the cloudy scent of damp earth and the sour perfume of rotting leaves.

After a moment Pieter relaxes, sitting back down on his haunches and playing with Willem's ear.

"Nothing?" François asks.

"Something," Willem says. "But it has moved away."

"What was it?" Jean asks.

"Only Pieter knows," Willem says. "Boar, wolf, deer. It could have been anything."

That isn't quite true. Pieter would have reacted a little differently had it been a boar or a wolf. From the way his whole body stiffened, whatever he sensed was a saur.

It is out of range now, but that does not mean it is not hunting them.

Willem reaches inside his satchel, checking once again that his father's apparatus is still there. It was when he had last checked and the time before that. But still he feels comforted by the presence of the two oval containers.

They set off once again, François in front. This is his way. Jean, with nothing to prove, follows, and Willem brings up the rear.

The cousins are alike but different in many ways. Some of that comes from their fathers. The brothers had spent too many years on the battlefields of Europe, in the service of Napoléon. Whatever they had seen, whatever they had done, it had driven one of the brothers closer to God, and turned the other from His sight. The sons follow their fathers. François is a pious and committed Christian, while Jean is a Sunday worshipper and in great danger of going to hell, according to his cousin.

They are different in other ways also. They both brandish mustaches; however, François's is soft and thin, like the saplings of the ridgeline, while Jean's is thick and coarse, like the old oaks of the forest. The cousins are both strong, but Jean is the taller and brawnier of the two, despite François's many hours swinging the ax. Their fathers being so similar, that difference may have come from their mothers' sides, for Jean's mother is a large and sturdy woman, robust in body and tongue, while the preacher's wife is a delicate flower given to long sullen moods and bouts of inexplicable anger and tears.

Willem was not always friends with the cousins. They are Walloon. Within a few weeks of his arrival in the village they waylaid him on the river path, simply because he was Flemish. They were big, strong boys even then. They beat him bloody, then dragged him to the riverbank and held his head under water until he blacked out. He was six years old.

He did not make it easy for them though. He fought back, hard, kicking and biting, leaving Jean with a permanent scar on the corner of his mouth. Nor did Willem cry. Not once.

It only happened twice more before he earned their grudging respect, and that slowly turned into friendship. That stopped the other beatings too. Once he came under the wing of the Lejeune cousins nobody else dared to touch him, not even the older children in the village.

Willem does not have the height nor the breadth of the other two, yet there is a wiry strength about him, and a cunning that would win games and fights that strength alone would not. He is also quick of hand and fleet of foot, and can step and run his way out of trouble if it comes to that—and it often does.

For although Willem, Jean, and François are the closest of friends, there is a rambunctious nature to the two cousins, and brawling usually only ends when there is blood.

"How is Mademoiselle Héloïse this morning?" Jean asks. "Did she try to eat you again?"

"Maybe we should have brought her with us." Willem laughs. "In case we do find this saur. It would surely run from her."

"François would have liked that," Jean says. "He yearns for more time alone with the wild girl."

"I think you dip a brush in your own heart and paint me with it," François says.

"Ah, cousin, but I am not the one who dallies by her gate, or feigns illness to gain her attentions." Jean laughs.

"It was a gash from a falling tree," François says, fingering a long scar on his forearm. "You would rather I bled to death?"

"It was but a scratch from a twig," Jean says.

"I saw this wound after it became infected," Willem says. "Without Madame Gertruda's poultice, you would have lost that arm, or your life."

"True, but my cousin is always correct, even when he is not," François scoffs. "I should take his counsel and seek Héloïse's hand in marriage without delay."

"You would not survive the wedding night," Jean says. "Your skin is not thick enough for her claws."

"There are ways to tame the wildest of beasts," François says.

"Not a saur. No one has ever tamed a saur," Jean says.

"Willem has," François says.

"Pieter? That is but a dog without fur," Jean says. "Even I could teach tricks to a microsaurus."

"Then why have you not?" François asks.

Jean does not answer that. Instead he asks, "And what tricks would you teach your new bride?"

The ribbing continues as they follow the ridgeline down to another stream, simmering coldly through rounded boulders.

François's fondness for Héloïse is easy to see, although he denies it vigorously. They have one thing in common, a soft heart for wounded animals. He often brings her injured creatures that he finds in the forest. Still, Willem is unsure whether François really does have feelings for the wild girl, or whether she is just another of his projects.

As far as Willem can see, Héloïse holds no return affection for François. But even if she does, he is not sure if she is capable of showing it.

Jean squats and puts two fingers in the water as if he can tell something about the movement of the water by doing so.

"Just a couple of kilometers more," he says.

"Which way?" Willem asks.

"Downstream," Jean says. "This takes us directly to the waterfall."

Pieter is becoming restless, stretching up and looking around, and shifting uncomfortably on Willem's shoulder. Willem lifts him down and sets him by the stream for a drink, but he ignores it and scurries back up Willem's arm to his perch.

"He seems nervous," François says.

"A little," Willem says. "I think he can smell something."

"A raptor won't stray too far from her nest, if there are eggs," Jean says. "So we must be cautious as we approach."

"I think Jean also is nervous." François laughs.

"Not nervous, just careful," Jean says.

"Do not worry, cousin," François says. "I will take great care of your crossbow if you die."

"It is not the raptor I am scared of," Jean says. "It is facing your mother when I return with just chewed-up scraps of her son for her to bury."

"Now you are making me hungry," François says. "Let us quickly replenish ourselves with water and bread, before facing the beast."

The talk of François's mother reminds Willem of the argument with his own mother. He is an only child, of an only parent. They are outsiders in the village, sharing a secret they can reveal to no others. He knows they have to support each other, and so he tries not to fight with her. But more and more he is feeling the pull of his own path through life, no longer a child hiding behind his mother's skirts. Even so, he knows he must go back and apologize before the rift widens to a chasm.

"We are so close, and you choose to snooze," Jean says.

"I merely wish to face it with food in my belly and strength in my arm," François says.

"He is right," Willem says. "We are better rested and revived."

"You are both clucky little ducks," Jean says, but Willem can tell that he also is glad of a break and a meal.

Willem has the baguette. Jean has a stick of hard cheese, and François has brought sausage. François slices the meat with a hunting knife he wears on his belt and they share the food, scooping up the cool water of the stream to wash down the dry fare.

Willem picks leaves off nearby trees and feeds them to Pieter, who holds them with both front claws, his head still twitching from side to side, scanning for danger.

François brings out his pipe while they eat and takes tobacco from a small pouch.

"No," Willem says.

"Each day you sound more like my mother," François says.

"If you fill the air of the forest with smoke, then Pieter will not be able to smell a predator," Willem says.

"Yes, Mama," François says, and he puts away his pipe and tobacco.

The stream cuts a clearing through the forest and sun pours into it, sparking off bursting bubbles in the water. It is only March but the heat of the day rises, and Willem finds he is sweating heavily.

"If we do not find this nest," Willem says, "then this whole morning is a waste of time."

"It is an adventure," Jean says. "And adventure is never a waste of time."

"Willem still worries about his act for the fête," François says.

"Is that the reason for his weak spirit?" Jean asks. "Why do you insist on these pipe dreams, Willem? There are many real jobs out there, even for a riverweed like you."

"These tricks conceal the devil's hand," François says.

"You will never be a famous magician," Jean says. "That is not possible for a boy from Gaillemarde."

"Why not?" Willem asks. "Why can I not be whatever I want to be?"

"You can." François smiles. "But you must want to be something sensible. And useful."

"I pity your lack of vision and ambition," Willem says, feeling that this is uncomfortably close to the conversation he just had with his mother.

Jean and François exchange glances.

"He's a feisty little dog," François says.

"All right, Willem." Jean sighs. "Come on. Practice your tricks on us."

"I have only a little magic," Willem says. "I will not squander it on you two fools."

"But now we insist," Jean says. "We are your friends. We should be the first to marvel at your skills, not waiting until the fête like all the common people of the village."

"It would have been easier had not someone's mother told my mother of my plans," Willem says, with a pointed look at Jean.

"You accuse me?" Jean asks. "But I said nothing to my mother."

"Nobody else knew," Willem says.

"Do you forget my father?" Jean asks. "You had me ask him if you could borrow his pistol."

Jean's father is one of very few people in the village with a working flintlock pistol. It had returned with him from the nightmarish Russian campaign of 1812.

"That's right," Willem says. "Perhaps he told your mother."

"No doubt," Jean says.

Willem nods. "I forgot to ask. What did your father say?"

"He wanted to know why you might need the weapon."

"I cannot tell him the details," Willem says. "Just that it is my finale, my grand illusion. Tell him it will be the highlight of the fête."

"Perhaps you should ask him yourself," Jean says. "You are the one with the slick tongue."

"We have delayed long enough," François says, standing. "It is still a long walk to the falls."

The stream merges with a river at a small set of rapids. The banks of the river here are a knobbly surface of rounded boulders, many of which shift underfoot, twisting at the boys' ankles. Even so it is easy going compared to the trek through the undergrowth.

Pieter becomes more and more agitated as they travel, which makes Willem nervous. He secretly hoped that this quest for raptor eggs would be fruitless, but the constant perching and pacing of the little saur makes him increasingly sure that fate has more in store for them this day.

If alone, he would turn back, but there is no way the cousins will agree to that. And if either of them suggested it, the other would accuse him of being fearful, and so they would sting each other into continuing.

"Jean, François," Willem says. "You are both strong and brave. And if we find a small raptor, then I am sure you could dispatch it with cold steel. But not a firebird."

"What do you know of firebirds?" François scoffed.

"More than I wish to," Willem says. "My father once told me of three soldiers, a hunting party, that trapped a firebird near Bruges. They were armed with sword and musket. Only one soldier survived, and he only barely."

"They were weaklings, and cowards," François says. "We are warriors."

"They were imperial grenadiers," Willem says.

François closes his mouth at that.

The story is a fabrication. His father told him no such thing. But it is the only way he can think of to make the cousins realize the danger they face.

The river flattens and widens as it sweeps toward a cliff, and from there comes the sound of rushing water.

Pieter clutches tightly onto Willem's hair, hurting him. Pieter's eyes are darting in every direction, his movements rapid and agitated. However, there is no sign of a nest of any kind. They look in the mud by the side of the river and beneath the long, hanging boughs of trees on the edge of the forest.

Jean even ventures a few steps into the forest, in case the nest should be secreted in the forked roots of a tree.

They reach the edge of the cliff, stepping carefully over a wet, rocky shelf along the side of the river.

Willem keeps about a meter from the edge, although Jean and François each seem to delight in stepping one toe closer than the other cousin. To their right the water thunders out over the falls, buckling and blossoming as it drops away to the small rock pool below.

"I see no nest," Willem says. "It is time we returned."

"But we have only searched one side of the river," Jean says.

"And your little friend seems to know something, from the way he twitches," François says. "Perhaps we need but open our eyes."

"Open your eyes now!" Jean says.

Willem stares out over the waterfall in the direction Jean is pointing. He expects to see a raptor emerge from the forest, but instead sees a small group of men.

They are walking in single file, like soldiers, but wear the smocks of local peasants. They carry long dark shapes on their shoulders, and with disquiet Willem realizes they are muskets.

Jean raises himself up and draws in breath, preparing to shout.

"No!" Willem says. "Get down."

Jean turns to look at him. "Why?"

Willem doesn't know. He just has a sudden bad feeling about these men, with guns, so deep in the forest. He cannot say that, so he says, "Do you want them to find the nest, and have our eggs?"

Jean drops down to his knees, and François squats beside them.

"You think they search for the raptor's nest also?" Jean asks.

"What else would they be doing here?" Willem asks.

They watch as six of the men cross the river downstream and disappear into the forest opposite.

"We shall find it first," François says. "It is our nest."

"They shall not take it from us," Jean agrees. "How can we get down there?"

"There is a track," François says.

Willem feels that the last thing the men are looking for is a raptor's nest, but cannot explain why he feels that. He ventures closer to the edge of the cliff, dropping to his knees before peering over. It is not as high as he imagined, no taller than a house of two stories. On the other side of the falls, a narrow ledge just below the cliff edge slopes down. From there a series of jutting rocks makes for a possible but difficult climb down the face of the falls.

"It is scarcely a track," he says.

"Perhaps we are being hasty," François says. "Pierre said it is at the top of the falls."

"And we have not looked on the far side of the river," Jean says.

They backtrack from the top of the falls and cross the river where the water is at its widest, and therefore most shallow.

It is no more than ankle deep, and there are many flat rocks to stand on, but even so Willem feels the tug of the water on his boots as if the river is a living thing that wants to feed him to the hungry mouth of the waterfall just a few meters away.

Pieter begins to show extreme alarm, and a few paces farther he begins struggling and scratching to get down from Willem's shoulder.

"Draw your weapons!" Willem says.

Jean does, and François holds his ax tightly in front of him. Willem opens his satchel and lets Pieter climb inside, closing the top and letting the little saur lie still, more secure in the darkness.

Willem's pulse is racing. A heady mixture of fear and thrill, and something more: a primal desire for revenge.

"The nest is here," he says in a voice that is not as steady as he would like it to be.

"Where?" François asks. The riverbank is rocky and flat. Jean has stepped toward the forest and is poking around in the undergrowth.

"Here," Jean says.

Willem and François join him in a V formed by the roots of a large beech. The ground has been dug out, forming a shallow bowl, and in it, partly covered by twigs and leaves, are five large eggs.

"Look at the size of them," François says. "How we will feast!"

The eggs are mottled brown in color and each is as long as Willem's foot.

"We must hurry," Willem says. "If the eggs are of such a size, how big do you think the mother will be? Let's take them, and get away from this place."

There is no argument from the cousins.

Jean has brought a sack and he carefully places three of the eggs inside it.

"Take them all," Willem says.

"No, leave some," François says. "Then if the mother returns she will want to stay and protect the eggs she has left, instead of chasing us."

Willem shakes his head. "It won't matter if we take one or all of the eggs," he says. "The mother will hunt us regardless. So take them all. Do you want more raptors roaming the forest?"

"No," François says.

Jean packs the other eggs carefully into the sack. "For our return, we stick to the river," he says. "Stay in the water. We do not want this saur to follow our scent back to the village."

He stands with the now-heavy sack, and all three step out onto the rock of the riverbank.

There is a terrified, high-pitched scream from Willem's satchel and he feels Pieter thrashing around inside.

Willem turns upriver and, for the second time in his life, looks a firebird in the eye.

THE NEW WORLD

In 1492, a little-known Italian explorer named Cristoforo Colombo set out to discover a new trade route to Asia. His small fleet
consisted of three ships: the *Pinta*, the *Santa María*, and the *Santa
Clara* (known as the *Niña*). On August third they sailed, first to the
Canary Islands, off the coast of Africa, for provisions and repairs.
They left the Canary Islands on the sixth of September. Colombo
was never heard from again.

Almost a year later the *Niña* sailed into Lisbon harbor, its sails
in tatters, its crew emaciated and ashen, telling tales of meat-eating
lizards as tall as houses. No one knew if they were telling the truth,
or had been driven mad by the voyage.

Two more expeditions were mounted to find Colombo and this
strange land that came to be called the New World, but no one ever
returned.

In 1499, another Italian, Amerigo Vespucci, mapped the New
World. The ships of his expedition stayed a safe distance from
land, content to trace the outline of the new "islands." What the
maps showed were two vast continents, hitherto unknown, that
lay in the middle of what had been called the Ocean Sea. His ships
came back with even wilder tales of giant saurs with heads that
rose above trees.

One specific account, given in great detail by Vespucci, was that
of a pack of meat-eaters, each twice the height of a man, trapping a

long-necked, long-tailed "land whale" on a beach within sight of their boat. The fleet furled sails but did not set anchor in case it turned out that these creatures could swim. They watched in horrified awe as the pack killed the creature and feasted on the carcass, bellowing with pleasure at the jungle and the seas around them.

Vespucci brought back detailed drawings of what he had seen. Scientists conferred and finally said what everybody else already knew: that the geckos and lizards of the forest, and the saurs of the known world, were in some way related to the gigantic beasts of the New World.

For reasons not understood, all but a few of the creatures had died out in the known world, and then only the smallest had survived. But in the New World, the giants reigned.

Once discovered, the New World, now named the Amerigo Islands, was left alone.

Any maps showed only the outline of the coast, with the warning in Greek:

Tromeró sáṿres. Oi deinósaṿroi.

Here there be terrible lizards.
Here there be dinosaurs.

THE NEST

"Run!" Willem shouts.

"My ax will sever its neck," François says, standing his ground.

"After my bolt pierces its heart," Jean says.

"It will get you before you can strike," Willem says. "We must escape, not fight."

He takes a step backward. The others move with him, not wanting to show fear, but deep primal instincts are telling them to keep far away from this creature. Willem considers reaching into his satchel, but knows that this time his father's trick will not work. He has to get close, but this raptor will charge at them, striking before he can even begin.

"Escape where?" François asks.

Behind them the sound of the rushing water grows louder as they step closer and closer to the cliff face.

"We leave the eggs," Jean says, placing the sack carefully on a small plateau of rock.

"No," Willem says. "If we cannot escape, then at the end I will hurl the sack from the cliff rather than let them grow into adults."

He picks up the sack and slings it over a shoulder. The thick shells jostle inside.

The firebird regards them, its head twitching from side to side.

"What is it doing?" François asks.

"I don't think it knows yet that we have stolen its eggs," Willem says. "It is probably just deciding which one of us to attack first."

They back away farther from the creature, which takes two quick steps then stops, one leg raised, examining its prey.

"It knows we are trapped," François says.

"What about the track down the cliff?" Jean asks.

"We don't have time," Willem says. "One of us maybe, but it would be on the other two before we could even start to climb."

"Then you go," Jean says.

"You are a brave friend and true," Willem says. "But I cannot leave you two to be torn to pieces."

"François and I will jump," Jean says.

"We will what?" François asks.

"The water is deep," Jean says. "Let Willem climb. We hold our ground. When the saur starts to attack, we run and jump."

"We will break our necks!" François says.

"A more noble death than at the claws of the firebird," Jean says.

"But—" Willem begins.

"Go swiftly, before it is too late."

Willem obeys. He steps to the edge of the cliff and slides over, his feet finding the narrow ledge.

Almost immediately there comes a splashing and a rustling of feathers from above as the firebird springs forward, sensing that its prey is trying to escape. The twanging of Jean's crossbow is followed by a curse.

Then comes the sound of boots on rock, and with incoherent cries Jean and François hurtle out over his head, plummeting into the pool below, landing with great spouts of water.

Willem has no time to look and see if they are alive. Giant talons sweep through the air above his head, the terrible hooked claw just grazing the side of his head as the enraged raptor stands on the cliff face above him. Willem slides along the ledge, feeling for the next foothold, then the next. The firebird's claws rake the side of the cliff, dislodging pebbles and dust. Willem shakes them from his hair and face. Spray from the waterfall soaks him, and the rocks are slippery. He loses his grip, regains it, loses it again, and only just saves himself by frantically scratching at the cliff face. In the satchel, Pieter is terrified, screaming, clawing at the leather.

The sack bangs against the side of the cliff and Willem hears a cracking sound.

His foot slips from the ledge and he grapples desperately for a handhold as his body swings out over the precipice. If he falls now he will not land in the water but on a bed of jagged rocks. He regains his footing and lowers himself farther, the screeching of the firebird all but drowned out now by the roar of the rushing water.

Angry bellowing comes from above him and the saur scrabbles at the edge of the cliff as it tries and fails to follow him. There is no path for the flightless bird's great claws down the near-vertical slope.

Willem reaches the bottom of the cliff to see Jean dragging his cousin out of the water, blood streaming from François's head.

"François!" Willem yells.

"He lives," Jean says. "Just a cut, I think, and a momentary stupor. I think he did this to himself, with his ax."

Willem bends over the unconscious body. There is a sizable dent in François's forehead and Willem doesn't believe it is as simple as Jean thinks. François opens his eyes, but they are dull and unseeing.

Above them the saur screeches and bellows its rage into the vast reaches of the forest.

THE EGGS

They pass Willem's house on the way to Madame Gertruda's. Willem's mother meets them at the gate.

"Willem! François! What has happened?"

Jean had hoisted his cousin onto his shoulders and carried him most of the way. Only on the last stretch did François begin to stir, then to wake, and he walked into the village himself, with only his arm around Jean's shoulders for support. His precious ax lies somewhere under the water back at the waterfall, but he does not notice or care.

"We went looking for a raptor's nest in the forest," Jean says. "It is my fault. I talked Willem into it."

"You went *looking* for a raptor?" Willem's mother is almost breathless.

"It was a firebird," Willem says. "We saw it. It chased us, but we escaped."

"Not without a price," his mother says, examining François's head. "Did the firebird do this?"

"No, he . . . fell in the river," Willem says.

The truth, he feels, might be a little too much right now.

"He has a thick bone," Jean says. "He will be all right."

"You will take him to Madame Gertruda, immediately," Willem's mother says.

"We go there now," Jean says.

"You angered a firebird, you foolish children. What if it tracked you back here?" she says.

"We walked in the river to hide our scent," Jean says.

"What is in the sack?" Willem's mother asks, noticing it hanging from Willem's shoulder.

"Eggs," Willem says.

"You stole the raptor's eggs?"

"We will feast on them at the fête!" Willem says.

"You will feast on the eggs?"

"Look at them," Willem says, opening the sack and showing her. Despite the risks, they had succeeded in their great adventure. Could she not see that?

"You look at them!" Her eyes steam and her face is red with anger. "Look at the color! You stupid boys!"

She takes the sack from Willem, reaches inside, brings out an egg and throws it to the ground.

"No!" Willem yells, grabbing at the sack to stop her from destroying the other eggs, after all they had been through to get them.

"Dear Father in heaven!" It is François who has spoken, his first words since the accident. He crosses himself with his free hand.

Willem follows his eyes to where the egg has smashed on the cobbles of the path. He expects to see a dense yolk and a translucent white, like a hen's egg.

Instead, the path is covered in blood and fragments of shell, and in the center of it is a creature, not yet fully formed. A long snout with buds of teeth protruding. A stump of a tail. Claws that are still like fingers. Spikes that have yet to turn into feathers.

And it is moving, convulsing, squirming on the cobbles.

"Jean, go now with your cousin," his mother says. "Willem, stay." She points at the abomination.

"Kill it, bury it, and clean that up," she says.

"Yes, Mother," he says.

"Kill them all," she says.

She comes to him later and the redness is gone from her cheeks. Her eyes are soft. "Perform your miracles at the fête. But only little ones. Tricks that any boy could learn. Do not show off the full range of your skills."

"Yes, Mother," he says.

LAFFREY

Major Thibault marches at the rear of the column as the road twists and turns up into the French Alps. They are making for the capital, Paris. It is not much of a column. Little more than a thousand men, and only a few horses.

Napoléon's garrison from Elba has been joined by soldiers from the fort at Antibes where they landed on the coast. They have been marching for many days. The road narrows as it climbs into the mountains, and patches of ice have turned to a constant sheet that coats the road with white and makes it treacherous underfoot. Even the sturdy mules slip and stumble, and although Thibault rode one for part of the journey, here it is too dangerous.

They brought two cannon from the fort at Antibes, but the weapons slithered from the road many days ago and have been left lying in a frozen gully. So too their carriages. Much worse is the fate of their horses, their hooves unable to find traction on the icy road. The horses are splendid animals, fearless in the face of musket and cannonfire, hardened on the battlefields of Europe. But too many times on this deadly climb Thibault has heard the agonized scream of an injured animal, followed by the sound of a musket. Then silence.

Napoléon's escape from the island was straightforward. *L'Inconstant*, a brig hired by Thibault, met them at Cavo, then sailed for the French mainland.

Already the light in the sky is dimming as the day draws to a close. The sun is an orange ball, looking for a place to hide amid the mountains.

They crest a steep rise onto a small plateau close to the village of Laffrey. The ground is flatter here, and although still icy, less treacherous.

The low sun throws their orange-rimmed shadows out across a frozen lake to the right of the road. An early-spring frosting of ice, nothing more, not strong enough to bear the weight of men or horses. The lake hems them in against the mountainside. It is a good place for an ambush. Even as Thibault thinks this, the column comes to a halt. Word quickly rustles down the line: soldiers block the path ahead.

"It was to be expected," Thibault says to the man at his side. "The garrison at Grenoble would surely have been alerted to our route."

"Then we will march forward and drive these vermin from the path," Count Cambronne says.

"Might I respectfully remind you, General, of our orders," Thibault says. "These soldiers are our brothers, merely doing their duty."

"That is *Napoléon*'s opinion," Cambronne says.

"They have chosen their arena well," Thibault says. "We are pressed into this narrow pass, while they have the luxury of the meadow."

To their left, woods rise steeply in tides of snow-covered trees. To their right is the smooth ice of the lake. With such a narrow front the column will be able to bring only a few muskets into the battle at any time, whereas the Grenoble troops can spread out across the width of the meadow, bringing many guns to bear on the narrow road.

"We make formation and march forward," Cambronne says.

"We would march to our deaths," Thibault says. He stands high on his stirrups and raises a spyglass to his eye.

"You forget," Cambronne says, raising his own spyglass, "we march with God on our side."

"God may be on our side," Thibault says, "but the devil has more muskets."

"Shoulder your muskets or be fired upon." The voice carries to them from a man on horseback in the front ranks that face them.

"A major," Cambronne says, lowering the spyglass. He snorts, as if to rid himself of a bad smell. "I will not waste my time. You go, Thibault. Tell him to get out of our way."

Thibault moves slowly through his own lines, which ripple to let him through. These are the Old Guard. The elite of the French army, loyal to their exiled emperor. Veterans of Italy, Russia, and the Peninsular War. There is a constant rustling sound as the men feel for paper cartridges in their pouches.

"Shoulder your muskets," the Grenoble major demands again, but stops as Thibault appears at the front of the column.

"Whom do I address?" Thibault asks.

"Major Lansard of the fifth infantry regiment."

Another officer, in a colonel's uniform, also on horseback, moves forward through the ranks behind the major. "Tell your men to shoulder their muskets."

"Like you, we are soldiers of the French army," Thibault says. "We are not enemies. I beg you to stand aside."

"I cannot do that," Lansard says. "I am set to my duty. Retire or be fired upon."

"Your duty to whom?"

"To the king," Lansard says.

"Then let me talk to him, face-to-face. I presume the king

travels with you?" Thibault says. "Or does that plump piglet yet wallow in his trough and preen before mirrors in Paris?"

"Retire, monsieur, I cannot ask again," Lansard says.

"You have spine, Major, but we will not retire," Thibault says.

He begins to move forward. Behind him the soldiers of the Old Guard advance at the same pace.

"Advance no farther," Lansard shouts.

"Make ready," the colonel shouts. The muskets of the Grenoble men are raised into the air.

Thibault is within pistol range now, and Lansard draws his sidearm and cocks it, but leaves it pointing at the sky.

"Present," the colonel shouts, and his men lower the muzzles of their weapons to aim at Thibault and the Old Guard behind him.

Thibault senses rather than sees the ripple in the lines behind him and turns, expecting to see Cambronne, but it is the prisoner of Elba who is making his way forward.

A man of average height, but dwarfed by the tall men of the Old Guard. One hand tucked into his waistcoat, which protrudes, potbellied. His unpowdered hair falls to his shoulders. His nose is royal, his eyes are deep-set, his complexion is sallow.

The guns of the Grenoble men waver, then lower as they recognize the familiar shape in his customary gray greatcoat and bicorne hat.

From somewhere in the rear of the column a voice calls out, *"Vive l'empereur!"* The cry is taken up by others. "Long live the emperor!"

There is a clatter as muskets drop to the ground and suddenly Napoléon is gone, disappearing amid a whirlwind of blue uniforms as the soldiers of Grenoble surround and embrace him.

"Take up your eagles again, for your emperor has returned and France shall once more rise to greatness!" Thibault shouts.

In shock and confusion the Grenoble colonel turns his mount and canters away, with just one disbelieving glance back over his shoulder.

The crowd parts and Lansard emerges on foot, the soldiers moving away from him as he approaches.

He draws his sword, touches it briefly to his hat, then reverses it, offering it hilt-first to Napoléon.

Napoléon takes the sword, but immediately reverses it and offers it back to Lansard.

"You, Major, had the spine to stand against Napoléon!" he says. "I am sure such courage would find a place in the emperor's army."

Lansard says nothing, bowing his head.

Napoléon nods. "How many men have you?"

"Six thousand in the garrison," Lansard says. "And four thousand more in Draguignan."

"Then tomorrow we march for Paris," Napoléon says.

THE BLACKSMITH

François awakes on the eighth of March, three days before the fête. He has been sleeping for five days.

He had lapsed back into a stupor by the time they got him to Madame Gertruda's.

She announced that his brain was swollen and there was nothing she could do beyond lowering his body temperature and treating him with herbs and potions to keep him asleep until the swelling subsided. She kept him covered with damp towels in a room with the windows open, and although he shivered terribly, she said this was for the best.

She also said that a surgeon in Brussels might be able to drill holes in his head to relieve pressure, but that it was a risky procedure.

In any case his father refused to allow it. He had seen the results of such operations in the battlefield surgeon's tent, and although Madame Gertruda assured him there had been great advances in such medicine, Father Ambroise insisted that prayer, plus Madame Gertruda's treatments, would heal his only son.

Willem's mother said that he was foolish, and was risking the life of his son, but she said this only to Willem.

A hunting party armed with swords and muskets, led by Jean's father, set off to find the firebird, without success.

* * *

François remains at Madame Gertruda's for the next three days under the constant care of the healer—and Héloïse, who fusses over him as if he were a newborn.

Jean and Willem visit him every day, but find him sullen and withdrawn. He speaks little and when he does speak it is usually to God. Even Jean cannot reach him.

"Give François time," Willem says. "It has only been a week since the accident."

"He is not himself," Jean says.

On that, Willem thinks Jean is wrong. François is still himself. He is everything he was before the accident, only more so. More prone to moods and brooding like his mother. More boastful. More pious and devout.

On the second Saturday of March, the day of the fête, Madame Gertruda finally declares François well enough to return home.

In celebration, Jean and Willem present him with a new ax to replace the one he lost in the river.

Willem paid for the iron and Jean tempered it to steel, hammering it to a fine edge. The best ax-head in Europe, he declared when it was finished. Willem carved the haft for the ax from a sturdy length of straight-grained oak, with guidance from Monsieur Antonescu, an old, blind, Romanian woodchopper, who selected the bough by touch for its strength and resilience, and guided Willem in the carving.

When they give him the ax, François looks at it dully and does not offer gratitude for their efforts.

The day of the fête is sunny and cheerful, and so it has been for every fête since Willem has lived in the village. The weather is warming toward the spring equinox and already the days and nights are of almost equal length.

Preparations begin at first light with children of the village gathering wood for the bonfire. This tradition goes back hundreds of years, although in recent times adults in the village carefully place random piles of wood in convenient locations not too far from the saur-fence to make it easier for the children.

This year an adult with a musket stands by at all times, and another armed man remains on alert at the saur-gate. The firebird has not been sighted near the village nor found in the forest.

By noon, the preparations for the feast are well under way. Another tradition, peculiar to Gaillemarde, is the fasting that precedes the feast. There is no bread for breakfast or the noonday meal. It is as if the villagers are to empty their stomachs to make room for what is to follow.

Willem and his mother have spent all the morning baking. He is collecting water from the river for the cleaning up when Monsieur Lejeune, Jean's father, sees him and waves him over. Willem crosses the dusty cobblestones to the smithy with more than a little trepidation. He has not spoken to Jean's father since the accident, and is expecting a weighty rebuke. He is afraid Monsieur Lejeune will hold him responsible for putting his son in danger, and for what happened to his nephew. Jean's father is a burly, coarse man, the skin of his hands and face turning black from years of blacksmithing. Most of the children in the village are wary and respectful of him. He is not slow with the back of his hand or the toe of his boot on the rump of a wayward child.

He was a cuirassier in Napoléon's Grande Armée. A horse-mounted soldier with armored breastplates and back plates, armed with a heavy straight sword and two pistols. Only the largest of men were chosen as cuirassiers, and they were mounted on the largest horses. Monsieur Lejeune was one of the elite, and he has been hardened in the fires of battle the way iron is tempered to steel in his forge.

The smithy is usually oppressively hot, even with all the windows wide open and the large open doors at the front and rear. But today the fire is not lit. The forge in the center of the smithy is cold. The fat brick chimney above it is lifeless, where usually curls of escaping smoke decorate its sides. Today is the day of the fête.

Although Jean's father is not working, he still wears his heavy black apron, as if by taking it off he would shed part of himself. It is so unusual to see him without it that Willem would not be surprised if he wears it to bed.

Monsieur Lejeune says nothing as Willem enters, and instead disappears through a back door, to his house on the other side of the street. Willem sets his pails of water down and waits.

Even without the fire, the smithy smells of charcoal and carbonized iron. Tacked to high beams around the smithy are rows of old horseshoes, perhaps for luck, or to ward off evil spirits, but Monsieur Lejeune is not a deeply religious or superstitious man. A set of large metal rings for wagon wheels is stacked against one wall and a number of sharp metal spikes are clumped against the edge of the forge. On hooks around the forge hang many sets of heavy metal tongs of varying shapes and sizes. A large tub of dirty water sits near the anvil, which is mounted on an old tree stump. It is a two-horned anvil, which, when silhouetted by the flames of the fire behind it, looks like a square-headed demon.

Marcel and Ambroise Lejeune were tearaways as younger men, even wilder than their sons would turn out to be. They fought, they danced, they chased girls and drank too much wine. They climbed mountains and swam rivers. They made lifelong friends, and mortal enemies. They gambled both their money and their lives.

It seemed a miracle to some in the village that the pair survived to adulthood. By the time of their conscription into Napoléon's

Great Army they were both married: Marcel to a girl from the village, Ambroise to a girl from nearby Fichermont.

But Napoléon wanted them for his army, along with most ablebodied men in the region, and in 1798 they both marched to war, leaving wives heavy with child.

Ambroise returned to Gaillemarde a year later, having left half a hand and a quarter of his blood on the wild desert sands of Syria. He stayed for a while in the village, recovering. But Ambroise was not the same person who had proudly donned his shako and plume in service of his emperor. He spent most of his time in the church, communing with God, and that led to the seminary in Tournai. During the six years Ambroise was studying for the priesthood, Father Constantin, the village priest, died. Mass was conducted by visiting priests from Brussels for nearly two years, until Ambroise was ordained. Now Father Ambroise, he returned to the village and became shepherd to the village flock.

Under church law, Ambroise, a married man who turned to the priesthood, was allowed to remain married, but he and Agathe were no longer permitted to live as man and wife. When he returned from the seminary, he moved into the small rectory on the church grounds, while Agathe remained in their cottage, with François and his older sister, Émilie.

Jean's father stayed in the army for much longer, surviving the long and devastating Russian campaign of 1812. The things he saw and the things he endured on that terrible winter retreat must have been horrific beyond comprehension. Half a million soldiers went into Russia with Napoléon, but fewer than thirty thousand returned. Cold, hunger, disease, murderous Cossacks, and the dreadful, shredding Russian cannonfire accounted for the rest.

On his return to the village Marcel Lejeune took over the family smithy and never spoke of the war. Nor did he attend church, except at Easter, Ascension, and Christmas.

Willem is beginning to wonder whether he has misunderstood Jean's father, and if he was supposed to follow him to the house, when the blacksmith returns to the smithy with a small leather pouch and an object wrapped in an oilcloth. Laying the object on a workbench, he unwraps it carefully.

It is his flintlock pistol. When he left the Great Army, one of his two pistols somehow remained in his possession.

Willem had completely forgotten about the pistol. He had done as his mother said and chosen just a few simple tricks for the fête, and no grand illusion. But he had also forgotten to tell the blacksmith.

Monsieur Lejeune looks deeply at Willem, and gestures toward the weapon.

"What is your purpose with it?"

Willem hesitates. "You would still allow me to use it, after what happened in the forest?"

Monsieur Lejeune picks up the pistol and turns it over in his hands.

"This is no mere thing," he says. "This weapon saved my life on countless occasions on fields wet with the blood of my brothers. And look what a vile thing it is. A tool designed not to create or shape or sow or reap, but only to take life. I should destroy it. Cast it into the deepest lake. Yet I keep it."

"Why?" Willem asks.

"Because it holds the memory of the fallen," he says. "In battles lost and won. I cannot remember them all. But the weapon remembers, as it remembers the lives of the others. The lives it has taken."

He replaces the pistol on the bench.

"I do this *because* of what happened in the forest," he says.

"I don't understand," Willem says.

"Jean told me about that day. How you warned them not to go, but when they insisted, you would not let them go alone. You are small, but show more heart than men twice your size."

"Jean overstates the truth," Willem says.

"I think not," Monsieur Lejeune says. "He told me also how you stopped them from fighting the meat-eater. Had you not done that, we would have had two, maybe three, funerals this week, instead of one patient at Gertruda's. Of all the young men in the village, you are the most levelheaded. The smartest in the village, from what Jean tells me."

That Jean considers him the smartest in the village is news to Willem. That Jean would say such a thing to his father is an even greater surprise.

Monsieur Lejeune says, "I will use the pistol for you, as part of your act, if that is what you ask. As long as nobody will be in danger. And thank you for saving the life of my woolly-headed son."

Willem hesitates again. "After the raptor, I had more or less decided not to use the pistol," he says. That is almost the truth.

"The decision is yours," Monsieur Lejeune says, wrapping the pistol up again.

"Can you show me how it works?" Willem asks.

Monsieur Lejeune considers that, then nods and removes the gun from the cloth.

"First you must prime the pistol," he says. "Pull the hammer back to halfway, and open the frizzen." The frizzen is a short piece of metal above a small pan. A cap at the bottom covers the pan when the frizzen is closed. "A little powder here in the pan, then the rest of the powder in the barrel. Close the frizzen to keep the powder safe. Then ram the pistol ball and the wadding tightly into the barrel."

"The wadding?" Willem asks.

"The paper," Monsieur Lejeune says.

He opens the leather pouch and brings out a paper cartridge, a small tube glued at each end and in the middle to create two distinct sections. In one half is a round object that Willem knows must be a pistol ball. The other half looks to be filled with gunpowder.

"Tear open the packet and pour the powder into the pan and barrel, as I told you," Monsieur Lejeune says. "Then ram the ball and paper into the barrel. The paper acts as wadding, keeping the ball steady. To fire, pull the hammer back all the way. This piece of flint"—he points to a small rock-like object clenched in a jaw at the top of the hammer—"strikes the frizzen and makes sparks. At the same time it pushes the frizzen back, revealing the powder. The sparks ignite the powder in the pan and that sets off the powder in the barrel."

Willem nods. It is much as he has read, although he has never seen a pistol up close before.

"I will fire the pistol for you tonight if you wish," Monsieur Lejeune says.

Willem stares at the pistol for a moment. He promised his mother he would not perform a grand illusion. But compared to the card and coin tricks he intends to show, this will be spectacular. An illusion worthy of the final act of the festival.

But he promised his mother.

"Merci, monsieur," Willem says. "Please bring the pistol tonight."

He is still undecided as he picks up the pails of water and carries them home.

It is his destiny.

But he promised his mother.

LA FÊTE
DU PRINTEMPS

The festivities commence with the lighting of the bonfire, and will conclude near midnight with fireworks.

The entire village is there, along with some invited families from nearby towns. It is the biggest event of the year.

All the gas lamps in the square have been turned up high and people radiate out from the focal point of the stage. Groups of families and friends have spread blankets on the grass, or sit on stools or upturned pails.

The stage is a low wooden platform, half a meter off the ground, with strong posts at each corner. It is erected each year on the river side of the square, in front of a large stone building, next to the stable that is the village market hall.

At the front and rear of the hall are large barn-style doors. The doors that face the square are open wide, and a heavy, dark curtain is draped across the entrance, so that the interior of the building becomes a kind of backstage area. Lamps hang from wooden posts at each corner of the stage, and from ropes strung between the posts. The wicks are turned up, and the stage is brightly lit.

Now fifteen, Willem is no longer required to sit with his family and instead sits with Jean and François in a group of other young men from the village, near to, but separate from, a group of girls of similar age that includes the Delvaux sisters, Angélique and Cosette, and François's sister, Émilie.

On a low wooden bench nearby, the old blind woodcutter, Monsieur Antonescu, sits alone, guzzling happily from a bottle of plum brandy. He hums to himself, tunelessly, although Willem is sure that in the old man's head the melodies are vibrant and joyful.

At seven, just after the setting of the sun, the mayor strikes a flint to light a tallow torch, then hands the flaming brand to the oldest resident of the village, Madame Gertruda. She has had this honor for five years, since the previous oldest resident, Madame Monami, passed over.

Madame Gertruda walks steadily toward the bonfire: a pile of wood and scrub in the center of the village square. After closing her eyes in prayer for a brief moment, perhaps thanking God for another year (or maybe cursing him for it, depending on her mood), she tosses the torch onto the pyre and steps back quickly as the dry brush, some of it dripped with pig fat, whispers, then howls into flame.

Within minutes there is a lively fire leaping in the square, putting out heat and light to counter the cooling air and slowly fading glow of the sky.

There is applause from the audience, and Madame Gertruda turns and curtsies happily.

Today, apparently, is a good day.

The feast is waiting on long tables around the edges of the square. Wooden plates are handed out by the children, who have to wait for the adults to fill theirs before helping themselves.

Willem, in his first year as an adult, is handed his plate by Cosette, and thinks as he takes it that she will be prettier than her sister when she is fully grown. She is nearly an adult already, at fourteen years. She has long, golden-brown hair just a little darker than her sister's. A narrow face but wide, straight teeth. A lazy eye adds to a kind of asymmetrical lopsided beauty. Unlike some girls in the village whose aspirations mainly revolve around finding a suitable husband, Cosette talks of being a writer and of living in Paris or Salzburg, two cities that hold some special romantic appeal for her. He smiles at her, but she ignores him and saves the white perfection of her teeth for Jean, next in line.

For a moment there is a quickening of his pulse with anger, with jealousy. But it fades quickly. Willem shrugs as he moves on. He should not be offended. This is the way of things. But that brief pain? What was that? Was that like the feeling his father had for his mother? She often spoke of love, but that is something alien to Willem.

Father Ambroise—François's father—raises his hands for silence when all have overflowing plates on their laps. One of those hands is half gone, shot away in the same war injury that had nearly claimed his life, over a decade ago. All that is left are the thumb and forefinger, all-important as without them he could not have been ordained. A one-handed priest cannot perform communion.

He offers a prayer for the coming season, blesses the food and the villagers, and wisely keeps it short, knowing that after a day of fasting, the people will be impatient for their plates.

After the prayer, Willem sees Cosette helping Monsieur Antonescu back to his seat. She holds his arm to guide him and carries his plate with her other hand. Once he is settled she hands him the plate and Monsieur Antonescu nods briefly in thanks. Only then does Cosette return to the tables to fill her own plate.

François eats just a small amount, then sets his plate aside. A moment later his pipe is in his hand and he tamps tobacco into it while he watches the others eat. He rises and finds a half-burned switch that has jumped from the bonfire. He blows on the end till it glows, then uses it to light his pipe.

As he returns to his seat beside Willem, a log collapses somewhere in the midst of the bonfire, sending up a shower of sparks, spitting at the stars.

The wine flows freely. Most of the other Flemings in the village prefer beer but Willem has never developed a taste for it, preferring the crisp tartness of the grape to the cloudy malt of the hop.

He is sparing with his wine, sipping slowly, not wanting to haze his mind before his act. Jean drinks freely, but it seems to have no effect on him. He has been drinking wine since he was four, and claims to be immune to its powers.

François also seems to have a mug constantly refilled and is happy, although already his words sound slow and blurred. In most ways he appears to have recovered fully from the accident. He smokes his pipe and drinks with them, wiping rivulets of red from his chin with the back of his sleeve.

The first sour note of the fête occurs during the feast.

"See the wild animal," Jean says, nudging Willem with his knee.

Willem follows Jean's eyes to where Héloïse sits on the ground, near a group of girls but not part of them. He has never seen her at the fête before, and he wonders how Madame Gertruda has convinced her to attend. Héloïse eats by bringing the plate to her mouth, and wolfing at the food like a dog from a bowl. The girls around her are staring, or laughing behind their hands.

Cosette laughs also, but her eyes do not share the humor.

Cosette and Héloïse were best friends before that day in the forest: the day of the firebird. Before Héloïse disappeared for six years, and returned as a wild animal.

There is a sudden clatter and Jean's plate goes flying across the ground, scattering the remains of his dinner in the grass.

"You think you are better than her, cousin?" François says. "You can eat from the ground, then we will see who is the animal."

Jean begins to rise, fists clenched, but Willem puts a hand on his arm and holds it there until Jean slowly subsides into his seat.

"He does not speak as himself," Willem murmurs. "And she tended him for many days."

Around them all eyes are on the two cousins. Jean nods his head and places a hand on his cousin's shoulder.

"Forgive me, François," he says. "I was not thinking."

It is one of the few times that Willem has heard him call his cousin by his first name.

"Ffft." François looks away.

Jean collects his plate and food from the grass and carries on eating as if the incident hadn't occurred. Food is never wasted in Gaillemarde. Not even during the feast.

The entertainment begins during the meal. The mayor is master of ceremonies, introducing the acts and encouraging applause before and after.

The first act is musical. The Poulencs are a large farming family that owns three of the prized river cottages, and a huge barley plantation south of the village. Most of them are talented musicians and they play every year. For this festival they offer two sisters and a brother, playing fiddle, bass, and cello. They play a sedate piece by the Austrian composer Mozart. Dinner music.

They are followed by a choir from the church, led by François's mother: Madame Agathe Lejeune. She is a thin, nervous woman with deep, anxious eyes. They sing a lively hymn.

After the choir comes a succession of other acts, mostly singing or dancing, although there is one short theatrical sketch from a small group that includes Angélique and Cosette Delvaux. It is a frenetic pantomime and they play it well, to many laughs. Cosette plays Pierrot, the sad French clown, and when she returns, flushed and giggling with the rush of applause, she sits even closer to the group of boys.

She has shown real talent, Willem thinks, and if she does not become a writer, she has a possible future in the theater. He congratulates her on her performance and she accepts with a brief nod but saves her attention for Jean.

Willem places his plate on the ground and stands as Jean begins regaling Cosette with stories about their hunt for the firebird, except the way he tells it, the cliff is surely a hundred meters high, and he and François actually flew like birds before diving into the rock pool.

Willem glances back as he leaves and thinks from the quiet smile on Cosette's face that she is not as impressed as Jean clearly thinks she should be.

Willem finds Monsieur Lejeune seated with his wife and some other families.

"Now?" Monsieur Lejeune asks.

"Soon," Willem replies. "I just wanted to check that you had brought . . . it."

"I have the essentials," Monsieur Lejeune replies, tapping the side of his coat.

Willem returns to his seat and waits, watching Cosette as she laughs and eats and sips delicately at her wine with pursed, moist lips.

He wills her to notice him, but when her eyes do fall on him it is only as they sweep past to Jean, François, or to look at someone else in the crowd. It is as if Willem exists on a different plane. There but not there. She sees him, but does not see him.

He is the boy who brings the bread, nothing more.

This is what decides him, in the end. Not the decree of his mother. Not the call of his destiny. Not the desire to follow in the footsteps of his father.

Just the eyes (one of them lazy) of a pretty, fourteen-year-old girl that look through him without seeing him.

It is nearly ten when the mayor nods at Willem.

Willem taps Jean on the shoulder, interrupting a long and intense conversation with Cosette and François's sister, Émilie.

Jean excuses himself and follows Willem into the market hall.

On a small table is a large burlap sack full of dirt. Jean hoists the sack, Willem lifts the table, and they move to the rear of the stage. A writing desk covered with a black cloth holds an assortment of other equipment for his act.

They wait patiently behind the rear stage curtain for the penultimate act, a young girl who plays a beautiful melody on a set of pipes made from saur bones, then for Monsieur Claude to announce Willem.

The crowd is still applauding the girl when he takes the stage carrying the table. They hush, expectantly.

He sets the table at the side of the stage and Jean places the sack of dirt on it. They both take an end of the writing desk and place it at the front of the stage, then Jean retires through the stage curtain.

Moths and other small insects hurl themselves at the lanterns, and fireflies dart in short bursts above the audience as Willem steps to the center of the stage.

The fluttering of the moths is echoed in his stomach, but he swallows a couple of times and finds his voice.

He introduces himself with a few simple coin tricks, then produces some scarves from the palms of his hands. All to no more than a little polite applause. Such trickery is common among street performers in the cities.

He performs his best card trick on a volunteer from the audience. He hopes that Cosette might raise her hand, but she does not, and in the end he performs the trick on the village tailor.

There are a few oohs and aahs when the card is produced, but this still is small magic. Safe magic, that his mother would approve of. What happens next is not.

"Monsieur Claude," Willem calls out, "please come to the stage."

With an expression of surprise that is almost convincing, the mayor rises, kisses his wife gallantly on the hand, and steps forward to the stage.

After just the briefest of pauses, to reconsider what he is doing, Willem motions Monsieur Lejeune to come forward also.

"And for my finale," Willem announces, as Monsieur Lejeune makes his way through the crowd, "an illusion such as has never been seen before in Gaillemarde." He lays it on thick, trying to build up the tension, sensing that the crowd is entertained, but not enthralled. "I will survive a ball fired from a pistol."

Now he has their attention, although Monsieur Lejeune is frowning at him. Willem gives him a surreptitious nod to let him know everything will be all right.

Monsieur Lejeune reaches the stage and draws his pistol from a leather holster at his side.

"We will need a pistol ball," Willem says, and a little reluctantly, Monsieur Lejeune produces a paper cartridge from his leather pouch. He tears open an end and removes the lead ball. Willem takes it using two fingers and hands it to Monsieur Claude.

"Monsieur le Maire, please scratch a symbol onto this ball," Willem says. "Something that I would not know, nor could have predicted."

He hands Monsieur Claude a horseshoe nail.

After a moment's thought, Monsieur Claude scratches something into the side of the ball and hands it back.

"Monsieur Lejeune, now please load the pistol," Willem says.

The audience shifts and ripples like a windswept lake as people strain for a better view.

Monsieur Lejeune expertly primes the pistol, then pours the rest of the powder into the barrel.

"The wadding please," Willem says.

Monsieur Lejeune hands him the paper, and after showing the pistol ball to the audience one more time, making sure they can see the mayor's symbol, Willem drops it into the small paper cartridge and twists the end shut before handing it back to Monsieur Lejeune, who inserts it into the barrel and rams it home.

"Monsieur, please step to the right of the stage," Willem says, "and take aim at this sack of dirt."

Monsieur Lejeune does as requested. The audience goes completely silent.

"I will place myself in between the pistol and the sack of dirt," Willem announces, and proceeds to do so, standing just in front of the table. "When the pistol is fired, the pistol ball will pass right through my body, doing no harm. It will hit the sack, and when we dig out the ball, it will bear the very marking that our beloved mayor scratched into it not a moment or two ago."

The mayor bows his head graciously at the small flattery, and waves to the crowd as though he, not Willem, is the center of attention.

Monsieur Lejeune has remained in position, aiming his pistol at the sack, even though Willem now stands in the way.

He seems uncertain, and as Willem spreads his arms wide and closes his eyes, a voice comes from the crowd.

"Do not do this." It is Father Ambroise. "The boy does not know what he is doing."

"I know exactly what I am doing," Willem says, his eyes still tightly shut.

If Monsieur Lejeune does not pull the trigger, then there will be no final trick. No grand illusion to finish his act. The best he can hope for will be polite applause and quiet sympathy.

He opens his eyes and catches his mother's face, near the front of the crowd. Unlike the others, which vary between wonder and apprehension, her face radiates anger.

"Pull the trigger, Monsieur," Willem says, closing his eyes again.

Nothing happens, and he risks a quick look. The barrel of the pistol has lowered a little as Monsieur Lejeune wavers. It is now pointed between Willem's legs.

"You aim at the wrong sack," Willem calls out.

The audience roars with laughter.

Monsieur Lejeune laughs also and raises the pistol back to Willem's chest.

"Do it!" a voice shouts out of the crowd.

"I command you not to do this," Father Ambroise says. "In the name of—"

That, more than anything, seems to make up Monsieur Lejeune's mind.

"No!" Father Ambroise shouts, but he is too late.

Willem imagines, rather than sees, the flash of the pistol and the spurt of white smoke, but he feels the impact on his chest and that is quickly followed by the rotten-egg smell of gunpowder wafting across the stage. From somewhere nearby, Pieter screams.

The crash of the pistol dies away into the still night air.

All eyes are on Willem, and his eyes hold shock and fear as he looks down at the spreading patch of red across the white of his smock.

He collapses to his knees, his hands clutched to his chest.

Around him the faces of the villagers echo the shock, creeping into horror. Only his mother's face remains unchanged, etched with a look of quiet fury.

The pistol drops from Monsieur Lejeune's hand, clattering onto the rough wooden floor of the stage. Willem coughs, once, twice, then spits something into his palm. He slowly raises his head and holds the object up to the crowd, who by now can see for themselves that it is a pistol ball.

Willem stands up and hands Monsieur Lejeune the ball. "Please show this to the mayor," he says.

Monsieur Claude has remained at the edge of the stage, and Monsieur Lejeune crosses back to him and hands him the lead ball.

"Does it bear your mark?" Willem asks.

Monsieur Claude nods and begins to laugh, a tight, high-pitched sound. "It is my mark, exactly as I scratched into it not a moment or two ago."

It is the simplest of tricks, as all great illusions are. The switch occurred as Willem dropped the ball into the wadding, palming the real pistol ball and replacing it with a ball of wax, filled with red dye. There is a box of the wax balls in one of his father's chests.

Willem turns to the audience to acknowledge the applause, the adulation, but there is none, only quiet murmuring.

There is movement in the crowd, and it is Father Ambroise, wending his way through to the stage.

He climbs up and stands next to Willem, turning to face the audience and holding up his hands for silence.

"This is not magic," Father Ambroise declares. "This is a conjuring trick that went wrong. Today you have borne witness to a miracle from God, who has saved this boy from his own foolish death."

"No—" Willem begins, but Father Ambroise is joined on the stage by his son.

"I prayed for Willem, and God listened to my prayer," François says.

Willem opens his mouth to protest, but closes it again, realizing the blunder he has made.

He cannot prove it is a trick without revealing how he did it. And he cannot argue with François and Father Ambroise without going against God.

He looks around at the audience, many of them now crossing themselves, or with their eyes closed in prayer.

He has pulled off a grand illusion, one that would have made his father proud.

But God is getting all the credit.

THE BONFIRE

The band is made up of members of the Poulenc family and Monsieur Antonescu. One of the Poulencs plays the piano accordion, and the blind woodsman plays a violin-like instrument with a trumpet horn attached.

The band starts playing even as Willem and Jean are packing up the equipment in the backstage area. They play a short popular song, pre-dance music. On the grass in front of the stage the villagers are already forming up into circles for the first dance.

Jean's father watches them work. "There was a magician in Paris, many years ago," he says. "The Great Geerts. He also performed this illusion."

Willem stops in his tracks and looks at Monsieur Lejeune.

"You saw the Great Geerts?" Willem asks, carefully. "Even I have heard of him."

Monsieur Lejeune laughs. "No, a lowly cuirassier could not attend such a show, but my captain did, and he described it to us all with such eloquence that it is as if I had been there. Had I not known of this illusion, I would not have pulled the trigger tonight." He pauses, considering. "When you handed me the wadding, the weight was wrong. A lead ball is much heavier. Even so, when I saw the blood spreading across your breast, I feared that some terrible calamity had befallen you. That you, or I, had done something wrong. You are a great young magician, Master Willem."

"They think it is God's doing," Willem says, indicating the audience.

"Not all of them," Monsieur Lejeune says. "And you may not realize it, but my brother, the priest, did you a favor tonight."

"A favor! How so?"

"These are not the sophisticated intellects of Paris, Moscow, or Berlin," Monsieur Lejeune says. "They are simple farming folk, and such a trick is so far beyond their comprehension that to them it can only be a miracle. Had my brother not claimed it for God, they would have thought this the work of the devil."

In the end it doesn't matter, magic or miracle—either way, Willem is a hero. All the girls of the village want to dance with him, Cosette most of all. Jean joins in the dance circle with Cosette's older sister, Angélique.

Cosette is a natural and artful dancer. Each time the circles bring them back together that slight quickening of his heartbeat tells him he is happy with the prospect of a further dance with her, if only for a moment. Again the thought occurs to him: What is love? Is this love?

During the dancing she asks him, with lips moistened by tongue, if he will tell her the secret of the pistol trick.

Despite the allure of those lips he replies firmly that he is sorry, but he will not.

The music changes to a waltz and Willem bows to Cosette and holds out his hand before any other young man can claim her for the dance.

Jean dances with Angélique, closer than would have been considered proper in more elegant society in the towns, or the cities. But here in Gaillemarde, in the flickering light of the bonfire, burning away the hardships of the winter months, the mood is light, and if the dancing is close, what of it?

Monsieur Antonescu's trumpet-violin sings, the other instruments provide accompaniment, and the rest of the dancers seem to slip away, leaving just Willem and Cosette with the bonfire, dancing to its own music, and the stars of the sky above.

As the dance finishes he sees that François also found a partner for the dance. It is Héloïse, which is a great surprise to Willem.

He hadn't known she could dance.

The second sour note of the fête is quite late in the evening, just before midnight. It is the last dance, before the grand finale of the fireworks display.

Again Willem offers Cosette his hand.

She turns away, and his heart stops for a moment, but then she turns back and looks up at him through lowered eyelids, and he takes her hand for the dance.

François, who is usually one of the first to claim a dance partner, does not even rise from his seat, and would have sat out the dance if not for Héloïse, who stands in front of him and waits until he offers her his hand. It is very forward, and had it been any other young lady of the village it would have been quite unseemly, but Héloïse is somehow outside of those normal conventions.

Willem looks at Cosette. At the powdered skin, the delicately brushed hair, the pretty dress, the graceful and delicate movements. Then he looks at Héloïse prancing clumsily behind her. They are opposites, yet once they were alike. Fate has chosen a very different path for each of them.

Jean dances with Marie Étoile, a girl from outside the village who is staying with her aunt and uncle.

François's father, as village priest, does not join in any of the dancing, so he sits on a chair near the stage and benevolently presides over the dance area.

When Willem looks around to see who else is dancing with whom, always a favorite game during the final dance, he sees that Madame Agathe, François's mother, is dancing with Monsieur Claude, the mayor. That does not strike him as particularly odd; they are both without natural partners for the dance, as the stout and shortsighted Madame Claude never dances, claiming a bad ankle.

But Willem sees François watching Monsieur Claude with narrowed eyes. Willem is just glad that his own mother has not been chosen by the village's lecherous leader. He looks around to see who she is dancing with, but cannot see her.

The dance finishes. Cosette dips her head and smiles at him as she turns away. It is quite girlish and unlike her.

But then he sees Monsieur Claude reach out a hand and cup the buttocks of his dance partner. It is perhaps not unexpected from such a man, but her reaction is the surprise. A frown, a scold, even a slap across the face is the appropriate response. But Madame Agathe dips her head and smiles just as Cosette had a few seconds earlier.

François turns abruptly and leaves the dancing area without bowing to Héloïse, who slinks off like a chastised dog.

Willem looks around for Jean but cannot see him in the swirling crowd. He takes off after François. When he finds him, François is returning to the square. In his hands, the new ax, still shiny and pristine. The tool is now a weapon.

Willem blocks his way, but François pushes past him.

"It is nothing, François," Willem says. "Claude is a man with hands like creeping vines and always will be. He means nothing by it."

"He means nothing?" François says. "What do you know? He comes to our house in the day, when I am out chopping wood in the forest. When I return, I smell his funk."

There is a quiet fury in his voice, and something more than that. A derangement.

"Perhaps he just comes to check on her, to help her out," Willem says. "You cannot know that he visits his desires upon her."

"I know it," François says, pushing forward.

"How could—"

"Because she is with child," François says.

Willem is silent.

As soon as François says it Willem knows that it must be true. There is a slight bulge to the belly of Madame Agathe that he had not given any significance to, but now he realizes that in these lean times, it is not the belly of a well-fed person.

There is a hotness to Willem's cheeks, and his fingernails cut into his palms as his hands clench into fists. To his surprise and displeasure, he finds himself angry to discover that his mother is just one of the man's mistresses. That the mayor is cheating on the woman he is cheating on his wife with.

François has almost reached the square when Willem tackles him from behind. He means to wrestle the ax off him and hide it, but François is surprisingly quick and far too strong. He twists under Willem, rolling on top of him, rage seeping from his face. Now it is Willem who is pinned, under the larger, stronger boy, and François has the ax, held midshaft. There is no sense in his eyes. He raises the ax. Willem struggles, but his arms are pinned by François's knees.

"François!"

It is the voice of the blacksmith, François's uncle.

François stops. He looks at Willem, then at the ax in his hand, as if surprised to find it there. He drops it to the ground beside Willem's head, then slowly stands, releasing Willem. With a quick glance at Monsieur Lejeune from beneath a lowered brow, he runs off and does not return to the fête.

The band is packing up as Willem and Monsieur Lejeune return to the square, and the villagers are spreading out, finding comfortable spots from which to watch the fireworks display.

Jean sees them coming and queries them with a raised eyebrow.

"François has great anger inside," Willem says.

"What did you do to incur his wrath?" Monsieur Lejeune asks.

"It was not about me." Willem glances over at Monsieur Claude. "That peacock has been strutting in the wrong farmyard."

"My brother's wife?" Monsieur Lejeune asks. He does not seem particularly surprised or angry, just seeking clarification. Most men in the village have mistresses at one time or another.

"What happened?" Jean asks.

Willem nods. "François went for his ax," he says.

"My idiot cousin did what?" Jean asks.

"Just a moment of fever," Willem says.

"I will conceal it until morning, when he is calmer," Monsieur Lejeune says, holding up the ax.

"And has less wine in him," Jean says.

"He will be all right," Monsieur Lejeune says. "It is still the shock from the accident more than anything. I will talk to him in the morning."

"And Monsieur Claude?" Jean asks. "Will you talk to him?"

Monsieur Lejeune shakes his head. "There is nothing to say."

"But Aunt Agathe!" Jean says.

"Your aunt sees me as a friend," Monsieur Lejeune says. "If she objected to his visits, she would come to me. She is a wife without a husband, thanks to my pious fool of a brother."

Willem thinks of that haunted, bleeding look in his mother's eyes and decides that his dislike of Monsieur Claude has turned into hatred.

He again looks around the square for his mother. The subject of the mayor's visits to their house is not something he feels he can discuss with her, but he could share the gossip about Madame Agathe. Perhaps that will dissuade her from further assignations.

He cannot see her. Suddenly uncomfortable and not sure why, he looks again around the square, searching for Monsieur Claude. Have they . . . ?

No. He is still there, holding court from his throne near the stage.

A series of loud bangs is followed by explosions overhead and the sky lights up with brilliant stars. More explosions; streaks of light shoot up from a paddock near the square, and sounds like cannon-fire shake the houses of the village.

Willem begins to walk back to his home. Behind him the sky is alive and the air reeks of gunpowder.

That fades as he nears his home, but there is another smell, that of burning. His brisk walk turns into a run.

Smoke is curling out of the door of his house when he arrives. His first thought is that their house is on fire, but there is not enough smoke for that.

He runs to the kitchen and bursts inside.

His mother kneels at the baking oven, the fire door of which is open, smoke pouring out.

Empty chests lie around the oven. His father's chests.

"Mother! What are you doing?"

Mixtures and potions are crackling and popping inside the oven.

His mother slams the fire door shut.

"You think word of tonight will not spread? You've announced our presence here to the world. You have struck a flint and the fire will spread."

There is a sudden cracking and popping sound from the oven, not the sound of wood burning, and a sulfurous smell leaks out.

"Mother!"

Willem races to the oven and opens the door of the firebox. Inside, all is flames. A bonfire of their former lives.

Thunder from the square shakes the stars, and bursts of light flash through the windows of the house.

"How could you do it?" Willem cries.

"How could *you* do it, Willem? This is all I had left of him," his mother says through the start of tears.

Then the fireworks end, and there is only silence.

THE MONSTER

On the fourth day of the fourth month in the year of Our Lord, eighteen hundred and fifteen, more than three weeks after the fête, the monster came to the village of Gaillemarde.

Willem's mother always said that four was an accursed number. That it was the sign of death. And so it was.

But it was not a monster, just a saur. Neither devil nor demon, not mythical nor fantastical. A creature of flesh and blood: a wild creature from a wild and dangerous world.

It came at night, hunting in the moonlight.

First to be taken was Angélique Delvaux, the eldest daughter of the schoolmaster. She was walking back from the nearby township, well after midnight. There was no shame in what she had been doing. Wars had ravaged this part of the world for more than a decade. The country was like its people: emaciated, cadaverous. It was a time of great hardship. There were few in the village who could count on food for the next day.

Yet a young woman of a certain age could return from nearby Waterloo with a purse that jangled with coin. No one would judge her for it. If anything, those with empty tables and bellies envied those with something ripe and luscious to sell.

It would be many weeks before the remains of Angélique's naked, maggot-ridden body were found.

Book Two

April 4–June 18, 1815

THE ARTILLERYMAN

G troop of the British Royal Horse Artillery is on the move.

The rain has stopped and the sun glares hot, but all that does is bake a thin crust on top of deep slush.

Three times on the way up the hill, the gun carriage, with its heavy nine-pounder cannon, breaks through the scab that looks like solid ground, and only the combined effort of all eight horses, and the men of the gun crew, straining against the wooden wagon wheels, convinces the carriage to start moving.

The fourth time the wheel sinks almost to its axle, releasing gas trapped deep in the mud. It smells like dead things. The gun carriage twists around as one wheel tries to continue forward, then stops.

"Ease off the horses," Sergeant Roberts orders immediately, "or you'll snap the wheel."

Bishop, the driver, lets the horses rest and seven men cease pushing. The cannon and the limber carriage with its heavy load of ammunition is stuck fast.

From here, they can see over a copse of trees to the red tile roofs and the fortified wall of the city of Brussels beyond.

A trio of crows caws and circles above them, black predators against a hard blue sky. Jack Sullivan looks up at the birds and crosses himself. Crows are a harbinger of death.

"We're going to need more horses," Roberts says. "Private Sullivan."

Jack straightens from where he still has his shoulder to one of the spokes of the wheel. "Yes, Sergeant."

"Back down the hill with you, lad. Find us a couple more horses. And tell the others this ain't going to work. They'll need to take the long way around."

"Yes, Sergeant," Jack says again.

He is covered to the waist in mud. Fortunately he removed his tunic and helmet before they started. But his boots and his gray uniform trousers will need a good wash in the river before next inspection.

He stumbles on trembling legs down to where the other five cannon of G troop are lined up in neat rows. A thin-faced young lieutenant rides forward and meets him at the base of the hill.

Jack almost salutes, then realizes he shouldn't, as he isn't wearing his helmet.

"Yes, Private?"

"Sir, my sergeant suggests that the rest of the troop take the long way around. The hill, it's like puddin', sir."

"Yes, I can see," the lieutenant says. "What do you need?"

"A couple of horses would be good, sir," Jack says. "Help us pull the carriage out."

The lieutenant nods and gestures to a sergeant. They have already unhitched two of the horses from one of the ammunition wagons, in anticipation of the request.

Jack leads the animals back up the hill.

Corporal Wacker is staring in the other direction. "Our new lieutenant has arrived," he says.

"And how would you know that?" Roberts asks.

"New officer down at the captain's tent," Wacker says. "Uniform looks like he just picked it up from the tailor. He's still riding on his horse like he has a bayonet up his bum and thinks he's on show for the king."

They all look.

Dysentery had claimed their last lieutenant just a week earlier and the arrival of the new one has been much anticipated.

"Just a little boy," Wacker says. "Barely weaned from his ma's tit."

Jack is the youngest in the crew at barely seventeen but even from this distance it is clear that their new lieutenant is much younger.

It is not uncommon to see officers of fourteen or fifteen in the British army, their commissions purchased for them by wealthy fathers. It is also not uncommon to see those same young officers shipped home in coffins.

"Get those horses put to," Roberts says. "We don't want to be still mincing around on the side of this hill when he gets here."

Below, the lieutenant dismounts and disappears into the tent.

Wacker helps Jack put the new horses to the traces of the exhausted team.

"Now put your backs into it," Roberts says. "Sullivan, you lead the horses."

Bishop, who has had that job up till now, blows Jack a kiss as he goes to lend his own shoulder to the gun carriage.

Jack tugs gently on the reins and the new horses take up the load. Their own team follows the lead, legs straining through the mud.

The carriage moves, but does not pull free.

At the captain's tent, Jack sees the new lieutenant emerge and remount.

"He's heading this way," Jack says.

"Move this bleedin' carriage!" Roberts barks.

Jack hauls on the reins and the horses strain, their hooves sinking through into the soft ground below.

There is a squelching sound, but the left wheel is firmly embedded in the ground.

"Hie!" Jack yells at the horses.

The lieutenant reaches the base of the hill.

"Come on, lads," Roberts cries, his voice straining with the effort. "Come on, Sullivan."

"Hie!" Jack roars at the horses, yanking on the reins. One of the new horses takes fright. It rears, and the other rears with it.

"No! Stop!" Roberts shouts, seeing what is about to happen.

The horse team twists and pulls to the left, hooves cracking the sun-baked crust of earth. The gun carriage twists, and the pressure, plus the weight of the cannon, is too much for the stuck wheel. One of the spokes gives way with a crack like a musket shot, then the others in quick succession. The metal rim twangs away like a watch spring releasing, then the outer wheel snaps off the remaining spokes and the side of the carriage collapses deeply into the mud as the men scatter and fall around it.

"Good morning, Sergeant." The new lieutenant has arrived. His horse is a mare, a beautiful chestnut with white stockings on its two rear feet. Two rear stockings is a sign of good luck, Jack's father had always said.

"Good morning, sir," Roberts says, standing up quickly.

The rest of the squad jump up from where they have fallen and stand to attention. Bishop, the only one wearing his helmet, salutes. The lieutenant returns the salute briskly.

"My name is Frost. I'm to be your new lieutenant."

His voice is high and gentle. He looks about fifteen years old.

"A pleasure to meet you, sir," Roberts says.

"Bit of a sticky situation," Frost says.

"'Fraid so, sir," Roberts says.

"Hardly the way to greet your new lieutenant," Frost says.

"No, sir. Sorry, sir," Roberts says.

"Sorry is not good enough, Sergeant," Frost says. "If this

happened in the heat of battle it could turn the tide in the enemy's favor."

"It's just one cannon, sir," Roberts says.

"One cannon missing at the crucial moment could be a catastrophe," Frost says. "This is not acceptable. Someone will have to be shot for this."

"I beg your pardon, sir?"

"You heard me, Sergeant. We are at war. We might overlook something like this during peacetime, but it cannot go unpunished in a war. Someone will have to be shot."

"But sir, you can't—" Roberts begins, clearly no longer happy to have accepted the responsibility. To his credit though, he did not attempt to shift the blame.

The boy lieutenant cuts him off brusquely. "I am new here, Sergeant, and have to learn the local customs. So tell me, in the Duke of Wellington's army is it sergeants who tell their officers what they can and cannot do?"

"Stupid little twat," Wacker mutters under his breath beside Jack, not loudly enough to be heard.

"No, sir," Roberts says.

"So whose fault is it?" Frost asks.

There is silence.

"It is my fault, sir," Jack says. "I scared the horses. I panicked a little when I saw you coming. I'm very sorry, sir. I'm usually very good with horses."

"And you are?"

"Sullivan. Jack Sullivan. Private," Jack says. "I'm not very bright, sir, but I'm a good lad."

"Is that so, Sullivan?" Frost asks.

"It is, sir. I heard the lieutenant tell Captain Mercer himself. I mean the old lieutenant, not you, sir."

"I see," Frost says.

"I really liked Lieutenant Gibson, sir," Jack says. "But he died."

"I will do my best not to," Frost says.

"Shame," Wacker mutters.

"Sir, I was in charge of the carriage," Roberts says. "It is my responsibility."

The lieutenant scratches his chin.

"Why were you going up this hill in the first place?" Frost asks.

"Orders of the captain," Roberts says. "He wants us ready to move out in a hurry."

"Well, we can't exactly shoot the captain, now can we?" Frost says.

"No, sir, you can't shoot the captain, sir," Jack says, when nobody else answers. "On account of he's the captain."

"So why did Captain Mercer want you ready to move out?" Frost asks.

"Duke of Wellington's orders, I would say, sir," Roberts says.

"And why should he order such a thing?" Frost asks.

"Apparently we're getting ready to invade France," Roberts says. "Bony—I mean Napoléon, sir, has escaped from Elba. That Frenchie King Louis has scarpered and now Bony's in Paris, raising an army."

"So you're saying it is Napoléon's fault that your wheel broke."

"In a way, sir," Roberts says.

"Then he will have to be shot," Frost says.

There is a brief silence, then Roberts asks, "Napoléon, sir?"

"Well, he's clearly the one to blame," Frost says.

"Yes, sir. I will see to it personally, sir," Roberts says. "First chance I get."

"Very good, Sergeant," Frost says. "Now in the meantime rustle up a new wheel from somewhere. Unload the limber and get my gun carriage back down this blasted hill. We'll take the long way around." He turns to Jack. "And, Private Sullivan."

"Yes, sir," Jack says, drawing himself up to full attention.

"Please don't go scaring my horses," Frost says.

"No, sir. Won't happen again, sir," Jack says.

Frost wheels his mount around and heads back down the hill.

"He might just turn out to be all right," Wacker says.

APRIL FOURTH

The dark pool of blood is not quite congealed on the ground. When Willem kneels and touches it, it is dense and tacky, not quite a fluid, not yet solid.

It has pooled in a hard, rocky depression on the path along the riverbank that leads to Waterloo, only a few minutes' walk from the village.

Monsieur Delvaux, the schoolmaster, woke the village at first light, covered in blood, yelling and screaming about a saur attack. His elder daughter, Angélique, had not returned from an evening in Waterloo, and when he went to look for her, he stumbled upon (in fact into) the pool of blood.

The weeks after the fête have been happy ones. François's recovery seems complete, with only occasional lapses. Crops thrive. Days have warmed in the village even further, and so has Cosette.

It is Cosette, not Angélique, who emerges each morning to collect the bread from Willem, and as her sister has so often done, her hand touches his as she accepts the loaf. But where Angélique did it as a tease, there seems something more behind Cosette's touch, a connection between the two of them expressed only in the quick, light caress of fingertip on palm.

After mass she will often linger with him and they will discuss the sermon and the events of the week. On occasion the milling crowd outside the church will force them to stand more close together than is generally considered acceptable for a man and a young lady; however, neither of them minds.

He finds himself thinking at night of the lines of her jaw, and the fall of her hair. Even the slow drift of her lazy eye seems something interesting, exotic.

As expected, Jean and François rib him mercilessly.

"Be careful, young Willem, or she will have you hooked," Jean says.

"And would that be a terrible thing?" Willem asks.

"You are young. There are mountains to climb, rivers to swim, women to woo. It is too soon for you to be ensnared."

"A cook must taste many broths to know which is best," François says.

Although Willem feels far from ensnared, there are moments, late at night, when he finds himself hoping she will not follow the path of her older sister to Waterloo. Whether that means something, he does not know.

But today that path has led to disaster.

"It was no saur," Monsieur Claude says. "There are no claw prints."

If there were any prints they would be well and truly trampled by the feet of the men who gather around. But Monsieur Claude is right. The ground is soft from recent rain, yet when they arrived, apart from the imprint of Monsieur Delvaux's bare feet, there were no marks. On the right of the path is dense forest, and the dirt at the base of the trees is dark and soft. On the left is the river, where the earthen bank is also unmarked.

Willem glances at Jean and they both look at François.

If it was a saur then it was a vicious one. A raptor. Maybe even a firebird. Willem knows they are all thinking the same thing: Is it the firebird from the waterfall? Has it somehow, after all these weeks, tracked them back to the village? Are they to blame for the disappearance of Angélique, and the appearance of this tacky, red-brown puddle?

"Do we even know that it was Angélique who was attacked?" Monsieur Lejeune asks. "Might not she have remained in Waterloo overnight, perhaps staying with the friends she is visiting?"

Willem notes that he is careful not to suggest anything unseemly about Angélique's nocturnal visit to the nearby town. Monsieur Delvaux's face lifts at that thought, but only slightly.

A girl is missing, who would have taken this path. There is blood on the path. It is a fool's hope that the two are not connected.

"Whoever was attacked was attacked by a saur." The voice comes from blind old Monsieur Antonescu. Monsieur Chambaux, the tailor, has his arm and guides him along the path with the others.

"How can you know this?" Monsieur Claude asks.

"I can smell it," Monsieur Antonescu says.

Willem, along with most of the other men from the village, sniffs the air, but can detect nothing. He has brought Pieter, curled up in the leather satchel, and the little microsaurus is moving and scratching around inside.

There is nothing nearby, or he would be showing signs of distress. Willem opens the top of the satchel and lets Pieter run up his arm onto his shoulder. Pieter is not alarmed, although he is nervous and skittish, his head darting in all directions. These are signals that Willem knows well.

"Monsieur Antonescu is right," Willem says. "A saur was here."

"You are sure?" Monsieur Claude asks.

"Pieter is sure," Willem says.

"Then where are the signs?" Monsieur Claude asks, and there are murmurs of agreement from other men in the group.

"If everyone will move back, I will let Pieter find them," Willem says.

"Do as he asks," Jean's father says.

Monsieur Claude is the mayor of the village, and the owner of half of it, but Monsieur Lejeune is the one the villagers most respect. They withdraw immediately.

Willem sets Pieter on the ground, then clacks his tongue a few times at the microsaurus and makes a rotating hand gesture.

Pieter runs first to the pool of blood, sniffing at it, then around to the forest side of the path. His small head darts in all directions, sniffing the ground, looking for signs that the human eye cannot see.

He darts off down the path, heading toward Waterloo, then returns. He still looks agitated, but seems unsure, if that is even possible for a saur.

It is only when he ventures onto the river side of the path that things start to go very wrong.

Pieter creeps across the earthen bank toward the river. The riverweeds are short here as beneath the soft dirt is rock and their roots are shallow. Pieter moves cautiously, pushing through the stalks with his nose.

A patch of long reeds rises out of the river itself, and as he approaches it he starts to become more agitated, darting forward, then retreating just as quickly.

He sniffs cautiously at the reeds, then suddenly screams in fright and freezes.

"What's he doing?" Jean whispers.

"I don't know," Willem says.

Pieter remains frozen in place for a long moment, then slowly topples to one side. He lies on his side, rigid and immobile.

"Pieter!" Willem yells and runs over to him.

He is breathing and his eyes are moving, but his body is not. It is as if he has been mesmerized, but somehow different. And there are no lights or flames here to mesmerize him. Willem picks up his

93

pet and strokes his stomach gently. Pieter looks at him, but does not otherwise move.

Although it is early, the sun has already risen above the trees to the east and at that moment a passing cloud releases the sun. A brief flash of white in the reeds of the creek catches Willem's eye. Something moves.

He jumps, stumbling and falling backward, Pieter clutched safely to his chest.

"What is it?" Monsieur Lejeune asks.

"Something in the reeds by the river," Willem manages.

A long sword that had been hanging from Monsieur Lejeune's belt is suddenly in his hands.

"Everybody stay back," he says.

Willem scrambles away, Pieter still held to his chest.

Monsieur Lejeune advances, the sword held in front of him.

He parts the reeds with it, then turns and shakes his head.

"It is nothing but an old rag," he says. "Moving in the current."

"Then why is Pieter so afraid?" Willem asks.

Monsieur Lejeune thrusts the sword into the reeds and lifts a dirty piece of cloth. It had been half in the river and is sodden. The rest is dirty and brown.

"Your pet is afraid of this?" he asks.

Monsieur Delvaux's legs collapse beneath him, and if Monsieur Claude had not been standing next to him to catch him, he would surely have hit his head on the rock of the path.

"That is not a rag," Monsieur Delvaux says. "It is Angélique's frock."

Now Willem can see it. What appeared to be a dirty bunch of rags is in fact clothing, shredded. It is covered not with dirt but the brown stains of blood.

"There are no claw prints," Monsieur Claude still protests.

"Nor drag marks," Monsieur Lejeune says, with a quick, embarrassed look at Monsieur Delvaux. "How could a saur drag her into the river without leaving marks?"

"It is a saur," Willem says, firmly, stroking the stomach of his pet, who is just starting to come out of his stupor. "It has to be a raptor, but I have never seen Pieter so petrified."

"It is the firebird," François says. "We should have killed it at the waterfall, but we ran like skinned chickens. Now it has found us and seeks revenge for its eggs."

"You did this!" Monsieur Delvaux cried, his eyes red and brimming with grief. "You brought this on our village!"

"This is not a firebird," Monsieur Antonescu says, but nobody listens.

There is heat in the group of men, and it is directed at the cousins, and Willem most of all.

"We left no trail," Jean protests. "We walked only in the rivers and streams."

"So it has been hunting the forest since that time, seeking out your scent," Monsieur Claude says.

"Brothers, you misdirect your anger," Father Ambroise says. He holds up his arms, asking for silence and calm. He says, "Now is not the time for recriminations or anger. Kneel with me, brothers. We will pray for the soul of the daughter of our friend."

And so they pray, kneeling on the hard rock of the path, beside the rocky pool of dried blood.

For some reason, when Willem closes his eyes, all he can see is the image of her breasts, pressed together by her arms after she opens the shutters to let in the morning sun.

DEFENSES

Tuesdays in the village are market days, when the traveling merchants from Waterloo and Brussels set up their carts in the village square. The market hall itself is home to the local merchants, including Willem's mother, with a table of freshly baked breads and rolls.

This Tuesday morning, however, customers are scarce. Word has spread quickly of the saur attack, and journeys that lead through or past the great forest are undertaken only if necessary. Gaillemarde is avoided. The square, normally bustling and busy, is all but deserted.

The merchant hall, too, is virtually empty. Only a few of the produce stalls are open. The menfolk are busy rebuilding the defenses that protect the village, long since fallen into disrepair.

A meat-eater is on the loose, and nobody will sleep easily until it is caught.

The gaps in the saur-fence are being mended. Rotten spikes are being replaced. The tarred wood in the fire pits outside the fence, sodden and useless, has been dug out and teams of men now venture cautiously into the forest, cutting wood with which to replace it. Always in teams. Never alone. Always one man on watch, armed with sword or musket.

Watch will also be kept by night, until the beast is caught. The church steeple, the highest building in the village, will be constantly manned, and the church bell will sound the alarm if anything is sighted.

Swords, hoes, shovels, and other makeshift weapons are left at locations around the fenceline, and tallow brands dot the fence at regular intervals, ready for the night.

The bird comes cartwheeling out of the forest in a flurry of feathers and leathery wings. Only as it lands, crashing into the reeds at the edge of the river, does Willem realize that it is not a bird, but a winged saur. They are common in the forest: not quite a bird, not quite a bat, but something in between. The larger ones have wingspans wider than Willem is tall, but this is a young one, barely more than a chick and no larger than a hawk. From the way it comes spinning down out of the trees, something is very wrong with it.

Willem perches on the edge of the old stone bridge, just outside the saur-gate, his feet dangling above the water.

Willem sits alone. Jean and François are in the forest with one of the cutting crews. Willem has offered to help, but was not needed. It is a job for big, strong men, and the building of the fence is skilled work. Nor has he been wanted as a guard. That requires skill with sword or musket, which he does not possess.

He does not want to stay at home. Every time his mother looks at him he can see the disappointment in her eyes. He did his chores, helped with the baking, then left the house as soon as he could. Not so much to avoid her gaze as to avoid showing her the fury in his own eyes.

He went around to the Delvaux house to see if there was anything he could do to help, but a sharp glance from one of the old women of the village warned him off. He is not wanted there either.

In the end he helped some of the women tar wood for the fire pits, and when that was finished came to sit on the bridge and wait for the others to return.

The winged saur thrashes around in the reeds for a moment or two, squealing in pain, and as it does, Willem sees the huge gash along one of its wings. A clean cut, made by a knife or a sword. Inflicted by man. Flying through the forest the little saur has had the misfortune to come across one of the woodcutting parties. Someone has slashed at it with a sword, crippling it in a way that can never be mended. Winged saurs do not attack humans. They pose no danger. But in the aftermath of an attack any saur becomes a target.

The saur goes quiet, but still makes pathetic struggling movements. Half of its body is in the water and half is out, the water pulling at it, dragging it into the river.

He should do something, Willem knows, but he can't bring himself to. The creature is beyond saving; the wing cannot be repaired. He should cross the river and wring its neck, but although he knows it is wrong to just sit and watch it die, he does not want to be the one to end its life.

Jean and François emerge from the forest together as Willem is watching the dying saur. They look sweaty and tired. Each holds an ax. They do not notice the winged saur and Willem does not mention it to them. François would try to save it, and he wouldn't be able to, and it would upset him. There is still a fragility about François. He seems, to Willem, like a spinning top, delicately balanced, with a brittle equilibrium.

"Is the fence finished?" Jean asks.

Willem nods. "And the tar pit is replenished."

"Good," Jean says. "We shall sleep safely in our beds tonight."

The saur-fence, newly repaired, stands strong and sturdy a few meters from the riverbank. The newly sharpened spikes of the crossbracing that extend through the fence make a jagged row of teeth.

In front of the fence lies the long black line of the tar pit, a ditch that surrounds the entire village.

Behind the fence rise the stone walls and thatched roofs of the river cottages, and behind those is the church with its tall steeple.

"Any sign of the raptor?" Willem asks.

"None," Jean says. "It is probably long gone by now."

"Or waiting its chance for another attack," François says.

There is a silence at the memory of the congealing pool of blood on the river path. Jean lays down his ax and sits on the edge of the bridge beside Willem. After a moment François sits too.

"We have brought this upon ourselves," he says.

"That is stupid," Jean says with some venom. "You are stupid, cousin."

"You don't even know it is the same saur," Willem says.

"It does not matter," François says. "This is a punishment from God."

"For what?" Jean asks.

"Your tongue did wag too much, cousin," François says, "and all of us gazed upon the form of the girl in her night frock."

"And you think God sent a raptor to punish Angélique because we said a few words in jest about her," Jean says.

"Not Angélique," François says. "She rests with Him in paradise. It is we who are punished. We who must live with this guilt."

"Quiet your mouth, cousin," Jean says, glancing back toward the village. "Look who comes."

Through the open saur-gate the mayor and the priest walk with the schoolmaster, propping him between them. Monsieur Delvaux seems in a kind of a daze.

Behind them Cosette holds a sheath of wildflowers.

"They go to lay the flowers at . . . the place," Jean says.

Willem rises as they approach, and turns to face them, steeling himself for the inevitable exchange.

"I am sorry for the loss of your daughter," Willem says.

Monsieur Delvaux stops in front of him, vacant eyes seeing him as if for the first time.

"You should be sorry." The voice comes out high and loud, spittle flying from his lips. His cheeks are unshaven and seem hollow. His eyes are dark-rimmed. "The three of you. You brought this horror to us."

"This is not true," Jean says, rising up beside Willem. "You cannot blame us for what happened."

Cosette has stopped behind her father. The wildflowers are clutched tightly to her chest. Her eyes are on Willem, waiting for him to respond. There is a look akin to pleading in her gaze.

Willem looks from her to her father, then back. He lowers his eyes.

"Do not blame Jean or François," Willem says. "It was I who took the raptor's eggs."

The schoolmaster stares at him, cursing him with cratered eyes, then with a dismissive shake of his head, walks on.

Cosette glances at Willem once, her left eye, the often lazy one, as fixed and focused as the other. Both eyes are cold and unforgiving. The colors of the flowers, caught in a shaft of late sunlight, reflect on her face. In her grief and anger, she has never looked prettier. She averts her gaze and walks silently in her father's footsteps. Willem watches her until she disappears around a bend in the river path.

"What is wrong with you, Willem?" Jean asks, as soon as they are out of earshot. "You know this is not our doing."

"Willem only speaks the truth," François says.

"Hush yourself, cousin, or I will hush you," Jean says. "Why, Willem?"

"Did you not see his eyes?" Willem says after a moment. "If Monsieur Delvaux cannot direct his anger elsewhere, then he will blame himself for allowing his daughter to visit the town at night, and that burden would be too great for him to bear."

"So you bear it for him? Why is that your yoke?" Jean asks.

Willem sits back down on the edge of the bridge without answering. A tender breeze ruffles the flowering lavender, bringing a heady perfume. In the river, the body of the dead baby saur dislodges itself from the reeds and floats gently away on the current.

THE FUNERAL

The funeral of Angélique Delvaux is held on Saturday, April fifteenth, almost two weeks after her death.

Her body has still not been found, and with desperate but quite pathetic hope her father has refused to allow the service before that.

When she has still not returned in the second week, and with her soul in need of introduction to heaven, Father Ambroise convinces Monsieur Delvaux that it is time.

An official from Brussels arrives on that Friday afternoon in an official carriage with a team of white horses, declares her officially dead, then takes off almost without his feet touching the ground. It seems a curt and perfunctory end to seventeen years of life.

In another Gaillemarde tradition it rains on the day of the funeral, although, perhaps in a portent of the deaths that are yet to come, it is more like a tropical downpour than a spring shower: heavy belts of water whip the dirt of the riverbanks into mud and batter the side of the church.

The schoolmaster and his daughter sit alone in the front pew, as is customary. As he did with both of his daughters beside him some years ago when his wife took ill and died. Relatives, some who have journeyed from as far away as Nivelles, sit in the pews behind them. Villagers fill the rest of the church.

It is a strained and awkward occasion. A funeral without a

body. A child taken before a parent. And there are other reasons for the discomfort of some present.

Madame Agathe does not lead the choir as she usually would. That is left to one of the Poulencs. Instead she sits at the back of the church where she can better conceal her growing belly.

The mayor sits next to his wife but there is a clear distance between them, and a tension behind their expressions of support and compassion.

After the service, in a ritual that seems cruel to the point of torture, Father Ambroise leads Monsieur Delvaux and his daughter down the aisle, past the mourners, so that every one of them can acknowledge and touch their grief.

Monsieur Delvaux seems determined to get through the ordeal with dignity and grace. In his mourning coat, he walks slowly behind the priest, nodding to the congregation, acknowledging their silent sharing of his pain.

Cosette walks beside him. Willem is seated at the end of a pew but she walks past without seeing him. He has ceased to exist.

Halfway down the aisle there is a minor disturbance, and when Willem turns to look he sees that Héloïse has stood and stepped in front of Cosette, wrapping her arms around her and clutching tightly.

After a moment Cosette's hands find their way around the shoulders of the wild girl, and that is how they stay for long awkward moments. Monsieur Delvaux stands silently, while Father Ambroise shuffles his feet impatiently.

Cosette begins to sob quietly, small sharp shudders that convulse her body in the arms of the other girl. Still Héloïse holds her, still everyone waits, until the tremors subside and Cosette slowly withdraws.

Their close friendship is a thing of the past. In the six years

Héloïse was missing they grew apart in ways that cannot be rejoined. But Héloïse, more than anyone else in the village, understands what Cosette needs. A comforting touch, a poultice to draw out the pain and suffering inside.

Although their lives, once close, have taken very different paths, they have now, in a way, again converged.

Both have lost a loved one to a saur.

SENTRY

The sound of the church bell is an unrelenting steely clanging that cuts through the night like a bayonet, and through sleep just as easily.

Willem has barely enough time to register the noise and wonder what it is, and if it is real, or part of a dream, before it cuts off abruptly. It is the sudden silence, more than the sound itself, that jolts him awake.

Pieter has been curled up at the end of Willem's bed, but now stands erect, his ears and nostrils scanning the air for danger. In the other room, Willem's mother gasps with fright.

Willem explodes out of bed, propelled by a terrible fear. He is halfway to the door before he spins back around, groping in the darkness for the leather pouch that hangs from his bedpost.

Others have been quicker to wake and react. Through the windows he sees men with lamps and weapons spilling out of houses. Some have swords, a couple have muskets, but most have farming utensils, spades, pitchforks, or just sharpened spikes.

He takes the stairs three at a time and flings open the front door.

"Willem!" his mother screams from the top of the staircase, but he ignores her and runs out into the darkness. An overhead haze obscures the stars and even the quarter moon is no more than a vague, malevolent smirk pressed against charcoal clouds.

In confusion and uncertainty people are running in every direction, unsure what is happening, unsure where it is happening, sure of only one thing: danger has come to the village this night. Shouts and screams come from all sides, but the voices are those of fright, not of terror or pain.

Around the saur-fence, tallow brands are being lit, adding a string of flickering lights to the darting fireflies of lamps that swing in the hands of the villagers.

Willem ducks around the confused and milling crowd and runs with clarity and purpose.

Others have the same idea, and there is a congregation of lights around the church. It is there, too, that he finds Jean and François bearing weapons and frayed nerves.

François's lips are moving and without hearing the words Willem knows he is praying. Jean's face is expressionless, but his eyes are moving constantly, flicking between the church and the saur-fence.

Now Willem sees why: the hole in the fence that gapes like an open, jagged-toothed mouth, the wooden poles that lie, broken and twisted, among the lavender plants along the riverbank.

The tar pit has been lit and a low blue flame races along the narrow trench, erupting here and there into bursts of orange and yellow that quickly spread. Within a few moments a wall of flame rings the village, visible to Willem only through the gap in the fence. Black smoke glows like the devil's breath in the light of the flames below and brings with it an oily stench. One of the broken poles from the fence lies across the pit, and begins to burn.

"What could do this?" Willem wonders.

"Is it not clear?" François asks.

"Not to me," Willem says.

"Nor me," Jean says.

"It is the firebird," François says. "It seeks revenge. It seeks us."

"No firebird could do this," Jean says, walking toward the hole in the fence.

"This part of the fence had not yet been replaced," François says. "The wood is old and rotten." He kicks at a broken pole, which looks neither old nor rotten to Willem.

"Get back from there." It is Jean's father, his flintlock pistol in one hand, in the other a burning brand. He is naked from the waist up. Across his stomach are the marks of battle, the rewards for years in the service of the French emperor: deep scars, vivid, white, and angry in the flickering flame of his torch.

Willem and the cousins step backward as men push past them, grim-faced, some holding muskets, some guarding the hole in the fence, while others, including Monsieur Lejeune, search the river-bank by torchlight.

Willem looks up at the steeple of the church. It is empty and dark.

"Why did the bell stop so suddenly?" he asks. "And where is the sentry?"

"I don't know," Jean says. "Who was the sentry tonight?"

Jean shakes his head, as does François. If there was no sentry, then who sounded the alarm? If there was a sentry, then where is he?

"Monsieur Antonescu was on watch tonight," Monsieur Claude says.

"Then where is he?" Jean asks.

After a quick discussion, someone is sent to check Monsieur Antonescu's cottage.

Whispers flicker through the crowd as quickly as the flames spread on the tarred wood in the pits. Antonescu was old; he was drunk; he fell; he went home, or forgot his shift altogether.

The news comes back quickly. Monsieur Antonescu is not at his cottage.

It isn't until someone climbs up into the open-sided bell tower and leans out, holding a lamp, that the evidence becomes clear.

There are scratch marks, deep and dark, on the side of the steeple, decorated with bursting floral patterns, crimson in the lamplight: blood.

"It climbed up into the tower to get him," François says, and crosses himself.

"Then it was not the firebird," Willem says.

"Of course it was the firebird," François says.

"A firebird cannot climb," Willem says.

"This one can," Jean says.

"Or it was some other kind of saur," François says. "One that can climb, or fly."

"Flying saurs don't attack humans," Willem says.

"This one did," Jean says.

"Nor would a winged saur have needed to make a hole in the fence," Willem says.

"So it was not a flyer. But this saur was strong enough to break the fence, and can climb," François says. "And that is how it took Antonescu."

"Why was he even on watch?" Willem explodes. "He was old and blind."

"He insisted." Monsieur Claude speaks quietly. "And not without cause. His hearing and sense of smell were the worth of any pair of eyes."

Jean nods. "At night, he was worth two men."

"You are certain of that?" Willem asks, indicating the side of the steeple.

"Unless he had been drinking," François says.

Whether or not he had been drinking, there is no question that he has been taken. The deep red spray patterns down the side of the bell tower lead to the discovery of a trail of blood on the dark ground. It runs from the church to the river through the crushed and splintered gap in the saur-fence.

"Are there any claw prints?" Willem asks.

"If there were, they are long gone," Jean says.

The lavender beds outside the fence are flattened, but whether that is from the saur or the footprints of men, it is impossible to tell.

Monsieur Lejeune reappears at the gap in the fence.

"Get the dogs," he says. "Quickly, we must give chase."

"In the darkness?" Monsieur Claude asks.

"Before it is too late," Monsieur Lejeune says.

"It is already too late," Monsieur Claude says. "Saurs do not toy with their prey."

There is silence. They all know it is true.

"We will hunt the beast!" Monsieur Lejeune says, gesturing with his pistol at the woods on the far side of the river.

"And risk more lives?" Now it is Father Ambroise who is speaking.

"So we should wait for the next time it invades our village?" Monsieur Lejeune shouts. "How many more of us must die before its hunger is satisfied?"

"We will send a message to Brussels," Monsieur Claude says calmly. "The English army, under Wellington, is encamped there. They will find and kill this beast."

Monsieur Lejeune is silent. He bows his head and takes three deep breaths. When he lifts his head, his eyes are firm and hard, and glint like steel in the torchlight.

"I did not call him friend," he says, "but I called him neighbor.

For many years Antonescu cut wood for my forge. He played music for our fêtes. He drank with us at our celebrations and our funerals. He was a good man. He was . . ."

There is silence as Monsieur Lejeune gathers his words. The moon shuffles into a fissure in the clouds and lights up the old soldier's face.

"They are all gone now, the founders of our village," he says. "Antonescu was the last of them. I will not sit by and let others avenge his death."

"Nor I," Jean calls out, and the shout ripples and echoes around the crowd.

Monsieur Claude looks about, like any politician, sensing the mood of his people. "I agree, but not now." He holds up both hands for quiet. "The darkness is this creature's ally, and our enemy. We will go at dawn."

"At first light," Monsieur Lejeune says.

INTO THE FOREST

The dawn sky is a cold gray pan of gruel, colored only by a creeping redness to the east, like dripping blood diffusing in a bowl of dirty water. As it spreads, it reveals a morning ground fog choking the trees of the forest.

Ten men wait at the gap in the fence, reluctant to venture into the hazardous brew of darkness and mist. Four more stand guard until repairs can be made. The fence will have to be strengthened all around the village, judging by the ease with which this firebird has pushed through it.

Birds and winged saurs paint the air with sound, a discordant dawn chorus of screeches and caws, a preposterous orchestra playing a grotesque score of dread and awe.

Willem hasn't slept since the attack, and nor, he is sure, has anyone else. Sleep for Willem would have been a blessing. If he slept too long, he would miss the hunt for the raptor and no one could blame him for that, least of all himself.

But when the blackness of the sky turns to dull gray, he rises and quickly dresses, then holds open a canvas bag for Pieter, who clacks with innocent amusement as he scampers inside. Willem cannot look at him. He is carrying the simple, trusting animal to an uncertain fate.

Willem is the last to arrive at the fence and his appearance causes a sudden silence and a slew of downward glances. He looks around at the faces. Monsieur Lejeune and Monsieur Claude he expects. Jean and François go without question. Others are farmers, hard-faced men, tempered to steel by a lifetime of working the fields. Some of them, like Monsieur Lejeune, are also ex-soldiers.

The surprise is Monsieur Delvaux. The schoolmaster is still in mourning. He seems weakened and made vulnerable by the loss of a child. Yet he comes to hunt the saur. The desire for revenge outweighs all else, except perhaps his distaste at Willem's presence.

"The child is not wanted," he says.

Murmurs from one or two others express agreement. Jean's father keeps silent, as do the cousins.

The weight of the deaths seems to have settled securely on Willem's shoulders. François and Jean's involvement in the raid on the firebird nest is now minimized, if not forgotten. It was Willem who took the eggs, who incurred the wrath of the saur. But perhaps worse, it is Willem who is the outsider, Flemish, in a Walloon village.

"He wishes to make amends for his actions," Monsieur Claude says, when Willem does not respond.

"You think he can undo what he has done?" the schoolmaster asks.

There is silence.

"I came to help," Willem says at last, with conflicting feelings. In many ways he will be happier if he is turned away, unwanted in the hunting party.

"He is a puny boy," Monsieur Delvaux says, refusing to address Willem directly. "A pathetic child. A Fleming. He can do nothing."

"Pieter is with me," Willem says. "He will give good warning of any danger."

"For that we have the dogs," one of the farmers says.

"The boy brings a saur to a saur hunt." Monsieur Delvaux emits a single, bitter laugh. His face is lined, his hair flecked with gray that has sprouted almost overnight. His eyes are sunken and sallow. It is hard to believe that this is the same man who stood in front of Willem in school, day after day, teaching him arithmetic and geography and the books of the Bible. That this is the man who once called Willem his best-ever student. Monsieur Delvaux has been transformed by his grief into a raw stew of emotions. And the focus of it all, in the absence of the firebird, is Willem.

No logic can defeat such inflammation, and Willem does not try.

"Willem's pet is sensitive to the mood of the forest," Jean says. "He will give us warning well before the dogs, and may help lead us to the raptor."

"It is so," François agrees.

"The boy comes with us," Monsieur Lejeune says before Monsieur Delvaux can respond.

"I will allow it," Monsieur Claude proclaims, as if it has not already been decided. "But he stays in the boat. We do not want him under our feet."

Now Willem sees the boat, a flat-bottomed riverboat, with a single oar for sculling at the stern. It is moored by the stone bridge. Two wicker eel traps sit near the bow.

"We search until midday," Monsieur Claude says. "We must be back before nightfall."

"We search until we find it," Monsieur Lejeune says.

"We return before dark," Monsieur Claude says.

Willem thinks the tension between the two of them is more than just a battle for the leadership of the hunting party. Monsieur Lejeune professes no anger toward the mayor, but Willem wonders what he really feels about the man who has cuckolded his brother.

By the time they set off, the sun is smoldering at the edge of the horizon. The tips of the trees make long shadows on the top of the fog as though drawn in long flowing strokes of charcoal.

The dogs pick up the scent by the base of the church, but lose it at the river, and no amount of scouring of the opposite bank can locate it again. It is as if the saur is using the river to disguise its trail.

Willem finds that a worrying thought. It implies a level of intelligence on behalf of the raptor such as has never been seen before. Jean clearly thinks so too. He says nothing, but his eyes are thoughtful.

Without a scent trail there is nothing to do but follow the river into the forest until they find the point at which the saur leaves the river.

There are eleven hunters, but only three of them are armed with muskets. Monsieur Lejeune has his flintlock pistol, François his ax, and the rest carry swords or long pikes. Monsieur Claude has a long, curved cavalry saber. Willem has only his leather pouch and its contents.

"We split into two groups," Monsieur Lejeune says. "And search both banks at once."

"There are only three muskets," Monsieur Claude says. "One musket should join the boy in the boat. Then they can cover either side of the river."

"From a moving boat?" Monsieur Lejeune says. "I wish I were that good a shot. They would likely do more injury to one of us than to the meat-eater. I have my pistol. One of the muskets comes with me across the river, and we leave the other two muskets here."

"Are you now in charge of this hunting party?" Monsieur Claude asks icily.

"You have missed our best chance of catching this meat-eater," Monsieur Lejeune says. "Had we followed the trail of this saur when it was fresh, we would likely be returning home with its head now, instead of hunting a cold trail. If you want to take a vote, let us do it now."

Monsieur Claude opens his mouth to object, then closes it again as there are murmurs of agreement from among the others.

"There is no need for a vote," he says. "With your experience as a soldier, you are clearly the best man to lead us. I appoint you as leader of this party."

With a few shreds of his dignity still intact, the mayor moves to stand next to Monsieur Lejeune.

Monsieur Lejeune picks two others, one man with a musket and Jean with his crossbow. Then he leads the group across the bridge.

Jean's head is high, and his shoulders are square with pride at being chosen by his father, although Willem wonders if the father wants to keep his son near, rather than having great faith in his aim.

The dogs are pinscher bitches belonging to a pig farmer, Monsieur Beauclerc. He takes one across the bridge. The other stays with Édouard Poulenc, the accordion player from the fête.

The dogs snuffle and circle fruitlessly on opposite banks of the river for a few moments, then follow the river to the west, into the depths of the forest.

Willem sits at the bow of the boat, with Pieter between his arms, curled up on the breasthook. He stares straight ahead, thinking that if the firebird is using the river, then the boat offers no more than the barest illusion of safety. Parts of the river seem quite deep, and he can only surmise that the firebird has kept near to one of the banks.

Willem looks back at Monsieur Lecocq, the eeler. He is tall and strong in a wiry kind of way. A bundle of tightly stretched cords under a thin, leathery skin. He smells like oily fish. He has long hair swept back and tied with a leather thong, and a sword thrust into a leather belt. He propels the boat forward in long, easy strokes of the single oar, twisting the handle as he sculls. He does not look at Willem even once, and Willem feels even more keenly his place. Not only is he responsible for what has happened, but he is a liability. A child who must be protected.

The bow of the craft pushes aside the mist as the boat slowly drifts with the river. Behind them, the still, clear water is perplexed by the passing of the boat. Moss hangs heavy on branches, stooping low over the river.

A breeze is rising with the morning sun, gusting through the forest, teasing the fog that flexes and billows, movements that catch the eye when nothing is there but vapor.

On the east bank, Jean moves with quiet confidence at the head of the group. His father is right behind him, one hand resting on the stock of his pistol, in a holster on his belt. Their side of the river is quite flat, although the bank is narrow.

On the western bank, the team has a more difficult trek. The bank is not flat, but peppered with large boulders that must be surmounted or passed.

An hour into the forest there is still no excitement from the dogs. It seems the raptor has disappeared into the mists, a phantom, not a creature of flesh and blood. An illusion like one of Willem's tricks.

They move past shrouded trees and water that murmurs beneath a thin, diaphanous film of vapor. They see remnants of an old jetty lying along part of the riverbank. A row of ravensaurs lines the jetty, perched on top of the rotten and warped posts and collapsed timbers. Among them are a number of crows. Birds and saurs living alongside each other and sharing the perch in the light mists of the morning.

Black, unblinking eyes follow the hunting party as it traverses the river.

One of the crows caws, a cruel, discordant sound that sets off a frenzied cacophony. The ravensaurs are silent, just watching as the men from the village pass. Somehow their silence seems more ominous than the raucous conversation of the crows.

Willem finds his hands clutching the sides of the boat, and when he removes them, the wooden hull is darkly moist from his sweat.

As the boat drifts past a patch of giant, flowering ferns on the east bank of the river, Pieter becomes agitated, squawking and jittering, running up Willem's arm to his shoulder.

The men on the riverbanks stop. All eyes are upon him. Weapons are unsheathed. Muskets, already primed, are now cocked.

"Something has come this way," Willem says.

"Why did the dog not find the scent?" Monsieur Claude asks.

"I do not know," Willem says.

The dogs are halted, and one is encouraged to scratch and sniff around the ferns. Eventually she disappears into the dense foliage. Monsieur Beauclerc and the hunters follow.

"Monsieur?" Willem asks, and Monsieur Lecocq nods. He eases the boat toward the bank and Willem climbs awkwardly over the side, foundering and splashing in the shallow water.

He looks back. The group on the west bank have stopped, and are watching intently.

He pushes into the foliage where the others disappeared. The edges of the fern leaves, although soft-looking, are sharp and hard, scratching his skin, but not cutting it. They are damp from the fog, and spring back behind him with soft slapping noises.

He emerges into an opening in the forest. Not a clearing but a swamp of dark, brackish water. The others, including Jean, wait on firm ground, staring across the swamp at something on the other side.

A voice calls from the far bank of the river. "What is it? What have you found?"

"A house," Monsieur Lejeune calls back.

It is not a house, nor a cottage. It is barely even a shack. It was once, but that was a long time ago. Its walls are stone, and stand firmly, although the roof has fallen in. A rusted old cooking pan hangs from an equally rusted hook by a shuttered window. The shutters barely exist. They have rotted to virtually nothing and sag beside the window. There is no glass in the window. Nor ever was there.

Nobody has been here for a very long time.

"What is this place?" Willem asks into the still, fetid air of the swamp.

Nobody answers for a moment, then Monsieur Claude says, "I have lived in Gaillemarde all my life, and have never seen this."

"Nor I," Monsieur Lejeune says.

One of the farmers thinks it belonged to an old trapper. Nobody is sure.

Jean steps into the water, his crossbow leading the way to the shack.

"Wait," his father says.

"Let him go," Willem says. "Something was here, but not for many days."

"You are sure?" Monsieur Claude asks. He sounds frightened.

Willem nods and wipes his hands on his smock. He is sure. Pieter is alert, but the nervous little saur shows no signs of immediate danger.

"The rain has cleansed this place since the meat-eater was here," Willem says. "That is why the dogs missed the scent."

But not Pieter. The sensitive nose of the little saur misses nothing.

Jean moves through the dark waters of the swamp, disturbing clouds of insects that rise up about him like a black mist. A ripple in the water makes Willem worry about snakes, but Jean seems unconcerned.

The swamp extends right to the door of the shack, as though the level of the swamp has risen over the years. Perhaps that is why the shack is deserted. Eventually the rising swamp waters will undermine the foundations and reclaim this area of the forest.

Flies buzz around Willem's head, and he waves them away, but they are persistent.

Jean reaches the doorway and looks inside before turning back and shaking his head.

"Here," says Monsieur Beauclerc. The dog, sniffing around the edges of the swamp, has found something. She is going wild at a patch of weeds, scratching and pawing.

The farmer with the pike investigates the area with the sharpened end of his weapon.

He hooks something, and lifts it. It looks like a pile of bloody rags, but it is too heavy for that. With mounting horror Willem sees the rotting, maggot-ridden flesh and realizes that it is the remains of a body. His stomach heaves and bile floods his mouth, burning his throat. He hawks and spits, but the fire in his throat remains.

"Antonescu?" Monsieur Claude asks.

"No," Monsieur Lejeune says. "It is too soon for maggots."

"It is, it was, the schoolmaster's daughter," Monsieur Beauclerc says.

"You are sure?" Monsieur Claude asks.

Monsieur Beauclerc nods. "The dog and I searched for her also in the days after she disappeared. She knows this scent."

How the dog could recognize any scent from the grisly tumble of flesh seems almost miraculous to Willem, but he knows it has to be true. The raptor brought the girl here and feasted on her.

"Leave it here," Monsieur Lejeune says. "We found nothing."

"Delvaux has a right to know," Monsieur Claude says.

"And he has a right not to know," Monsieur Lejeune says.

"He cannot have a burial without a body," Monsieur Claude says.

"He had a funeral. That will have to suffice," Monsieur Lejeune says. "Do you want *that* to be the last image he has of his daughter?"

The farmer with the pike lowers what is left of the beautiful seventeen-year-old daughter of the schoolmaster back into the putrid waters of the swamp. A girl killed by a beast that Willem brought to the village.

Willem's stomach heaves again and this time hot fluid rushes from his throat. It is all he can do to lean forward and keep it from his clothes and shoes.

There is silence except for the buzzing of the flies and the occasional burp of swamp gas.

FIREBIRD

Pieter's find at the swamp house has restored a little of Willem's standing. The blame for what has happened is still cast in his direction, but at least now he has contributed to the hunt. He strokes Pieter's belly and plucks a leaf from a low-hanging branch for him as a thank-you snack.

By the time the party reaches Lightning Rock, where the river forks, the mood among the men, at first focused and determined, has turned to frustration and anger. There is still no scent of the firebird.

"Which way?" Monsieur Lejeune asks. He takes dried beef from a pocket and chews on it slowly. Many of the others do the same. Willem had not thought to bring food, and his stomach gurgles for breakfast.

Monsieur Beauclerc allows his dog a long rope. It sniffs briefly at the undergrowth, then toilets against a tree. He shrugs.

"We should split into two groups," Monsieur Delvaux calls from the other side of the river.

"We do not have enough muskets," Monsieur Lejeune says.

"Then we are wasting our time," Monsieur Claude says. "We should return home and use our time to better reinforce our defenses."

"I would not give up so easily," Monsieur Lejeune says.

"Nor I," Jean says.

Monsieur Claude looks away.

"Perhaps Willem's precious little pet has an opinion," Monsieur Delvaux says.

Pieter has been sitting quietly on the breasthook without any sign of nervousness. Nor is there now any.

Willem points to the right fork of the river. "There is no sign here. However, this way leads to the base of the waterfall. This is the path we took with François after the . . . accident."

"So that is how it followed you," Monsieur Delvaux says. The words fall into a cold silence.

Willem had been so sure that the raptor could not have followed them. Now he is less certain. Perhaps it hadn't had to. Perhaps it had simply followed the river. Eventually that would have brought the saur to the path where it had taken Angélique. And farther, until it came to the village.

The boat ferries the group on the western bank across to the center of the fork. Then both teams set out once more.

The water is sluggish under the boat. It seems still, as if frozen in time, although Willem knows it is flowing steadily toward the sea. The breeze makes ephemeral faces out of the mist and in the distance a wolf howls a question into the heavy air.

He offers to take over the sculling for a while and Monsieur Lecocq agrees with a sinewy shrug of his shoulders.

It is not difficult work, just a back-and-forth movement with a twist at each end, creating a figure-eight motion. Standing in the stern of the boat, he has to duck occasionally to avoid low boughs.

Standing also finds spiders' webs, stretched between branches. Several times he has to wipe the strands from his face, taking one hand from the oar to do so, which earns him a sharp glance from the boat owner.

Once, after looking around to check the waters behind the boat, he turns back in time to catch a thick web across his face. He gasps in surprise and fright and sucks a large spider into his mouth. There is a bitter taste and frantic scrabbling on the soft skin of his cheeks and tongue. He spits twice, unsuccessfully, before hooking it out with a finger.

The boat has drifted perilously close to a sharp-ended log and Monsieur Lecocq glares at him as he works the oar frantically, steering the boat back on course, spluttering the taste, and at least one leg, out of his mouth.

Ravines rise on either side of the river as they head into a steep-sided gully. They are deep in shadow, but looking up he can see the trees on the tops of the hillsides bright with light, two glowing lines that frame the valley.

The river and the forest are alive with sound. Insects, birds, scrabbling noises in the undergrowth. Hissing noises through the trees around and above them. Are these the sounds of the forest awakening, magnified by the hillsides, or are they the result of every sense in his body operating at high intensity?

He is working much harder now to keep the boat moving forward and he realizes that the flow of the water is swifter; the gradient of the river is steeper. His muscles burn, but he does not stop. He is not a passenger.

Another sound begins to intrude: thundering water. The falls cannot be far ahead. Even as he hears it, there is sudden excitement and frenzied yelping from the eastern bank of the river. The dog has picked up the scent.

Without needing to speak, Monsieur Lejeune motions to Monsieur Lecocq, who takes over the oar and steers the boat to the west bank, picking up the four men and one dog, and ferrying them across, reuniting the party. The riverbank here is a wide, flat bed of pebbles and four of the men haul the boat out of the river. The dogs strain at their leads, sniffing and pawing at the ground.

Part of the hillside has collapsed in front of them and the way upriver is blocked by a heavy ramp of earth topped with thick, low brush, like the head of a broom. The scent trail leads up the ramp into the forest.

"Ssshhh!" François says abruptly, holding up a hand for silence.

Even the dogs are still for a moment. Then Willem hears it too; they all do. The sound of pebbles shifting. Something is moving on the opposite side of the earthen ramp.

Pikes and swords are raised. Muskets are cocked and presented.

The crunching, shuffling sound gets closer.

"Spread out," Monsieur Lejeune says. "If it comes toward you, hold your fire until it is almost upon you. You will only get one shot."

"It is not the firebird," Willem says. Pieter shows no signs of panic.

Monsieur Lejeune seems not to have heard him. He crouches, using his knee to support his elbow and the weight of his pistol. "Aim at the base of the neck. It is your best chance to hit the heart, or the spine."

Monsieur Claude moves behind the boat, using it as a shield, and draws his saber.

"It is not the firebird," Willem says again, and is proved right almost immediately as voices are heard ahead of them.

Muskets lower. Swords are sheathed.

Moments later four men in gray peasant smocks push their way through the brush. They, too, carry muskets, although theirs are shouldered.

The first of the men is the tallest, but all of them look strong and well fed. That is unusual for peasants. Monsieur Lejeune is stone-faced. He says nothing, and it is left to Monsieur Claude to offer a greeting.

"You are deep in the forest," the tall man says, after returning the greeting cordially.

"We seek a firebird," Monsieur Claude replies. "It raided our village two weeks ago, and again last night."

"A firebird?" the man asks. There is meaning behind the question but Willem cannot discern it.

"Yes, a firebird!" Monsieur Delvaux jumps in vehemently, and crooks a finger at Willem. "This one raided its nest and stole its eggs. It followed his trail back to our village."

"A foolish boy," the man says with a quick, derisive glance at Willem. But he seems satisfied somehow with the answer.

"Have you seen a firebird around here?" Monsieur Claude asks.

The tall peasant shakes his head. "We have not. But we are not from here. Hunting has been scarce in our part of the woods, forcing us farther afield today."

Today he says. Yet Willem saw these men, or men like them, a few weeks earlier. Perhaps game was scarce that day also. He and Jean exchange glances.

"If you see this beast, kill it, with our gratitude," Monsieur Claude says.

"Of course," the tall man says. "And you would have us send word to your village?"

Monsieur Lejeune starts to intervene at that point, clearly uncomfortable with the conversation, but the mayor has already answered. "Yes, we would wish to know. We are from Gaillemarde, to the south of the forest, east of Waterloo."

Monsieur Lejeune smiles and nods, but the smile is fixed and the nod rigid. They bid the men farewell at the riverbank and climb the earthen ramp into the forest, following the noses of the dogs up a rocky path.

"Those peasants were not Walloon," Monsieur Beauclerc says quietly. "Their accent is French. Parisian, I think."

"Those were not peasants," Monsieur Lejeune says. "Their muskets were too new. Too clean. Did you not see the white skin on their cheeks? Sideburns, recently shaved. Or the holes in their ears? Earrings, since removed. Those were French soldiers. Grenadiers of the Imperial Guard."

"French soldiers!" Monsieur Claude's voice suddenly drops as if the men at the river can hear him. "What could be their purpose here?"

"Wellington's army camps at Brussels," Monsieur Lejeune says. "French soldiers in disguise so near to his camp can only be spies."

"We have seen those men before," Jean says.

"When?" Monsieur Lejeune asks.

"On the day we raided the nest," Willem says.

"That is many weeks ago." Monsieur Lejeune seems disturbed by this information, although Willem cannot see how it changes things.

He looks back down the path toward the river. The soldiers in peasant smocks had been watching them, but now turn and make their way along the riverbank.

There is something strange about one of the muskets. Even at this distance he can see it is no ordinary weapon. It is larger than the others. The barrel is wider and the end curved outward like the mouth of a clarinet.

He points it out to Jean, but the men disappear around a bend in the river.

"We must return to the village," Monsieur Claude says.

"Return now?" Monsieur Lejeune says. "What about the meat-eater?"

"It is almost noon," Monsieur Claude says. "We must leave soon to be back before dark."

"The day is young," Monsieur Lejeune says. "We are almost upon the beast, I can sense it. We do not give up now."

"We are close to the nest," Jean says.

Monsieur Claude is silent, but all eyes are upon him.

"We continue our search," Monsieur Lejeune says. "At least to the waterfall."

Monsieur Claude raises his head in a gesture of indifference, as if the whole conversation, indeed the whole expedition, is beneath him.

Monsieur Lejeune nods to Monsieur Beauclerc and Monsieur Poulenc, who give the dogs a long leash.

The rocky path brings them to a clearing, then to a wide track that leads deep into the bush. The dogs leave the trail at the base of a steep ridge where the earth has slipped. It has exposed the rocky core of the forest and is devoid of soil and vegetation. In a zigzagging pattern the scent leads the dogs and the raised muskets and swords of the hunting party up the ridge to the crest, where the ridgeline has been cleared by fire and is thick with recent growth. Willem recognizes it as part of the same ridge they traversed when searching for the firebird eggs.

"The dogs lead us toward the nest," Jean says.

"As expected," Monsieur Delvaux says.

Willem nods, a little reluctantly.

"Have no fear, little Willem," François says. "We shall find the firebird this time and kill it."

"You are more confident than I," Willem says.

"My confidence is not without warrant," François says. "God is with us today."

"You are sure of this?" Willem asks.

"Of course." François smiles.

Willem is silent.

The dogs follow the ridgeline down to the stream where, once again, the scent trail disappears.

"Now which way?" Monsieur Poulenc asks.

"Toward the waterfall," Monsieur Lejeune says.

Side by side, weapons ready, the men of the hunting party move along the uneven rocky banks of the stream.

They emerge from thick forest where the stream joins the river and shade their eyes against sudden bright sunlight. Here on the high plateau the overhead sun is no longer blocked by trees and it sparkles and burns off the undulating surface of the river.

The dogs jump and strain at their leashes. The scent is strong here.

Pieter has gone quiet and without warning topples from Willem's shoulder. He would have landed on the rocks on the side of the river, had not Jean seen it happening, and caught the microsaurus as he fell.

"Pieter?" Willem asks quietly, rubbing the creature's belly. "Pieter?"

Pieter is unresponsive. This worries Willem more than anything. He looks around, but can see nothing. Yet something must be there, to have had this effect on Pieter.

Monsieur Lejeune has drawn his pistol from its holster again.

Willem places Pieter gently in his bag and wipes his hands on his smock.

The men, tough farmers, ex-soldiers, look around nervously.

There are no bird sounds here. The only sound is that of the waterfall.

High above them, a ravensaur crosses the sun briefly, then glides off over the forest.

"Where is the nest?" Monsieur Lejeune asks.

Willem points across the river to the location, as best he can remember.

Monsieur Lejeune nods and picks three of the men. "The rest of you remain here. Stay alert."

He leads the way across the river and the four of them merge into the trees.

Willem scans the forest around the river. He can see nothing, but any of the trees could hide a saur.

Monsieur Lejeune reappears, followed by the others. He shakes his head.

"We found the nest," he calls softly. "But it is deserted."

The sound of the rushing water calls to Willem and he steps quietly along the riverbank, his shoes trembling over rounded stones, toward the brink of the cliff.

"Then we return home," Monsieur Claude says.

"We continue our search," Monsieur Lejeune says.

Willem stands next to the fall. It seems louder and stronger than he remembers it, thundering out over the precipice.

"It is after midday," the mayor says. "We must return now to be back before nightfall."

"The return trip is mostly downriver," Monsieur Lejeune says. "The journey will be a faster one."

"You risk our lives with your bravado," Monsieur Claude says. "The English army has many soldiers, well trained and well armed. We are but a few with rusty muskets and old swords."

"You are the mayor of our village," Monsieur Lejeune says, his voice growing louder. "Perhaps your concern should be more for your citizens and less for your own skin."

"You overstep yourself," Monsieur Claude says, his voice also raised. "My concern is for my village. I love these people as brothers and sisters."

"And some of them even more," Monsieur Lejeune says, "judging by the state of my brother's wife's belly."

Into the angry silence that follows, Willem says quietly, "I have found the firebird."

When there is no response he repeats it. "I have found the firebird."

The others move up alongside him. They see it too. It lies on a blood-spattered rock by the side of the river at the bottom of the cliff. It is not moving.

The mighty firebird. So terrifying in life. So resplendent in death. For all its feathers and wing-like arms, it could not fly.

"Our job is done," Monsieur Claude says. "It has slipped and fallen to its death."

"How could it have fallen?" Jean asks.

"Perhaps it has thrown itself over the edge in its grief over the eggs," Monsieur Poulenc says, a weak attempt at humor.

Willem shakes his head, but says nothing.

"We will return home. But first we must check that it no longer breathes," Monsieur Lejeune says.

"There is no need," Monsieur Claude says.

"It is a long way around," Monsieur Lecocq says.

"There is a path down the face of the cliff," Willem says.

"I will go," Jean says.

"I will show you the way," Willem says.

When François does not offer to join them, Willem hands him the canvas bag with Pieter, still unconscious, inside.

Willem leads the way down.

At the base of the cliff he reaches up to steady Jean as he clambers over the last of the rocks.

Looking up, he sees muskets trained down on the saur from the clifftop, just in case.

"Stay back," Jean says, the crossbow held in front of him.

Willem allows him to approach the beast first, although it is clear that the animal is dead. Its neck has been almost severed, and this is where most of the blood has come from, leaking out of the shattered body and staining the rock on which it lies. The blood is wet, and oozing down the rock.

"It is dead," Jean says, poking it with the stock of his crossbow. "We should take its head back to the village as a trophy."

Willem squats by the dead animal and examines it. The feathers are thick and the skin is leathery except under the chin, where the deepest wounds are. He presses on the skin around one of the puncture marks, surprised at how soft and supple it is, compared to the scaly leather of the rest of the creature.

"It is dead," he agrees eventually, "but not from the fall."

Jean looks at him silently.

"Look at the neck," Willem says. "It is almost parted from its body."

"I do not take your meaning," Jean says.

"See the feathers," Willem says, pressing his fingers into them. They are coarse and bitter to his touch, and the ends are sharp, crushed and broken.

"What is this?" Jean asks.

"Teeth marks," Willem says. "This creature did not fall. It was flung from the cliff."

"By what?" Jean asks.

"I do not know," Willem says. "But whatever it was, it has nearly bitten the firebird's head off."

"Your imagination takes flight," Jean says. "Even the bear and the wolf fear the firebird. There is nothing in these forests large enough to do this."

"Until now," Willem says.

The climb up the cliff face was easier than the climb down, and strong hands hauled them up over the edge. Now the others are circled around them, disbelieving faces turning slowly to looks of horror.

"The firebird is dead," Willem says. "But it was not the firebird that attacked our village."

"You seek to cleanse yourself of blame," Monsieur Delvaux says.

"Willem speaks the truth," Jean says. "A firebird could not have pushed through the saur-fence. A firebird could not have flown, or climbed, to attack Monsieur Antonescu in the church tower. Whatever killed the firebird is what attacked Gaillemarde."

"You cannot know this," Monsieur Delvaux says.

For answer Willem reaches inside his smock and brings out a bunch of feathers from the dead saur below. He holds them out toward the dogs, who sniff at them indifferently.

"It is not the firebird's trail that we have been following," Willem says.

"Then what?" Monsieur Lejeune asks. "What could challenge a firebird?"

"A new kind of meat-eater?" Monsieur Claude utters the words as though it is a preposterous idea.

"One from the Africas, perhaps," Willem says. "We have all heard the tales of packs of vicious raptors that roam the savannas."

"One that can fly?" Monsieur Lejeune asks.

"I do not think it flew," Willem says. "I think it climbed the tower."

"Where is it now?" Monsieur Beauclerc asks with a nervous glance around.

"If it can climb a church tower, then it can climb a tree," Willem says. "We have been searching the forest floor. Perhaps we should have looked higher."

All eyes immediately rise to the trees around them, scanning for movement. Leaves shift in the breeze and shadows creep between the branches. Every tree may be hiding a monster.

"The firebird's blood is fresh," Jean says. "The attack was recent. Whatever flung it from the clifftop stood here, where we now stand, and not many hours ago."

"It is time to return to the village," Monsieur Claude says, and for once Monsieur Lejeune does not disagree.

When they reach the boat, the dogs start barking and sniffing along the riverbank.

"What is it?" Monsieur Lejeune asks.

"A new trail. A fresh one," Monsieur Beauclerc says.

"It was here," Monsieur Claude says. "While we were up at the waterfall, *it was here*."

The dogs race along the wide pebble bank until the bank narrows. There the scent trail once again disappears into the water.

"Hurry!" Monsieur Lejeune shouts, running back to the boat, grasping the stern and pulling it toward the water. Others scramble to help.

"What is it?" Jean asks, wide-eyed.

"It hunts," Monsieur Lejeune says. "It follows our trail."

He does not have to elaborate. Their scent will lead the raptor back to the village.

Frantic hands grab the sides of the boat and drag it into the river.

With eleven people it is low in the water, but stable enough. Stringy muscles stand out in Monsieur Lecocq's neck as he hauls on the sculling oar.

There are paddles in the bottom of the boat and Monsieur Lejeune is the first to add the strength of his arms to their flight.

Willem had sculled the boat upstream, and the going had been hard. Now the boat surges along on the river flow, the bow rising with the dipping of the paddles and the thrust of the sculling oar.

Nobody speaks.

* * *

When they reach the village it is still light, although the sun has gone below the horizon.

The saur-gate is open, and although that initially causes a swell of concern in the boat, they soon see people walking down to the river for water, and children playing inside the fenceline.

"Where is the saur?" Monsieur Lecocq asks.

"It is a night hunter," Monsieur Lejeune says. "It waits till dark."

SMALL BEER

The Wood brothers are busy converting their blankets into tents when the lieutenant arrives. Not having muskets or bayonets, they are achieving this using branches and rocks. Ben, the elder brother, is convinced that heavy rain is expected. Lewis says that his brother is always right about the weather.

Not that there is any sign of it. The skies are warm and clear, the sun just resting a little above the horizon.

If it does rain, Roberts, the sergeant, will drape his blanket over the nine-pounder and bivouac under the gun carriage. The rest will fight for places at nearby trees.

"Good evening, men," Frost says, drawing his horse to a halt. "Everything all right?"

The men stand, but do not salute, as they are not wearing their helmets.

"This small beer," Wacker says, holding up his tin mug, "tastes like muddy water, sir. How's a man supposed to get drunk on this?"

"Have you considered, Wacker," Frost says, "that His Grace does not want you to get drunk? That when you are pointing your cannon, Wellington wants you sober enough to point it in the right direction?"

"If he could point his cannon in the right direction, there wouldn't be a puddle around the toilet bucket every morning," Richardson, the ventsman, says, to laughter.

Townshend, the firer, stops laughing quickly. "What toilet bucket?"

"That one," Richardson says, jerking a thumb behind him.

The others peer over his shoulder. There is a silence.

"That's the water bucket, you pillock," Roberts says to groans from the crew.

"I thought the water tasted funny in Flanders," Wacker says.

Frost swings a leg over his saddle, handing the reins to Jack.

"Lovely horse, sir," Jack says, stroking the muzzle of the mare. "What's her name?"

"Molly," Frost says. "Don't go scaring her now, Sullivan."

"Wouldn't dream of it, sir," Jack says.

Frost pulls a silver hip flask from an inside pocket and offers it up. A flurry of mugs present themselves and he pours a quick tot of clear rum into each, then sips briefly at the flask, pursing his lips and sucking in air afterward, his young palate clearly not used to the strength of the alcohol.

"Some'at's up," Wacker mutters, swirling his mug to mix the rum with the beer.

"Very generous of you, sir," Roberts says. "Are we by any chance moving out for Paris in the morning?"

Frost shakes his head. "There's no word on the invasion yet. In fact I heard a rumor that it will be postponed until July."

"July?" Townshend asks. "What are they trying to do? Give Bony enough time to build up another grondee armee?"

"Is one a little impatient, Townshend?" Frost asks.

"One is a little bit, sir," Townshend says. "I've heard a lot about the Frenchwomen. Can't wait to meet them."

"Problem is," Wacker says, "they've heard about you an' all. They'll run a mile."

"We should go now, sir," Roberts says. "Before he's ready."

"Unfortunately we're not ready either," Frost says. "Our orders are to maintain a defensive position on this side of the border, until the Austrian and Russian troops arrive. Then we will invade in full force and hammer that little Corsican corporal into the ground."

"So why the rum, sir?" Richardson asks. "What are we celebrating? Is it your birthday?"

"Yes, he just turned twelve," Wacker mutters so Frost can't hear him.

"Don't you like rum?" Frost asks.

"Indeed I do, sir," Richardson says. "In fact I'd accept another tot, if it was offered, sir."

He holds up his mug.

Frost smiles and ignores it. "There is to be a ball next week," he says. "The Duke and Duchess of Richmond have invited all the senior officers."

"Are you going, sir?" Townshend asks.

"As a matter of fact I am, Townshend," Frost says. "I received a special invitation."

"Helps to have an uncle on Wellington's staff," Wacker mutters.

"What is that, Corporal Wacker?" Frost asks.

"I said, it helps, a tot of rum, when you're swilling this draught," Wacker says, holding up his mug cheerily.

NIGHT

Someone has decided to blockade the bridge, to prevent the meat-eater from crossing it. Willem thinks the idea is stupid but does not voice his opinion.

This creature uses the rivers. Blockading the bridge is useless. But it gives people something to do.

They barricade the bridge with a wagon, turned on its side, tied in place with long ropes that loop around and under the stonework. The execution of the blockade is as stupid as the idea. Have they already forgotten that this creature can climb?

Other villagers go about different tasks. Everybody finds something to do.

The church tower has not one but two sentries, one watching the river, and the other scanning the farmlands to the south and east, in case the beast comes from either direction.

And it is coming.

Some want to kill it. Others just want to keep it out of the village.

The mayor has assembled those with muskets into a small squad and is making them march in unison back and forth along the edge of the square. There are four muskets altogether, the three from the hunting party, plus one that had remained to protect the gap in the saur-fence.

"They are idiots, playing at being soldiers," Jean says, watching the squad march back and forth across the square with Monsieur Claude at its helm. "We have a fool for a mayor."

Willem murmurs a sound of agreement, but thinks that the mayor is smarter than Jean is giving him credit for. A squad of muskets, with even a small amount of discipline, has a greater chance of killing the raptor than panicking individuals.

The saur-fence has been strengthened with additional poles crossbracing the existing supports. The tops of the sharpened posts have been interlaced with strong rope for added strength.

The preparations have not been limited to the fenceline. The shutters on windows are closed and barred. Lengths of timber are placed inside doorways, ready to brace the doors. Many of the village children have gathered in the church for safety. Monsieur Beauclerc's pinschers are chained at the church doorway. The outside of the church has been strung up with lamps, all brightly lit. Inside, Father Ambroise is doing his best to protect the village through prayer.

Cosette finds Willem at the blacksmith's, where he is helping Jean sharpen crossbow bolts. She stands at the entrance, framed by the doorway, her hair not let down or brushed for bed. Like the others in the village she clearly does not anticipate sleep this night. Lamplight trembles across her face and in the faint glow and the flickering shadows, Willem thinks she is the most beautiful thing he has ever seen.

She says nothing, but waits for him to put down the metal file and newly sharpened bolt and to cross to her. It is as if she dare not enter this place, this dark, smelly, manly place, as if it would corrupt her.

Pieter starts to follow, but stops as Willem makes the stay signal with his hands. Pieter sits back on his haunches and crosses his front legs across his chest indignantly.

As Willem approaches she backs away until she is clear of the entrance, out of earshot of Jean, who has glanced up briefly, then returned to his work.

"My father has wronged you," she says, "and so have I."

"It is not important," Willem says, "not now."

"It is," she says. "It was not a firebird that killed my sister. So it was not your doing. I came to apologize."

"On whose account?" Willem asks, more roughly than he intends.

"On my own account," she says.

"And your father?"

"He does not yet see the truth, but he will," she says. She reaches out and takes his hand.

Willem looks away, now feeling bad. "He has lost a daughter and you have lost a sister. You are both suffering."

She says, "My father is not thinking, he is only feeling. Sense and reason will return when the pain subsides."

"I believe it," Willem says, awkward and unsure what to say next. "Thank you for your words."

"I must go," she says. "I am helping to look after the children at the church. Besides, I did not mean to interrupt your work."

"There is much to do," he agrees, glancing behind at the row of shiny new crossbow bolts.

As he turns back to her, she leans forward, catching him by surprise. She presses her cheek to his and her lips touch his skin momentarily, then she lets go of his hand and is gone, out into the dark of the nighttime village.

He looks after her, a little confused, but with a slowly diffusing warmth that disappears in an instant at the sound of Jean's voice. "Willem!"

Willem turns quickly.

Pieter is standing tall on his hind legs; his body is completely rigid, except for his beak, which twitches constantly.

"Pieter!" Willem calls.

With a squawk Pieter scrambles down the leg of the workbench, across the floor, and up Willem's leg into his arms. The little saur is shaking violently.

"It is here," Willem says.

"Why have the lookouts not sounded the alarm?" Jean asks.

"It approaches. That is all I know," Willem says.

Jean rises and takes his crossbow, attaching a quiver of bolts to his belt. "Good. Let us see if it likes the taste of steel. From which direction does it come?"

"I don't know. Perhaps from the river," Willem says. "It seems to like the water."

"Then we go to Antonescu's cottage," Jean says. "It has a high roof and we shall have a good vantage point."

A heavy wooden ladder leans against one wall of the smithy. Jean picks it up easily in one hand and hoists it onto a shoulder.

Willem places Pieter into a sturdy wooden bucket and covers it with a sack. When they leave the smithy, he braces the door. It is the best he can do to keep Pieter safe.

Although the hour is late, the village square is abuzz with movement, men with weapons, tools, or just sticks. Women with lamps. The faces are strained, lips pressed tightly together. Heads flick around at the slightest sound.

Monsieur Lecocq, the eeler, sees them. His eyes take in the ladder and the crossbow and he crosses quickly to them.

"What is happening?" he asks.

"Go to the church," Willem says. "Tell them to sound the alarm."

"What have you seen?" Monsieur Lecocq asks.

"Do as he asks," Jean says. "There is no time for questions."

Monsieur Lecocq nods and has turned toward the church when a sound comes echoing from the direction of the forest. A deep, undulating, gurgling howl. A primal bellow. It sounds just once, and lasts little more than a second, but that is enough.

Around them everyone stops. All eyes turn toward the river. There is a moment when the entire village seems frozen in tableau: a Christmas ornament, porcelain figures posed on a painted backdrop.

Then the illusion is broken as everyone begins to run, all in different directions. Some to their homes to barricade themselves inside. Others to their weapons. Some seem to run aimlessly in one direction, then another, panicked by the sound to the point of folly.

"What in God's name was that?" Jean asks.

"I do not know," Monsieur Lecocq says.

Jean begins to run and Willem runs with him, leaving Monsieur Lecocq still standing openmouthed and unsure.

The church bell now sounds. The alarm seems unnecessary. The bellow of the beast was warning enough.

François meets them at the edge of the square. "Where is it?" he asks. He does not carry his ax, but rather a hatchet in each hand. The blades look newly sharpened. Willem wonders where he got them and suspects they belonged to the old Romanian woodcutter.

"We are mounting Antonescu's roof to look for it," Jean says.

"Remember that this creature can climb," Willem says.

"I hope so," Jean says, raising his crossbow.

At the cottage, Jean flips the ladder up against the wall. François tucks the hatchets into his belt and is the first one up. Jean steadies the ladder for Willem, and then climbs himself.

The tar pit is beginning to flame, combining its light with that of the torches on the saur-fence, lighting up the lavender along the riverbank. There is a mild moon but it is behind a cloud, and does not assist.

As Willem clambers from the ladder onto the spongy thatch, he sees François standing on the apex, near the chimney, one foot on either side of the roof. The light from the fires below throws him into silhouette, backlit with a skittish yellow glow. His arms are extended and held high, a hatchet in each hand. He is ready to face the saur.

Willem scuttles on hands and feet over the reeds of the thatch and stands behind François, balancing himself with a knee against the stonework of the chimney.

Nothing is moving. Not on either bank of the river, nor on the now-barricaded bridge. Not that Willem can see. The torches and the tar pit are a hindrance, not a help, the brightness of the flames burning his eyes and throwing everything behind them into deep dark.

Willem blocks the flames with his hand and scans the trees of the forest, straining his eyes, imagining that he sees vague shapes up in the high branches. But there is nothing.

"Where did that roar come from?" Jean asks.

Below them people are climbing up on the supports of the saur-fence, trying to locate the source of the sound.

Jean is right. It sounded close. Yet they can see nothing. It is as if the meat-eater is invisible.

"That is no firebird," François says so quietly that at first Willem doesn't realize he has spoken, until the meaning of the words creeps into his brain like a tendril of fog.

"Where?" Jean asks.

"In the river," François says. His words are slow and disconnected.

"There is nothing in the river," Jean says. His voice comes from right behind Willem.

Willem cannot see it either.

"That is no firebird," François says again, and this time Willem looks to the center of the river, still shading his eyes from the fires. Then he sees it.

There are eyes in the river, two pale disks against the dark of the water. They gleam dully in the light of the fires. The water is rippling slowly alongside the eyes, and by following the ripples forward, Willem finds nostrils, also jutting out of the water. The eyes blink slowly. The nostrils close to narrow slits, then open again.

"It cannot be," Jean says.

"It is a crocodile," François says.

He is wrong. This is much bigger than any crocodile.

The eyes turn to face the village. They blink once again, languorously.

"It's in the river," someone cries from the fenceline, and more people climb up to get a glimpse.

"Get away from the fence!" Willem shouts. Don't they remember what this creature did to the fence by the church?

His foot slips on old crumbling thatch and he has to clutch at the chimney for support. It takes him a moment to relocate the circles that are the eyes, and when he sees them they appear to be floating upward, as if detached from the body. But it is not the eyes, Willem realizes. It is the whole head of the creature that is rising from the river. The water has been a kind of camouflage, allowing the saur to sneak up on its prey. And its prey is the village.

Water streams from the snout. It is no crocodile. A crocodile is low and squat. It cannot raise its head like this. The eyes, now well above the water, flare with the lights from the tar pit and the flaming brands.

Up, up comes the head: heavy, ridged skin; long, straight teeth in a single, even row jutting out over the lower jaw. Willem cannot watch, and yet he cannot take his eyes off it. His heart does not seem to be beating in his chest. The head does look like that of a crocodile, yet it is intolerably large. And still it rises, water draining in long rivulets, creating dancing strings in the firelight.

Then the river itself seems to flex and bulge up behind the creature. But it is not water. In the dim light Willem sees what it is surely impossible to see. The river is the monster. The monster is the river. What he had thought was a dark shadow behind the creature is actually the backbone of the beast and that is now high in the air as the bulk of the creature emerges from the water.

"It cannot be," Jean breathes. "It is like an elephant with the head of a crocodile."

"It is bigger than that," Willem whispers. "Much bigger."

He looks at the saur-fence and at the ropes and extra poles that strengthen it. They now seem so puny, so inconsequential.

People still cling to the fence, where they have climbed to get a view.

The front legs have just emerged from the water, more like arms with long bony claws for hands. The surface of the river wallows as water surges in to fill the void created as the saur stands upright on great tree trunks of hind legs.

It snorts, and misty vapors jet from its nose, orange in the firelight.

A slapping sound comes from behind the animal. Its tail is flapping back and forth on the surface of the river, splattering huge sheets of water to either side.

It takes a step forward, toward the village, and now Willem realizes that however large he had thought this creature, he was wrong.

It has been standing in the deep of the river, and only now as it moves toward the bank, and shallower water, is its true size being revealed.

"Get away from the fence!" Willem screams down at the onlookers, frozen in place.

"Get out of there!" Jean joins in, waving his arms.

Still the onlookers pay no heed and it is not until the monster steps out onto the riverbank, crushing the lavender plants, that they tumble and scatter, then run, shrieking, away from the fence.

This meat-eater did not climb the tower to take Monsieur Antonescu. It did not need to climb. It is as tall as the church tower.

Willem watches as the giant saur stops at the fire pit, its eyes caught for a moment by the leaping flames. Willem hopes for the briefest of moments that the fires will deter it, but it shakes its great head and simply steps over. It towers over the saur-fence, then lifts one of those great hind legs, pushing through the fence as though it was made of matchsticks. The newly intertwined rope splits like cotton.

The beast roars again, the same gurgling, low-throated sound, and Willem feels the thatch of the cottage vibrate beneath him.

There are shouted commands from behind him and he turns to see Monsieur Claude's musket squad: two kneeling, two standing behind them. The front row fires, then the back, but if there is any effect on the beast, other than angering it, Willem can't see it.

Perhaps they have missed; perhaps the musketballs cannot penetrate the thick, scaly skin. The small troop scatters, the men running as the beast roars and steps toward them.

It passes right next to the cottage, so close that he feels he could reach out and touch it. It seems to be sniffing around, picking a victim. Willem is conscious of Jean's presence above him and looks up to see Jean standing over him, his crossbow to his shoulder.

"No!" Willem screams, but it is already too late.

The crossbow twangs and silver flashes in the sky. There is a grunt of pain from the beast and the end of the bolt is protruding from its upper jaw, close to its eye.

The head of the great lizard swings toward them, so close that the disks of the eyes are like twin moons in the night sky.

"Move," Willem yells.

Jean turns and starts to run, but slips on the thatch, sliding and disappearing over the edge of the roof. Willem hears a thud from below.

"It is a creature not of this earth," François says, unmoving. "It is a demon from the depths of hell. We have sinned. Our mayor has sinned. This is God's wrath visited upon us."

François seems spellbound by the sight of the huge head that is now swinging toward him. Willem pushes him and he falls, the hatchets slipping from his grasp and sliding over the edge of the roof. François follows, hands scrabbling for purchase, then he, too, is out over the edge, and Willem hears another thud and a curse as he hits the ground.

Willem runs for the ladder, but the creature is upon him and he can only dive and slide headfirst over the edge of the roof, falling, landing on Jean in a tangled cluster of arms and legs. On the other side of the cottage the giant saur bellows again, in frustration.

"Run!" Willem yells, and does not wait to see if they listen.

The beast moves past Antonescu's cottage into the road. It steps through the village, untouched and untouchable as people scatter out of its path, hiding behind houses, or just running. The creature seems in no hurry, aware that there is food all around it, and content to take its time. It is dark of skin and with no moon it is visible only by how it blocks out the lights of the burning brands and the lamps behind it.

The dogs chained at the gate of the church begin to bark, then to whimper. They tear at their chains, again and again until their necks are bloody, finally wrenching the wooden stake out of the ground and running together, yelping into the night.

It is then that the mighty tail of the creature swings around, accidentally it seems, and smashes into the church. A wall collapses, exposing the innards of the church: pews, drapes, and finery, along with a crowd of women and young children.

The nostrils of the creature flare and it turns back in that direction. The air fills with the sound of children screaming, trapped in the rubble. Mothers covers their children with their own bodies. Father Ambroise steps forward, blood streaming from a cut on his head, a cross in his one good hand; Willem doesn't need to see his lips to know that they are moving. He is praying. Invoking the name of the Lord to ward off this evil demon. The beast does not seem to hear.

But when all is lost there is sudden movement. By the light of the lamps that still festoon the church they see the schoolmaster, Monsieur Delvaux, brandishing a sword that gleams brown and rusty in the lamplight. He charges at the creature, screaming incoherently in a voice hoarse with madness.

Then Willem remembers: Cosette is in that church. He remembers the softness of her lips on his cheek and it is like gravity, pulling him in that direction.

Monsieur Delvaux actually gets within striking distance of the great head before the snout of the creature flicks to the side—a careless movement, nothing more—sending the schoolmaster flying sideways into the graveyard, where he lands at the feet of a statue of an angel. The angel looks out at the demon over the fallen man, who shudders and tries to rise, then collapses.

Another scream rends the air. It comes from the church, and a figure is running toward the graveyard. Willem recognizes the dress and the hair. Cosette is running to her father.

The meat-eater wavers for a moment between the children cowering in the church and the girl and her father, exposed in the graveyard.

It turns toward Cosette.

Willem himself is now a statue. He watches, unable to move. The huge clawed feet of the beast shake the ground as it moves toward Cosette. She shrieks again and again, but makes no move to flee. She covers her father's broken body with her own. He is pushing her away, wanting her to save herself, but still she clings to him.

Willem's hand touches the apparatus in his leather satchel. But his feet will not move. What use would it be anyway? What works on a microsaurus and a firebird could not possibly have any effect on this behemoth.

He knows he should try, that he can't just watch as those dreadful jaws close on her gentle flesh. But still he does nothing, paralyzed by fear.

Jean has his foot in the stirrup of his crossbow, drawing back the string to reload the weapon. Behind him, he can hear François praying.

Cosette screams once again, a shrill, primal, piercing sound, and now the beast is upon her. The long, crocodile-like snout swoops down toward her.

But there is another movement, and a flickering light bound with the screeching of a feral animal. Some kind of small creature scuttles over the ground toward them. At first Willem thinks it is a dog or a small saur with a burning brand in its mouth, but then he realizes it is a human. It is the wild girl, Héloïse, a flaming torch in one hand, running with the other on the ground like an animal.

The beast turns, its eye drawn by the flame, and Héloïse hurls the torch at the creature's head, where it impacts with a shower of sparks. The saur snaps at her but she is too quick for it, rolling along the ground beneath its jaw and between its massive legs, then running toward the gap in the fence.

It almost works. It almost turns to chase her, but then some part of its brain remembers the easy pickings in the graveyard.

Cosette has somehow dragged her father to his feet and together they are stumbling away, but now it is back on their scent. It takes a step forward, the huge clawed foot crushing gravestones and flower beds alike.

It takes another step, but this time Willem is there, and Jean is right behind him.

Somehow Willem's feet have found the will to move. Perhaps it is the sight of Héloïse, or the way the saur's eye followed the flaming torch.

He is terrified, shaking, almost unable to stand. His heart thuds painfully in his chest, but he steps toward the awful creature with a shout and a wave of his arms.

The snout turns toward him and the eyes blink once, slowly, as the creature evaluates him.

"Don't fire your weapon," he says to Jean. "Stay behind me. Do exactly what I tell you to do."

The beast growls, not the undulating bellow of before, but just a deep rasp from its throat. It sounds like a laugh.

The breath of the creature brings forth the stench of death. Of putrefied flesh and the sweet odor of decay.

It growls again, perhaps unsure what to make of this fragile man-thing that steps toward it, seemingly without fear. A beast such as this must never have encountered such a thing, for even in the remote depths of the jungle there could be no creature that would not flee, gasping and screaming, from these teeth, these claws, these cold, dead eyes. Even the breeze sputters to nothing, as if not daring to approach the creature.

It shuffles its feet, the movement shaking the earth so much that Willem is unbalanced and nearly falls.

The meat-eater waits. Its prey is coming to it. The tongue is ridged and pointed and drawn back in the open mouth. A cluster of mottled white teeth at the end of the jaw are larger than the rest, each longer than Willem's forearm.

The creature draws in breath, preparatory to a strike. But there is a clap of Willem's hands and a flame appears between his palms, burning bright yellow in the blackness of the night.

The meat-eater pauses, watching the flame. Willem steps closer. Within easy range now of those long, evil teeth.

He separates his hands and the flame leaps from one palm to the other, then back. He moves his hands in a circle and each time they cross, the flame jumps to the other hand.

The meat-eater watches, transfixed, mesmerized by the flame dancing in Willem's hands. Its giant head moves closer.

William begins to whistle, gently, and the creature cocks its giant head.

The flame leaps to Willem's left hand and stays there as he brings it closer and closer to the eye of the creature, now transfixed, unmoving.

He can scarcely breathe, so pungent and foul are the fumes that envelop him from the creature's throat.

"Jean, get down on the ground," Willem says, in a singsong voice.

Behind him there is a rustle of clothing as Jean drops down.

"Move forward slowly," Willem says.

Willem loses the eye of the creature as it notices the movement but he catches it quickly with the flame, weaving a glowing spell in the night air.

Jean has passed him now, crawling forward beneath the massive jaw.

The creature snorts and the flame in Willem's palm goes out in a whirl-storm of droplets. Willem coughs and chokes, panicking and fighting the urge to turn and run. He holds himself in place, just barely, and manages to clap his hands together again. The eye of the beast is once more caught by the leaping flame.

"The skin is soft where the jaw meets the neck," Willem says, in the same singsong voice.

Jean says nothing. Crouched on the ground beneath the jaw of the beast, he aims his crossbow upward. The beast tilts its head to one side.

"Wait for its head to straighten, then fire straight up, into its brain," Willem says.

Jean nods silently. The head stays on its side, then cocks the other way. Willem makes small, intricate movements with the flame and slowly the head returns to level.

There comes the twanging, punching sound of the crossbow firing, and the creature rears up, bellowing in pain, a long, agonizing rattle of sound. The crossbow bolt is nowhere to be seen, but a trickle of blood marks a small hole on the underside of the beast's neck.

Jean has rolled to the side. It snaps at him but misses, then turns back to Willem, who falls and grunts as the hard earth slams into his back.

The terrifying jaws close together millimeters above Willem's prone form, the long front teeth grazing his smock, then as the head raises again, the creature seems to stiffen. It staggers. The damage is already done. The bolt has entered its brain. It is dead, but not yet aware of it.

The head of the creature begins to fall. Had Willem been

underneath, the creature would have got its revenge, for the weight of the skull that crashes down where Willem had lain is far more than enough to crush the life out of him.

But a strong hand has grasped his arm and hauled him out of the way.

A few meters away Jean is just getting back to his feet.

It is François whose hand is on Willem's arm.

The chest of the beast moves for a few moments with the beating of its heart, then is still.

Willem tries to stand, but his legs collapse. François has him, supporting him with a strong arm under his shoulders.

Around them people start to gather, slow and cautious, not yet convinced that the creature is dead.

Monsieur Claude stands with a musket aimed directly at the eye of the beast, as if it will suddenly rear back to life. Glancing around, Willem sees the looks on people's faces. They see Monsieur Claude standing over the head of the beast like a hunter standing over his kill. He does nothing to dispel the idea that it is he, the mayor, who has saved the village.

Over in the graveyard Willem sees Cosette crouched by her father, who is being tended to by the mayor's wife. Madame Gertruda has yet to unbarricade herself from her cottage. Monsieur Delvaux seems to be having trouble breathing.

Willem finds his legs, and with a quick thank-you to François, who deserves more than that, he moves across to the graveyard.

Cosette strokes her father's forehead and in that simple touch of love from a girl to her father, Willem sees that the crazy man who has been making his life miserable is no more than a father, grieving terribly.

Cosette senses him behind her and looks up.

"How is he?" Willem asks.

She does not answer but rises suddenly and wraps her arms

around him, enveloping him in an embrace that exceeds all bounds of propriety.

Then she turns back to her father.

Monsieur Delvaux is conscious but clearly in great pain. He looks up at Willem and nods mutely. He says nothing, and yet says everything.

Then his eyes close, but not before Willem catches a glimpse of such agony and suffering as he has never seen before.

Before, he had Willem to share the blame for what happened to Angélique.

Now he only has himself.

"Willem!" It is Jean's voice.

He is with his father and a group of other men who are gathered around the creature.

Willem touches Cosette briefly on the arm to let her know that he is going, then crosses over to Jean.

The creature is no longer in darkness. People have appeared from everywhere with lamps. It lies on its stomach, one of its front legs splayed out to the side, the other caught underneath its body. The rear of the animal is on its haunches as if it might at any moment rise and resume the battle. The jaw is closed, but even so the huge teeth are terrifying. The eyes are glazed and the pupils have narrowed to slits, like cats' eyes.

Monsieur Lejeune is examining some rags, remnants of cloth that are caught on the bony protrusions at the top of the creature's spine, at the base of the neck. Not just fabric, shreds of leather as well. It makes no sense, and all Willem can think is that it is the remains of the clothing of another victim.

The beast shudders once as Willem leans forward, and he jumps backward, but it is just a death rattle.

"What is it?" Jean asks.

"Look at these scratches," Monsieur Claude says, pointing to deep gouges on the skin of the beast around where the fabric is caught.

"Claw marks," somebody says.

It is only when Monsieur Lecocq drops to his hands and knees and peers under the neck that the awful truth starts to become clear.

"There is a buckle here," Monsieur Lecocq says. "These rags are not caught on its back, they are strapped around its neck."

"Like a collar," Monsieur Claude says.

"A *collar*!" The word is repeated around the crowd, and there is consternation as the ramifications of that sink in.

"These scratches are from its own claws," Monsieur Lejeune says. "As if it had been trying to remove the collar."

Jean is examining the fabric, tearing it with his hands to reveal more of the shredded leather underneath. He pieces two fragments together and looks up, confused.

There is embossing on the leather and, with an awful feeling in the pit of his stomach, Willem recognizes the markings of the French emperor Napoléon. Now he notices the royal blue of the cloth, the imperial color.

"It is not a collar," Jean says. He has unearthed a molded hump of rounded leather. Willem has seen this shape before, but cannot place it in his mind. Then with sudden, horrible clarity, it comes to him.

"What is it?" François asks.

Monsieur Lejeune speaks what Willem already knows.

"A saddle horn," he says.

The great beast shudders a final time, then moves no more.

A good deal of time passes after this before Willem remembers his pet, hidden in the smithy. He unbraces the door and uncovers the bucket to find Pieter still frozen, comatose. The last time, it took many hours for him to return to normal.

Willem whispers soothing words to him and blows gently on his face. But as he goes to pick Pieter up he notices the eyes. They are not wide and flickering around as before. They do not move at all.

Pieter is not comatose.

The cheeky little microsaurus has simply died of fright.

THE MEETING

Town meetings in Gaillemarde are usually held in the church, but the church is damaged, so this meeting is held in the square.

The mayor is flanked by the brothers, Father Ambroise and Monsieur Lejeune.

Monsieur Claude holds his hands up for silence. There is a respectful hush. By now the entire village knows that it was Jean and Willem who brought down the meat-eater, but most of them will never forget the sight of Monsieur Claude standing heroically over the beast with a musket aimed at its eye.

Madame Claude is not present, that Willem can see. He suspects that she is off tending to the injured. Some villagers were hit by debris from the saur-fence as the animal crashed through, and a number of the children received cuts and bruises in the church. Madame Claude was everywhere last night, patching minor injuries and helping Madame Gertruda with the more serious ones. It is more than he expected from the mayor's stout wife.

Monsieur Claude thanks Jean and Willem for their role in helping to kill the giant saur. Willem accepts the nods and pats on the back of those around them with a gracious nod of his head, although he feels it should be Héloïse receiving the praise. If not for her, he would have been frozen in place. But he knows that even if such praise was offered, it would not be accepted.

When the adulation dies down enough, Willem turns to François, who is at his other side.

"They praise me and Jean," he says. "But I would not be here to accept it, if not for you."

François smiles but says, "It is God you should thank, Willem."

"I have done that already, in my prayers," Willem says. "But last night you were his instrument and I will be forever grateful for it."

François accepts this with just a slight bow of his head.

"We have all heard the stories of the terrible lizards," Monsieur Claude says. "The 'dino' saurs that Colombo and Vespucci were said to have discovered in the New World. We now all see the truth in those tales."

"But what was it doing here?" someone calls.

Monsieur Claude phrases his answer carefully. "I know no more than you. But it wears a saddle and bears the emblem of the French emperor."

It is some moments before the mayor can continue, and before he can, Monsieur Lejeune speaks. "Yesterday when we were hunting the firebird, we saw French soldiers in the forest. I believe now that they were searching for this very beast."

When the hubbub dies down he says, "I don't know what it is or where it came from. But I do know that the body of Napoléon's dinosaur lies dead in our field."

"What if there are more of them?" a voice calls from the crowd.

"I do not believe that is possible," Monsieur Claude says, and it is the first time that he smiles. "If a herd of dinosaurs was rampaging around the Sonian Forest, surely someone would have noticed them before now."

"But what if there is another one?" Monsieur Lejeune says. "We must alert the British. Already there is talk of invasion by the

French. The British cantonment is close to the forest. Imagine the carnage if a creature such as this was set loose among their ranks."

Monsieur Lecocq walks to the front, just below the podium. Already tall, he stretches himself up to his full height and turns to address the crowd. "An invasion by the French? An invasion? Do you forget that we *are* French? Even as we speak, those fools in Vienna seek to carve up Europe to their own map. They are about to sign agreements putting us under the rule of those Dutch pigs in the North. Why? Did we ask for this? We are not Dutch, we are Walloon. We are French. And you want to pass information to our enemies?"

From the cheers, it is clear that there are many in the crowd who think the same.

"Like Lecocq, I am Walloon," Monsieur Lejeune says. "Like Lecocq, I have lived here all my life. I speak like the French, I eat like the French. I make love like the French." He pauses at the crowd's laughter, then continues. "I shed blood for Napoléon. I fought at Austerlitz and Borodino. But I am not French. I am no more French than I am English or Italian. I am Walloon, and I will not be ruled over by a Corsican who fancies himself emperor of Europe. Napoléon's time is past. There is peace on our continent. I for one do not want to see a return to the blood and mayhem of the European wars."

Monsieur Lecocq now climbs up next to Monsieur Claude, as Father Ambroise, who is surprisingly subdued, steps out of the way.

"Europe stands divided," he declares. "A pathetic collection of weakling states. There may be peace now, but it is a fragile little bird. We face threats from the Ottomans in the East, from the Russians in the North. Europe must be united to be strong, and there is only one man who can do that. A man sent by God. Napoléon Bonaparte, the rightful ruler of Europe!"

There are cheers and applause for his speech.

Monsieur Claude steps forward. He speaks more softly than Monsieur Lecocq but there is power in the timbre of his voice. "We are but a small village in a small country. We risk being caught between the boot of the French and the rock that is the allied army. If Napoléon discovers that we have killed his dinosaur, then I fear the consequences. If he discovers that we have sided with the British and the Prussians, then I fear we will pay a heavy price."

"This is madness," Monsieur Lejeune thunders.

Monsieur Claude says calmly, "We are not English. We are not French. We are Walloon. We must remain neutral for now, and then we can align ourselves with the victor."

"There is no remaining neutral," Monsieur Lejeune shouts. "To do nothing is to side with the French."

"There will be a vote," Monsieur Claude declares. "Right here. Right now. All able-bodied men, over the age of fifteen. If you vote to warn the British about what we have discovered, raise your hand now."

He makes a show of counting the hands although the result is already clear. The hands are few and scattered.

"And if you vote to remain neutral, please raise your hand."

This time many hands are raised.

"Then I think it is clear. We do nothing that would align ourselves with either side," Monsieur Claude says.

"Then be it on our heads," Monsieur Lejeune says quietly, and steps down from the platform.

"Marcel!" The mayor stops him.

Monsieur Lejeune turns back to the stage.

"The village has decided, and we act as one," Monsieur Claude says.

"So I saw," Monsieur Lejeune says.

"You were not thinking of acting against our decision, of warning the British yourself?"

"Of course not," Monsieur Lejeune says. "I would not go against the village."

He turns away, and the crowd parts like the sea of Moses to let him through.

Jean looks at Willem and François and jerks his head after his father.

They wind their way through the crowd and see Monsieur Lejeune heading to the smithy.

Jean stops them halfway there, and checks that nobody is around to listen.

"They are fools," Jean says. "My father is right. To do nothing is to side with the French."

"I feel the same," Willem says. "But I am Flemish, how else should I feel? I am one of the Dutch pigs that Monsieur Lecocq spoke so eloquently about."

"Well, I am not Flemish, but neither am I French," Jean says. "Like my father and his father, I am Walloon and proud of it."

He stops for a moment, thinking.

"Jean?" François asks.

"My father will not go against the village, but somebody must," Jean says. "What if there is another one of these creatures? What if there are more? Someone must warn Wellington what hides in the Sonian Forest. Despite what our dithering, philandering mayor says."

"The village has voted," François says. "The decision is made."

"The village is swayed by Monsieur Lecocq, who plants his lips firmly on the emperor's arse," Jean says. "And they follow the lead of that clown who calls himself mayor. A storm is coming and they hope to ride it out by shutting their eyes. But they are fools."

François seems about to argue, but thinks better of it. "You are right," he says. "I will go. I know these woods better than anyone."

"I will come with you," Jean says.

"I can move faster and more quietly by myself," François says. "It takes but one pair of lips to deliver a message."

Willem shrugs, but Jean insists. "Cousin, when have I ever let you do something by yourself? God save something as vital as this. I will come with you to make sure you don't trip over your own feet."

"There is no need," François says.

"I do not agree, cousin," Jean says. "And what if you are spotted, and captured by the French soldiers we know are patrolling these woods? Who then will pass on the message? We both go, and if one of us is taken, then the other can deliver the message, as well as return to the village to let them know what has happened."

"Cousin—"

"There can be no more argument," Jean says. "We must leave immediately if we are to make it by nightfall. I will go home quickly to gather some provisions."

He leaves before François can argue further.

"My cousin is crazy," François says. "He goes against the village. I will reason with him as we walk."

"He does what he believes to be right," Willem says, then smiles. "And he is not one to be argued with."

"That has always been true," François says, and there is a strange sadness to his voice.

He takes out his pipe and a packet of tobacco, and takes his time filling it, tamping it, then lighting it. Willem waits, sensing that François has something more to say. He moves upwind of François, disliking the pungent smell of his pipe smoke.

"The way in which you entranced the dinosaur. How did you learn that?" François eventually asks.

This is a question that Willem has been dreading. But he knows that soon others will be asking the same thing. "It is a simple trick," he says. "It is the same trick I used to train Pieter."

He has avoided answering the question but even so it seems to satisfy François, whose mind is clearly on a different trail.

"Héloïse says that when she was attacked by the firebird, in the forest, there was a boy. She doesn't know where he came from. The firebird attacked him and that was how she was able to escape."

Willem's mouth drops. He is stunned by this. Firstly that Héloïse saw, and remembers that day, and secondly that she has told François. Then he remembers all the hours the two of them spent together during François's convalescence. They must have talked about many things.

"I thought she was dreaming," François says. "No boys were missing from the village. It made no sense until I saw you bewitch the monster last night."

Willem stares at him mutely, then finally nods. It would be foolish to deny it. "That boy was me."

"And you did to the firebird what you did to the dinosaur."

"Yes, then I cast pepper into its eyes and it ran into the forest."

"Yet you have not told her," François says.

"I have told no one," Willem says.

"Why, Willem?" François asks. "You saved her life. As you saved ours last night. You are a hero."

"I was no hero last night." Willem almost spits the words out, so great is his distaste for himself, and the person they think him to be.

"What are you saying?" François asks.

"I was terrified," Willem says. "I could not move. If it had been left to me, then Cosette and her father would have been food for the beast, and perhaps the children in the church also."

"But you—"

"I could not move," Willem says. "I did nothing. It was Héloïse who attacked the dinosaur, throwing the burning torch. Only then, after a girl had shown greater courage than I, could I persuade myself to step forward."

François shakes his head. "You do not understand it, but God is working in you. You did what you had to do, despite the cost to yourself. Like Jesus sacrificing himself on the cross." He stops for a moment, closing his eyes, reflecting on what he has just said.

"I was—I am—no hero," Willem says.

"You saved her life. She deserves to know," François says, opening his eyes again. "And she deserves to know that the boy who saved her did not perish. I will tell her."

"No!" Willem says.

"Why?"

"Because she will hate me," Willem says. "Because I could have saved her mother. But I was afraid."

There is silence for a moment. François says, "We all must face things that terrify us."

"Do not say anything to her," Willem says.

"I must go and prepare for the journey," François says, and abruptly turns.

As he walks off, Willem reflects that it was the most normal conversation he has had with François since the accident.

LA FORÊT DE SOIGNES

"The well-used trails are the easiest to travel," François says, "but we can save time if we avoid them."

"And there is less chance of encountering soldiers dressed as peasants," Jean agrees.

They are on the bank of the river by the old stone bridge. François squats and draws a rough map in the dirt with his knife. "The shortest distance is a straight line through the forest," he says. "We keep to the river until the fork at Lightning Rock, then branch left. It will take us to the old trails through the deepest heart of the forest and past the abbey."

"You can find your way through this part of the forest?" Jean asks. "It has been a long time since we ventured this way."

François shrugs as if it is a stupid question. "From there we can follow the ridgeline down to the north river, which will lead us to the Waterloo–Brussels road. We can be there in a few hours if we walk swiftly."

"Then let us be on our way," Jean says, rising.

François stops him with a hand on his arm. "Cousin, regardless of the outcome of the battle, you know that many in the village will hate us for what we are going to do."

"I know. And it does not deter me at all," Jean says. "A man must be true to what is in his heart. I cannot sit by and see Wellington's troops slaughtered because they were not forewarned. Whatever the cost."

"And no one could persuade you otherwise," François says.

"No one," Jean agrees.

"Not even me," François says.

"Especially not you." Jean laughs.

The dinosaur looks smaller in death than it had in life, now just a flaccid sack of flesh, sagging on the ground in the church graveyard. Willem circles it, inspecting the remains of the saddlecloth, scarcely able to believe that men could actually ride these great beasts.

The small statue of an angel stares implacably out over the corpse, as if it, not Willem and Jean, had killed the beast. Perhaps it had, Willem thinks. Perhaps it was, as many think, a miracle from God, and Willem had merely been His emissary on earth.

A group of men is approaching, including the mayor and Monsieur Lejeune. Through the gap in the saur-fence Willem sees Jean and François cross the bridge to the far side of the river. He wills them to hurry up before they are spotted. For the moment, at least, the men are more preoccupied with the dinosaur.

"We must get rid of it," Monsieur Lejeune says as they reach the corpse.

"What do you mean?" Monsieur Beauclerc asks. He walks up to the animal and kicks it. It does not even ripple the hide.

"On this, the mayor and I agree," Monsieur Lejeune says. "Napoléon will not be pleased when he learns that his dinosaur is dead. I suspect it came to them at great difficulty and expense. If he discovers that we were the ones who killed it, there will be a heavy price to pay."

Willem grasps hold of the wide leather strap that encircles the neck of the beast. He uses it to climb onto the neck, and straddles it, looking at the remains of the saddle, imagining what it would be like to ride this creature when it was alive. Living, breathing, moving under him. He imagines also what it would be like to ride it into battle.

"He is right." Monsieur Claude nods. "We must dispose of the carcass. Repair our church and the fence. And we must never speak of this to anyone outside the village."

"How?" Monsieur Beauclerc asks. "It would take a month to dig a grave for something this size."

"We will have to dig many graves," Monsieur Lejeune says. "Out on one of the farms. Then we dismember the beast with axes and saws. We take it out piece by piece." He starts to glance around at the gap in the saur-fence, through which Jean and François are still clearly visible on the river path.

"There are no reins," Willem calls out.

"What do you say?" Monsieur Lejeune asks, turning back to the carcass.

"Reins," Willem says. "If there is a rider, then he must be able to steer the animal. But there are no reins."

"Perhaps they were torn off with the rest of the saddle," Monsieur Beauclerc says.

"Probably," Willem says.

"Assemble as many men as have strong arms and backs," Monsieur Lejeune says. "It is a monster, and a monster job to render it down. But it must be done."

On the neck of the beast Willem sees two metal wires protruding from the skin at the rear of the animal's head. He shuffles forward on the neck, reaches out and grasps one of the wires. It does not move. It is clearly deeply embedded within the flesh. He points out the wires to the others.

"Could these be the reins you seek?" Monsieur Claude asks.

"They seem too fragile to control such a massive creature," Willem says. "But perhaps."

In the distance the cousins disappear into the trees.

The forest closes in more and more as Jean and François venture deeper into the forest. The banks narrow and the trees join up overhead, turning the lively river into a grim tunnel.

"I would not want to meet a dinosaur here," Jean says.

"Nor anywhere else," François says. "Do you really think there are more of them?"

"I hope not," Jean says. "But even so we must take great care."

"It is a vast forest," François says.

"Then let us hope our paths do not cross with those of the soldiers," Jean says.

They reach a set of rapids, bubbling vigorously over rounded rocks. After some thought, François declares that this is where they must leave the river, that there is an old path here.

It takes him a long time to find the path. Eventually he pushes aside a thick bush and declares that this is it.

It is not a path, although clearly it once was. It is long disused and the undergrowth has filled in the void. The brush is so dense and the going is so slow that they keep off the path, instead moving through the forest adjacent to it.

"I think that I will never see such a thing in my life," Jean says, pushing through a patch of prickly blackberry vines, "as little Willem standing up to the giant saur."

"Don't say that to him," François says. "He does not see himself as a hero. He says he is a coward."

"Willem? A coward?"

"That is what he says."

"Cousin, you have known me all my life." Jean laughs. "Have you ever seen me afraid of anything?"

"Apart from the tongue of your mother?"

"Apart from that," Jean agrees.

"Seldom if ever," François admits.

"Yet when that monster came to our village, I was terrified. I could never have approached it as Willem did, without even a weapon in his arms. Had he not walked toward it, I would have run in the other direction."

"As would I, cousin," François says.

"Yet he thinks himself a coward? I will have to set him straight when we return from Brussels," Jean says.

"He is a good man," François says, and adds, "for a Fleming."

"He is not strong, or tall," Jean says, "but he is clever and quick and brave. And he has a heart that is true. I like him immensely." He laughs again, this time a big booming sound that echoes off the trees. "But tell him I said that and I will kill you."

François laughs too but at the same time puts a finger to his lips and Jean immediately hushes. There are predators of many kinds in this forest.

They step from the forest out onto another path, at a right angle to the first. The paths couldn't be more different. The first is overgrown and knotted. But this new path is clearly well used. The dirt is flat and free from growth.

"We must find another way," Jean says. "I am uneasy here. A well-trodden path in the heart of the forest? This is very odd."

"There is no other path," François says. "We can only continue to fight our way through the trees. But the bush is dense here. At the rate we are going, we will not make Brussels by nightfall. The forest is a dangerous place at night, even without giant saurs."

"Then we stick to the path," Jean says. "But move silently and keep your ears open."

The stench of the blood and the saur flesh is almost overpowering, even from the single barrow-load that Willem wheels out through the gap in the fence, across a heavy plank that has been laid across the tar pit, and along the riverbank to Monsieur Canari's barley farm, to the east of the village.

Oxen have been working all morning to plough deep furrows, and men with shovels have followed behind, deepening them into trenches.

Other men, naked from the waist up, swarm over the carcass. Their trousers and torsos are stained completely red with the blood of the beast. They work with saws, ripping through the tough flesh. When they get to a bone, the men with axes move in.

Before they started, Father Ambroise came to bless the beast. To sanctify it, because it had tasted human blood and dined on human flesh. After that, he stripped off his cassock and picked up a saw with the others.

Willem has little taste for the sawing of flesh, and not the strength for the chopping of bones, so he volunteered to help barrow the macabre cargo out to the farm.

Even that is hard work, and after the first few loads his muscles are aching, but he looks at the far greater exertions of the other men, and does not complain.

After many trips out to the farm, he arrives back to find the cutters waiting, while the ax-men hack into the huge bones of the creature's hind legs.

He waits behind Monsieur Lejeune and his brother the priest. A girl brings water and scoops some out for each of them with a ladle, so they do not have to use their hands, now black and sticky with dried and drying blood.

At the head of the animal, Monsieur Claude stands, still un-bloodied, directing the operation, but not participating in it. Such is the right of a mayor.

"Our mayor buries his head in his own arse and does not see what is happening in the world," Monsieur Lejeune says.

"Our mayor is more interested in his own affairs than the affairs of the village," Father Ambroise says bitterly.

"You leave an empty nest and cannot be surprised when the cuckoo moves in," Monsieur Lejeune says.

"I did not say I was surprised, brother. I am never surprised at the depravity of man."

"Yet you say nothing to him," Monsieur Lejeune says. "You ask nothing of him."

"What could I ask?" Father Ambroise says. "As a man I want to kill him. As a man of God, I must forgive him. I am his neighbor, but I am also his priest."

"You are a fool."

"And you are an unbeliever."

"I choose to be an unbeliever."

"And I choose to be a fool."

The conversation ceases as the mayor approaches.

"The bones of the legs and the spine are thick," he says. "We could use the strong back of your boy, and his ax."

"I do not know where he is," Father Ambroise says.

"What about Jean?" Monsieur Claude asks. "I have not seen him since we started. It is not like either of them to shirk their duties."

He looks closely at Monsieur Lejeune, who shakes his head. "I do not know where they are. I was looking for Jean myself earlier."

"If you have sent them to warn Wellington, you go against the whole village," Monsieur Claude says. "We made a decision."

"I do not know where they are," Monsieur Lejeune repeats, and Father Ambroise also shakes his head.

"Boy," Monsieur Claude says, "where are those friends of yours?"

"I don't know," Willem says truthfully. He knows where they are going, but not where they are at this moment.

Monsieur Lejeune turns, a little surprised to find Willem standing right behind them.

"Willem, what is that bull-brained son of mine up to?" he asks.

"I really cannot say, sir," Willem says.

"Willem," Father Ambroise says, "have Jean and François gone to Brussels to warn the duke?"

Willem turns red, and is silent, unable to lie to his priest.

"Willem?"

"They left this morning," Willem says.

"Idiots!" Monsieur Claude shouts, staring at Willem as if it is his fault.

"I had nothing to do with it," Willem says. "It was their idea and their decision."

"But you could have told us what they were doing, and you chose not to," Father Ambroise says.

"There will be retributions," Monsieur Claude says. "No one in the village will be safe!"

Especially not the mayor, Willem thinks.

"What time did they leave?" Monsieur Lejeune asks.

"Straight after the meeting," Willem says.

"Idiots!" Monsieur Claude shouts again.

"We will not catch them," Monsieur Lejeune says. "They have many hours' head start on us, and nobody knows the forest better than François."

"This is treachery," Monsieur Claude says.

"Calm yourself," Monsieur Lejeune says.

"It is a crime, and they will be made to pay," Monsieur Claude says. "They will be arrested and put to trial, as soon as they return." He is also the town magistrate and Willem thinks that the result of such a trial has already been decided.

"There is no need for a trial," Father Ambroise says.

"It is our only hope," Monsieur Claude says. "If we punish the crime ourselves, we may deflect the anger of the French. We must show that we do not condone these actions."

He looks at Willem. "This one also, for aiding the criminals."

The first glimpse Jean and François get of the abbey is through a gap in the trees where a huge oak has fallen, taking several smaller, younger trees with it. An old bell tower, its top fractured and jagged, juts above the forest canopy.

It is impossible to tell how tall the tower once stood, but even now, crumbling back into the earth, it still soars above the forest around it.

"I remember this place," Jean says.

"We came here once before," François says. "When we were children."

"We were on a bear hunt, I think," Jean says.

"Lucky we didn't find one." François laughs.

"Lucky for the bear," Jean says.

"I will always treasure those days," François says.

Jean looks at him oddly, then shrugs. "Life was simpler then," he agrees. His nose wrinkles and his smile fades. "Do you smell that?"

"Cooking fires," François says.

"I think the abbey is not as deserted as it once was," Jean says.

"You think it is the French soldiers?" François asks.

"I doubt that it is the ghost of the abbot," Jean says. He looks around at the thick, dense bush and closely packed trees. "We could move into the forest, but it would mean hacking a trail," he says. "However, if we stay on the path, then we may run into one of their patrols."

"It is my fault," François says. "It was my idea to come this way. I'm sorry, cousin."

"It is no matter," Jean says.

"If we return now we can be back before dark," François says. "Tomorrow we can take the longer path, toward Waterloo and around the outskirts of the forest."

"No. We have come too far to turn back," Jean says. "We will proceed, but with greatest care. If we encounter a patrol, and cannot hide from them, we will protest our innocence. We took a wrong turn and are lost in the forest."

"And if they do not accept our deceit?" François asks.

"Then we shall convince them," Jean says, putting a hand to the stock of his crossbow.

"We should turn back," François says.

"What, cousin, you are afraid of a few French dandies?" Jean asks.

"I fear nothing," François says.

"Then lead the way," Jean says.

They reach a stream that crosses the path, creating a small ford. It flows from a clearing created by a rocky plateau and there they see the decaying glory of the abbey in full for the first time. It sits atop a hill, rising up out of the forest that surrounds it like a saur emerging from an egg. A thin line of water glints down the face of the hill, a natural spring giving birth to the stream that flows across in front of them.

The walls of the abbey still stand, and in one place, where it had collapsed, there are repairs. The gates look new, and stand firmly in a great stone arch, tall enough for even a dinosaur to enter. The stone of the walls is mottled green with moss and creeping vines, and the tops of the walls are rounded, weathered by the centuries.

Behind the ancient walls rise steep roofs, most of them newly thatched. The windows of the outside wall are tall and narrow, giving the appearance of battlements.

On either side of the main gate are statues, now gray and green with lichen, but still intact. To the left is the Virgin Mary, her arms enfolded in her robes, spread out in supplication. To the right is Christ in a crown of thorns, his head bowed in agony.

As they look, there comes a bellow from the direction of the abbey. It sounds distant and echoes hollowly, as though in a dungeon or a cave.

François and Jean look at each other. No words are necessary. They know that sound.

Napoléon has another dinosaur.

François turns his head quickly at another sound. This one from the pathway.

"Someone comes," he says.

They scan the forest around them. The rocky clearing is of no use for concealment. It is a flat plateau of shale-like rock. The other side of the path is a dense alluvial thicket of alder and dogwood, but it is their only choice. Jean pushes into a tangle of roots, brush, and vines, spreading the branches of a thorny bush and finding a gap at its base. He drops down into it, holding back the branches until François slides in beside him. Behind them is the sound of gentle water: the stream that runs from the abbey.

They hear more sounds now, the steady tramp of heavy boots and something else: a scratching, slithering sound interspersed with a strange rattle.

"What is that?" François asks, but Jean just puts a finger to his lips. Whatever it is, it is close now. They hear breathing: the rough, raw panting of an animal, with a small, inward whistle as it inhales.

A smell comes to them, like the sulfurous stench of an unemptied bedpan or the bitter-rotten perfume of gangrenous flesh.

François crosses himself, daring to make only the smallest

movement with his index finger on his chest. Jean swallows repeatedly, trying to rid himself of a sudden metallic taste in his mouth. He reaches for the stock of his crossbow and lets his hand rest there. Something crawls across the back of his legs, a sensation that would normally have him jumping and twisting around, but he ignores it. Snake, spider, or rat, it concerns him less than what approaches down the forest path.

"It is not of this world," François says in a voice that barely disturbs the air.

He is wrong. It is of this world, just not of the known world. A creature surely from the New World, the Amerigo Islands.

The hands of the creature are the first thing they see, through small gaps in the mesh of plants and twigs that shelter them.

Each hand has three long, bony fingers, jointed like a human hand, but ending in a vicious hooked claw. The arms come into view. They are long and skeletal with sharp elbows. The hide of the creature is ridged and muscular, as a human being would look without its skin, but not red; rather it is the charcoal black of old burnt wood.

The creature is the size of a large goat. Its snout is short and its mouth is open, revealing two rows of sharp, yellow teeth. The one eye they can see is red, and seems to glow against the dark of its body.

Sweeping back from its head are spines, and similar spines, but much longer, protrude from its back. Its hind legs have hocks like those of a horse. Its tail is long and ends in another cluster of spines. Such a creature surely cannot exist outside of a nightmare, and yet it walks in front of them, shackled by a leash fastened to a leather collar around its neck.

It passes in front of them and twitches its head to one side, examining the bushes where Jean and François lie. It seems to sense them concealed in the bush and starts to move in their direction, but a whip cracks behind it and the creature recoils from a sting on its left flank. It moves on, followed closely by a soldier.

"Surely this is the face of the devil himself," François whispers.

"It is just a saur," Jean says, but he doesn't sound convinced.

A second of the creatures follows, with its own handler. It also stops, sensing something in the bush.

Jean and François wait, hoping this one too will move on. But this time there is no crack of a whip. Instead, with a sudden movement, the head of the creature bursts through the vines and creepers that hide them. Its yellow teeth snap together, just centimeters from Jean's face.

Jean and François recoil from the snout and the evil yellow teeth. It hisses, spraying them with saliva.

It is only one short lunge away, but the leash has snagged in the thorny thicket. Jean and François scramble backward on their hands and knees, desperate to get away from this abhorrent thing. It thrashes and shakes as it tries to reach them but only succeeds in tangling itself further.

Muskets fire on the other side of the thicket and lead balls rip holes in the thin branches. Leaves jump and wood chips fly.

Jean and François emerge into dense forest, jumping up and running without thought or direction. The sound of the water beckons and Jean leads the way to it as shouts come from behind them and they hear knives slashing at the thicket.

They stumble and splash into the stream but have gone only a few steps when Jean catches François by the arm and points back upstream.

"This way!" he says.

"But that takes us back toward the abbey," François says.

"Which is why they will search downstream," Jean says.

"No . . . but . . ." François freezes, panicked, unable to move.

The sound of the creatures is closer now.

"God is telling me to go this way," Jean says.

Confused and stumbling, François follows him, copying his movements, both sliding their feet through the water to avoid making sounds.

They are just around a bend when they hear splashing from where they entered the stream, along with snarls and rattles from the creatures and more shouts from the men.

Jean and François continue upstream but stop as the stream reaches the path they were on a few moments before.

Ahead at the monastery, they see men in peasant smocks, with muskets, pouring out through the gates in the great archway.

They stop, unable to go forward or backward.

"What do we do?" François asks. "What can we do?"

Then, from the west, comes the roar of cannonfire.

BRUSSELS

"What is wrong?" Willem's mother asks. She knows him well and although he has done his best to hide his distress, she can sense it.

The dismantling of the dinosaur carcass is finished and Willem has come home to try to wash the stink of blood and meat from his clothes and body.

His mother is baking. No baking was done the previous day, and the village needs its bread. Her hands are covered in flour and her apron is streaked with dough.

Willem stares at the floor.

"Jean and François have gone to tell the British about the dinosaur," he says.

"At least someone in this village has a backbone," his mother says.

"The mayor has found out. He will put the cousins on trial to convince Napoléon that the village had no part in it."

"It will be a sham," his mother says. "But do not concern yourself. The mayor is a fool. I will make him see reason."

"He blames me for helping them," Willem says. "I too will face trial."

"Not when I have finished with him," his mother says. "You are the hero of the village after last night. The people will not let you be put on trial." She pauses, then smiles. "But if I ever see you approach a dinosaur like that again, I will kill you myself."

"Yes, Mother," Willem says. At that moment he hates himself.

That his mother would use her relationship with the mayor to save him is bad enough. That he wants her to do it is much worse.

"Do not let this sham trial concern you," she says. "There is something else I want to talk to you about."

"Yes, Mother."

"You know that Monsieur Delvaux is at Madame Gertruda's while he recovers," she says.

Willem nods.

"That leaves Cosette alone in her house," she says. "It is not good for her to be on her own. She has suffered greatly in the last few weeks."

"More than anyone should have to bear," Willem says.

"Perhaps she would like to live with us for a while," his mother says. "We have plenty of space, and ample food."

Willem hesitates, wondering if his mother knows of his feelings for Cosette, and whether that would influence her thoughts.

"Something worries you?" she asks.

"I was just thinking about her father. He was terribly injured. I hope he is all right," he says.

"Madame Gertruda will be doing everything she can," she says.

"I will go to find Cosette," Willem says.

She nods. He turns to go, but stops and turns back, sensing that she has more to say.

"You did a brave thing, facing that animal," she says.

"So everyone tells me," Willem says bitterly. "But I was not brave."

"There is something you should know," she says.

"What is it?"

"You know that your father fell out of favor with the emperor. But you do not know why."

"He never spoke of it," Willem says. "Nor did you."

His mother acknowledges this with a short nod. "Napoléon was very taken with your father's dancing saur. He felt that if a micro-saurus could be trained, then so could raptors. He thought they could become weapons. He even spoke to your father of an expedi-tion to the Amerigo Islands to recover dinosaur eggs. Your father refused to help, and that is why he had to flee the palace."

"Then how . . . ?" Willem asks.

"It seems Napoléon found someone else to help him with his plans," she says.

"I should have been told this," Willem says.

"You are right," she says. "And now I fear for our safety if word of your skills reaches the ears of the emperor."

"My skills?"

"Napoléon has a new weapon. But you have shown it can be defeated."

"The mayor has sworn everyone to silence," Willem says.

"Do you think that will be enough?" she asks.

Almost at the edge of the forest is a path. Not a track or a trail, but a proper path, laid with smooth gray pebbles. Perhaps it is here that the ladies of Brussels take their forest airs. The pebbles must make for easy walking even when the forest floor is damp, but they are not quiet, and as Jean and François reach the path they hear the crunch of footsteps close by and the sound of voices, unmistakably French.

When the cannonfire began, the soldiers in front of them stopped in their tracks. They seemed confused, then concerned, then began to return to the abbey.

Since then François and Jean have made a rapid but uneasy transit through the forest, running where the trails allowed it, both of them keen to put as much distance as they could between them-selves and the black creatures behind them.

There was another burst of cannonfire after the first, but since then, silence.

They reached the north river without incident and followed it to the very edge of the forest.

Now Jean places a foot carefully on the path but withdraws it immediately as the pebbles start to shift under his foot. They cannot cross the path without making noise.

The thick stone walls of the city seem so close. The road to it is smooth and wide, atop a low ridge. Below that in a grassy field is a troop of British artillery conducting a training exercise. It appears to have finished. The British artillerymen are now packing up their cannon and drawing into formation, ready to move. They look like toy soldiers, tall and thin in their crisp blue-and-red uniforms.

A dash across the path and a wild run through the field and Jean and François would be safe. Surely the French soldiers would not dare to fire on them within sight of British soldiers.

"Quickly," Jean says, "before the French get any closer."

"No!" François says.

Jean hesitates, and even in that short time the opportunity is lost. The footsteps sound now just around a bend in the forest path.

Jean eases back into the trees, François beside him, dropping to the ground and crabbing sideways toward a fallen log. It is not a tree but a heavy bough, at the base of an old dead birch. The tree still stands, but only just. It bulges with rot, its bark peeling away in long strips. The bough is not substantial, but smaller branches off it have collected old leaves, and it provides adequate concealment.

The tread of boots on the stones of the path grows louder, and the cousins press themselves into the mulch and moist earth.

As the soldiers draw level with them there is a one-word command, given in a hushed voice, and the soldiers stop.

There comes the shuffling of feet and low conversation, too faint to make out the words.

François closes his eyes for a moment, and his lips move slightly as he utters a silent prayer.

"Just stay still," Jean whispers, peering over the top of the bough. "And do not worry. They have not seen us. They are watching the British."

François nods, but Jean has not understood the meaning or the reason for the prayer.

François draws his hunting knife from his belt, and starts to rise.

"Do not be stupid," Jean hisses. "There are too many of them, and they are armed with muskets. In any case they are moving on."

The sound of footsteps has resumed and recedes as the French soldiers continue onward.

"See, we are safe now," Jean says. "Now let us go and deliver our message."

"Wait just a moment," François says. "Stay here."

He rises to a squat and crosses over Jean's prone form, straddling him.

"You will undo us both," Jean says, and starts to say more but cannot, and there is only a slight gasp of air as François's knife slips in between his ribs.

Cosette is just closing the gate to Madame Gertruda's. She steps lightly and smiles briefly when she sees Willem.

"How is your father?" Willem asks.

"He will be fine," she says. "Some bones were broken, but Madame Gertruda has tended to them, and says he will be up and around in a few weeks."

"That is good news," Willem says. "Where will you stay in the meantime?"

"I hadn't considered that," she says. "At home, I suppose. I am going there now."

"May I walk with you?" Willem asks.

"If it pleases you," she says.

She walks quickly and he has to lengthen his pace to keep up. They walk in silence at first, Willem choosing his words carefully before revealing them.

They are almost at the square when he says, "My mother asked me to invite you to stay with us. Until your father is well. There is a spare room and we have ample food. She says you can choose your own bath day."

On the far side of the square, by the church, the cadaver of the dinosaur has disappeared as if it had never existed. As if the memory of that dreadful night was no more than a nightmare. Men with spades are turning the earth to hide the bloodstain, and it will soon be planted with flowers. A pretty garden to hide a terrible secret.

"You saved my life, and that of my father," Cosette says. "I already have too much to thank you for."

"It was Jean who killed the beast," Willem says.

"But you who stood before it, so that he could fire his bow," Cosette says. "I still do not understand why it did not eat you."

"Perhaps it did not like Flemish food," Willem says.

Cosette laughs prettily, and her lazy eye wanders out, gazing at something far away. "People are saying that you were sent by God to protect the village. Some say that is why God saved you at the fête."

Willem shakes his head, smiling with her. "Is that what you think?"

"I think that I would be joining my sister in heaven if not for you," she says, and her face grows sorrowful once more.

"You must miss her unbearably," Willem says.

"It is true," Cosette says.

"So will you come and stay with us?" he asks. "The living arrangements will be entirely proper."

He regrets those words as soon as he says them.

"I know what you thought about my sister," she says. "But you are wrong."

"I did not think badly of her," he protests.

"Yes you did. You all did," she says.

He is silent.

"There is an artist who lives in Waterloo," she says. "A painter of some renown. Angélique would model for him. And his students."

"That is nothing to cause discomfort," he says.

"She posed unclothed," Cosette says. "But the pay was generous and there was no impropriety."

"You don't have to tell me this," he says.

"I know," she says. "But I wanted you to think better of her. Just a little."

"She was always nice to me, even when others weren't," Willem says. "That is what I will remember of her."

"You are a kind person, Willem," Cosette says. "I think that I would like to get to know you better." It is the first time since her sister died that he has seen her looking happy. "Tell your mother that I would be honored, and grateful, to accept her invitation."

Jean lies on his back, his face contorted with pain. He grasps at François's arm with hands in which the strength is already fading.

"What is in your heart is not what is in my heart, cousin," François says. He eases his arm out of the other's grip. "Do not look at me with such eyes, filled with confusion and hurt. With all of my being I wish there were another way, but I could not have fought you. You were always the stronger one."

Jean's mouth opens, trying to form a question, but no sound emerges.

François puts a finger to Jean's lips, hushing him.

"Your heart has stopped, Jean. You have but a few seconds, so listen," he says. "You are my cousin but I have loved you like a brother and that is why I have done this thing for you. I have saved you from transgression. We are Walloon. We are French. Napoléon is our one true leader, sent by God to unite all of Europe under His name. Yet you would have aided His enemies.

"It would have been a mortal sin, cousin, and one that would have condemned you to an eternity in the roasting fires of hell. But I have saved you from that. Do you not see? Do not fear, or hate, but rejoice, for you shall live forever in the kingdom of the Lord."

He stops, seeing that the eyes of the other are cold and still, like those of a fish. Tears begin to fall from his own eyes and he weeps unashamedly, making no attempt to wipe them away.

"I could have turned you over to those soldiers," he says. "That would have been the easy path, but you are my blood, and I would not have a stranger take your life."

A thin wind whistles up through the trees around them as the young man crouches, weeping, over the body of his cousin.

"And so you rise to heaven," he says. "And I shall go to hell in your place."

The patrol is almost out of sight when François steps out from the bushes. They stop at the sound of his footsteps on the path, and turn back, muskets sliding off shoulders into their arms.

"*Vive l'empereur,*" François says.

FRANÇOIS

Despite the death of the dinosaur, lookouts are still posted in the church tower, and it is one of the younger Poulencs, so posted, who is the first to see François walking in the fading light of evening along the river path to the bridge. It is a day since he and Jean set off.

The lookout calls out the sighting and the saur-gate is unbolted and open by the time François reaches it. Men are waiting to meet him, Monsieur Claude at their head. The mayor has detailed two men with muskets to arrest the cousins when they arrive back, and although François is alone, they make a great show of tying his arms behind his back with strong cord.

It is completely unnecessary, Willem thinks, and clearly all for the sake of the emperor, should he ever get to hear about it.

Willem keeps to the back of the small group that quickly gathers, hoping the mayor will not notice him.

François carries Jean's crossbow in a sling on his back and one of the men takes it from him as if he would use it against them.

That is when Willem feels a weight, like a boulder, in the pit of his stomach. *Why does François carry Jean's crossbow?*

François makes no move to resist as his hands are tied and just stands with his head bowed.

He either does not hear his uncle's question, "Where is Jean?" or chooses not to answer.

Monsieur Claude repeats the question a few moments later, after marching François to the center of the village square where a crowd is starting to form. He wants everybody to see this.

"Where is your cousin?" he asks.

Again François does not answer.

Father Ambroise watches the affair but does not attempt to intervene on behalf of his son.

Willem's mother stands at the back of the crowd, her face set. Watching her, Willem has a strong suspicion that she has had her "talk" with the mayor, and the mayor has not been as responsive as she would have liked. Or is that perhaps the reason why Willem is not now standing, hands bound, at François's side?

"Where have you been?" is Monsieur Claude's next question, followed by, "What have you been doing?"

Now François lifts his head defiantly. "We went to Brussels, to warn the Duke of Wellington about the dinosaurs."

There is quiet shock in the crowd at this frank admission of guilt.

"Yet you know that we, the village, had expressly voted against this," Monsieur Claude says.

"I know that you were against it, and you made the rest of the villagers afraid to go against you," François says.

"If Napoléon hears of this treachery, he will demand blood," Monsieur Claude roars. "And it will be your blood we will give him. Yours and that of your cousin."

From the look on Monsieur Lejeune's face, Monsieur Claude will not find that as easy to do as it is to say.

"I did something that I truly believe in," François says. "Regardless of the consequences."

"Where is Jean?" Monsieur Lejeune asks. He sounds concerned. It is the third time this question has been asked.

François begins to weep.

"Where is your cousin?" This time it is Father Ambroise who asks.

Willem now has a growing dread of what the answer will be.

"We were spotted by a French patrol," François chokes out between sobs. "I got away, but . . ."

"They captured Jean?" Monsieur Lejeune asks. "Did they capture my son?"

"Jean is dead," François says.

There is a sudden and shocked silence.

"What happened?" Monsieur Lejeune asks finally.

"The French soldiers fired at us," François says.

"He is shot. That does not mean he is dead. Perhaps he lies wounded somewhere," Monsieur Lejeune says.

"He is dead," François says. "I saw the breath leave his body and the light leave his eyes."

There is a scream from somewhere in the crowd and Jean's mother drops to her knees, wailing and keening. Several people move to help and comfort her. Monsieur Lejeune glances at his wife, but does not move toward her.

"Untie his hands," he says.

"He is still under arrest," Monsieur Claude says.

"Untie his hands," Monsieur Lejeune says again in a voice that is calm but so cold that the air freezes around the words.

Monsieur Claude nods and one of the guards moves to do so.

"Go home, François," Monsieur Lejeune says.

François looks at him for a few moments, his eyes full of unbearable pain. But he does not move.

"All of you, go home," Monsieur Lejeune says.

Madame Lejeune is now screaming hysterically. A group of ladies lead her away toward the church, arms around her shoulders, supporting her.

"I am sorry for your loss," Monsieur Claude says.

"My son made his own decision, and has suffered the consequence," Monsieur Lejeune says. "As must we all."

Willem becomes conscious that François is still standing there. He has not moved from the spot where he was taken. He now holds the ropes that had bound his wrists, and his hands are moving, twisting and pulling the cords like rosary beads.

He looks small, isolated by his grief.

Willem stares at him, lost in his own world of disbelief and utter desolation.

A shape moves in front of him, and Cosette walks to François. She seems a small and fragile bird standing in front of the hulking shape of the woodchopper, yet it is he who is the fragile one.

She puts her arms around him and pulls his head down onto her shoulder as he begins again to weep. Awkward, embarrassed, themselves suffering from the shock of the loss, the crowd starts to disperse. Father Ambroise stays. He walks to his brother and touches him gently on the arm, but says nothing.

Monsieur Lejeune looks at him. "Brother, I am not a religious man," he says. "I wish this were not so. But I have seen too many things and done too many things to believe that there is a great Father who watches over us. Even now, as my son lies alone in the great forest, food for the wild things that roam there, I cannot find faith."

Father Ambroise listens quietly and nods.

"I have asked for little from you these last years, brother," Monsieur Lejeune says. "I did not want to take from you because I had nothing to give you in return. But I must ask something now. I am not a believer. I cannot pave the way for my son into the afterlife."

There are tears in his eyes and he does not try to blink them away.

"I beg you to do that for me, Ambroise, despite our differences. Ask the Lord to accept him. To allow him to join his ancestors in paradise."

"Marcel." Father Ambroise reaches out and lays his hand on his brother's shoulder. "I cannot administer the last rites to someone who is already dead. How can I ask for penance if they cannot reply?"

"I know that, brother. But do whatever you can," Monsieur Lejeune says. "He was my son."

LIGNY

The church is burning. So are the houses around it. From every window and every doorway the long, sharp needles of muskets project, fire, then withdraw to be reloaded. The stone of the church appears diseased, so badly is it pockmarked from ball and shot.

In gardens, men kneel among the bushes, behind walls and fences. They crawl through hedges and ditches and clamber across rooftops.

The French cannon unlimber within sight of the walls and unleash a hell of ball and grape against the Prussian defenders. Twelve-pound iron balls make gaping jagged holes in the stone walls, and in the sides of houses.

Through the gaps pour French infantry. This is not the neat lines and precision marching of battle in the open field. This is dirty, ragged, urban warfare.

Before dawn on the previous day, Napoléon and his army crossed the border near Charleroi, aiming to drive a wedge between the English and the Prussian armies. Ligny is the key to that strategy. A win here and the Prussians, under Blücher, will be prevented from linking up with the English, under Wellington. It is a vital and brutal engagement.

Into this fiery netherworld trots Thibault on a thoroughbred charger he took from a dead colonel after his own horse was shot from under him.

In a courtyard he finds a platoon of grenadiers preparing to spike a row of Prussian six-pounders.

The clash and crash of battle is everywhere, on every street. Smoke swirls around the houses, and the three houses on the far side of the courtyard are burning fiercely, flames gushing from the windows, although the stone walls remain impervious.

The Prussian artillerymen are lined in a row on the ground near the wall of the courtyard. At first Thibault thinks they are all dead, but then he sees the two guards, muskets presented, who stand above them.

Many other Prussians lie where they fell, at their cannon.

There are numerous French dead also in this courtyard, and Thibault can picture the battle in his mind's eye. The grenadiers entering the courtyard to be met by a hail of grapeshot from the row of Prussian artillery. Rushing forward before the cannon are reloaded, and capturing them.

The leader of the grenadiers is a young captain. His uniform is black with smoke and red with blood. Not his own, judging by the efficient way he salutes as Thibault approaches.

"Hold," Thibault shouts, seeing one of the soldiers remove a fuse from one of the cannon, preparatory to spiking it. The soldier stops, holding the fuse, while another stands behind him, an iron spike and hammer ready in his hands.

"Why do you spike the cannon? Can you not commandeer them, and turn them against the Prussians?" Thibault asks.

"Sir, we have more cannon than we have cannoneers," the captain says. "The Prussians have been targeting our artillerymen. I would see that these are not used again against us."

"Well, think twice before spiking that one," Thibault says. "Especially when I am in front of it."

"Sir?"

"This cannon is loaded, Captain," Thibault says. "One spark as you hammered that spike into the touch hole might have set off the charge. As I was in its path, that would have caused me great displeasure."

The captain turns red, and bows his head in an apology. "How did you know it was loaded, sir?" he asks.

"The fuse was already inserted," Thibault says. "Did you not notice, or did they not teach you that at Saint-Cyr?"

"In the confusion, I confess I did not see it, sir," the captain says. "What mission brings you here?"

"I seek the headquarters," Thibault says.

The roof on one of the houses collapses, sending up a shower of flames and sparks. Smoke drifts through the courtyard.

"But that is to the west, at Fleurus," the captain says.

"I was told we had captured this town!" Thibault says.

"We did, sir. Three times so far," the captain says.

The sound of a musket, close by, removes the last word of his sentence, and the young soldier with the fuse still in his hand collapses back against the cannon behind him, a shocked look on his face.

"To arms! To arms!" the French captain shouts.

There are more shots before the soldiers can react and another of the soldiers flies backward, arms flailing.

Now the gates on the eastern side of the courtyard are filled with Prussian uniforms. A sea of dark blue speckled with smoke from the muskets. The first rank kneels as a second rank fires over their heads. Two more of the French soldiers drop.

"Retreat!" the captain shouts.

"Damn that!" Thibault shouts. "I will shoot the first man who retreats. Present arms."

The remaining grenadiers aim their muskets from where they stand, or from the cover of the cannon.

"Fire!" Thibault shouts.

Holes are cut in the Prussian ranks, but already the first row is rising again, reloaded.

"Help me," Thibault shouts to the nearest French soldier, running to the trail of the loaded cannon. Musketballs zing past his ears and his sleeve explodes in a puff of fabric.

The soldier runs with him but drops almost immediately, coughing blood.

The grenadier captain takes the soldier's place, grasping one of the handles. Together they lift and spin the cannon around.

Thibault snatches the fuse from the dead private and rams it into the touch hole. There is no portfire, so he holds his pistol to the fuse and pulls the trigger.

The pistol fires, and a second later, ignited by the sparks from the flintlock, so does the cannon.

There is a roar and the courtyard fills with smoke.

The effect is more than Thibault could have hoped for.

The cannon is loaded with grape—iron balls tightly packed into a metal canister—and at such short range the effect is devastating.

When the smoke clears, those Prussians who are not dead are dying, lying wounded, or running for their lives.

The captain orders his men to gather up the wounded and force them to lie down in the row with the other prisoners.

"Why do you keep these Prussians?" Thibault asks. "You have more prisoners than you have soldiers."

"I cannot spare the men to escort them to the rear," the captain says. "And many of them are too wounded to move."

"Then I think you have a problem, sir," Thibault says.

"Indeed so, sir," the captain says.

"Do they have information that you need?" Thibault asks.

"No, sir," the captain says.

"Then they are of no use to you," Thibault says.

He rests the tip of his saber on the back of the nearest Prussian. The man is bleeding heavily from a wound to his shoulder. The sharp blade cuts the cloth of the Prussian's uniform and pricks the man's skin.

"No! In the name of God, sir," the Prussian pleads in heavily accented French.

"Sir, these are not the actions of a gentleman," the captain says.

"This is not a gentle war," Thibault says.

"If we kill their prisoners then they will kill ours," the captain protests.

"Only if there are witnesses," Thibault says, and presses the saber home. Blood spurts. The Prussian shudders once, then is still.

"Sir, I cannot condone . . ."

"Now, Captain, there are witnesses," Thibault says, gesturing at the other captives.

"Sir, they are my prisoners!"

Thibault moves to the next man in the row and again the saber does its work.

"Do you want them to spread word of this?" he asks. "Will you be responsible for retaliation against French prisoners?"

"But, sir!"

"See to them directly, Captain, or would you have me do it all for you?" Thibault moves to the third prisoner in the row.

The captain shakes his head and signals to his men.

The screams are still sounding as Thibault gallops out of the courtyard heading west. He rides through the rubble of the town wall, past cannon that lie in shambles, their carriages and limbers burning fiercely.

Behind a stand of trees he can see the windmill. A wooden

observation platform has been erected around the outside and as he draws closer he can see Napoléon standing on the platform, studying Ligny through a spyglass.

Count Cambronne is at a table at the base of the windmill poring over a map when Thibault arrives. He only looks up when Thibault salutes. He scowls.

"You came through Ligny! Are you a fool?"

"I was informed that it had been captured," Thibault says.

"The report was wrong," Cambronne says.

"So it seems," Thibault says.

"What if we had lost you, Thibault?" Cambronne says. "So close to our first battle. Who would have commanded the emperor's new army then?"

"Sir, I came to get news of the progress of the campaign. There is no sign of Wellington in the fields around Waterloo. I must know when to move up my unit."

"Wellington is not retreating toward Waterloo, because that damned fool Ney has not managed to dislodge a few stubborn Dutchmen from the crossroads at Quatre Bras."

"Perhaps it is more difficult than we think, to bend the Iron Duke to our will," Thibault says.

"Mont-Saint-Jean," Cambronne says, jamming a finger down on a ridge on the map. "We have found the perfect defensive position for him. If I could only persuade him to use it. Ney must capture Quatre Bras. If he does not, then our battle will be fought here, out of reach of our new war beasts."

Thibault is still studying the map. "General, Wellington is trying to link up with Blücher's army. But if you defeat the Prussians here at Ligny, then there is no longer any point to his action and he will have to fall back anyway."

Cambronne looks at the map, then looks directly at Thibault.

"You are right, Major. I must be old, or tired, or both. When we defeat Blücher, Quatre Bras will cease to be of importance."

"It is so," Thibault agrees.

"Ready your men and their great beasts," Cambronne says. "Your battle is coming."

FIELD HOSPITAL

The British Field Hospital arrives at Gaillemarde in a series of wooden carts and carriages, loaded with portable cots, orderlies, surgeons, a physician, and assorted medical equipment.

Casualties begin to arrive before they have finished setting up.

Within a few hours it is clear that the staff of the hospital are never going to be able to cope with the influx of wounded, and many of the villagers volunteer or are drafted in to help.

Madame Gertruda moves among all the patients, anointing wounds with powders and giving soldiers sips of liquids she says will prevent infection.

The two surgeons look on her as a mild nuisance, but the patients seem to appreciate the attention.

Madame Claude is everywhere, bathing and bandaging wounds, applying leeches, helping the surgeons with bloodletting.

The surgeons are Mr. Sinclair and Mr. Grace, and both seem professional and efficient in their work, which mainly appears to involve removing limbs that have been shattered by musketballs or cannon shot.

Everyone from the village has been given a stern talking-to by the mayor, reminding them not to mention anything about the secret that lies buried, in a thousand pieces, on Monsieur Canari's farm to the east.

Willem was one of the first to volunteer to help. His job is to unwind bloodied bandages from those who arrive already dead, or who do not survive the surgery. The bandages are rinsed in the water trough outside the stables next door, then hung up to dry. It is not pleasant work, but still substantially less onerous than wheeling bloody barrow-loads of dinosaur meat.

Cosette is another of the helpers and he often sees her bringing pails of water from the river, some of which end up in his trough. They seldom have a chance to speak, but each time their paths cross there is time for a quiet smile.

Sometimes Willem thinks he would not make it through the day if not for those smiles.

When there are no bandages to wash, he helps in whatever way he can.

He brings a mug of tea to Mr. Sinclair, who is taking a short break after operating nonstop for four hours. He sits outside the market hall on a wooden chair.

"Thank you, son," Mr. Sinclair says in perfect, unaccented French.

"May I ask you a question?" Willem asks.

"Of course," Mr. Sinclair says.

"I do not understand why the soldiers always are shot in the arms and legs," Willem says. "They never take musketballs to the body. Yet surely that should be more often hit; it is a much larger target."

"You are right, son," Mr. Sinclair says. "Most soldiers get shot in the chest or abdomen."

"Where are those patients taken to?" Willem asks.

"Nowhere," Mr. Sinclair says. "They do not generally make it off the battlefield. And if they did, there would be nothing we could do for them here."

"It is a terrible war," Willem says.

"This?" Mr. Sinclair waves a hand vaguely behind him. "This is a squall before the storm. I shall be much busier soon." He sighs. "They call me a doctor, but I am merely a butcher, slicing meat. I hack off arms and legs to try and save these men's lives, and half the time they die anyway from gangrene and infection."

The sight of a wagonload of casualties, bodies jumbled up on top of each other, causes him to rise and hand the half-drunk mug back to Willem.

"Thank you for the tea, son," he says. "It looks like I am back to work."

In the evening, after a short break for a meal, Willem is back at the hospital in the market hall.

"Son, could you come here?" Mr. Sinclair says.

Two orderlies are holding down an officer with a mangled left leg. He is young and looks terrified as the surgeon readies his saw.

"This is empty," Mr. Sinclair says, indicating a rum bottle beside the table on which he operates. "There is another in the trunk by the door. Would you mind?"

Willem takes the empty bottle and replaces it in the trunk, swapping it for a full one. He returns it to the surgeon, who nods at a small metal cup on the table. "Just a tot in there, thanks."

Willem pours a little into the cup and holds it to the officer, who sucks at it greedily.

At the other table Mr. Grace is preparing a young corporal for a similar operation. Willem pours another tot into the cup and is about to take it to him when Mr. Sinclair stops him with a shake of his head.

"The rum is for officers," Mr. Sinclair says.

Mr. Grace places his saw on the man's leg and an orderly places a leather strap in his mouth, for him to bite on.

On the other side of the room there is a sudden commotion.

"Where are the leeches?" the physician asks, throwing his hands in the air. "How can I help these men if I do not have enough leeches?"

Behind Willem a man is screaming in his sleep. Next to him a tough-looking sergeant is weeping.

Two orderlies brush past Willem with a man held between them. A body. They are taking him out the back to pile him on a wagon with the others.

Willem's breath is short. The room seems to be spinning; the ground is unsteady beneath his feet. He sucks in air and stumbles to the entrance, bending over with his hands on his knees, gasping at the fresh, cool air of the evening that flows past the hall.

"Willem."

Willem looks up at the sound of Monsieur Lejeune's voice. The blacksmith is standing right in front of him. He hadn't known he was there.

"Are you all right, Willem?" Monsieur Lejeune asks.

Willem nods. "I needed some air."

"I must know what happened at Quatre Bras yesterday," Monsieur Lejeune says. "There is an officer here from the Second Dutch Division but he speaks no French. Will you translate for me?"

"Of course," Willem says. He straightens, takes a deep breath, and follows Monsieur Lejeune down the long rows of blood-spattered cots to where a man in a colonel's uniform is resting with his eyes closed. His left arm is gone below the elbow. A lucky wound, Willem has learned, because the odds of survival are much better than they are if the amputation is higher up.

Monsieur Lejeune gently touches him on the leg to let him know they are there, and the colonel opens his eyes slowly. He seems tired.

"Ask him about the battle," Monsieur Lejeune says.

Willem does so in Dutch and almost immediately a red fire comes to the man's cheeks, and he clenches his one remaining fist.

"Quatre Bras." He spits out the words. "I cannot believe it. All day we fought for Quatre Bras, and although several times the French dogs took it, every time we beat them back. We had but a small force against a large army, but we were resolute. The French did not . . . they could not take the crossroads. And yet for all our sacrifice, Wellington just gives it up. So many men died, and he just hands Quatre Bras to the French. The fool!"

Willem translates quickly.

"Wellington is no fool." The voice comes from a man in the next cot. His uniform also is Dutch and bandages cover one of his eyes. "He retreats to the ridgeline at Mont-Saint-Jean. He draws the French to a battleground of his own choosing, where he has the high ground, and strongpoints like the chateau at Hougoumont and the farmhouse at La Haye Sainte. Had he stayed at Quatre Bras to engage the French, he would have been out in the open, and easily outflanked."

"Mont-Saint-Jean?" Monsieur Lejeune asks, after Willem has translated. "But that will put his back right up against the forest."

"The forest is the least of his concerns," the second man says.

"Monsieur, the forest is the greatest of his concerns," Monsieur Lejeune says.

Willem does not translate that.

That night Willem is woken by the sound of crying from Cosette's room, and lies awake waiting for the sound to subside, before himself drifting back to an uneasy and broken sleep.

MONT-SAINT-JEAN

The four-pounders in the valley below sound again, like yapping dogs. The white gasps of smoke that briefly obscure the cannon are followed by the familiar whistling sound of cannonballs in flight.

Jack does not flinch, as he has the previous few times. The French guns are out of range.

This time they are firing spherical case shot, but these also fall well short, except for one that, with the vagaries of gunpowder, wadding, and wind, outflies all the others to land just a few yards from Jack's position.

It embeds itself in the mud, the fuse sputtering and fizzing.

"Get your head down, boy," Roberts yells from behind him, and Wacker grabs his arm, pulling him down just as the projectile explodes, spraying iron balls and fragments of the metal casing up into the air, clanging off the cannon, showering them with mud.

"Stand fast, men." It is Frost's voice. He rides up behind them on Molly, his chestnut mare.

"Why don't we have at them, sir?" Wacker says. "Our nine-pounders would sort them out."

"Captain's orders, and they come down from the duke himself," Frost says. "We are not to engage enemy artillery."

"We're not engaging anything at the moment," the older Wood brother says.

"Afraid you're missing out?" Frost asks.

Another volley of shots comes from down in the valley and Molly rears and wheels around at the sound, showing them the white stockings on her back legs. Frost brings her back to face them.

"We've been here all day," Wacker says. "Ain't even lit the linstock yet."

Embedded in the ground at the rear of the cannon the linstock is a metal staff holding a slow match, which will be used to light the cannon fuse.

"Don't worry, Corporal," a new voice says. It is Captain Mercer himself, riding up behind Frost. "Some of our chaps are having a pretty thick time of it. They'll find something to do with us before too long."

The guns sound again and Jack looks out down the valley as the smoke gradually clears. If the shot has fallen anywhere nearby, there is no sign of it.

The valley is a wide plain, with vast fields of head-high corn. Here and there are scattered small woods and thickets. It is a pleasant country scene, Jack thinks, like a landscape painting.

Except for the soldiers. And the cannon. They are overlaid onto the canvas like an afterthought, by a different painter with a different style.

The gently waving stalks of yellow corn are a silky blur of restful movement, but imposed on that are the straight, vibrant lines of the infantry ranks, neat and precise, the colors softened by the veneer of smoke that drifts over them.

In front of the infantry is the long straight line of the grand battery: Napoléon's "beautiful daughters," his twelve-pounder cannon. In between the two are the artillery support teams: limbers and wagons, hundreds of them, and thousands of horses.

Earlier, a quiet mist drifted up from the valley as the fields of corn, soaked in the overnight rain, were warmed by the morning sun.

Then that mist turned to dense clouds of smoke as eighty cannon began to speak, leaping back in ragged formation before being returned to their neat straight lines.

Again and again the massed cannon fired, their voices the only discordant thing on this otherwise serene and tranquil vista.

The cannon fall quiet and the colors of the infantry muddy as they march in file, threading through the long lines of limbers and wagons. It is as though the artist is mixing paints on his palette. What were neatly defined segments now blur, then separate again as the infantry passes through the lines of cannon and assembles again just in front of them.

The smoke that has muted the scene is now clearing and the hues stand bold and strong.

Jack likes these colors, just as he likes the music of the trumpets and fifes and the stir of the drums.

The banners of the French eagle flutter above the fields of gaudy dancing flowers that are the massed ranks of the infantry.

Lines of horses create outlines for the colors as they flow down into the valley. The cannon behind them now burst back into life, shouting encouragement for their troops in the form of lead shot.

Beneath the trails of the cannonballs the French troops flow like an ocean wave, sweeping up the ridgeline to where the British artillery waits.

Smoke from their own lines matches that from the French.

The British cannon draw long strokes through the French columns, as though the painter has taken a brush and daubed a streak across the picture. That must be round shot, Jack thinks, by the way it cuts such perfectly straight lines through the ranks.

Other cannon fire grapeshot, each recoiling cannon matched by a bite taken out of the French lines as though by the jaws of a giant.

Muskets open up also from the British lines, the crackling sound making little cotton wool lilies, and sending delicate ripples through the approaching columns.

But the French ranks are a never-ending sea, and they cannot be tamed by the roar and flash of metal. The French cannon once again fall silent as their troops flood up to the top of the ridge like the crashing of a wave on a sandy shore.

Then come the horses, the British Heavy Cavalry, sunlight glinting off the steel of their blades, another ocean, this one a sparkling, glittering sea, as it cuts through the smoke and pours into the sides of the columns. It is wonderful to watch the way the horses swirl and pivot and the way the colors of the French fall, like flowers beneath the blade of the gardener.

The neat formations are broken, and still the cannon and the muskets sound, and now the flow is reversed, as the wave of color that has swept up the ridge now ebbs back out to sea, foaming and sputtering as it withdraws.

Still onward race the British horses, through the ranks of the French. Jack marvels at the speed and majesty of it all. Now the neat colors are well and truly scattered, a mosaic of individual dots as the cavalry races right up to and around the grand battery of French cannon.

Then the British tide turns as French horses race toward them: Napoléon's famous and dreaded lancers.

Jack thinks he will never again see such a spectacular, picturesque sight, as the two sides whirl and twirl in a wonderful, colorful waltz, and more and more of the beautiful flowers of this giant garden turn to scattered petals on the ground.

Jack looks around at the sound of a horse, galloping fast. It pulls to a halt behind the captain and the lieutenant.

The rider's face is as black as powder and his uniform also is covered in soot to the point where it is impossible to recognize who he is. The right sleeve of his jacket is torn open and the flap that hangs down is stained red with blood. If the rider even notices the wound, there is no sign of it.

"Left limber up, and as fast as you can!" he shouts. It is an officer of some rank, that is clear.

"Limber up." Mercer repeats the order, and it is taken up by the lieutenants.

Jack races with the others to prepare the cannon for transport. The two Wood brothers grasp the handles on the trail of the gun carriage and hoist it as Bishop backs up the horses to attach the limber.

Jack has already mounted his horse and glances quickly behind, seeing the other gun crews forming up into the column.

"At a gallop, march!" Captain Mercer orders.

The ridgeline is not flat ground but rough countryside, and the carriage bounces and bucks along behind them. The smell of smoke fills the air and the sounds of battle get louder. They are the first crew in the column, but the others are close behind. The horses throw their heads back, enjoying the freedom of the gallop. They jostle against the wooden traces.

"Who is that officer?" Jack asks.

"That is Colonel Frazer himself," Roberts answers. "Commander of the Royal Horse Artillery. That includes you, Private Sullivan."

Captain Mercer and Colonel Frazer ride ahead of them, and their conversation flows back over the sound of the horses and the rumble of the carriage behind.

"It's going to be a big one," Frazer says. "Right in the heart of our line. They are assembling a cavalry charge such as I have never seen. They've been bombarding us fiercely and it'll start any minute, I warrant."

"My men will not falter, no matter what comes at them," Captain Mercer says.

"That may be," Frazer says. "But when the charge comes, the duke's orders are positive. That in the event of their persevering and charging home, you do not expose your men, but retire with them into the adjacent squares of infantry."

The gallop up to that point has been downhill, but now they turn and race up the slope. Behind them stand the tall trees of the Sonian Forest. From the other side of the ridge come the sounds of battle. Constant musket- and cannonfire, but something else. A drumming. A vibration that seems to well up through the dirt of the ridge itself. Jack has never heard anything like it. It is loud enough to almost drown out the roar of the cannon.

The summit of the ridge approaches, and they pass through the infantry, frightened-looking men formed into squares, prickly with muskets like a hedgehog's spines. They are Brunswickers, German troops fighting in the British army.

As G troop comes up toward the top of the ridge Jack hears the sound of cannonballs, and up over the ridge comes the black blur of round shot. Most crash down into the ridge, or fly over their heads into the gully, but some smash into the packed squares of infantry, sending men and muskets flying. The Brunswick officers yell and push their men, closing up the gaps.

The artillery team has to slow as they come to a sharp dip down into a sunken road, and up the other side.

Still the thunder of the earth rises up around them, and only now, as they emerge up onto the front slope of the ridge, in between two other artillery troops, already unlimbered and firing, does Jack see the origin of such an earth-shattering racket.

Cavalry. A blue mass of them. As far as the eye can see in every direction, a horse-and-human tidal wave. With it comes the smoke and the dust kicked up by the shoes of thousands of horses, so that the front lines are completely obscured.

"Unlimber your guns. Form the line!" Captain Mercer shouts.

"Form the line! Form the line!" The call is echoed by the lieutenants.

"Do not wait for my command. Fire as soon as your gun is sighted," the captain calls. "Double load."

From behind him Jack hears the call from the Brunswick officers: "Prepare to receive cavalry!"

The infantry tighten their squares, the front rows on their knees, the stocks of their muskets braced on the ground in front of them. The rear row stands tall, their muskets held at the ready. The bayonets gleam sharp and deadly.

The horse team wheels around to bring the gun to bear. Wacker and Roberts are already off their horses, pulling the key and lifting the lunette off the pintle hook.

The Wood brothers are right behind them, grabbing the wheels and helping haul the carriage into position.

Jack slides out of his saddle and grabs his swab and ramrod from the back of the caisson. There is no time to set the elevation, or properly aim the gun. But nor is there any need. The briskly trotting horses of the French cuirassiers are less than a hundred yards away, rising up over the crest of the ridge.

Townshend runs to the closest crew and uses their linstock to light his own. Jack twists the tampion out of the muzzle. Wacker appears with a case shot and drops it into the barrel, whipping his hands out of the way as Jack rams it home. There is a metallic clunk as it hits the cannonball that is already loaded in the barrel.

The double loading, ball and grape, will shorten the range

considerably, but range is not the problem. The front row of the cavalry is barely seventy yards away.

"Ready!" Jack shouts, hauling his ramrod out of the barrel.

"Fire!" Roberts yells, and Townshend touches the portfire to the firing tube that is already in the fuse hole.

Jack has barely time to spin away from the muzzle when he is enveloped in smoke and noise, with no time to cover his ears. A sheet of flame bellows out of the mouth of the cannon.

He can see nothing. He can hear nothing apart from a ringing in his ears. Then the other cannon speak too, with flames and smoke of their own, and the French cavalry disappears behind a solid wall of smoke.

Jack reverses the ramrod without even thinking about what he is doing, coughing and spluttering through the foul, sulfurous stench of burnt gunpowder. Aren't they supposed to be running for the safety of the infantry squares? But there has been no such order. Or has there been and has he missed it in the roaring of the cannon and the ringing in his ears? Have the other members of his crew run to safety and he is still here, by himself?

He dunks the sponge end of the ramrod into the water bucket and shoves it into the muzzle. No time even to worm the barrel.

The younger Wood has a charge ready and Townshend and Richardson are there with another round shot and another canister of grape.

Jack rams it home, expecting at any moment to feel a cavalry saber slide between his shoulder blades.

He hauls out the ramrod and only then turns to see the damage the first round has caused.

It is chaos. The ground in front of them is littered with the dead and dying, both horses and men. The scattered shot from the canister has torn into the wall of cavalry, cutting them down like the scythe of a mower. The solid cannonball that followed has plowed through the ranks behind.

Horses have fallen. Men have died. Some riders, now horseless, have dropped their armor and run. Some horses, now riderless, have panicked and turned into the paths of those behind.

Jack glances around. Nobody has run to the infantry squares. The men of G troop still man their guns, right along the line.

The next row of cuirassiers are fighting their way over the ones in front and just as they succeed in doing so, the cannon roar again. There is a metallic punching sound audible as the roar of the cannon dies, and Jack realizes it is the sound of steel balls perforating the armor of the cuirassiers.

"Stay at your posts." Now Jack hears the order. "Do not retreat into the squares!" That is followed by, "Hold. Hold."

This time they hold their fire until the order is given. The cuirassiers are allowed to wend their way past the killing ground before the cannon retort. Those not felled by the grapeshot and round shot are struck down by musketballs from the Brunswick squares to either side of them.

The cavalry turns and tries to retreat, but those coming along behind are forcing the front rows forward. Again and again the cannon fire their lethal double dose, tearing great holes in the ranks, trapped between the barricades of bodies and the relentless swell behind.

Finally the French horsemen begin to retreat, those at the rear wheeling around to create a gap through which the front rows can gallop.

There are cheers and shouts from the gun crews along the line and Jack feels himself filled with a wild exhilaration, partly at sending the seemingly unstoppable French cavalry back in its tracks, and partly at still being alive and uninjured.

And then the screaming starts.

ATTACK

All is wild confusion. All is terror.

Men run past the gun, toward the sweeping blades of the cavalry. The sound of sabers meeting flesh and bone melds into the screams as the unarmed soldiers run to their deaths. Running from . . . what?

"Turn the gun." It is Frost's soft, high voice. He is yelling, but even that sounds impossibly calm amid the chaos and the unearthly screaming. "Turn the gun."

Jack does not understand what is going on, and so does nothing except stay at his position by the muzzle of the cannon, first dipping his sponge in the bucket of water. The cannon swings around to face the rear and he moves with it. It makes no sense at all, and yet that is where the screaming is coming from. He swabs out the barrel as it turns to the north and west.

He can barely see anything. The sun is low on the horizon, burning through a low slot in the clouds, which are blood-red to match the field below. The swirling smoke, white, lit red by the sun, comes and goes in eddies. It is like staring into a fog bank.

"Round shot." Frost's voice again, a single sane thing in an insane maelstrom.

Someone's hands put a charge in the barrel, and Jack rams it home in the smoke and the fury, then waits for the cannonball.

"Round shot, please." Still the lieutenant's voice. What can he see that Jack cannot? Still men are streaming past him, many have thrown down their muskets and run in a blind panic.

A pair of hands appears out of the smoke, carrying a cannonball; then Jack sees Wacker's face. Where are the others? Why is the loader bringing the shot? It makes no sense.

Jack looks up at a blur of movement overhead. It is a soldier, in Brunswick colors, arms flailing as he flies through the air.

Jack rams the rod down on top of the cannonball and has just withdrawn it when the impossible happens. Something from a fantasy. A nightmare. Jack wonders if he has died, and does not know it, for surely this is hell.

A vast shadow darkens the red smoke and through it comes a mouth such as Jack could not have imagined. A jaw the size of a gun carriage. Teeth as long as bayonets. Behind it are eyes—black, evil eyes.

The mouth closes on Wacker, who has just turned and so has seen his fate, yet does not scream or cry out. His head, arms, and upper torso disappear into the maw.

The mouth—that abominable mouth—flicks to one side and pieces of Wacker, *pieces*, fly off into the red smoke.

Now the eyes see Jack and the mouth swings toward him. It opens and in some kind of instinctive reaction Jack shoves the ramrod as high and as hard as he can up into the gaping throat. The mouth recoils for a moment, then it lunges forward again.

There is a roar like thunder and new smoke billows. The teeth, just a yard from Jack's face, jerk upward, then backward into smoke, disappearing from sight.

"Sullivan! Sullivan!" It is the lieutenant, and only then does Jack realize that the cannon has fired.

It will be the cannon's last shot.

He instinctively goes through the motions of swabbing out

the cannon. But now there are French soldiers sifting through the smoke, with muskets and swords.

One of them sees him and aims, but there is a gleam of silver and the soldier drops, clutching at his throat. Lieutenant Frost emerges from behind him, now in battle with two French grenadiers, both with bayonets fixed to their muskets. The lieutenant is a swordsman of no mean skill and the flash and clang of steel is constant as he darts and whirls, keeping both of the men at bay, but unable to get close enough to either to inflict any damage.

A musket fires close by, creating a distraction. One of the grenadiers glances away and Frost slips inside his blade and sinks his own sword home. But the other Frenchman is behind him now, leaning in for the kill. Frost is off-balance, his sword in the wrong position, trying to turn with too little time. The Frenchman strikes but just as he does so the solid wooden end of the ramrod smashes down on the top of his head. He staggers, the musket drops from his hands, and he falls to Frost's sword.

"Behind you," Frost shouts, and Jack turns.

Something steps out of the smoke, towering over him. At first he thinks it is a horse, but no horse was ever this big. Then he sees the teeth, those terrible, terrible teeth. It is the creature returned. He stumbles backward, tripping over something or someone and falling.

The giant beast casts the gun carriage aside with just a twitch of its jaw and steps toward Jack. The cannon flies backward into the limber, which collapses in a pile of fractured wood. The ammunition case is crushed, the powder barrels have split open, and the still-lit linstock is spinning in the air. Then there is a sheet of lightning and a roar as though the earth itself is rent apart.

CASUALTIES

There is something different about the next arrival at Gaillemarde.

The carts are by now a familiar sight; the trails of blood they leave on the riverbank have turned the stone and dirt of the path to a deep ochre. The men they bring are mostly alive, and sometimes dead, although all were alive when they were placed on the carts at the battlefield.

But these men are different. The eyes of men who have faced cannon and massed volleys of muskets stare into the distance as though they sleep and are in the grip of a terrible dream.

Always, following the carts, are the walking wounded, men with arms and heads wrapped in red bandages. But this time the carts bring with them also soldiers on whom no apparent injury can be detected. Soldiers who still carry their weapons, yet trudge with the reluctant shuffle of defeated men.

A senior officer on horseback comes with them. He dismounts and strides quickly into the hospital while an adjutant takes hold of his horse.

Willem is outside, washing bandages in the water trough. He can tell that something is wrong, but is not sure what.

When the officer emerges, it is to confer with several other officers who have arrived with him. There is some discussion over maps, and much pointing of hands, before he and his adjutant ride off. They ride fast. They are in a hurry.

It is Mr. Sinclair who gives Willem the news.

"We are leaving," he says, in tears. "At first light."

"Leaving?" Willem asks.

"Our army is retreating toward the coast," he says. "We have been cut off, and so must head east and try to link up with the Prussians. But they are also withdrawing. The situation is dire."

"What will happen to the wounded?" Willem asks.

"We will take as many as we can," he says.

A heartbeat.

At first Jack thinks it is his own, pounding in his ears. But it can't be. It is too gradual. Too heavy. Like a regimental bass drum sounding the beat for a slow march.

He cannot move. When sense returns in measured amounts, he realizes this is because his arm is caught on something. Not on, but under. He lies flat, staring at a clear sky in which smoke still twirls in spiraling columns from fires that must be burning nearby. The stars are bright. Too bright, he thinks, as if the sky itself is on fire in some far distant place.

He can see only half of the sky. The other half is blocked by something that blots out the night. Understanding brings with it a new horror.

That is where the heartbeat is coming from.

Then blackness covers him once again.

NAPOLÉON

The emperor of France is receiving the Duke and Duchess of Richmond when Thibault arrives. Thibault waits at the back of the drawing room where Napoléon has set up his war office. Marshal Ney is seated to the left of an ornate desk.

"Again I must thank you for the use of your house," Napoléon says. "And I assure you that my staff will leave it in pristine condition."

"A kindness greatly appreciated," the duke says. He bows his head graciously, but it is clear from the tension in the neck of his wife, the duchess, that she is far from pleased with the arrangement.

"I hear that you had a great ball here, just three nights ago," Napoléon says. "Had I left France a little sooner, I could have attended myself."

Ney laughs at his joke. The duke and duchess do not. Nor would Thibault, in their situation. Most of the officers who attended that ball are surely now wounded or dead, their elegant wives now nursemaids, or widows.

"My men will accompany you to the coast, and arrange passage for you to England," Napoléon says. "They will ensure you are not harmed."

"Thank you again, monsieur," the duke says.

"I await your king's reply with great eagerness," he says.

"I expect that England will not surrender quite so easily," the duke says. "After just one battle."

"Then the next time I ask for her surrender will be on the steps of Buckingham Palace," Napoléon says. "And my terms will not be as generous."

The duke and duchess sweep past Thibault as they leave, the strain showing through the powder that cannot conceal the dark circles under her eyes, or the gray pallor of his face.

Ney waits until the door closes, then summons Thibault over.

Thibault bows in front of his emperor.

"Ah, the late Major Thibault," Ney says.

"I must apologize for our untimely arrival at the battle," Thibault says, still bowed. "The forest was crawling with British patrols and we had to proceed slowly lest we lost the advantage of surprise."

"Your timing could have been a little better," Napoléon says. "Many men were lost because of it. However"—a great smile breaks out on his face and he embraces Thibault warmly, kissing him on both cheeks—"victory is ours."

"A victory that will resound through history," Thibault says.

Napoléon gestures to an aide, who steps forward with a tray of crystal glasses. Thibault takes one and sips. It is fine champagne. Napoléon retrieves his own glass from the desk, next to an intricately patterned black oval snuff box. He tosses the champagne back as if it is water.

"The British run away with their tails between their legs, and we drink their champagne from their own crystal," Napoléon says. "And the beauty is that from now on I will scarcely even have to fight! Fear now rides at the head of my army. The Netherlands have surrendered without so much as a skirmish, and the Prussians are already pressing for terms!"

Napoléon laughs and takes a pinch of snuff. "These battlesaurs of yours win actions without setting foot on the battlefield."

"The Russians do not forget 1812, and England has its moat," Thibault says.

"Ah, Major, even my generals do not dare to so insult me," Napoléon says.

"Sire! I never—"

"Hush, hush," Napoléon says. "You speak your mind, and your heart. Too many of my pampering squibs say only what they think I want to hear."

"Sire," Thibault says.

"You seek to remind me of my greatest defeat. You think perhaps I have forgotten the long retreat from Russia. Or the hundreds of thousands of men we left on those frozen fields. I have not, Thibault. Nor has Marshal Ney, the last man to leave Russian soil. But this is a new war and we have new weapons. As for the English?" Napoléon passes the snuff in front of his nose, smelling it, then discards it without inhaling. "John Bull thinks the channel makes him safe. That the water that surrounds his pathetic little island will stop me from crushing him. Not this time, Major!"

"The Royal Navy still commands the channel, sire," Ney says.

"The English are foolish and unskilled in the art of war," Napoléon says. "King George lies at death's door. Liverpool's puppet, no more. I will give the ships of his majesty something else to do, while we cross the water unmolested. And let me tell you this, Thibault. This time my plans are not so limited. After England and Russia we will take Austria, and the Ottomans. Then perhaps we will look toward Asia."

"Yes, sire," Thibault says.

"But I cannot have a mere major commanding my new army,"

Napoléon says. "That would not do at all. I will need to put a general in charge."

Thibault bows his head. "Sire, with the utmost respect, I have spent years with these creatures. I understand them, and how to use them in battle. To replace me, in the midst of a war, with a new officer might not produce the results you intend."

"I agree, Major," Napoléon says. "And yet it is only appropriate that a general should be in command."

"I do not understand, sire," Thibault says.

"You will, General Thibault," Napoléon says. "Ney will see to the paperwork."

"Of course, sire," Ney says.

"Thank you, sire," Thibault says, bowing again. "It is a great honor."

It is a big promotion, from major to general. Almost unheard of.

Napoléon looks up at the sound of the door. A valet opens it and Count Cambronne approaches in long confident strides.

"Faithful Cambronne," Napoléon says. "I did not expect to see you again tonight."

"Sire, I bring serious news from Wallonia," Cambronne says.

"What can be serious in Wallonia?" Napoléon laughs. "I have just conquered Wallonia."

"There is talk of a boy, in a small village near Waterloo, who has command over saurs," Cambronne says.

"Not over my saurs," Thibault says. "They would devour a boy without noticing."

"They say he charmed a saur, and then killed it while it was under his spell," Cambronne says.

"A microsaurus, perhaps?" Napoléon asks. "Or a small raptor?"

Cambronne shakes his head. "My men say it was a dinosaur, one of Thibault's."

"Thibault?" Napoléon impales him with a glance.

"It is true that we lost a saur," Thibault says cautiously.

"You lost one of my battlesaurs?" Napoléon flings his arms wide. The snuff box crashes to the ground but he does not notice. "An animal the size of a house?"

"It escaped, sire," Thibault says. "The equipment failed and it threw off, then ate, its rider. It escaped into the forest. We hunted it for many days."

"Which kind of saur was it?"

"The one we call the crocodylus, sire."

"I warned you that that big one would be difficult to control," Napoléon says. "Where is it now?"

"I do not know, sire. I assumed it was dead at the bottom of a gully or still roaming wild in the forest. We were preparing for battle and did not have time to worry over one lost beast."

"One lost beast." Napoléon repeats the words as if he cannot believe that he has heard them.

"There is more, sire," Cambronne says. "This village, Gaillemarde—it was the site of a so-called miracle, a few weeks ago."

"A miracle?"

"A boy was shot, by pistol, accidentally," Cambronne says. "He was shot in the chest, but was unharmed, and produced the ball through his mouth."

"That is nothing but a conjuring trick," Thibault says. "An old trick."

But Napoléon is now leaning forward, his relaxed pose giving way to a ramrod stiffness.

"A boy performed this trick?" he asks.

"Yes, sire."

"And a boy charmed and killed one of my battlesaurs?"

"So they say, sire."

"It is the son," Napoléon says. "It must be."

"They are just stories, sire," Thibault says.

"We conquer Europe with an army of fear," Napoléon says. "If word spreads that even a child can kill one of your terrible lizards, then who will fear them?"

"You speak wisely, sire," Cambronne says.

"Bring me this boy," Napoléon says.

"Of course, sire," Cambronne says.

"Not you, Count," Napoléon says. "This is Thibault's pickle. He can clean it up."

"As you wish, sire," Thibault says.

BATTLEFIELD

Jack hasn't moved. Neither has the beast next to him, which still traps his arm. The all-enveloping thud of the creature's heart seems slower now. With each beat he waits longer for the next, the anticipation building up like a wave crashing onto a beach.

He tries to free his arm, but cannot. It is firmly trapped under the flesh of the animal. There are dark shapes to either side of him and he spends some time trying to decide what they are.

Legs, he decides. The creature is lying on its side and he is trapped against the underbelly.

He wants to call for help, but he is afraid. If there are any soldiers still on this battlefield, they will be French. Worse than that are the peasants. Locals who will plunder the dead and dying. The wounded they will silence forever with a knife across the throat as they steal their jewelry, watches, and coin.

He could wait for first light, but that would bring no benefit and the idea of lying all night against this hellish creature brings waves of nausea and despair.

"Help," he calls, praying that any reply will come in English. "Help."

"Who is there?" a voice calls back.

"Private Jack Sullivan, G troop," Jacks says. "I'm a good lad." His voice has caught in his throat and he is not sure why. He shuts his eyes to blink out tears. "I'm a good lad," he says.

There is a kind of laughter from the other, just two short, muffled huffs, then the voice asks, "Is that so, Private Sullivan?"

"Lieutenant?" Jack asks cautiously.

"Are you wounded?" Frost asks.

"I'm not sure, sir," Jack says. "But I'm trapped."

"Trapped?"

"I can't move. My arm is trapped under . . . it," Jack says.

"Under what?" Frost asks.

"I don't know, sir," Jack says.

"You mean the saur?" Frost asks.

"If that is what it is," Jack says.

"Is it dead?" Frost asks.

"Almost, I think, sir," Jack says.

"I'll come to you," Frost says.

There comes the sound of shuffling movement.

"Where are you?" Frost asks.

"Under the . . . saur," Jack says.

"Yes, but where is that?" Frost asks.

Jack thinks for a moment how to answer this. The moon has risen and the battlefield, what little he can see of it, flat on his back next to a giant carcass, is silvered.

"Can't you see it, sir?" he asks.

"I can't see anything," Frost says.

There is silence for a moment while Jack thinks that through.

"Keep talking. I'm following your voice," Frost says. He sounds close.

Jack, unsure of what to say, begins to sing. A children's rhyme about a wooden toy. He barely gets through the first verse when Lieutenant Frost appears, clambering over the carcass of a horse. His face is a mask of blood, except where a red-stained rag is tied around his eyes. His uniform is dirtied and torn, and he has lost his beautiful bearskin crested helmet.

"Is it safe, sir?" Jack asks.

"Safe?" Frost asks back.

"I mean are there any Frenchies around?" Jack asks.

Frost shakes his head. The bloodied rag around his head flaps with a soft slapping sound. He feels around Jack's body, finding the arm where it is trapped under the beast.

"I haven't heard any for hours," he says. "There were many earlier. I played dead and I guess I was lucky. There were so many bodies that they just didn't have time to check them all. Stay here."

Perhaps it is the lieutenant who isn't very bright, if he thinks Jack is going to go somewhere.

Frost is back a few moments later with a bayonet, feeling his way across the ground.

"Lieutenant Frost, sir," Jack says.

"Yes, Sullivan?"

"Please don't cut me arm off, sir," Jack says.

Frost gives the same half laugh as earlier. "I'll try not to," he says.

He stabs at the ground on either side of Jack's arm, cutting the turf and loosening the damp soil underneath. He scrapes away underneath the arm, taking care not to cut it.

"Try and wriggle it free," he says.

Jack pulls and is rewarded with an agonizing bolt of pain. He clenches his teeth but does not cry out. Who knows who else is lurking around this absurd charnel house this night.

"Can you do it?" Frost asks.

"No, sir," Jack says. "I think it might be broken, sir."

"All right," Frost says. He begins to dig again. This time he is more thorough, digging farther and more deeply than before.

Slowly Jack feels his arm come free. But with it comes the pain. Not the stabbing, piercing pain of the first time, but a long, slow, constant burn.

"What happened tonight, sir?" Jack asks. "I can't make head nor tail of it."

Frost digs deeply into the ground with the bayonet.

"Nor I," he says. "Try now."

Jack reaches into the hole that Frost has dug and supports his trapped left arm with his right. He pulls. It is still agonizing, but the arm slips free and he rolls over, away from the beast. The arm flops around, beyond his control, and he clutches it to his body with his right hand.

"How is it?" Frost asks.

"Good as gold, sir," Jack replies, somewhat amazed that the arm isn't flattened. "Just a wee bit broken, I think."

"You have the rain to thank for that," Frost says. "Soft ground. Otherwise that arm would be pulp."

Working by touch, Frost straightens Jack's arm as best as he can and fashions a makeshift splint out of the bayonet, tying it with a lanyard from his uniform.

"What happened to the men, sir?" Jack asks.

There is a long silence. There is a shout and a gunshot somewhere in the distance, down in the valley. A looter perhaps, who met a wounded soldier with a pistol.

"I do not know," Frost says. "Perhaps they were able to retreat."

Jack presses him no further on that. He hopes it is true, but cannot shake the memory of Wacker's body, in pieces, hurtling through the blood-red smoke.

"Where are we going to go, sir?" Jack asks.

Frost sits down on the rump of a dead horse. He looks even smaller in the moonlight. Not like a British officer at all. More like a frightened little boy on his first day in school. But when he speaks, his voice, although still soft and high, has authority and determination.

"The French were moving on to Brussels," Frost says. "If they are going west, then we must head east. There is a field hospital in the village of Gaillemarde. That is less than an hour away."

"Will it still be there?" Jack asks. "The field hospital I mean, sir, not the village."

"We will find out when we get there," Frost says. "Won't we, Sullivan?"

"Lieutenant Frost, sir," Jack says. "My name is Jack. Sullivan was me dad, sir."

"All right, Jack," Frost says. "And mine is Hunter."

"I'll just call you sir, sir," Jack says. "If that's all right, sir."

Frost nods. "What does your father do, Jack?" he asks.

"Ship's carpenter," Jack says. "Helped carve the figurehead on the *Victory*."

"Nelson's ship?"

"The same, sir. And he served on her at Trafalgar."

"That was a great victory," Frost says.

"Not for Nelson, sir, he died," Jack says. "And not for me dad, neither."

Frost is quiet.

"We should leave now, sir," Jack says. "I don't know what the time is, but we should try to be off the battlefield before it gets light."

"Indeed, a wise observation," Frost says. "But first I need you to do something for me."

"Yes, sir."

"Can you see the beast that trapped your arm?"

"Yes, sir, the moon is out, and I can see it plain as day," Jack says.

"Describe it for me, Jack," Frost says.

"Describe it?"

"Yes, what does it look like?"

"Terrifying, sir," Jack says.

"So I remember," Frost says. "But give me some details. Tell me everything you can see."

"Bloody great beast from hell, if you'll pardon me language, sir," Jack says. He walks around to the other side of the dead animal. "It's a saur, sir, no doubt about that. But it's much bigger than anything I've even heard of before."

"Or I," Frost says.

"It's got a saddle, sir," Jack says.

"A saddle?"

"Yes, sir. With a Frenchie in it."

"A French soldier?" Frost asks.

"What's left of 'im, sir," Jack says. "'E's a bit squished."

"What about the animal itself? Any feathers?" Frost asks.

"Not that I can see," Jack says.

"Spines?"

"No, Lieutenant, sir. It's got very hard, thick skin. Lumpy, sir."

"And the legs?" Frost asks.

"Very big back legs, sir. Got big claws on them too," Jack says. "Funny little front legs though. Like little arms. I think he walks on his back legs, sir."

"I think you are probably right, Jack," Frost says. "How tall do you think it is?"

"Standing up or lying down, sir?"

"Standing up." Frost smiles. "In your best guess. Compared to you."

"Oh, it's definitely taller than me, sir," Jack says.

"Yes, but how many times?" Frost asks.

Jack walks around the carcass examining the feet and the giant legs in the moonlight. "Two or three times me, sir," he says. "If it was standing up."

"All right, good work, Jack," Frost says. "Now tell me every little detail you can see."

And so Jack does. But there is one detail that he leaves out, and it does not pertain to the dinosaur, but rather to the dead horse on which Lieutenant Frost has made his seat.

It is as well that the lieutenant cannot see for himself that he sits on the rump of a beautiful chestnut mare with two rear white stockings.

"Is it still dark?" Frost asks when Jack has run out of words to describe the beast.

"It is still night," Jack says. "But there is a fine moon."

On Saturday the fields around Mont-Saint-Jean were carpeted with softly waving stalks of corn. Now it is Sunday and the carpet is vastly different.

Jack and his lieutenant move through a bloody nightmare of corpses, carcasses, and much worse. It is a smoke-filled inferno of mud, blood, guts, and excrement. The dank night air is filled with the pathetic whinnying of dying horses and the cries of wounded men. Hands grab at their ankles as they pass but they wrench themselves free without even looking to see the color or rank. There is nothing that can be done. Only one thing comes for these men.

Several times they see bodies being pillaged by looters, who scatter when they see Frost and Jack approaching.

In the distance they see the lamps and ambulance wagons of French corpsmen and litter-bearers checking for wounded.

Footing is treacherous as the ground is a tangle of crushed cornstalks, slick with blood. The breeze carries the stench of the battle, the acrid smoke, the rotten-egg residue of gunpowder, the cloy of freshly slaughtered meat.

There is something else in the air. Something that cannot be seen, heard, smelled, or explained. But Jack can taste it. He can feel it. He does not mention it to Frost, but knows that Frost can sense it too. The souls of so many: invisible, silent, odorless. They swoop and swirl a spirited dance of death above the battlefield: those who died gloriously, those who died in hopeless futility, and those who just died.

At first they think the soldier is dead, but he emerges from a tumble of bodies like Lazarus rising from the grave. He wears a British uniform but his skin is dark like that of an African. His teeth shine in the moonlight.

"Who goes there?" His musket is presented.

"Lieutenant Frost, Royal Horse Artillery, G troop," Frost says. "And Private Sullivan of my troop."

The musket lowers.

"Corporal Mathan Mogansondram, Royal Indian Brigade, twenty-five battalion," the dark soldier says.

"I thought your brigade was at Halle, with Prince Frederick," Frost says.

"We were, sir," Mogansondram says. "The prince sent my colonel to report on the progress of the battle. We were caught up in the fighting when the British lines collapsed."

"Are you injured, Corporal?" Frost asks.

"Yes, sir, in the leg, sir, but I can walk," Mogansondram says.

"Then walk with us, Corporal. We are on our way to the field hospital at Gaillemarde," Frost says.

"I cannot do that, sir," Mogansondram says. "I must stay here." He indicates a man lying nearby, who Jack had assumed was dead. "My colonel, sir. He made me promise to stay with him, to protect him from looters, until he can be evacuated."

"I would talk to him," Frost says.

"He is sleeping, sir," Mogansondram says. "I do not like to wake him."

"Where is he?" Frost asks. Jack takes him by the arm, leading him to where the colonel lies. Frost examines him with his soft, small hands, now blackened and bloodstained. He presses his ear to the man's chest and listens.

"Your colonel is dying," he says.

"Yes, sir," Mogansondram says. "I believe so."

"His journey has begun," Frost says, feeling the officer's pulse. "It will not be a long one."

"I believe that too," Mogansondram says.

"Then come with us. Get that leg looked at," Frost says.

"I cannot do that, sir," Mogansondram says. "I promised that I would stay with him."

"He will never know," Frost says gently.

"Even so, sir," Mogansondram says, standing to attention.

"Of course," Frost says. "Gaillemarde is to the northeast. Just follow the roads."

"Indeed, sir," Mogansondram says. "I hope to see you there, sir."

Frost stands up straight, facing the soldier. He salutes.

Mogansondram, surprised at being saluted by a lieutenant when he has not saluted first, takes a moment to react, then quickly raises his hand to his forehead.

"He is returning your salute," Jack says.

"I know," Frost says.

It is only later that Jack realizes that neither of them were wearing their helmets.

RETREAT

It is late, but still Willem makes the rounds of the temporary hospital in the marketplace building.

The surgeons and nurses have gone, with their orderlies and carts full of medical equipment. With the help of the villagers they packed up their equipment and left, men with lanterns walking the eastern path in the darkness to light the way for the carts and the carriages.

The British army is retreating. There is little Willem can do, except keep an eye on the patients who remain, and cover the faces of those who die.

Jean's father enters quietly and moves down the rows, looking at the names written in chalk on the ends of the wooden cots. He seems to find what he is looking for and kneels by the side of the cot. It is a young British captain with long red hair. His right arm is missing and his face seems yellow in the light of Willem's lamp.

Monsieur Lejeune waits, trying to ascertain if the man is asleep or just resting. After a few minutes the captain seems to sense the villager's presence and his eyes open. Willem moves in that direction. Monsieur Lejeune notices him and nods.

"Where is the doctor?" the captain asks in English, but Monsieur Lejeune shakes his head.

"Where is the doctor?" the captain asks again, this time in French. His French is rudimentary, but sufficient.

"The doctors are gone," Monsieur Lejeune says. "Your army has withdrawn."

The captain nods his understanding.

"You are the one who says he saw monsters?" Monsieur Lejeune asks.

The captain frowns.

"Beasts. Giant saurs," Monsieur Lejeune prompts.

The captain's face rises briefly in understanding, then sinks into a private hell. "It is neither a dream nor a lie," he says. "My men ran, but they were not cowards."

"I believe you," Monsieur Lejeune says.

"You are the first," the captain says. "The doctors say I have imagined it. That I am suffering from melancholia."

"What did you see?" Monsieur Lejeune asks.

Even in his basic, stumbling French, the picture that the captain paints is of such confusion and terror that it is no wonder the doctors thought he was mad.

"You do believe me?" he asks, when he has finished.

"I do," Monsieur Lejeune says.

"Even I start to doubt my own sanity," the captain says. "Surely such creatures exist only in fairy tales."

"I wish that were true," Monsieur Lejeune says. "But were you not warned about these creatures?"

"We had no warning," the captain says. "We were taken by complete surprise."

Monsieur Lejeune excuses himself and hurries away. It is the second time Willem has seen him quizzing soldiers on the battles and he suspects there is more to his questions than just interest.

Willem turns to resume his walk around the makeshift hospital, but the captain stops him with a quiet, "Monsieur."

"Yes?" Willem asks.

"My ring," he says.

Willem shakes his head, not understanding.

"They took my arm," the captain says. He shuts his eyes and swallows a few times.

"Others have lost much more," Willem says, a little more harshly than he intends. A few moments ago he covered the face of a pretty young woman. The wife of an officer who was at his side during the battle.

"Monsieur," the captain says. "Please help me."

"There is little I can do," Willem says.

"I was not myself when they took my arm," the captain says. "I am not as resolute as many of the others, to my shame."

"There is no shame, monsieur," Willem says quietly.

"On my hand was a ring. It is gold," the captain says. "It is very important to me. It is important to my family. It is very old."

And now Willem sees the problem.

"I will ask someone to look for it in the morning," he says. What he does not say is that he cannot go *there*.

There is the back of the marketplace. Beside the rear doors. In the street that runs by. It is a place of such horror that Willem does not even allow himself to look in that direction for fear that he will see through the walls to what lies behind. A jumbled pile of limbs. Arms and legs, hands and feet, tossed in a heap, their neatly cut ends and sawed bones a contrast to the mangled flesh of the wounds that caused their removal.

And in his imagination the limbs are not still and silent. Fingers grasp, toes wriggle. The arms and legs writhe and crawl like a nest of maggots.

He opens his mouth to tell the captain that he cannot do this, that he cannot face the horror that lies outside the rear doors. But he does not utter the words. He looks at the void under the thin blanket where the man's right arm should be. Just a few hours ago it was being cut from his body with only a few drops of rum to ease the parting. How can he compare his suffering to that of the captain?

"How will I know it?" he asks.

"It has my family crest on it," the captain says. "A lion over a crown. I will be forever grateful if you find it."

His amputation is a high one, just below the shoulder. Forever is not likely to be long for this captain.

Cosette finds Willem in the street at the rear of the marketplace, seated, his back to the wall. She has come to bring water for the men. She rests her bucket and lamp at his feet and sits beside him for a minute.

"You should sleep," she says. "It is late."

"I should, but I cannot," he says.

"To your bed, Willem," she says. "I will attend the patients for a while."

"There is something I must do," he says.

She waits.

"I promised an officer that I would find his ring," Willem says.

She understands immediately. "And you cannot find it?"

"I cannot look," he says.

Her hand covers his. Her words are soft.

"Describe the ring for me," she says. "I will find it."

"No, Cosette," he says. "The promise is mine."

"Then come with me," she says. "The promise is not broken if we search together."

He rises up with her and her strength becomes his strength.

Cosette wets a rag with water from her bucket and cleans dried blood off the ring before they take it together to the captain.

His eyes fill with tears and he clutches it tightly in his remaining hand.

"Thank you," he says.

"It was an honor to help you," Willem says, with an apologetic glance at Cosette.

"If I do not survive this injury," the captain says, "I beg you to find a way to return this ring to my family."

"I will try, sir," Willem says.

Cosette touches the captain gently on the shoulder. "What is your name, sir?" she asks.

"Wenzel-Halls," he says. "Captain, Coldstream Guards."

Cosette smooths hair away from his forehead where a loose lock has covered his face.

"Cosette is my name," she says.

"And Dylan is mine," the captain says. "I am pleased to make your acquaintance."

"I wish you had not had to," Cosette says.

Afterward they sit together on the cold wooden bench outside the hospital. Cosette is shuddering, and clearly trying not to cry. Willem puts his arm around her to ease her burden and she turns in to him, and for a while they are one.

There is dried blood on his hands, and the same on hers. She begins to sob, and he realizes that it was no easier for her than it was for him. But she did it all the same. She did it for him. And in that moment Willem wonders, amid the blood and the guts and the gore, if he has discovered what love is.

FIRST LIGHT

"Why are we stopping?" Frost asks.

"Don't rightly know which way to go, sir," Jack says.

"North and east will take us to Gaillemarde," Frost says.

"Yes, sir, but I am not sure which way east is," Jack says. "Not till the sun comes up."

"But we've been traveling east until now, is that not right, Jack?" Frost asks.

"Yes, sir."

"How have you managed that, without the sun?"

"I could see the forest, sir. I knew that was to the north, so I kept it to my left."

"Jack, I think you're a lot brighter than you give yourself credit for," Frost says. "But what is the problem now? Can't you see the forest anymore?"

"No, sir. I mean yes, sir. I mean no, sir." Jack stops, in a muddle.

"I'm afraid I don't understand," Frost says.

"I mean we're right in the middle of it, sir," Jack says.

The forest surrounds them. Tall black trees that reach up to the sky, blotting out the moon and the meager light of the stars.

"Time for a break then, Jack," Frost says.

"Good idea, sir. Bit of sleep wouldn't hurt. First light we'll be off again," Jack says.

"Indeed," Frost says.

But sleep does not come to either of them. The horrors of the previous day are too bright, too vivid, too huge in their memories.

"Lieutenant, sir. Why did you want me to describe the beast?" Jack asks after a while.

"To help identify it," Frost says.

"How can you identify some'at like that?" Jack asks. "Nobody's ever seen anything like it before. Have they?"

"I doubt it," Frost says. "But there are men of science who can link it to other, smaller saurs that we do know of. Like a lion is related to a cat. That might help us understand the beast. And we will need to understand it, if we want to learn how to kill it."

"I like cats," Jack says.

He thinks for a while on what the lieutenant has said. Then asks, "Do you really think they'll be able to kill those . . . things?"

"Perhaps," Frost says. "We killed one already today."

"Two, I think, sir," Jack says.

"Two?"

"That one that was on top of me, I don't think it was the one we shot. I been thinking about that and that one would have a bleedin' great hole in its chest. This one didn't."

"Then what killed this one?" Frost asks.

"When the ammunition cart blew up," Jack says. "I think that was what killed it."

"So what happened to the other one?" Frost asks.

"Dunno, sir. Maybe it rolled away down the hill."

For some reason the image of a dead dinosaur rolling down a hill seems funny, so Jack laughs. Frost laughs with him.

"So they can be killed," Frost says. "With shot or with powder. This might well be our counter."

"Counter, sir?"

"If we cannot match these new weapons," Frost says, "then we will have to learn to counter them."

"That's why you wanted me to describe the dead one," Jack says.

"Exactly. I suspect few if any British soldiers have seen what we have seen, and lived to tell the tale," Frost says. "We must somehow return to England and tell them everything we can about this beast."

Jack stands abruptly. He has fallen asleep despite everything and the sun has already risen.

The movement wakes Frost, who is curled on a bed of soft leaves like a child. There are dragonrat tracks around them both. Jack is just happy that nothing larger came across them during the night.

"What is it?" Frost asks in a hushed voice. He sits up and his hand goes automatically to touch the bandages that cover his eyes.

Sleep has been a respite from the horrors that surround them, but as consciousness rushes back, so does reality, and Jack can see the weight of it on the lieutenant's face.

"Sun's up, sir," Jack says.

"Then let us be on our way," Frost says.

Gaillemarde is close, they find out. Much closer than they had realized. The eastern road takes them through a short stretch of the forest, then along a riverbank path. Ahead Jack sees a stone bridge and a saur-fence on the other side of the river.

If Lieutenant Frost had his eyes, he might have realized sooner, but he does not. Jack is exhausted, trudging along with his eyes on the path in front of him. Which is why he does not see until they are at the saur-gate itself.

There are guards inside the gate.

But their uniforms are not the red coats of the British.

They are the blue and white of the French.

Book Three

June 19–June 25, 1815

THIBAULT

Thibault is already dressed when his wife wakes.

He stands at the window, staring out at the darkened roofs of Brussels and the fortified wall beyond. He breathes in deeply, savoring the smell of smoke, the sweet perfume of victory, that still drifts this way from the fields near Waterloo.

"Marc?" A soft voice from the bed.

It is still dark but his movement must have disturbed her for she sits up as if taking a fright.

"Rest, Nicole," he says. "It is not yet light."

"You are leaving?" his wife asks. "And so early?"

She turns and lights the candles on her nightstand. A warm smell of paraffin quickly fills the room. Like the rest of the apartment, it is small and sparsely decorated. A house suited to a colonel or a major perhaps, but not to a general of France. That will change.

"The emperor himself commands me to run an errand. A trifling thing and a waste of my time, particularly when there is so much else to do. But it was the emperor who gave the order and I must obey."

"You are now a general of the Imperial Guard, not a manservant," she says.

"Not for long," Thibault says.

There is a pause, then Nicole says, "I do not follow your meaning, my love."

Thibault turns, leaning across her and brushing loose hair back from her face with his hand.

"Bonaparte is a conqueror, not a ruler," he says. "He has neither the nature nor the temperament for it. He is an attack dog. The states of Europe will quickly fall under him. But then the new empire will need a leader. A peacetime leader. Perhaps someone like myself."

"You think you can overthrow the emperor of France?" she asks. The idea excites her and she catches his hand with hers and gently kisses his palm.

"I do not think it, I know it," Thibault says. "I know it without question. As of yesterday, I am the source of Napoléon's power. And there are greater things to come. There are secrets deep in the caves of the Sonian Forest that even the emperor does not know about."

"Does that not make you the most powerful man in all of Europe?" she asks.

"In fact, if not in title."

"And when do the two combine?" she asks.

"That day is coming," he says. "But for now I need his brilliance. Let him conquer Europe. He need not know that he conquers it for me."

"If you imprison him, the people will rally to his cause," she says.

"Without question." Thibault nods. "But Napoléon is a relic. An emperor who strides the battlefield with his army like the great conquerors of old. And a battlefield is a dangerous place. A musket shot or a cannonball does not discriminate based on rank or uniform. If Napoléon were to die—heroically—on the battlefield, France would have a martyr, and a legacy that will resound through the centuries."

"And you?"

"I would have an empire," Thibault says.

"And I would have you," she says.

"And all the fineries of the world would be yours," he says. "But that time is not yet. For now I must continue to play my part, and run this fool's errand. There is a boy in a village not far from here. Napoléon wants him captured."

"And you?"

"I would see him killed," he says.

"Will it take long?" she asks.

"It is but a trifle," he says. "He will be dead by noon."

HÔPITAL DE CAMPAGNE

The French doctors arrive at Gaillemarde first thing in the morning in a well-organized convoy of ambulance and supply wagons. They impress Willem with their efficiency.

A detachment of French soldiers had arrived earlier to secure the village, but found only the wounded, the dying, and the dead.

Under the supervision of the head surgeon, a small team of surgeons and physicians begin to examine the patients, preparatory to evacuating them to French field hospitals.

For two days British and Dutch wounded had arrived on the backs of carts, or on makeshift stretchers, dragged in by their comrades. By contrast the French have dedicated ambulance wagons, with bandages and blankets, manned by corpsmen and litter-bearers.

A number of women accompany them, acting as nurses, tending to patients, and bringing them water. At first Willem thinks they are nuns, but they do not wear habits, although all dress uniformly, in black gowns, with black bonnets and shawls.

They are not the only women in the hospital. Madame Gertruda seems not to have slept since the hospital arrived. She is everywhere, administering herbs and medicines to the patients. The British doctors allowed this and now the French doctors encourage it, seeing the light of hope that it kindles in the eyes of desperate men. Madame Claude, the mayor's wife, is also tireless. She changes dressings and cleans wounds in a bustle of activity.

The wounded continue to arrive, as they drag or crawl their way off the battlefield. The French surgeons set up an area they refer to as triage, where the casualties are seen quickly and assessed, so the most urgent cases can be treated first.

The French are courteous but also suspicious, and although most of the detachment of soldiers leaves, some remain as guards. They are posted at the gates, in the church tower, and throughout the village.

Once examined by the doctors, the patients are loaded onto carts, carriages, or ambulance wagons and start the journey to French field hospitals, or in some of the more serious cases, to the main hospital in Brussels.

In typical French efficiency, an orderly or a nurse travels with each vehicle, tending to the men on their journey. A soldier sits up next to the driver, as a guard.

There are many wounded, and with more filtering in throughout the morning, it is a slow process. By midmorning all the available transports have left, and those who remain must wait for them to return.

When Willem enters the hospital, the head surgeon is examining a cavalry officer who has lost both his legs. The surgeon glances up at Willem, smiles briefly, then goes back to his work, tut-tutting over the standard of the British surgeon's workmanship.

Captain Wenzel-Halls is conscious, and motions to Willem.

On the cot next to him is an artillery lieutenant, barely in his teens. A new arrival. He has been blinded and a fresh dressing covers his eyes. He is with a tall, strong-limbed private, who reminds Willem of Jean. The private sits on the floor beside the lieutenant's cot. His only injury appears to be a broken arm, which has been set and splinted, and wrapped in clean white bandages.

Wenzel-Halls's color is not good. He reaches out and grasps Willem's arm, although there is no strength in the grip.

"I grow weaker," he says in a voice that is little more than a dry croak. "A fever takes hold. Do not forget your promise."

Willem looks at the ring, now on the middle finger of the captain's left hand. "You have my word," he says.

"The creatures I saw," he says, indicating the young blind lieutenant next to him. "Lieutenant Frost here saw them too. As did his man."

The private appears not to understand, and Wenzel-Halls speaks briefly to him in English.

"Private Jack Sullivan," the soldier says, standing up and extending a hand in the British way.

Willem shakes it. "Willem Verheyen."

"Do you speak English?" Jack asks.

"A little," Willem says, in English. "You saw the dinosaur?"

Jack says, "I did, sir. But not properly until after it was dead."

"What did you see?" Willem asks.

"Right horrid it was, sir," Jack says. "Bigger than an elephant with teeth as big as . . . as big as . . ." At a loss for words, he goes quiet.

"As tall as our church steeple?" Willem asks.

"No, not as big as that, sir," Jack says.

"The snout, it was long and thin like that of a crocodile?" Willem asks.

"Well, I ain't actually seen a crocodile," Jack says. "But I don't think so, sir. The snout was stubby, like a raptor. At least the two we killed was."

"Jack!" Frost says.

"Sir?"

"I suggest you hold your tongue when you are talking to our captors," Frost says.

"Sorry, sir," Jack says.

"I am not your captor, Lieutenant," Willem says. "I am neither French, nor a member of Napoléon's army."

"But you are Walloon, and I fear that your allegiance is with the emperor," Frost says.

"I am not, sir," Willem says. "I am Flemish, of a Flemish father, and Napoléon is my enemy as he is yours. I, too, have seen one of these beasts."

There is a long silence as Frost considers that.

"How can that be?" Frost finally asks.

"Sir, I would beg that you keep close counsel on this matter," Willem says. "I fear what would happen should the emperor's men learn of this."

"Then it seems we both have secrets we would keep to ourselves," Frost says. "I would know of the circumstances. This is of great importance."

"And you will treat this information in great confidence?" Willem says.

"As will you," Frost says.

A young nurse moves toward them, carrying a jug full of blood. She smiles briefly at Willem as she passes. He is silent, using a ladle to give Wenzel-Halls a drink of water from a bowl beside the bed.

"Prior to the battle, one of Napoléon's creatures escaped," Willem says when the nurse is out of earshot. "A great beast, even larger than the animals that Jack describes."

"A creature as tall as a church steeple with a snout like a crocodile," Frost says.

"It is so," Willem says. "It attacked the village."

"Do you not fear its return?" Frost asks.

"We do not," Willem says. "It lies in a deep grave."

Frost considered that. "You expect me to believe that the

menfolk of your village killed a dinosaur with nothing but rusty swords and pitchforks?"

"It was killed by . . . a friend of mine," Willem says. "With a crossbow."

"A good story, but not possible," Frost says. "I have seen these beasts with my own eyes." He stops speaking and touches the bandages that now cover his eyes. He seems to withdraw into himself for a moment before continuing. "A bolt would merely bounce off its hide."

"I tell the truth," Willem says. "There is a way to mesmerize such a creature. It does not move and a brave hunter is able to draw in close."

"Who has such knowledge?" Frost asks.

"I do," Willem says. "And that information will get me killed if you are not careful with it."

"Willem," Frost says. "I must talk to you with grave urgency."

THE ABBEY

The guards at the abbey open the huge wooden gates the moment they recognize Thibault, riding along the forest path.

He is met inside the crumbling abbey walls by Captain Baston and Major Lansard, who salute in unison. They are in disguise in their peasant smocks. Even now, the location and purpose of the abbey is a great secret.

"How are the saurs?" Thibault asks, returning the salute before taking off his gloves and clapping them together to remove some of the dust from the journey.

"They are secure, and resting," Baston says.

"And the wounded ones?"

"Superficial wounds only," Lansard says. "A few places where musket shot penetrated the armor, but the skin of the beasts is thick, and their flesh is dense. They scarcely notice the injuries."

"Splendid," Thibault says. "What about the two that were killed?"

"A platoon went out at first light to recover the bodies," Baston says.

"Good," Thibault says. "It is important that our enemies believe the saurs are invincible."

"You return early, sir," Baston says. "We were not expecting you until tomorrow."

"I return at the emperor's command," Thibault says. "He knows of the saur we lost and he knows about Gaillemarde."

"Can this story even be true?" Lansard says. "A boy who can mesmerize a saur? Impossible."

"Why? We did it," Thibault says.

"After years of trial and error," Baston says.

"The emperor believes this to be true. He seemed to know something of this boy," Thibault says. He reflects on this for a moment. "In any case I find it unlikely that this other boy, this François, could have invented such a tale."

"I agree, General," Baston says.

"I will march a company to the village to capture the boy," Thibault says. "And a cage of demonsaurus to sniff out the carcass of the crocodylus, if indeed it is there."

"If it is true about this boy," Lansard asks, "can you be sure he has not taught these skills to others?"

"I cannot," Thibault says. "We must find out who else knows what the boy knows, and guarantee their silence." He hands the reins of his horse to Baston. "Ride immediately to Gaillemarde. Ensure that nobody leaves before I get there."

THE MAGICIAN'S MOTHER

Willem's mother is baking when he arrives. Her arms are coated with flour up to the elbows. Like most of the village she has been tireless. Working around the clock to provide the extra food required for the soldiers.

She sees Willem hurrying up the path and meets him at the door.

"What has happened?" she asks.

Willem shakes his head. "Nothing," he says. "But I must leave Gaillemarde."

"In the middle of a war?" she asks. "It is not safe."

"Because of the war," he says.

"What do you mean, child?" she asks.

He takes her by the hands, not minding the flour, and draws her to the kitchen table.

"Mother, there are two British soldiers in the hospital. I must help them escape, get back to England."

She shakes off his hands and sits upright. "This is what you have come to tell me?"

"No," he says. "I have come to ask your permission."

This softens her. "Why these two?" she asks. "There are many soldiers in the hospital."

He lowers his eyes. "It is not just the soldiers who must get to England," he says.

"You? Why you?"

"Mother, the British officer says Napoléon's new army cannot be beaten. The war is already lost. Unless . . ."

"Unless you go to England and teach them how to fight the dinosaurs."

"Perhaps to breed and train dinosaurs of their own."

"And then both armies would have these terrible creatures? And you think that is a good thing?"

"I think it is better than if they are only in the hands of a tyrant," Willem says.

"And for this you ask my permission?" she says.

"It is not just about the British. What about me? What about you? If Napoléon conquers Europe, there will be no place for us to hide."

She is silent for a long time. She says eventually, "I am your mother, and I could never give permission for such a thing."

"Mother . . ."

"A child must ask permission from a parent," she says. She rises and moves to his side of the table and when he rises to meet her she embraces him fully, for the final time as a mother with her child. "But you are no longer a child," she says. "Do not ask my permission for I will not give it. But do what you know you must."

At first Héloïse is regarded as a curiosity by the French soldiers who now guard Gaillemarde. A strange, wild-haired thing. Half-human and of no appreciable intelligence. By the end of the first day she is forgotten, unnoticed, paid no more account than a wild dog, or a free-ranging microsaurus.

So it is that when Baston arrives at the saur-gate, the guards see her, yet do not see her, slinking in the wild lavender outside the fence.

"Hold there," the first guard says, presenting his musket at Baston. The second guard does likewise.

Baston dismounts. He wears the simple smock of a local peasant, but removes it, pulling it up over his head to reveal the uniform of a French captain.

Both guards lower their muskets and salute.

"I wish to see your commanding officer," Baston says.

The captain of the guard, a squat, heavyset man, is in the middle of the village square, deep in discussion with a doctor and the mayor of the village. The doctor's hands are bloody.

"Good morning, Captain," the doctor says, looking up at Baston's approach. Like the others, he does not see Héloïse drifting along behind the new arrival.

"Captain Baston, attached to the staff of General Thibault," Baston says.

"Gronnier," the captain says. "Captain of the Guard, Medical Division."

"I am Dominique Larrey, chief surgeon," the doctor says.

"Jacques Claude," Claude says. "I am the mayor of this village."

"How can I help you, Captain?" Gronnier asks.

"I bring orders from my general," Baston says. He looks around to make sure no one is within earshot. "He comes soon to this village. No one is to leave until he gets here."

"No one, Captain?" Larrey says. "But we are in the middle of evacuating a hospital."

"No one," Baston says.

"I must protest, Captain," Larrey says.

"You may protest all you want, sir. The village is to be sealed," Baston says.

"I will not allow it," Larrey says. "We do not have the facilities to properly treat these people here. They must be evacuated."

"I have my orders, sir," Baston says.

"And I have mine," Larrey says.

"I answer to General Thibault, and he answers directly to the emperor," Baston says.

"Sir, it is clear that you are poorly informed," Larrey says. "I am Dominique Larrey, Commander of the Legion of Honor and Chief Surgeon of the Imperial Guard. On matters of health and medicine, the emperor answers to me."

Baston holds his poise for a full minute, then bows his head.

"The wounded shall continue to be evacuated," he says. "But ensure that no natives attempt to slip out with them. Pay particular regard to any boys or young men who may try to escape." He stops, noticing Héloïse. "Who is that?"

Gronnier smiles and taps the side of his head with a finger.

Baston scrutinizes the girl for a moment. She sees him looking and growls at him like a dog.

"I shall remain here to ensure the general's orders are carried out," Baston says.

"Who is it that you are looking for?" the captain of the guard asks.

"A boy who can talk to saurs," Baston says. His eyes move quickly to the mayor, who has suddenly stiffened. "You know who this is?"

"I do not, sir," the mayor says.

"The emperor of France knows of this child," Baston says, "yet the mayor of his own village does not?"

"Perhaps your emperor is mistaken, sir," the mayor says.

"The emperor is never mistaken, monsieur," Baston says. "And he is also of the belief that somewhere in your village lies the carcass of a crocodylus."

"A what, sir?" Larrey asks.

"A giant saur, bred and trained for battle," Baston says.

"Ah, that Thibault," Larrey says, with sudden understanding and more than a little distaste. "I have not seen a dead dinosaur here, and I daresay it would not be easily missed. But then again, I have been a little busy. As I am busy now."

He turns and hurries away without excusing himself.

"I do not know what you are talking about," Claude says. "A dinosaur, in Gaillemarde? Look around, see for yourself."

"We will, monsieur," Baston says. "As soon as my general and his men get here. In the meantime, tell your people that they may not leave the village. Not for any reason."

"Of course, Captain," Claude says, and bows a little as he leaves.

Baston waits till he is out of earshot, then says, "I will personally inspect every wagon."

Turning to tend to his horse, he sees a young man walking toward him.

"François, is it not?" Baston says.

"Monsieur, I do not know you, and you do not know me," François says quietly.

"So be it," Baston says. "Tend to my horse, and I will walk with you as you do."

François nods, and takes the reins of the animal, leading it to a water trough. He finds a rag and wipes the dust of the journey from the horse's hide.

Baston makes a show of looking for something in the saddlebags.

"Is the boy in the village?" he asks.

François nods.

"Where is his home?" Baston asks.

François looks to his right and says, "The one with the fire lit."

Baston looks and sees a house with smoke trickling from the chimney. He raises an eyebrow. It is too warm for a fire.

"His mother is a baker," François says.

"Thank you, François, you shall be rewarded," Baston says.

"My reward will come when Europe is united under our great emperor," François says.

"So it shall," Baston says.

COOPERATION

François slips quietly into the church through the priest's door. He stands at the back of the sanctuary, behind the altar, hidden from view by thick velvet drapes. Behind him sunlight streams into the church through stained glass windows, casting a mottled, colored light over the altar and the polished floors.

"Give up the boy," Monsieur Lecocq is saying. "They will bring dogs and those dogs will find the grave of the dinosaur. We must give up the boy."

Most of the menfolk of the village have gathered in the church. Monsieur Claude stands beside the pulpit.

"My son has already died because of this," Monsieur Lejeune says. "Now you would sacrifice Willem as well?"

"We don't know why they want the boy," Monsieur Beauclerc says.

Monsieur Lejeune shrugs. "I doubt they wish to see his magic show."

"It was Jean and Willem who slew the beast," Monsieur Lecocq says. "Jean is already taken from us. That only leaves Willem. If we hide him then the whole town will suffer."

"How do they even know about the boy?" a voice calls from the congregation.

François shrinks back behind the curtain, afraid to breathe. He stares at the figure of Christ on the cross.

"I don't know," Monsieur Claude says. "But it is clear from the captain's words to me that they do."

"They will need something. Someone," Monsieur Lecocq says. "They will not be appeased by the spirit of a dead boy."

"We can turn Willem over on condition he comes to no harm," Monsieur Claude says.

"You would trust the French?" Monsieur Lejeune asks.

"They treated us fairly when we were under their rule," Monsieur Lecocq says.

"Lecocq, you would use your tongue to clean French arses," Monsieur Lejeune says.

"And, Lejeune, you are a puppet of the Dutch, who do not even speak our language."

"This is not about the French, or the Flemish, or the Dutch," Monsieur Claude says. "It is about the penalties that will be exacted if we do not cooperate with this army that has invaded our country."

"Give up the boy," Monsieur Lecocq says. "Before it is too late. If they find him first, then we will suffer."

Father Ambroise stands and walks up to the sanctuary, next to Monsieur Claude.

"You would do this?" Father Ambroise asks, shaking his head. "You would even say this, in a place of God?"

"Do we have another choice?" Monsieur Claude asks. "But we must be fair. We will take a vote."

"I will not be part of this," Monsieur Lejeune says. The door of the church slams so hard that dust jumps and hazes the air as he leaves.

François waits for a moment, then quietly slips back out through the priest's door.

KITCHEN

Willem hears the front door open, then quiet voices in the kitchen. He has been packing a bag for the journey, and takes it with him as he goes downstairs.

Héloïse sits on the floor in a corner of the kitchen. She eats a bread roll, crumbling it between her fingers.

Willem's mother is crying.

"What is it, Mama?"

She takes a moment to answer.

"A French officer has arrived at the gates. He has sealed the village. No one may get in or out except the wounded British soldiers."

"Why?" Willem asks.

"I warned you that word of your deeds would escape the village," his mother says.

"What are you talking about?" Willem asks.

"They are looking for you," she says.

The room seems to grow cold with those words, and Willem digests them slowly for a moment before responding.

"I should have heeded you," Willem says. "But now it is even more important than before for me to leave."

"Now it is impossible for you to leave," his mother says.

"I am a magician, like my father," Willem says. "I will make myself vanish."

"You are flippant when you should be serious," she says.

"If I am in danger, then surely you are in danger also," he says.

She nods. "I know. Neither of us is safe here."

"Come with me," Willem says.

"Perhaps you can make one person disappear, but not two," she says. "I will go to the river for water, and slip away into the forest when they are not watching."

"You are sure?"

"Of course," she says. "I have escaped from Napoléon's men before, and I can do it again. I, too, learned a few things from your father."

They are both startled by footsteps on the path and turn, expecting only to see soldiers and muskets, but it is Lejeune.

"Willem, you must leave the village," he says, as he enters.

"I know," Willem says.

"The mayor will make a sacrificial lamb of you," Lejeune says, "in the hope of appeasing the great French gods."

"Claude does what he does for the good of the village," Willem says.

"The mayor is a weak-livered goose," Lejeune says.

"That also is true." Willem smiles.

"They are watching the gate," Lejeune says. "No one may leave."

"So I have heard," Willem says.

"Go and find François," Lejeune says. "He has a way to slip out of the village that nobody else knows about."

Willem shakes his head. "No. I will find my own way. The fewer people who know of this, the better."

"That is true," Lejeune says. "Take this."

He hands Willem a small sack. He hesitates in his offering, almost reluctant to hand it over. It is heavy. A glance inside shows why. It contains the pistol and ammunition pouch. Willem places them carefully in his bag.

"Are you sure?" Willem asks.

"You remember how to fire it?" Lejeune asks in return.

Willem nods.

"Try to get to England," Lejeune says. "You will be safest there. Show your bewitching ways to the British. Teach them how to fight the dinosaurs."

"That is my plan," Willem says.

Willem's mother moves suddenly to him, embracing him, crushing his arms to his sides. Her grip is so tight that Willem can scarcely breathe.

"Go now," Lejeune says.

"Willem is all I have," his mother says through tears.

"Willem is all we all have," Lejeune says.

His mother lets him go.

"Go to Antwerp, Willem. There is a woman there you can trust. Her name is Sofie Thielemans."

"My father's teacher?" Willem asks.

"The same. Did your father speak of her?"

"Many times," Willem says.

"Good. I will meet you there in a day or so. She will help us arrange passage to England."

"How will I find her?" Willem asks.

"Avenue Quinten Matsys. Number twenty-five. Do not write it down. If you are captured and the address is found, that will put her life in danger also."

Willem nods, and quickly commits the address to memory.

"I must go," he says.

She hugs him one more time. "Goodbye, my son. I will see you in Antwerp."

"Goodbye, Mother."

"On your way, say goodbye also to Cosette," she says.

"Cosette, why?"

"I am not blind." She smiles. "You cannot just disappear from her world as you would disappear from Gaillemarde."

"I cannot bid her farewell," he says. "She would ask questions. It would put her life in danger."

He hopes to avoid Cosette altogether, but cannot. As he leaves the house she is opening the gate, returning from the hospital. She wears a white smock streaked with blood.

"What is happening?" she asks. "The saur-gates have been shut, in the middle of the day."

"The French have locked us in our own village," Willem says.

"Why?" she asks.

"Who knows?" he says. "Who can understand the mind of a Frenchman?"

"But you are leaving?" she asks.

"No one may leave," he says.

"Then why do you have this bag?" she asks.

"I take food to the wounded," Willem says, and moves past her, carrying the bag as lightly as if it contains nothing but bread.

She stops him with a hand on his arm and leans in to him, kissing him softly on the cheek.

"Goodbye, Willem," she says.

"I am just going to the hospital," Willem says.

"I know," Cosette says.

THE ESCAPE

The hospital cart is an uncovered wagon with a two-horse team. Three soldiers lie sideways across it, tended by a young nurse.

One of the soldiers has lost an arm. Another is blinded. The third has an arm in a splint.

It stops at the saur-gate, and Captain Baston climbs up onto the running board, casting his eyes over the patients. He draws a leather-bound notebook from his satchel and makes notes, then catches sight of Larrey and waves him over.

"I am Captain Frost of the Royal Horse Artillery," the blind officer says as Larrey is walking toward the gates. "Who is it that delays us?"

"Captain Baston of the Imperial Guard," Baston says. "And with respect, sir, you are my prisoners, and I shall delay you for as long as I deem it necessary."

He turns to the soldier with the broken arm. "Tell me your name and company, soldier."

"If you are speaking to my man," Frost says, "his name is—"

"I would hear him speak with his own tongue," Baston says.

Still the man is silent.

"Tell him who you are," Frost says.

"Me name is Jack," the soldier says quietly. "Private Jack Sullivan, G troop, under Captain Mercer."

Baston nods and makes a note. The soldier's accent is clearly English. He is not the boy they are looking for.

Larrey arrives and stands at the rear of the wagon.

"You know these British soldiers?" Baston asks.

"I have examined them personally," Larrey says. "One of them is gravely ill."

"The man you speak of is Viscount Wenzel-Halls, son of the Earl of Leicester," Frost says. "A valued prize indeed to your emperor but worth nothing at all without breath in his lungs."

"And dead he will be by morning if I cannot transfer him to a proper hospital," Larrey says.

Baston examines the man. A bloodstained bandage covers half of his head. From under it drifts a flow of dank reddish hair. Under the blanket there is a flat area where his right arm should be. On his left hand he wears a gold ring with the insignia of a crown and a lion.

"I would hear him speak," Baston says.

"He is asleep with the fever, and I doubt he can be roused," Frost says.

Baston prods the man's foot, but there is no response.

"I will take responsibility for this man," Larrey says.

"So you shall," Baston says. He nods his head to the guards. They open the saur-gate and the wagon drives out. He steps out after it and sees it crest the bridge and then turn to follow the river path.

Baston turns back to the gate, hearing voices. A woman in a gray smock stands just inside the gate, a pail in her hand. From the light way she carries it, it is empty. The guards have blocked her way.

"Monsieur," she says. "I fetch water for the wounded."

Larrey's eyes are now upon Baston.

"Of course, madame," Baston says. "We treat the British wounded as we treat our own. But I cannot allow you outside the gates."

"But, monsieur!"

"However, I would be happy to take the pail for you," he says.

"Of course," the woman says. "Thank you."

Baston accepts the pail from the woman, and fills it at the river's edge, before returning it to her.

"You are too kind, monsieur," she says, and carries the pail back into the village.

Baston turns to look back at the river path, watching the ambulance until it is almost out of sight. His eyes narrow. He runs outside the gate. "Halt!" he shouts.

The ambulance does not slow, the driver perhaps not hearing him over the rumble of the wheels on the rocky path. The ambulance disappears into the trees.

"My horse," Baston orders, and mounts it as soon as it is brought to him. "Shut the gates, and let nobody out until I return," he says.

The guards comply, pulling the gates shut as Baston gallops out.

"Halt!" Baston calls again as he nears the wagon, and this time it does slow, drawing to a stop just past a rocky depression that is strangely red-brown in color, as if stained with dried blood.

Baston pulls up behind the wagon and dismounts.

He draws his pistol and walks to the rear of the wagon.

"The viscount. Remove his blanket," he says.

"He is very ill," Frost says.

"Show me his right arm," Baston says.

Carefully, nervously, the nurse reaches down and lifts the blanket from the unconscious soldier. He stirs and opens his eyes. Bloodied bandages encase the stump of what was once a right arm.

"Can I help you, Captain?" he asks, in perfect, unaccented English. His voice is weak, barely a breath of air.

Baston shakes his head briskly. "My apologies, Viscount. You may go."

*　*　*

It is not long after this that the saur-gates open again and sixty French soldiers enter, marching three abreast. Thibault rides at their head. They are followed by a formation of cuirassiers on horseback, resplendent in their shining armor chest plates and fine helmets. The soldiers do not stop until they reach the village square. At the rear of the column a team of four horses skittishly pulls a cage wagon with bars of solid steel. Women grasp children to their skirts to avoid them seeing what lies within. But they cannot stop them hearing.

A large, four-wheel ambulance wagon loaded with the last of the patients waits outside the market hall where the doctors and hospital staff are busy packing and loading their own wagons.

Baston joins the procession at the gate and rides into the square alongside Thibault.

"Any sign of the boy?" Thibault asks.

Baston shakes his head. "No, General, but I have verified that he is here, and sealed the gates as you asked."

"We saw an ambulance wagon on the Brussels road. Did that come from here?"

"Yes, General. Three British casualties on their way to the hospital," Baston says.

"Get it back," Thibault says. "Send a horse, and find that wagon. It will return here without delay."

He turns to the column of men. "Round up everyone. Every man, woman, and child. Bring them to the square. Go house to house. Check barns and stables."

He stops the last three soldiers before they can head off with the others. "Baston, take these three. Check these wagons. Confirm the identity of everyone in them. Check the supply and hospital wagons just as thoroughly."

"General, these are my own wagons, and I am anxious to be on my way," Larrey says. "I assure you that whoever you are looking for is not among my caravan."

"So noted, and as soon as they have been thoroughly searched you will be allowed to leave," Thibault says.

"Allowed to leave? General, every moment you delay me, more men die," Larrey says.

"Most of whom will die anyway," Thibault says.

"There is a coldness about you that exceeds even what I had heard," Larrey says. "In case you do not recognize me, I am—"

"I know who you are, sir, and it does not move me," Thibault says. "The favor you curry with the emperor will have little currency if this boy escapes. Your wagons will be searched and that is an end to this discussion."

Not all the casualties are leaving. Some still lie in their cots in the shade inside the market hall. These are men who would not survive the journey, and will probably not last out the day.

Among them, in full vestments, walks Father Ambroise, administering last rites to those who request it. François is at his side.

Father Ambroise stops suddenly alongside the cot of the schoolmaster, Monsieur Delvaux, who has been moved here from the house of the healer. Father Ambroise is watching the new arrivals in the village square. His face drops, then hardens to stone. "François," he says.

"Yes, Father?"

"Go and find your uncle, and quickly."

François is back within the minute with Lejeune in tow.

"Ambroise?" Jean's father asks.

"The general." Father Ambroise nods toward the doorway. "You know him? Or know of him?"

Lejeune shakes his head.

"His name is Thibault. I served under him in Syria, back in ninety-nine," Father Ambroise says. He stops, and seems to be gathering breath.

"You know something of his character?" Lejeune asks.

Father Ambroise shuts his eyes. "For four days in early March we laid siege to a town called Jaffa. We breached the walls and invited their surrender. They answered with the head of our emissary on a pike above the town wall."

"I did not know you were at Jaffa," Lejeune says.

"The shame is deep," Father Ambroise says.

"What happened at Jaffa?" François asks.

"Our troops pillaged the town," Father Ambroise says. "There seemed no end to the raping and killing. Then under orders from Thibault, we marched the survivors, thousands of them, men, women, and children, to a beach, south of the city. It took two days to kill them all. We ran out of musketballs and formed squares with fixed bayonets. Then we advanced on them."

"Spread the word quietly," Lejeune says. "Tell our people to gather tools or knives. We outnumber the French. We will not lie down and accept such a fate."

"No. No resistance," Father Ambroise says. "We must give him no cause to do here what he did at Jaffa. But any that can get out should do so."

"What about the children?" Delvaux asks from his cot. "What about my daughter?"

"François," Father Ambroise says, "there is a priest's hole in the rectory."

"I know where it is," François says.

"Take as many of the children as you can," Father Ambroise says.

François nods and walks off.

"François." Father Ambroise catches up with him out of earshot of Delvaux.

"No more than a dozen, François," he says. "Just the youngest. The hiding place is not large. Instruct them to be silent. No matter what they hear. They are not to come out until we come to get them."

"And if we don't come to get them?" François asks.

"Then they are to wait for at least a day, then head to the east. To La Hulpe. The priest there will care for them."

It is as the ambulance wagon reaches the crossroads and slows to take the turn toward Waterloo that the guard hears something and turns to see the nurse reaching up under her skirts. Knowing that something is wrong, but not knowing what, he fumbles for his musket, but it is long and unwieldy and he feels the muzzle of a pistol, terrifyingly cold against his cheek. Still he tries to turn.

"I am not a soldier, but I know how to fire this pistol and I cannot miss at this range," Willem says, taking off the nurse's bonnet. "Now stop the wagon."

A few moments later the musket is in the hand of Wenzel-Halls.

Willem and the others climb down from the wagon, Jack helping Frost, who cannot see.

"Willem!" Wenzel-Halls says as Willem turns to depart. The officer extends his hand. "I would remove the ring myself, but I have no hand with which to do it. Take it, and return it to my family."

Willem nods and steps forward. The ring slides off easily, sized for a different finger. Willem finds it too loose for his own fingers, and puts it on his thumb.

"Sir, I shall return this ring to you when I see you in England," Willem says.

"I shall look forward to that day," Wenzel-Halls says, smiling.

Willem reaches forward and shakes the captain's hand. Frost salutes, as does Jack. The captain returns the salute left-handed.

"Driver, a fast trot if you don't mind," Wenzel-Halls says, and prods the driver lightly in the back with the bayonet when the driver does not immediately respond.

Tree leaves flutter and whisper to each other as the lieutenant, the artilleryman, and the magician disappear into the forest.

"Go to the church, wait for me there, say nothing to anyone," François whispers.

When the guards are not watching, he taps the girl on the shoulder and she slips quietly down the alley between the market hall and the stables. François moves slowly through the crowd, and finds Pierre Chambaux, the son of the tailor. He is four years old. "Let me take your son to the church, he will be safer there," he whispers to the father.

The tailor nods. He smiles at his son as François leads him away.

HUNTING PARTY

The hunting party consists of ten cuirassiers on horseback, and two saurmasters on foot. The saurmasters hold leashes, at the ends of which black and evil things drool and strain at their chains. Baston rides at the rear.

The rider sent to bring back the ambulance wagon returned with only the guard, one prisoner, and a disturbing story.

The hooves of the horses raise dust as the hunting party heads out and over the bridge. Their quarry lies ahead of them and so they do not look down, and therefore do not see the small girl with the ragged hair who peers out at them from the waters beneath the stonework, then quickly draws back, lest she be spotted.

They left the forest path many minutes ago, Willem leading them through tall trees with sparse undergrowth. He uses the sun to get his bearing, and his instincts are right. It is not long before they reach the river.

It has been difficult going for the lieutenant, stumbling along without eyes to guide him, but Jack has been there at every turn, at every tree, guiding him with a hand on his arm, catching him when he trips.

"I am slowing you down," Frost says, in French. "More than I expected. Perhaps it would be better if you continued without me."

Jack looks at him quizzically and Frost repeats what he had said, this time in English.

Jack shakes his head but says nothing.

Frost turns back to Willem. "He does not agree. But my father is wealthy. I would be a good prize. I will come to no harm and will fetch a fair exchange in a month or so."

"And what will happen when I reach England?" Willem asks. "Without an introduction from you, what kind of reception would I get? The Netherlands have capitulated. They now side with the French. That makes me the enemy."

"There is some truth in what you say," Frost says.

"I need you as much as you need me," Willem says. "Whatever we do, we do it together."

Frost turns with alarm, looking back the way they have come. Without eyes, his ears seem to be increasingly sensitive.

"Shh," he says. "Listen."

They all stop on the bank of the river.

"I hear the French soldiers," Jack says. "I hear their dogs."

"That is not the sound of dogs," Frost says.

SISTER

Madame Marie Verheyen, the mother of Willem, walks with dignity and grace as soldiers with muskets march her and Cosette from her home to the village square, stopping in front of the general. She says nothing and takes great care to keep any emotion from her face. What will show, if she allows it, is contempt, and that is likely to antagonize this man.

"Ah, the mother. And an unexpected bonus," Thibault says. "Perhaps a sister?"

Willem's mother is silent, as is Cosette. The girl stares straight ahead, but one eye drifts off to the side.

Thibault regards them both for a moment, his gaze lingering on the simple frock of the girl, then he abruptly turns to the captain at his side.

"Lansard, this boy has knowledge, and knowledge is a contagion," Thibault says. "Unchecked, it may yet defeat us."

"Yes, sir," Lansard says.

"Look around you." Thibault points to one of the Poulenc children. "Is she infected?" He indicates Madame Gertruda. "What about her? What about the blacksmith or the tailor? Any of these people might carry the disease."

"We can question everyone in the village," Lansard says. "Find out how far this knowledge has spread."

Thibault steeples his fingers together in thought.

"Sir?" Lansard asks.

Thibault explodes into unprovoked anger, clenching his fists and throwing them up against the sky. "Why do such burdens so often weigh on my shoulders? Is it a test of my character, of my will? For my character is strong, and my will is unrelenting."

"Your orders, sir?" Lansard asks.

"The boy's mother and sister will come with us. If we fail to locate the boy we may well make use of them."

"This is the schoolmaster's daughter, not mine," Willem's mother says, pushing Cosette away from her. "She is of no value to you."

"She lies!" Father Ambroise calls out, to a shocked look from Marie.

Thibault looks from the mother to the priest and back again. "Where is this schoolmaster?" he asks.

"I am here," Monsieur Delvaux says from his cot at the entrance to the market hall.

Thibault grasps Willem's mother and Cosette each by an arm and leads them over to where Delvaux lies. Madame Gertruda moves away as Thibault approaches.

"Is this your daughter?" Thibault asks. "If you lie, I will know it, and I will kill you both."

Delvaux's eyes close and his breathing seems labored in his chest.

"Answer my question, or face the consequences," Thibault says.

"My daughter died three weeks ago. She was attacked by a saur in the forest," Monsieur Delvaux says, his eyes still closed.

"And you have no other daughter?" Thibault asks.

Now Delvaux opens his eyes. He looks not at Thibault, but at Willem's mother. "I have no other daughter," he says.

"You see, madame, I am not fooled by your lies," Thibault says. "But I understand that you think to protect your child. I will give you one last chance for the truth."

Willem's mother still looks at Delvaux and in the depths of his eyes she sees what he knows.

"This is my daughter. Willem's sister," she says with trembling lips, drawing the girl to her. "Please do not harm her."

"Then she comes with us," Thibault says, his eyes once again roaming Cosette's body, his lips drawing back into a rare smile.

As Cosette is forced up into the caged wagon, her eyes, wide, terrified, and helpless, are fixed on those of her father. She opens her mouth to speak but the schoolmaster, who has found the strength to sit up, shakes his head, the barest of movements, and only watches as the gate of the cage is shut.

The floor of the wagon is covered with straw, and the droppings of animals. It reeks with a sulfurous, rotten smell. Willem's mother fights the urge to gag and clears a place to sit for both of them. When she looks up, Cosette and her father are still staring at each other through the thick bars of the iron cage. And Willem's mother can see that for the first time since the death of Angélique, the schoolmaster is at peace.

The other villagers are assembled in the square, and Willem's mother looks at their faces, confused and frightened. Father Ambroise stands with his wife, his arms around her, her hands on her swollen belly, their daughter, Émilie, at their side. The Poulencs make a huddle in front of the stables with the Beauclerc and Lecocq families. Marcel Lejeune and his wife stand together, holding hands, their chins high and defiant. Next to them is Madame Gertruda. She smiles as the wagon is drawn away toward the open saur-gate. She is having a good day.

Willem's mother draws Cosette to her, pulling her face in to her shoulder so Cosette cannot see what she sees: the French soldiers forming into squares.

UNDER THE BRIDGE

Major Jerome Lansard of the Imperial Guard is stationed on the stone bridge outside the wall of the village. This is the job of a conscript, not a captain. But had he remained in the village he would have been given orders that he would have refused to carry out, even knowing that the punishment for such insubordination would likely be death, summarily executed.

Here on the stonework of the bridge he can not only avoid such orders, he can avoid seeing what is taking place behind him, although he cannot pretend he does not know. The bells of the village church have been tolling for many minutes, on Thibault's orders, to cover the sound of the screams.

So Lansard guards the bridge, walking occasionally from side to side, although mostly just standing in the center, his back ramrod straight, his chin proud.

The river catches the sunlight as it meanders beneath the bridge, and, perhaps feeling the need to see something peaceful and clean, he walks to the edge and looks down.

A flash of movement catches his eye. Just a ripple in the water, nothing more. Perhaps a duck, or a fish. Maybe a sudden eddy in the current. He waits, but it is not repeated.

He crosses the bridge to the riverside, from where he can see most of the way under the arch of the bridge. He can see nothing. Yet his eyes did not deceive him before. He moves upriver and peers into the shadow under the bridge from that side. Was that a trick of the light, or a blur of movement? A tangle of weeds, or was it a wild mop of hair?

To see fully under the bridge will involve wading into the river, and the prospect of spending the entire day in wet footwear does not appeal to him. He almost turns back, then sighs and sits on the riverbank, removing his boots.

The sun is out strongly today and the lavender glows in the light. There is a gentle breeze running along the river. Even the bells of the church add a melodic resonance to the day. It seems a shame to spoil such a beautiful day with the sound of shot and the smell of gunpowder. But Major Lansard is not a man to shirk his duty.

He draws his pistol and cocks it before wading into the shallows of the river at the side of the bridge.

FRANÇOIS'S PRAYER

The sound of the church bells does not quite drown out the sound of the screams.

François runs through the forest and he does not look back.

He moves, and he prays. He prays with his eyes open, gliding on paths that are not paths. Filtering through trees, finding gaps that only someone with a lifetime of living in the forest could know.

After guiding the children to the priest's hole, he had slipped quietly across into the church and retrieved the crossbow, and a full quiver of bolts, from where he had secreted them, behind the pulpit. Then, carefully avoiding the guards, he moved to an area of the saur-fence where a rotten, loose post can be pushed easily to one side, creating just enough room for a young man to slip through. Now, as he moves, so do his lips, asking questions that only God Himself can answer.

"Is this what You want?

"What more can You ask from me?

"Is this a test of my faith?

"My faith is unshakable, but how can I accept the murder of my family, of the people of my village?

"Is this the sacrifice they must make for Your glory? Is this the price I must pay for being an imperfect servant? As You sacrificed Your Son to the cross, did I sacrifice the people of my village?

"But if I turn from this now, then the death of my cousin has no meaning."

He comes to the river and stops, listening. Every sound of the forest is known to him, from the twitter of the microsaurus to the rasp of the wings of the hawks.

He hears the soldiers. A group of them, blundering through the forest ahead of him.

They are moving upriver and they are moving quickly. No doubt scouring the riverbank for Willem's scent.

He rises and moves in that direction.

And as he does so, the answers come to him. Not as a sign or a voice in his head, but as a dawning understanding, a realization of the truth.

As Jesus had his Judas, so Napoléon has his Thibault. The evil of evil men does not make all men evil.

Napoléon has been sent by God. Thibault by the devil.

François stops running. He lifts the crossbow from its sling on his back and starts to turn back to the village. He even takes a few steps in that direction before he realizes: Thibault must wait. For now he has a higher purpose. Willem cannot be allowed to reach England.

He moves swiftly along the bank of the river, careful to keep a good distance from the crashing sounds of the soldiers and their beasts, who move in front of him.

He tries to think like Willem. Why would he take this route? If he stays in the river he will be forced to move slowly, against the running water, and the soldiers will easily catch him. If he leaves the river, they will find his scent and track him.

But Willem is too smart for that. He must have a plan.

It is only after François has passed a thick stand of ferns by the riverbank that it occurs to him. He doubles back, drawing the crossbow again and pushing aside the fronds of the thicket. He presses through into the swamp area, seeing the old shack slowly dissolving into the ground on the other side.

It is deserted, but as he steps forward there is a click at his ear and he spins with the crossbow in his hands to face the muzzle of a flintlock pistol.

"François!" Willem says, lowering the gun.

François keeps the crossbow steady at Willem's heart.

"What has happened at the village?" Willem asks.

"I am sorry, Willem," François says, and his finger tightens on the trigger.

But now there are more people, two British soldiers who emerge from the bushes behind Willem. One is blind and easily disposed of, but the other is tall and strong. He has one arm in a splint, but his other hand holds a bayonet. The crossbow holds only one bolt.

"I am sorry, I don't know," François says, and the crossbow lowers.

"What about the bells?" the blind soldier asks. "We heard them ringing."

"I heard them, too," François says. "But I saw nothing."

"Did my mother escape?" Willem asks.

"Yes," François says, then shakes his head. "I mean no. She and Cosette were taken away in a caged wagon."

"Cosette also?"

"Both of them," François says.

AMBUSH

"Come quickly, we must go," Willem says.

He leads the others back through the fern grove and out to the riverbank.

"Willem, no," François says. "The soldiers have taken this path with their raptors."

"And that is why we take it also," Willem says.

"That makes no sense," François says.

"They know we head to Brussels," Willem says. "So they head there also. We will follow them. They seek my scent. But they will not find it, because they are only searching what lies in front of them, and we are behind."

"Your tactics would rival those of Napoléon himself," Frost says.

"Hurry," Willem says. "Be as quiet as possible and do not speak unless necessary."

They stay on the riverbank, close to the treeline where they can quickly hide. They listen carefully for the boot steps in front of them. The cuirassiers are easy to follow; in their heavy armor they thunder along the riverbank like a herd of gardensaurus.

Always, mixed in with the sound of the soldiers, is the other sound. An ungodly sound.

Frost stops and turns back the way they have come. They all stop with him.

"Someone, or something, is following us," Frost says.

"I can hear nothing," Willem says.

"It is very quiet," Frost says.

"He is right," François says. "I have heard something, too."

"It makes no difference," Willem says. "We must continue."

It seems so long ago that he was in Monsieur Lecocq's eelboat, floating through the center of the river, watching the same trees and rocks. They seem different now. Dirtier. Tarred with the brush of all the events since that time. What had seemed grave then, an attack by a firebird, now seems no more than a frivolity, a diversion, compared to what is happening around them.

Frost trips on an edge of rock and falls, despite Jack's desperate attempt to save him. His outflung hand catches a branch of a small tree. It is dry, and snaps with a loud crack. They all freeze, waiting to see what the soldiers ahead of them will do, but there is no change in the sounds from upriver, and after a few moments they continue on.

When they near Lightning Rock, where the river splits in two, the noises in front of them stop, and they hear loud conversations. It is an easy guess that they are discussing which branch of the river to take. The left and most obvious one leads toward the abbey, and on to Brussels. The right would take them to the northeast and into the heart of the forest.

The discussion ends and the soldiers move out, toward Brussels. Willem smiles. That is exactly what he wants them to do.

To cross the river to get to the left fork is a tricky balancing act across slippery boulders. François scrambles across easily but Willem almost falls several times. When he gets to the other bank, he looks back to see Frost on his hands and knees, being assisted by the tall, strong private.

"Go on," Frost whispers. "We will catch up."

Just a hundred meters farther on, Willem's careful plan falls apart.

* * *

Perhaps the French soldiers have cottoned on to Willem's plan. Or perhaps they heard the crack of the breaking branch and made a lucky guess. But the two cuirassiers who hide, waiting for them, are so well concealed that Willem and François walk straight by them without seeing them.

The ambush site is well chosen, just past a sharp bend. The river narrows here, the water running rapidly through high, steep banks. There is no way to escape.

The cuirassiers wait for Willem and François to pass before emerging from heavy foliage.

"Hold!" is the shout.

Willem and François spin around.

Somewhere in front are the rest of the soldiers and now behind them are two cuirassiers, pistols raised. There is no time for Willem to reach for his own pistol, or François for his crossbow.

At almost the same time they see what the Frenchmen do not see: Frost and Jack rounding the bend behind them.

Jack acts, seemingly on instinct. Leaving Frost standing uncertainly on the riverbank, he starts to run.

At the last moment the French soldiers hear his footsteps and try to turn, but it is already too late. Jack cannons into them, pushing one into the other, then both overbalance on the narrow path, toppling down the steep bank into the river. The heavy armor the soldiers wear now becomes a hindrance as they struggle against the rapid waters of the current. Their pistols are useless, the powder soaked.

The damage is done, however, for even if the other cuirassiers had not heard the noise of the fall, they can certainly hear the shouts of the two soldiers in the river.

"Run!" Willem says, and they all turn back toward the village.

Away from the soldiers. Away from the shouts and running boot steps intermixed with the snarls and rattles of the dark creatures.

Jack guides Frost as best he can, but the footing is uneven and several times Frost falls, each time bodily hauled back to his feet by the strong artilleryman.

They round another bend in the river just as a shape rises up, seemingly out of the rock of the riverbank before them. A wild, tangled thing, in damp clothes.

It is so unexpected that even though he knows this girl well, it takes Willem a moment to realize that it is Héloïse. Her mouth is smeared with blood, as though she has wiped it, but indifferently. Dark red also stains the top of her smock. Has she been injured? There is no time to ask.

"Run, Héloïse," Willem yells. "The French are behind us!"

Héloïse does not move as they run toward her.

"I hear the rattle of the demonsaurus," she says. "You cannot outrun a demonsaurus. Come with me."

She leaves the riverbank, scampering through a dense area of trees. Willem follows without argument. Héloïse is nimble and quick, darting like a bird through the low branches. Willem and François are at her heels, but the other two slip farther and farther behind.

"Wait," François says. "We must use the river. They will follow our scent. We cannot escape them this way."

"Follow me or die," Héloïse says. "There is a place the demonsaurus will not go."

"Why?" Willem asks through heaving breaths. "Why won't it go there?"

"Because it is afraid," Héloïse says.

MAJOR LANSARD

The lines are formed, precise, neat, exactly the way Thibault likes them. The soldiers stand in rows of three with other soldiers of equal height, which gives a pleasing uniformity to the column.

What is displeasing to his eye are the blood splatters that stain the uniforms, but that, as always, is an unfortunate consequence of war. And this is war. War against an insidious disease.

The cuirassiers would normally ride at the rear of the column, but they are off with Baston, chasing the boy.

It has been a difficult day, but Thibault is at peace, knowing that despite the difficulties, he has done his duty. He waits on his horse at the front of the column. He is keen to move out. To get away from this unbearable place.

The only real concern on his mind is the disappearance of Major Lansard. The village has been thoroughly searched, without result. As he waits, a patrol inspects the circumference outside the saur-fence.

The leader of the patrol, a gruff sergeant, arrives back through the saur-gate at a trot.

"Sir, you must come."

Thibault dismounts and follows the sergeant down to the river beside the bridge. In the water two privates are retrieving the body of a soldier, and as it is hauled up onto the riverbank and rolled over, he can see that it wears the uniform of a major.

There are gasps of horror from the soldiers who have waded into the river to bring the body out. Were it not for the uniform there would be no way to identify him. Certainly not by his face, which is a bloodied mess. His neck also is a raw red mass, and his nose and ears are missing.

"He has been attacked by a raptor, sir," one of the soldiers says.

"Or a wolf," says the other.

"Undoubtedly," Thibault says.

THE SONIAN CAVES

The tree is a giant spruce, hundreds, maybe thousands of years old. It is entwined with creepers that have somehow merged into the bark to give the tree a lumpy, ridged skin that reminds Willem of the skin of the dinosaur.

Héloïse slides to a halt at the base of the tree, waiting for the others to catch up.

She looks behind them at something Willem dares not turn to see.

"Hurry," she says, and in the quiet of her voice is a warning more chilling than if she had screamed.

She pulls back the branches of a thick bush that grows at the base of the tree, revealing a vertical shaft that descends into blackness.

Willem reaches the tree just after François, who moves quicker through the forest than he does.

"Down," Héloïse says.

François hesitates.

"Just go," Willem says.

François sits on the edge of the hole, turns and grasps the rocky lip of the shaft, then lets himself down. He dangles by his fingertips for a moment.

Willem looks behind to see Jack arrive, no longer leading Frost, but carrying him on his shoulder.

There is a thump that echoes up the shaft.

"François?" Willem calls.

"It is not deep," François shouts back. "The fall is not great."

"The lieutenant is first," Willem says. "Help to catch him."

He doesn't wait for a reply but helps Jack lower the small frame of Lieutenant Frost into the hole.

The dreadful rattle of the demonsaurus sounds through the trees behind them.

"Jack, go!" Willem says, but for answer Jack shoves him backward into the hole, catching one of Willem's arms as he falls and lowering him down with one strong arm. Hands grab at his legs, and then he is safely on the ground. Jack arrives headfirst just after him, and Willem, looking up, sees black skeletal hands scrabbling down into the hole behind him. Jack lands on top of them, collapsing the group into a pile of bodies on the ground.

Willem looks around for Héloïse, and sees her extricate herself from underneath François. He hadn't even seen her climb into the hole.

At the surface, the demonsaurus are silhouetted against the light of the sky and the forest above. They scrape at the edge of the cave, and long spines on their head rattle furiously. The sound echoes down the shaft and off the hard rock walls in the cave.

The cave is narrow and dark, except for the rod of light that falls from the entrance. There is a muddy, earthy smell here, along with something else. A faint but bitter smell of animal dung.

Abruptly the creatures above are pulled back.

"Muskets!" Frost shouts, and they all scramble away from the area beneath the shaft.

The explosions are deafening in such a small space and lead balls ricochet off the rocky floor and the walls.

Jack grunts and staggers, but when they turn to him he shakes his head and points to a small tear in his uniform at the shoulder. The ball that hit him has ricocheted at least once, and although it will leave a nasty bruise, it has not broken his skin.

Already Héloïse is leading the way deeper into the cave. The roof slopes down, lower and lower until they must crawl to get through.

Behind them Willem hears one then another of the soldiers drop into the cave.

Héloïse is humming, softly and tunelessly, and at first Willem cannot work out why, but as the thin light from the entrance fades he realizes. It is pitch-black underground. Only by following the sound can he follow her.

There are passageways here, forks and branches. He cannot see them but he can feel them. A honeycomb of tunnels through solid rock.

The sounds behind them cease, then he hears the soldiers retreating. But he knows they will be back. With lamps.

For now though, they are safe, and as soon as he is sure the soldiers are gone, he calls out names, to make sure no one has missed a turn in the blackness.

Everyone answers.

Here, deep in the bowels of the earth, there are sounds. Animal sounds. Roars and growls that echo in the distance.

They follow Héloïse. There is no way to gauge time, but it seems like hours. Sometimes they stand and walk, other times they crawl below low rock ceilings. How she knows where she is going, Willem cannot imagine, but eventually a faint glow appears in front of them.

The glow intensifies and they emerge onto a high rocky ledge in a vast underground cavern.

The light comes from oil lamps hung from hooks on the walls at regular intervals, and now they see the source of the animal sounds.

Dinosaurs.

Héloïse puts her finger to her lips, then repeats the gesture. Her meaning is clear. Utter silence. Although the ceiling is high here, they crawl, so they can't be seen from below.

Willem places his hands and knees carefully, feeling the ground in front of him before trusting it to take his weight, wary of any pebble or loose rock that might move and create sound.

The smell of dung is strong. Below them, a cart piled high with animal waste is hauled off by four men in gray peasant smocks. There are no horses to pull the carts, nor mules. Not even demon-saurus will enter this place.

The dinosaurs are chained to huge metal anchor points in the floor and walls of the cave. They are not as large as the giant croco-dile that attacked the village, but still at least twice the height of a man. Immense heads on massive bodies are counterbalanced by long, heavy tails. The front legs are small, and seem to serve no purpose, but the back legs are enormous, with vicious claws like those of a firebird. They have the same protruding bony brow as the crocodile, but a shorter jaw. They are meat-eaters. There is no doubt. Only meat-eaters have teeth like these. The beasts strain against their chains, shifting their huge feet, scratching and stamp-ing at the rock floor of the cavern. Some kind of leather mask cov-ers their eyes and nostrils. Willem suspects they can neither see nor smell. Heavy leather straps run around the creatures' massive jaws, preventing them from opening more than a few centimeters. Wil-lem has seen the remnants of one of these masks before, on the beast that attacked the village.

Willem taps Jack on the shoulder and points at the creatures. Jack nods. These are the saurs that attacked the soldiers at Mont-Saint-Jean.

Willem counts. There are a dozen dinosaurs just in this one sec-tion of the cavern, but the rock walls bend away around a corner and echoing from that direction come more grunts and occasional growls. There could be any number of the creatures here below-ground.

They follow Héloïse, crawling along the ragged rocky ledge and under a low overhang that leads away from the cavern.

A series of interconnected caves takes them upward and here the air is slightly fresher, drifting in through natural vents in the rock, and the barest blush of natural light filters down somehow through a series of crystals in the ceiling.

They crawl beneath old, dead tree roots into another small cave.

There is just enough light to see, and what they see is both shocking and yet somehow not really a surprise. Some rough bedding is pushed against a wall. A wooden pail sits against the opposite wall. Old, dried food scraps litter a corner.

The surprise is the pictures. The walls are decorated with hundreds of them, crude images of flowers, trees, the sun, a boat on a river. One of them shows a woman cradling a baby. A wretched and yet touching vision. A desolate young girl's only reminder of her mother.

Willem looks around in a kind of horrified awe. This is where Héloïse spent six years of her life, fending for herself, feeding herself. Hiding from French soldiers. Sharing a vast dungeon with terrifying giant saurs.

"Are we safe here?" Willem asks.

Héloïse nods. "For now. They know we are here and will search the caves, but it will take them a long time to find this place," she says. "I go, but will return soon."

She scuttles out of the cave, leaving them in the almost dark, and the almost silence, broken only by the distant growls of the dinosaurs.

They wait without conversation, overwhelmed by the events and the sights of the day.

The light through the ceiling crystals shifts slightly as time passes, although how long Héloïse is away, Willem cannot tell.

When she returns she has two gray peasant smocks. She gives them to the British soldiers and indicates that they should cover their uniforms.

She also brings a small sack of food. That she can so easily raid the soldiers' supplies gives some clue to how she survived down here on her own for so long.

Willem glances again around the walls, looking at the world through the eyes of the girl, spending her childhood in this rock-walled cage. Suddenly he can bear the guilt no longer. He puts down the morsel of bread he is eating.

"Héloïse, I must tell you something," he says.

She looks at him curiously, but says nothing.

"That day in the forest. When the firebird took your mother," Willem says.

"It was you," she says without expression.

"You already knew?" he asks.

"Since you killed the dinosaur in the village," she says. "I knew then."

"I am so sorry about your mother," he says. "If I had done something sooner . . ."

"You could not have saved her," Héloïse says. "And I am alive because of you. But this memory holds great pain for me. Please do not speak of it again."

"I will not," he says.

"I also must tell you something," she says. "About your mother."

"Please," he says.

"She did not escape as she said she would," Héloïse says.

"François told me," Willem says.

"She was taken away in a cage. As was Cosette," Héloïse says. "They were lucky."

"Lucky? What do you mean?" Willem asks.

294

Héloïse looks at François, who looks away.

"He knows," she says.

"I saw nothing," François says. "I don't know."

"He knows," Héloïse says again.

François just stares at her, and when he will not talk, Héloïse does.

The cave seems to grow cold as she speaks and when she is finished, Willem is sobbing. François sits facing a wall, refusing to look at them. Shaking his head as if to shake out her words.

There is silence for a long time. The distant sunlight, filtered by the crystals, drifts farther and begins to fade.

"Where did they take Cosette and my mother?" Willem finally asks. He realizes even as he says it that, without thinking, he asked about Cosette first.

"I do not know," Héloïse says.

"I must find out," Willem says. "I cannot go to England while they are being held captive by the French."

"You must go to England," Frost says. "If you do not, then Napoléon has already won."

"I cannot leave them here in the hands of the French," Willem says.

"What will you do?" François asks. "Break them out of a French prison?"

"I will do whatever it takes," Willem says. "But I will not leave here without them."

The conversation has been in French, but Frost has been quietly translating for Jack, who now speaks. It is in English and although Willem understands the words, he cannot understand the meaning.

"What did he say?" Willem asks.

"A strong man can move a boulder. A wise man can change the world," Frost says.

"I understood the words, but not the meaning," Willem says.

"He means that you, by yourself, can do nothing to help your mother or the girl. You are just one man. But you can teach the world how to defeat Napoléon's monsters, and that is your best chance to rescue those you love."

"Jack said that?" Willem asks.

"That was his meaning," Frost says.

"I cannot go to England," Willem says. "Yet I cannot stay here. I cannot win."

"What do you mean?" Frost asks.

"They have my mother and Cosette," Willem says. "If they know I am here, and alive, they will use them against me. If they think me to be dead, or in England, they will . . . have no further use for them."

Frost relays this in English to Jack, who nods his understanding and mutters something.

"What did he say?" Willem asks.

"Jack thinks it would be easier if you just disappeared," Frost says.

One of the dinosaurs along the corridor roars, and the reverberation is so strong through the narrow passageway that dust falls from the walls.

"Jack is much smarter than he thinks he is," Willem says.

"I keep telling him that," Frost says.

ANTWERP

They stay overnight in the cave, sleeping with the smell of dinosaur in their nostrils and the grunts and occasional growl in their ears.

When they awake, Willem is surprised to see Héloïse curled up in the arms of François. François himself seems just as surprised a few moments later when his eyes open, and he moves quietly away, to spare her the impropriety when she wakes.

Underground routes take them to the north, emerging in a cave by a stream. That takes them out to the very edge of the forest.

They spend the next night in a disused house barn on the outskirts of Brussels, not daring to enter the city.

The next day they find a horse in a field. A war horse from the British Heavy Cavalry. It is nervous and skittish but Jack somehow finds calming words and after removing any insignia, it becomes Lieutenant Frost's horse.

The crossbow fits neatly into one of the saddlebags, which relieves Willem. He has been worried they would have to discard it, as it would attract attention. They have few enough weapons as it is.

Keeping to farm tracks and open fields they avoid seeing any French patrols. They circle around Antwerp to the south and arrive at the gate in the great wall that protects the city. A pair of Dutch soldiers, their helmets now adorned with the red plume of the French emperor, glance at them incuriously as they pass through, not in a group, but individually, mixing with the other travelers and farmworkers who stream in and out of the gate.

Willem was concerned that someone might recognize the saddle and realize it was a stolen horse, but on arrival at Antwerp it becomes clear that is not a problem. They pass many other military horses, torn of their color, and now the property of whoever had found them.

Antwerp is a bustling port city, and French soldiers are everywhere. Finding a place to hide here looks impossible until Frost suggests selling the horse. An unscrupulous stable keeper takes her for a fraction of what she is worth, but still enough to pay for a room at a local inn.

"Up here, General," Baston says.

There is a steeply sloping ledge, impossible to traverse if not for the ropes that have recently been rigged top to bottom. It is an arduous climb, but mercifully short, and at the top a series of passageways is well lit by lamps placed on the floor.

In a cave hidden behind the roots of a tree there are clear signs of habitation.

"Someone was living here?" Thibault asks.

"The girl, we think," Baston says. "Possibly for years."

"Incredible," Thibault says. "How many in the group now?"

"Five," Baston says. "Willem, two British soldiers, the girl, and our man, François."

"You are certain he is your man?" Thibault asks.

"That is what I wanted to show you," Baston says, pointing.

The writing has been scratched roughly and quickly into the stone of the wall by a crossbow bolt that lies nearby. There is only one word: *Antwerp.*

"It could be a trick," Thibault says.

"Perhaps. But I don't see what they would gain by it," Baston says. "François had a crossbow with him when we met him in the forest. I think he leaves the bolt for us to find, so we will know the author of the note. And if it is, then we should act with all haste. From Antwerp it is but a short sail to England."

"They would not succeed. The port at Antwerp is already under guard," Thibault says. "As are all the coastal ports. But go to Antwerp, Captain. Blockade all the gates to the city. If they are inside the city walls, we will keep them there like flies in a trap. We will hunt them down, house by house if necessary."

"Yes, General," Baston says.

"Where are the demonsaurus?" Thibault asks.

"Back in their cages," Baston says.

"And the woman and the girl?"

"Safe in Brussels," Baston says.

"Not safe enough," Thibault says. "Have them brought here."

"At once, sir," Baston says.

"I will follow with the demonsaurus," Thibault says.

OLD FRIEND

Twenty-five, Avenue Quinten Matsys, is a large villa on the edge of a park, in the heart of the city. Willem watches it for many minutes before approaching, to ensure that no one else is showing interest in the house.

The connection between his father and this woman may be known to people other than his mother.

Satisfied that there is nobody watching the house, Willem takes a side street, then a narrow lane that brings him to the rear of the house.

He taps quietly on the scullery door and a few moments later what sounds like the thundering of a herd of elephants comes from within. The door is opened by an enormous man, in both height and girth. His hair is long and tied back in two pigtails, and his mustache would rival that of a walrus.

He glares down at Willem from a very great height and says nothing, waiting for Willem to speak.

In Flemish, Willem says, "I am Willem Verheyen."

"So?" the man asks. "What do you want?"

"My real name is Pieter Geerts," Willem says, and it is strange saying those words, sounds that he has not made with his mouth for a very long time.

The man stares at him. A voice comes from behind him, the voice of an old lady. "Get him off the street, Lars, and quickly. It is Maarten's son."

Lars leads him to the parlor, where the owner of the voice is rising to meet him. She is younger than she sounds, or perhaps older than she looks. Her hair is gray and tied up in a neat bun. She is dressed elegantly in a flowing gown of some indeterminate dark color that shifts as she moves.

"Pieter?" she says.

Willem nods.

The lady steps toward him, surprisingly nimble. She wraps her arms around him tightly, then releases him and kisses him on both cheeks.

"It has been many years since I have seen you," she says, and smiles. "You were much smaller then."

"I do not remember," Willem says.

"Naturally," she says. "Come and sit down."

"Is my mother here?" Willem asks, hoping against hope that his mother has found some way to escape. But Sofie shakes her head as she returns to her armchair.

Willem looks around for Lars, but he has gone. Willem hadn't heard him leave, and realizes that Lars can move as quietly as a cat when he wants to.

"It is true that you taught my father magic?" Willem asks.

"Do not be too surprised," she says. "I, too, was quite famous in my day. Never to the heights of your father of course. Only a man could scale the heights that your father did." Her face grows serious. "What brings you here, Pieter? And why do you ask about your mother? Is it to do with the war?"

"It is," Willem says, and although he had intended to say as little as possible, there is something about this woman that makes him feel he can trust her, and over the next hour, he tells her everything.

"These are desperate times," she says, when he has finished. "But we will do what we can to help."

"We?" Willem asks.

She nods. "We lived under the boot of the French for twenty years. A year ago we exchanged one foreign ruler for another: in The Hague. Now it is again reversed. Our leaders may simper and bow down to Napoléon, our armies may fight for him, but there are many of us who would see Flanders independent once again."

"You take great risks, helping me," Willem says.

"You take greater risks, coming here," she says.

"We must get to England," he says.

"It will not be easy," she says. "The ports are barricaded. Not even a fishing boat can leave without filing papers with the dockmaster and an inspection by the French army. This morning a party of British soldiers broke through the cordon, commandeered a packet, and tried to sail down the Scheldt out to the North Sea."

"What happened to them?" Willem asks.

"There is a battery of forty-two-pounders on either side of the channel," she says, "and the gunners are highly skilled."

Willem thinks about that for a moment.

"I have an idea," he says. "But I will need your help."

"Of course."

"I need to disappear," Willem says. "In front of their eyes. It is the only way to keep my mother and Cosette safe."

"It is not easy to disappear," she says.

"I think I have a way to do it," he says.

"You have much of your father in you," Sofie says. "Tell me your plans."

"If you have paper and pen," Willem says, "I will draw them for you."

The plans are complex, and although Willem explains as he draws, it is over an hour before he has finished.

"It is a daring scheme," Sofie says, when Willem finally lays the pen to rest. "A grandiose illusion, to rival—perhaps even better—those of the great masters. But it depends on exact timing, and perfect coordination."

"What magic trick does not?" Willem asks.

"Indeed, young Pieter," Sofie says. "And the financial cost will be great."

"I do not know how I would repay you," Willem says.

"I would not take your money if you tried," Sofie says. "I am an old woman, and have wealth that I can never use. Besides, it will be worth it just to see this performance."

"I fear it will not have the audience it deserves," Willem says.

"And the audience it will have does not deserve such an illusion," Sofie says, laughing. She grows serious. "Now, Pieter. For a trick half as complicated as this I would expect to practice for months. But your first practice is also your performance. Respect your timing. It is a cruel and unforgiving master."

She studies a rough map that Willem has drawn of the Western Scheldt, then stabs a finger on it. "There. No closer to shore. But that will mean running past the fortresses at Breskens and Vlissingen. They are the ones I told you about with the heavy cannon."

"Do you think we can make it?"

"It is possible. The boat will be something small and quick, perhaps a brigantine. It will be light and maneuverable. That will help. But still you will need God looking over your shoulder."

"How long will it take to be ready?" Willem asks.

"Not long," Sofie says. "The equipment you ask for is relatively simple. The boat will be ready by tomorrow morning. The crew will do what you ask, but you must be seen to threaten them, in case they are caught."

"We have a pistol," Willem says. "And a crossbow."

"That will do," Sofie says. "But we still need to get you to the wharves. They are strictly cordoned. One person, alone, might slip through, but you say there are four of you?"

"Five," Willem says.

"You will never make it," Sofie says. "Not aboveground."

"Aboveground?" Willem asks, but Sofie is thinking aloud.

"It must be at night, after curfew, but you will not be able to leave until they open the lock gates at high tide." She ponders some more. "Where are you staying?"

Willem gives her the address of the inn.

"Sleep well tonight, Pieter," she says. "And be outside the inn tomorrow morning at five. I will send Lars for you."

"We will be there," Willem says.

"Do not be seen," Sofie says.

A door opens at the rear and the giant, Lars, enters again. He bends, and whispers in Sofie's ear.

Sofie looks up sharply at Willem. "Do the emperor's men know you are here in Antwerp?"

"I don't think so," Willem says.

"Someone has seen you. Someone has talked," Sofie says. "The French have just blockaded all the gates into the city."

LARS

Lars, it turns out, is Sofie's youngest son. He carries a tall, narrow lamp and looks around constantly as they hurry through the still-dark streets.

At this early hour of the morning, there are few people, but fewer patrols. Still they keep to the shadows, moving only when Lars says it is safe.

"Wait," he says, stopping abruptly at a corner. "Stay back." He covers the lamp with a thick black cloth and the meager light it gives off disappears.

Willem draws back a little and the others fall into line behind him. Lars stares at a second-story apartment where a curtain has just been drawn back.

A woman's voice sounds from a few streets away. She sounds drunk and giggly. A cart clatters along cobblestones somewhere in the distance.

The curtain is drawn shut.

"We go," Lars says. He uncovers the lamp and begins to move.

They move through the outskirts of Antwerp, one street at a time, always watching, often waiting. A mysterious and unseen network of sympathizers guides them through the streets of the city. In the east, the not-yet-risen sun leaks blood into the morning sky.

They are nearly at the main road when they hear the thud of

boots and shouted commands. Lars leads them into a small garden to wait, out of sight, and a few moments later a group of British soldiers appears. They have no weapons and do not march, but trudge dejectedly, heads down. The reason for that is immediately clear as behind them walk a team of Dutch soldiers, muskets at waist level, bayonets fixed. Captors and their captives.

"A few days ago they were helping us kill the French," Frost says when the soldiers have passed by. "Today they are helping the French."

"It's because they've changed sides, sir," Jack says.

"And if Napoléon conquers England will you fight for him, Jack?" Frost asks.

"I don't think I'd like that, sir," Jack says after a while.

At a wide road, busy with wagons and carts despite the early hour, they wait for a clearing in the traffic before crossing.

A few streets farther on Lars leads them into a brick archway.

"This is as far as we can go," he says. "The French have closed off all the streets around the port."

"Your mother assured me there is a way," Willem says.

Lars nods. "The Ruien," he says.

"Ruien?" Frost asks.

"Come," Lars says. A heavy wooden door in a wall at the back of the archway is bolted and padlocked, but the padlock opens easily to an iron bar that Lars produces out of nowhere. The air that wafts out when he slides back the bolt and opens the door has the foul reek of a cesspool, and Willem involuntarily puts his hand over his mouth and nose.

"Who passed gas?" Frost mutters, holding his sleeve to his nose.

"Not me, sir," Jack says, and in a confidential whisper says, "I think it was the big fella."

"This is nothing," Lars says with a huge grin. "Wait till you get down to the tunnels."

Inside, there is a bare room, with unadorned brick walls. The only thing in the room is the large hole in the center of it, and the circular metal staircase that leads down.

"You don't think the French will guard these tunnels?" Frost asks.

"I do not think so, monsieur," Lars says. "And even if they do, there are many entrances and many exits. The tunnels themselves are a bit of a maze. In any case I think you have no other choice. Here is a map," he says, handing Willem a piece of paper on which rough scratchings have been made. "If you lose the map, follow the water. It flows always to the sea."

Willem takes the map and folds it carefully into a pocket.

"The smell is not so good," Lars says. "But it mostly will not kill you."

"Mostly?" François asks.

"There are patches of firedamp in the tunnels," Lars says.

"Firedamp?" Willem asks.

"Gas. From the sewer water. Most places are safe, because the gas floats above air, and the ceilings are high. But there are many pockets that are very dangerous. Strike a flint, or light a lamp and . . . boom!"

He hands Willem the odd, tall lamp. A fine metal mesh surrounds the flame.

"You said no lamps," Frost says.

"This is a miner's lamp," Lars says. "It is safe to use, but you must keep a constant watch on the flame. See here."

He indicates a graduated series of lines marked on the metal handle that runs up the side of the lamp.

"If the flame starts to burn higher, and bluer, then there is firedamp," Lars says. "Firedamp rises, so crouch down and move on quickly. But if the flame starts to burn low, then there is low oxygen. You must move out of there immediately."

"When we get to the estuary, what then?" Willem asks.

"Everything you asked for has been done," Lars says. "The brigantine is called the *Épaulard*. It is moored in the dock."

"You are not coming with us?" Frost asks.

Lars laughs and shakes his head. "No man would go into the Ruien unless he had no other choice."

"I guess that's us," Frost says.

Lars turns to leave, then stops. From inside his voluminous coat he produces a narrow oilskin wallet.

"I almost forgot," he says. "Your papers. File these with the dockmaster before leaving the port. No boat can leave without authorization, and an inspection."

"Thank you, Lars," Willem says. "And Sofie also."

"Good luck," Lars says.

Willem, holding the lamp out in front of him, leads the way down the metal staircase. It is old and rusted, and the steps shift as he stands on them, sending metallic creaks reverberating out into the tunnel below.

The black shapes of the demonsaurus rasp and pace inside the small cage. The sun has just broached the horizon and the creatures need food.

The saurmasters appear with feed buckets, but Thibault stops them before they reach the caged wagon.

"Keep them hungry today," he says.

"That is dangerous, General," says the first of the saurmasters, a stocky man named Bolcque.

"I do not care," Thibault says.

"They will be much harder to control," the second saurmaster says. He is a thin, skeletal man named Alain.

"Half-rations only then," Thibault says.

The commandant of the garrison approaches, walking quickly, with a soldier trailing behind him.

"General, sir," he says.

"Yes, Commandant?"

"We may have found something," the commandant says, indicating the soldier.

"Speak," Thibault commands.

"Sir, we were patrolling the east side," the soldier says. "We found a door with a broken lock. It leads into the Ruien. I left my comrade to guard it, and came straightaway."

"What is this Ruien?" Thibault asks.

"Ancient sewers," the commandant says, with an expression of distaste. "Could this be your fugitives?"

Thibault shrugs. "A broken door on a sewer entrance. Possibly. Where do these sewers lead?"

"To the estuary," the commandant says. "Close to the docks."

"We must check it," Thibault says, turning to the saurmasters. "Bring the demonsaurus. Let us see if they pick up a trail."

THE RUIEN

The first thing Willem is aware of, other than the darkness and the suffocating stench of the old sewers, is the sound of fluids dripping. Perhaps water. Perhaps not. And not the sharp plunk of liquid into a bowl. Each droplet seems long and drawn out as though things move more slowly here in these ancient bowels of the city.

At first the sounds make him flinch, but soon they just merge into the background, unnoticed unless he thinks about them.

Not so the smell. The stench is aggressive, forcing its way through his nostrils and down his throat. He can taste the stink. He can feel it in his lungs.

A sharp turn at the bottom of the stone steps leads them into the first of the tunnels. A steeply walled brick corridor with a vaulted ceiling, supported by heavy arches of stone.

Ceramic pipes jut from the walls and it is from these that the dripping sound comes. Tongues of green slime hang from the ends, and sewer juice bloats on their tips before dropping into the channels below.

The light of the miner's lamp is dim, but enough for them to see that the surface of the water in the channels is bubbled and uneven with drifting blotches of scum. Foot-long sewer worms writhe in the sludge at the sides of the channels.

Willem is grateful for the floating scum. It shows him which way the water is flowing, and he does not want to rely on the map in these lightless innards.

Another sound encroaches: tiny, scuttling feet, and from on top of one of the pipes a large rat regards them curiously.

The tunnel curves twice before leading them out into a larger chamber where the ceiling is supported by huge pillars that curve up and outward in spouting fountains of brickwork.

They avoid wading in the effluent by following a stone walkway along one of the walls. Where it crosses the tunnels there are stone blocks in the streams, a pace apart. It is easy going, but runs out at the far end of the chamber where the flow surges into a low out-flow tunnel. There is a little air gap at the top of that tunnel, and when Willem stretches out from the walkway and holds the lamp in the entrance, the flame almost extinguishes.

"No oxygen," he says, barely opening his lips, unwilling to allow the fetid breath of the Ruien into his mouth.

"Then which way?" Frost asks.

The soldier holds a broken padlock, the metal bent and twisted.

"Has anyone come out?" Thibault asks, raising the back of a finger to block his nostrils as he peers into the entrance.

"No, sir, but I have heard movements down below," the soldier says.

"Let us see if the demonsaurus can pick up a scent," Thibault says.

The two patrol soldiers back well away as the black creatures are clipped to leashes, then released from the cage.

They latch on to a scent immediately and follow it through the doorway to the circular stone steps that lie behind it. They paw at the ground and strain at their leashes.

"The boy's scent is here," Bolcque says. "And it is fresh."

"Release the demonsaurus," Thibault says.

"Sir?"

"Release them and bolt the door behind them," Thibault says. "The boy and his group can only get out through the pipes at the dock. We will go there and wait for them. We will see if the demonsaurus are still hungry when they emerge."

"Yes, sir," Bolcque says.

The demonsaurus are unleashed and disappear quickly into the depths of the stairway.

Bolcque shuts the door behind them, and bolts it.

"You men." Thibault addresses the two soldiers of the patrol. "Good work. You will be rewarded. For now, return to the garrison. Tell the commandant what we have found. I want every available man down at the docks immediately. Search every wharf. Every building. Every ship. No vessel leaves unless I personally authorize it. Is that clear?"

"Yes, sir."

The two soldiers hurry away as Thibault and the saurmasters turn west and head toward the docks.

The garrison is close and the soldiers of the patrol, unsettled perhaps by the sight of the black creatures, and excited at the prospect of a reward, do not notice the large man who emerges from the shadows behind them, nor the iron bar in his hand.

Not until it is too late.

Willem is checking the map. "The first tunnel back on this side connects with another series of passages that also lead toward the docks. Let's try our luck that way, if you all agree."

No one objects.

Willem folds the map back into the canvas bag. He takes one step but stops almost immediately at a new sound. A rusty metallic creak reverberating through the chamber.

"Someone is on the stairs," Frost says.

The noise is quickly replaced by a splashing sound. Although they have traveled some distance from the staircase, the noise echoes clearly off the hard, enclosed walls.

"Something is in the water," François says.

There comes a low growl and a rattle of spines.

"Demonsaurus," Héloïse says.

"We have to get out of this chamber, now!" Willem says, and moves past the others, leading the way back to the tunnel.

The sounds of their pursuers get rapidly louder.

"The lamp," Héloïse says. "Cover the lamp!"

"We cannot see where we are going without it," Willem says.

"Cover the lamp," Héloïse says again, and Willem argues no further. He pulls the black cloth down over it. He stops walking as he does, unwilling to take another step in the total blackness that now surrounds them.

"Keep moving," Héloïse whispers. "But be quiet. They cannot smell us here, and they cannot see us. Be careful they do not hear us."

Silence envelops them except for the gurgle of the sewage around the central columns and into the outflow. That and the movement of the demonsaurus in the tunnel at the far end.

Afraid of stepping off the edge of the walkway into what lies below it, Willem feels his way back along the wall until he gets to the opening to the tunnel. The brickwork is uneven and slimy to the touch.

There are loud splashes as the demonsaurus enter the chamber; unconcerned about the walkway, or not seeing it, they have waded straight into the underground river of filth.

Placing his feet carefully to avoid making even the smallest sound, Willem eases into the tunnel. The bottom of this passageway is lightly curved and slippery. If any one of them loses their footing, the demonsaurus will be on them.

Willem moves farther into the tunnel and stops, the others behind him, waiting as the sounds in the chamber move closer.

Standing still, silently waiting is excruciating. Willem wants to turn and run, to scream and flee from the terror that approaches, but he knows that would bring certain death.

They hear the demonsaurus, at least two of them, hunting around in the chamber for a few moments. Willem cannot see it, but imagines them probing each of the tunnels that lead off the chamber.

There is a regular thudding sound in his ears. He is not sure if it is the drumming of his heart in his chest cavity, or the thrum of blood in his skull. Surely if it is so loud in his own ears, then the demonsaurus can hear it too. He can hear himself breathing, the air rushing in and out of his nose. He opens his mouth and inhales and exhales through it. It brings the taste of the sewers to his tongue, but it is quieter.

Finally the sounds of the demonsaurus start to diminish, then disappear.

"Move quietly," Héloïse says. "And do not uncover the lamp until we are well into the tunnel."

"Where are they?" François asks.

"The tunnels are all interconnected," Willem says. "They could be anywhere."

Even in front of us, he thinks, but does not say it as they creep through the narrow tunnel in total darkness.

He finds his way by feel, running a finger along the wall of the tunnel. When the wall abruptly disappears, he knows they have reached a cross-tunnel. It is confirmed by a mild, sideways movement of air.

Stepping around into the cross-tunnel he uncovers the lamp and it is a welcome relief to be able to see once again.

François has his crossbow in his hands. That makes Willem remember the pistol. He takes it from the bag and opens the frizzen to check that there is powder in the pan. They move deeper into the entrails of this ancient, brick-skinned creature.

Always they follow the flow of the scum in the channels. They pass through a low archway into a new tunnel, still made of bricks, but a different color, more of a light yellowish clay.

It is louder here than in the other channels, but there is a curious timbre to the sound, a distant, high-pitched wail that quickly resolves itself into a completely separate noise.

It gets louder and seems to be coming toward them. Willem stops, uncertainly, scanning the darkness beyond the reach of the lamp. He turns up the lamp as high as it will go, checking first that the flame is yellow, and that there is no risk of firedamp.

Now they see the cause of the noise. Rats. Thousands of them, running across the stone floors of the tunnel toward them. They flow around the fugitives' legs like water battering boulders in a stream, the sound of their feet a steady hum and their squeals merging into a single voice.

Héloïse turns abruptly and starts to follow the flow of the rats.

"Héloïse," Willem hisses above the sound of the rats.

"Come quickly. This way," she says.

"Why?" Willem asks. "The water flows the other way."

Héloïse gestures down at the rats. "They run from what we run from," she says.

"Turn off the light," Frost says.

The rats have gone, to their own hiding places deep in the Ruien.

No demonsaurus has shown. Do they sit quietly in the tunnel, lying in ambush, or just waiting for them to make a sound?

"Which way?" Willem asks.

"This way," Frost says, pointing.

"How do you know? There is no water."

"Do you not feel the breeze?"

Willem shuts his eyes and can feel a faint breath of air against his face.

"It must come from the estuary," Frost says. "If we keep the breeze to our face, we must eventually find our way there."

That plan holds for no more than a few minutes, when they hear the sounds of a demonsaurus in the tunnel ahead of them.

A cross-tunnel beckons and they reluctantly leave the light breeze that was leading them to safety and turn into the unknown.

The new tunnel narrows as it goes and makes unexpected turns. In the corners the ceilings curve down lower and in these places the flame on the lamp starts to elongate and a bluish tinge grows at its tip.

"Firedamp," Willem warns each time, but as they pass the flame reduces and the blue disappears.

The tunnel finally comes to an end, opening out into a small circular underground lake filled with brackish, sludgy water, and topped with a low dome. In the center is a wide brick column that holds up the ceiling. Willem can see no exit from the lake, but there is no other way to go, so they wade into the pool. Several times something brushes against Willem's legs and he thinks of eels or something much worse. But whatever it is, it is either uninterested or afraid.

They reach the central brick column and circle around it, dimly seeing the mouth of a tunnel on the far side.

The dome that is the sky above the lake starts to darken as they cross and François says, "The lamp!"

The flame has been getting lower and lower as they have crossed the lake, and is now almost gone. With that understanding Willem realizes that he is struggling to breathe. His lungs are working harder and faster, yet he feels as though he is suffocating.

"Hurry," he manages to say in a voice that is just a hoarse whisper. "No oxygen."

They try to move faster, wheezing and gasping for air, although their footsteps are sluggish in the pond water, which at times seems as thick as treacle.

Jack, guiding his lieutenant, has taken the lead, but Frost stops suddenly, holding up his hand for silence. Willem can barely see it, so low is the flame, and almost collides with him. He hears Héloïse and François come to a halt behind him.

Frost says nothing, but then they hear what he has heard. The sound of movement. The soft rattle of spines.

A demonsaurus has just entered the lake.

The lamp is so low as to be invisible, but still Willem covers it, quickly, but silently. He is again acutely conscious of the loud sound of his breathing in the thin air.

There is complete silence apart from the sound of the demonsaurus's breathing, laboring in the unbreathable atmosphere. They hear each footstep as it circles them, hunting in the blackness.

Bright spots have appeared inside Willem's eyelids and his head is beginning to waver. There is a slight noise in front of him and he realizes that Frost has slumped over, to be caught by Jack's strong arms.

Still the demonsaurus circles, hunting by feel in a place where all its other senses are useless. It is close now. So close in front of him that he could reach out and touch it.

Willem can feel his head spinning and knows he is losing

control, losing consciousness and there is no way he can bear it any longer.

Then with a series of splashing footsteps the creature is gone, like the humans, unable to stay in a place with no oxygen.

Willem sucks in a breath, and it is not enough.

He bends down closer to the water. Although the putrid smell is stronger, the air that he brings into his lungs seems less suffocating.

"Get lower," he croaks. "More air lower."

Jack has gone and when Willem uncovers the light, by its feeble beam he sees Jack almost at the edge of the lake, wading into the passage on the opposite side.

Willem follows him. The passage rises sharply and is joined by a cross-tunnel. Through that flows the freshest, sweetest, foul air he has ever breathed in his life, and it is wonderful. He glances back, worried about Héloïse, but she is at his heels.

Jack stands in the passage, the lieutenant in his arms, breathing in huge great gulps of air. Jack's face looks gray in the light of the lamp, which here burns bright and clear.

It is then that Willem realizes. One of Jack's arms is broken. Yet still he has picked up the young lieutenant and carried him across the lake. The pain must have been excruciating, yet Jack made no sound.

"The lieutenant?" Willem asks, and points toward Frost.

Jack nods and mumbles something incoherent in English. He places his hand on Frost's chest and Willem can see its movement. Frost is unconscious, but alive.

"Light," François says, arriving beside Willem. At first Willem is unsure what he means, then he sees the faint glow of daylight at the end of the tunnel. This is the reason for the breeze here and the clearer, more oxygenated air. The channel in the center of the tunnel is wide and flows swiftly down toward the glow. This must be the exit to the estuary.

Jack hoists Frost onto his shoulder and holds him there with his one good arm. They start to stumble down the slope, getting faster as they go, and their bodies recover from the lack of oxygen. Something about the light is a magnet that draws them to it. Here is air; here is light; here is safety.

The tunnel rises up slightly and as it does so the tip of the flame starts once again to turn blue.

Jack is almost running, anxious to get out of this dreadful place. François is right behind Jack and Willem tries to keep up, but can't. He urges his legs to hurry, but there is still no strength in them. It might be the firedamp, he realizes, and tries to bend down as he walks, breathing lower to the ground.

François, Frost, and Jack are well ahead. Héloïse is still at his side and now he realizes why. She has stayed back with him, to help him in case he should fall, or fall unconscious. The wild creature that would hiss and spit at him in Madame Gertruda's garden is making sure that he makes it out of the Ruien alive.

There are no words for what he feels about this.

They reach the highest point and see daylight down a ramp ahead of them. They start to descend when they hear the rattle behind them. He turns; so does Héloïse.

The demonsaurus is there.

The rise in the roof and the slope down to the entrance have created a dome-like effect in the top of the tunnel, and rising firedamp has accumulated here. The flame burns even higher and bluer with sudden bright sparks shooting off like miniature fireworks. The air is thick and muggy with the fumes and Willem can feel his head swimming. He and Héloïse back away from the black creature, just visible in the thin light that ekes its way up from the entrance. The entrance: so tantalizingly close, but so very far away.

The demonsaurus cannot smell them; the air is too thick. It cannot hear them, so silent are their footfalls on the stone ledge. But it can see them, silhouetted by the light from the entrance behind and below them.

The demonsaurus cocks its head from side to side and the spines on its back rattle, that awful, blood-chilling sound. It takes a step forward.

Willem raises the pistol, knowing he cannot fire it. Not here. Not in the midst of the firedamp. If he can get lower, where the air is clearer, he might have a chance.

"Willem," Héloïse says. "Go."

"We go together," Willem says.

"No. Then it will attack. If I stay here, you may get clear."

"No, Héloïse."

"Do not argue," she says. "I return a favor, long owed."

The demonsaurus takes three quick steps forward and Willem involuntarily backs away. Héloïse does not.

Willem takes another step and that is the cue for the saur to attack. It rushes at Héloïse, who raises up her arms to defend herself from it, and stumbles backward, falling into the channel, into the gray-green flow of effluent that runs down to the sea.

The demonsaurus is above her now, raising its claws to plunge them into her chest, and Willem hears himself scream. The demonsaurus looks up at the sound, and even as its eyes flick toward Willem there is a hand on his shoulder pushing him sideways and a sound that Willem remembers from a long time ago.

The crossbow bolt buries itself in the chest of the saur, which throws its head back in an enraged howl of pain that echoes off the walls, filling the tunnel with sound. But it does not stop. It slashes at Héloïse, but she has rolled to the side of the channel and its claws rake only sludge. It traps her with its back foot and raises its claws again.

Beside him François is desperately trying to draw the crossbow string and fit another bolt. But there is not enough time.

"Run!" Willem screams, shoving François backward down the pipe. Willem takes three quick steps forward, bringing him face-to-face with the creature. He raises the pistol to its head, covers his eyes with his hand, and pulls the trigger.

The boom of the pistol is followed by an unbearable heat and flash of light and he spins and dives backward into the nauseating flow in the channel, soaking himself in it as the insides of his eyelids turn bright red and a great sheet of flame gushes over the top of him.

For a second there is no air in the tunnel, then it rushes back in a strong gust, bringing with it the fresh smell of the sea.

Willem sits up, coughing and gagging, reaching out for Héloïse. He cannot find her, until a small hand latches on to his collar from behind, helping him to his feet. He looks around. The demonsaurus is dead, a crossbow bolt in its chest and a bloody, ragged hole in its head. Its spines are on fire.

Farther down the tunnel, François lies on the slimy ledge beside the channel. He looks shocked. Whether that is at finding himself alive, or at seeing Willem and Héloïse, Willem can't tell.

The pistol is gone and Willem does not wish to search for it. Even if he found it, it would be soaked and useless.

François picks himself up and waits for them, and together they walk down the slimy bricks to where the two British soldiers wait for them in the fresh air outside.

They are almost at the lip of the entrance when a voice comes from the side.

"Hold there, Pieter Geerts."

A French officer emerges from a side tunnel, a pistol in one hand, a saber in the other. Beside him are two French saurmasters, one stocky, one tall. They both also have pistols.

"Move no farther," Thibault says.

MERCY

"You have led us on a merry chase," Thibault says. "But it is now over. The emperor wants you alive. Myself, I have less desire to see breath in your body when you are taken to the royal chambers. Of course we may have to do something about the smell."

"The breath of the Ruien is nothing in comparison to the stench of your evil," Héloïse says.

"So it can speak?" Thibault says. He glances up the tunnel at the now-blackened roof and walls.

He shakes his head with disapproval. "What have you done with my demonsaurus?"

"One is dead," Willem says.

"And the other?"

"It is behind you," Willem says.

The two saurmasters glance backward into the night of the tunnel. Thibault does not take his eyes off Willem.

"He lies," Thibault says. "This one is full of trickery."

"Are you sure, sir?" the stocky man says, with another nervous glance behind. There is nothing there.

"You can't see it," Willem says, "but I can hear it."

"He is trying to fool you, Bolcque," Thibault says. "There is nothing behind you."

But there is.

With a sudden scream and a flurry of movement, the saur-master disappears backward into the indelible darkness.

"What time did they leave?" Baston asks.

"Need I remind you that I am a commandant, and you are a captain?" the commandant of the garrison says. "You will rephrase your question in a more decorous and appropriate manner."

"I will phrase my question however I damn like," Baston says. "General Thibault answers directly to the emperor and he is missing. As for your rank, I suspect it is likely soon to be that of a common infantryman, if you still draw breath when this is over."

The commandant regards him for a moment, his jaw tight, about to retort, then clearly thinks better of it.

"The general took . . . those saurs, and went to investigate a break-in at a sewer tunnel," he says. "It was nearly six."

"Two hours ago," Baston says. "And you did not think to check?"

"He had two of my men with him," the commandant says. "Good men. Plus he had the two that work with the saurs. He is in no danger."

"Why would the general investigate a problem with a sewer?" Baston asks.

"The old tunnels lead down to the docks," the commandant says.

"And you have done nothing since that time?" Baston asks.

"And what would you have me do?" the commandant asks.

"What a good French soldier would do," Baston says. "Have you alerted headquarters?"

"The emperor and his staff are no longer here," the commandant says. "They have moved to the fortress at Breskens while we mop up the last of the British."

"Then what happens is up to us," Baston says. "I want a full company of men ready immediately. They will come with me to the wharves. In the meantime, you will take a platoon to check these sewers, starting at the break-in."

"I will not, Captain," the commandant says, with emphasis on Baston's rank.

"Then your replacement will," Baston says, drawing his pistol.

The taller saurmaster, dead or unconscious, lies half in and half out of the tunnel where it joins onto the main outlet. The body of the other man lies facedown in the stream, which is slowly staining red.

Thibault sits astride the back of the beast, pinning it to the ground, one of its front legs twisted up behind its neck. The other leg scratches at the ground, but is not strong enough to dislodge the soldier. Thibault's sword lies nearby, knocked from his grasp. He stretches out for it, but cannot reach, and with the shifting of his weight, the demonsaurus is almost up from under him. Quickly he leans back, keeping his weight on the arm that pins the creature. It snarls and snorts. Its back feet flail on the slippery surface, sending rancid water and foul muck spraying against the walls.

"Come on," Willem says, climbing out of the mouth of the tunnel, onto the ledge that leads up to the dock.

"In the name of God, have mercy," Thibault says.

"No mercy," Héloïse says.

"François!" Thibault calls out, but François looks away.

"No mercy," Héloïse says.

Thibault's pistol lies near him, discharged without result, and now useless against the beast. Willem eyes it for a moment, then climbs back into the tunnel, picks it up, and places it in his canvas bag.

"It makes no difference for you," Thibault shouts. "You cannot escape. The wharves are swarming with my men."

"Then we must hurry," Willem says.

They leave the two predators locked in a final battle that neither can win, and exit the pipe into the clear morning sun.

REFUSE

Antwerp's two docks, the Bonapartedok, and the larger, adjoining Willemdok, named after the emperor of France and the king of the Netherlands respectively, are separated from the tidal estuary that is the Western Scheldt by a lock, the gates of which are closed during low tide.

But it is nearly high tide and the gates are open, jutting out from the stone wall that protects the dock area from the sea.

A narrow rocky shore runs along the base of the wall, contracting by the minute as the tide continues to rise.

Héloïse strips naked, unconcerned by the eyes of the others. François immediately averts his gaze, muttering to himself in what Willem assumes is a prayer. Out of politeness, Willem also finds something to look at. Jack just stares.

Héloïse wades into the water and bathes, rinsing her smock at the same time. The estuary water does not look particularly clean, but it is certainly better than what they have recently been soaking in.

"What is happening?" Frost asks, hearing the splashing. He still seems dozy to Willem, and his voice is thick, but he is improving constantly.

"You don't want to know," Willem says. But Héloïse's idea is a good one, and after placing his bag carefully on a flat rock, he wades into the estuary also, fully clothed, sitting down in the water and thrashing his arms and legs about to rinse his clothing as thoroughly as possible.

When he gets out, Héloïse, still naked, is wringing water out of her smock. Willem stands in his saturated clothes and wonders which of them is really the more civilized.

They follow the shore, looking for steps up to the docks. There are none, but they find a kind of ladder: a column of rusted metal rungs in a wooden post not far from the outer lock gates.

Willem risks a quick climb and eases his head over the top. There are sailors and shorehands going about their business, but no soldiers, apart from a small group checking wagons on the road that leads to the south. They are looking the wrong way, although he knows it would only take one to turn around and he would be spotted.

"Thibault's soldiers aren't here yet," he calls down to the others. "We may yet escape if we are quick."

The others climb up after him and they walk as quickly as they can, without attracting attention, past a series of small wooden buildings, and one large stone one. After that they must cross the road in full view of the barricade, but the soldiers' attention is taken by a row of wagons waiting to pass through, and they do not see the five fugitives walking casually across behind them.

There is no sign of the brigantine here, and they turn onto a wide central pier that divides the two docks. At the end of the pier they turn again, and there they find her, a sleek and modern two-masted vessel. There is a man up the mainmast with a spyglass.

Tied to the stern is a small dory, a flat-bottomed boat, almost as narrow at the back as at the front. It does not look very stable to Willem. Aft of center, a number of items, rectangular in shape, are covered by a tarpaulin.

The skipper of the brigantine is a heavily bearded man with a strong Dutch accent.

"Willem?" he asks, as they arrive.

"Yes," Willem says.

"We must hurry," he says. "There are a large number of French troops heading toward the docks."

"We are ready," Willem says.

"Have you filed the papers with the dockmaster?" the skipper asks.

Willem shakes his head. "Not yet."

"If you do not, then they will close the lock gates on us as we try to leave," the skipper says. "You must file the papers. I would do it for you, but we must get ready to cast off, and I fear we do not have long, with Napoléon's men on the march."

"I will do it now," Willem says. He opens the bag and retrieves the papers in their oilskin wallet.

"The office is in the stone building by the lock," the skipper says. "Be quick."

"We just passed that," François says. "I will take them."

"No, I will do it," Willem says.

"In soaking-wet clothes?" François asks. "That will look suspicious. And you still smell worse than I do."

"François is right," Frost says. "On both counts."

Willem nods. There is no time to argue. "Here." He hands François the papers. "And take this also. In case you are stopped." He reaches back into the bag and withdraws Thibault's pistol, then a paper cartridge.

He tears open the cartridge as he has been shown and loads the pistol quickly and efficiently.

"Be careful, and be quick," he says, handing the gun to François.

"I will return soon," François says, tucking it out of sight somewhere inside his coat.

He disappears around the corner of the pier.

"Héloïse, what will you do?" Willem asks. "Will you come with us to England?"

"What would I do in England?" she asks. "I know nobody. I do not even speak the language."

"Where will you go?" Willem asks.

"I do not know," she says. "Goodbye, Willem."

"Thank you, Héloïse," Willem says.

She nods a farewell to the others and is quickly out of sight.

The dockmaster's office is just inside the door of the stone building. A guard, a Dutch soldier, stands in a corner. He looks bored and his musket leans against the wall beside him.

A clerk glances up as François enters, then looks back to a logbook he is writing in. François slams the oilskin wallet noisily down on the counter and waits.

The clerk looks up again after a moment, sniffing the air, then screwing up his face.

"When did you last bathe, peasant?" he asks, with a glance and a grin at the guard in the corner.

"Do not mock me," François says. "This is of great importance."

"My chamber pot would not piss on you," the clerk says. "Get out of my office."

"French soldiers will be here shortly, seeking a fugitive," François says. "That person aims to escape on a brigantine called the *Épaulard*. Here are its papers."

That seems to perk up the clerk's interest and he rises and crosses to the counter, picking up the wallet with an expression of distaste. He extracts the papers and flicks through them.

"These papers seem to be in order," he says.

"I have no doubt," François says. "But the boat must not be allowed to leave."

"You say the French will be here soon?" the clerk asks.

François nods.

"Then I will show them these papers, and discuss it with them," the clerk says.

"That may be too late," François says. "Close the gates or the fugitive will escape, and it will be on your head. Napoléon himself will hear of your incompetence."

"And Willem will learn of your treachery," a small voice says from behind him.

François whirls. Héloïse is crouched in the doorway.

"Héloïse," François says. "Why did you follow me?"

"It does not matter," she says.

"I wish it were not you," he says, the pistol coming out from under his coat. He cocks it without thinking. The guard in the corner no longer looks bored, and reaches for his musket.

"You would shoot me?" she asks.

"Against my will," François says.

"I tended you when you were ill. I danced with you at the fête. You saved my life in the Ruien. You would shoot me now?"

"Those were but small moments," François says. "God makes far larger demands."

He looks away for a moment and there is genuine sadness in his heart. The pistol wavers.

She takes advantage of his indecision and leaps away from the door, running out along the wharves. He races after her and takes aim. Still something stays his hand: could it be a kind of love, or is it simply compassion for a wild but damaged creature? She is almost to the safety of a wooden shed when God guides his finger to the trigger.

The sound of the explosion echoes off the buildings around him. A puff of smoke surrounds the muzzle and he wishes it were thicker, to hide what he does not want to see. But it is not and so he sees the blood spurt from her spine as her body arches backward. She collapses onto a low wooden rail, looks back at him for a moment with pleading eyes, then rolls off into the water.

François runs to the edge of the dock and watches for a moment. In death she looks so fragile, stripped of the savagery that gave her size and purpose. Now she is just a small, dead girl, face-down in the center of a spreading red mist in the water, floating away under the docks with the fish heads and the rum bottles and the rest of the refuse.

"Hold where you are."

François turns to see the guard from the dockmaster's officer, his musket leveled.

Down the road at the barricade the French soldiers are looking in his direction.

"Place the pistol on the ground at your feet," the guard says.

François obeys, and cannot quite understand why he is crying.

DEPARTURE

"What do we do?" Jack asks.

The sound of the shot is still echoing off the wharf buildings.

"We don't know that was François's pistol," Frost says.

"It was," Willem says.

"We must wait for him," Frost says.

"You heard the pistol shot," the skipper says. "I do not know what has happened, but if we do not get out of the dock before they can shut the gates, then we will not get out at all."

"We would not have made it this far without him," Frost says.

"My instructions are to get Willem to safety," the skipper says. "They did not mention François."

Crewmen scurry up the masts, unfurling sails, and within a few moments the mooring lines are cast off and the brigantine starts to ease away from the pier.

"Wait," Willem says. "Look!"

"On your feet," the guard says, and François reluctantly complies.

"Let us go to the French, and see what they want to do with you," the guard says.

As he stands, François sees the bow of the brigantine emerge from behind the pier. He glances at the lock, where the gates stand wide open.

"Shut the gates," he says.

"That is not my concern," the guard says. "That is up to the dockmaster."

"They will get away!" François says.

"And that will be on the head of the dockmaster," the guard says. "Move."

He kneels to pick up François's pistol, balancing his musket on his knee so that his aim does not falter. He tucks the pistol into his shoulder belt, then gestures with the musket. He keeps well out of François's reach as they head toward the barricades and the waiting French soldiers.

Every few paces François glances back. The brigantine is now gathering speed, slicing through the water toward the lock, leaning over under the weight of the wind that now swells its sails.

Ahead, beyond the barricades where a large covered goods wagon is being inspected, he can see the ranks of the French soldiers approaching at a quick march. There is at least a company of them, an officer on horseback at their head.

Without warning there are shouts from the barricades and a musket shot. Red British uniforms are suddenly everywhere, scattering in all directions out from the wagon as the French soldiers kneel and take aim.

More muskets sound and, taking advantage of the distraction, François spins around, dropping below the guard's musket and springing forward. The musket fires but the aim is high and now the discharged gun is no more than a club. It is not a fair fight. The Dutch soldier is no match for arms and shoulders that have spent their life swinging axes, and a solid uppercut lifts the man off the ground, sending him flying backward in an untidy pile where he lies still.

The soldiers at the barricade are still busy dealing with the escaping British soldiers, but eyes now are turned in his direction, alerted by the shot.

François snatches up the pistol and scrabbles in the guard's ammunition pouch for a handful of paper cartridges. Then he starts to run.

The outer gates are slowly starting to close, but the brigantine is already entering the lock. It will be tight, but he thinks the brigantine will win the race. He sprints along the wharf to the lock.

Faces on the boat look up at him now. Willem, Jack, even Frost turns in his direction.

"François!" Willem shouts.

The crew on the boat ignore him. The skipper especially is focused on the angle of his boat. The sails are trimmed for maximum speed but the gap ahead of them is closing fast.

The end of the lock approaches and François reaches it just about the same time as the brigantine does. He does not hesitate, but runs out across the top of the still-moving gate. It is barely the width of a man, and its movement threatens to topple him into the estuary, but somehow he keeps his feet, balancing with his arms out wide, racing to the end of the gate that scrapes the side of the brigantine as it slips past. He leaps, landing half on the deck and half on the side of the ship, winding himself on the low gunwales.

Then the gate is past them and they are out into the open estuary.

Hands haul him up onto the deck and he lies there gasping for air, surprised to find the pistol is still in his outstretched hand.

The ship is coming about now, bearing away up the estuary, the start of the long, winding voyage toward the open sea.

"Get down," the skipper shouts, and François sees the others flatten themselves on the deck beside him as musketfire comes from behind. Holes rip in the sails and splinters fly from the gunwales.

François turns his head to see a row of French muskets on the edge of the stone wall, busily reloading. They fire again, but already the distance has increased and this time the shots do not come close.

By the time the soldiers can reload for a third time the brigantine is well out of range, her sails full, water surging up past her bow.

BRESKENS

Baston's horse seems to float effortlessly down the undulating roads that lead to Breskens.

Stones fly from the hooves and dust rises in a cloud around him. The blue streak that is the Western Scheldt glitters to his right and a white patch on the blue is the sails of the brigantine.

It is a three-hour ride from Antwerp, but he has made it in little more than two and a half.

He is furious that they arrived at the docks too late for him to stop the brigantine from leaving. The commandant at the Antwerp garrison will pay dearly for his inertia.

But the Western Scheldt is a long and winding estuary with many turns, while the road between the two towns is fast and straight.

The gates of the fortress are closed, a precaution against the bands of British soldiers, leaderless and aimless, that still roam the area.

Muskets up on the battlements cover his arrival and a voice calls down a challenge.

"Open the gates," Baston calls back. "I must see Count Cambronne immediately."

The count is in discussion with the emperor and Marshal Ney when Baston enters, hot and dusty from the ride. After a hurried discussion with an adjutant he is allowed to approach.

They all glance up as he clicks his heels together and stands at attention before them, but continue with their conversation without acknowledging his presence.

"Excuse me, Count Cambronne," he says after a moment.

This earns a glare from Ney, but no more than a raised eyebrow from Napoléon.

"Captain Baston," Cambronne says, indicating the emperor. "You can see who I am with. I am sure that what you have to say can wait."

"It cannot, sir. My apologies, sire," Baston says.

"Who is this brazen young man?" Napoléon asks.

"Captain Baston of the Imperial Guard, Second Dragoons," Cambronne says.

"You are from the Sonian?" Napoléon looks up with sudden interest. "Where is General Thibault?"

"He is missing, sire, and I bring news that cannot wait."

LA GRANDE ILLUSION

"There is activity on the fortress, sir," Jack says.

"What kind of activity?" Frost asks.

"Soldiers, sir," Jack says.

"What are they doing?" Frost asks.

"I think they might be readying the cannon, sir," Jack says.

"That was to be expected," Willem says.

"Perhaps it is just a drill," Jack says. "We was always doing drills, wasn't we, sir?"

"I don't think this will be a drill," Frost says.

The Western Scheldt has proved a demanding sail; many times they have come about to make the most use of the wind, or to round one of the sharp turns in the estuary.

But since passing the coastal town of Terneuzen they have only had to bear away once, as they approached a large sandbar. This new bearing, the skipper assures them, with a little careful rudder work, will take them straight down the mouth of the estuary.

The brigantine is close-hauled, leaning over and running fast as it makes for the open sea.

"Skipper," Willem says. "I thank you for your efforts. We will soon be on our way to England, and unless you wish to come with us, I suggest you take your leave. Can your men swim?"

"Of course," the skipper says.

"We pass close to the sandbar," Willem says. "It would be an opportune time for you to depart."

"Good luck," the skipper says.

"Give my thanks to Sofie and Lars," Willem says.

"I do not know these names," the skipper says.

The observation platform is a robust stone tower in the center of the circular fortress. It rises high above the ramparts, giving it commanding views out across the Western Scheldt. Arrayed below it are huge forty-two-pounder cannon on heavy wooden carriages. Some of those cannon face north, controlling the entrance to the estuary. Others aim to the west, out over the North Sea, where even now a flotilla of mighty British men-o'-war, bristling with guns, maintain a constant patrol.

Only half of the fortress's fifty cannon are manned, the sudden outbreak of hostilities catching the commander of the fort unprepared. But one land-based cannon, with its solid footing, is worth three shipboard cannon, and these forty-two-pounders have greater range, and hurl a larger, heavier iron ball. The British ships keep well clear.

"The crew is leaving the ship," Cambronne says, his eye pressed to a spyglass. "They swim to the sandbar."

"Send a detachment and arrest them all," Napoléon says. "In case the boy tries to slip away among them." He stops, thinking. "You are certain that the boy is on this boat?"

"Without a doubt, sire," Baston says.

"Sire, the brigantine is within range." The voice of the gun captain floats up from the battlements below the tower.

"Then, Captain, what are you waiting for?" Napoléon says. "A shot across the bow and signal her to lower her sails. If she does not, then sink her."

The boom of a cannon and a puff of smoke from the fort are followed by the whistle of a cannonball. It raises a column of seawater well short of the ship.

Willem has been below, and climbs up through the open hatch just aft of the mainmast, staring at the fortress.

"I think they want us to give ourselves up," Frost says.

"I don't think we should, sir," Jack says from the wheel. He has been steering the ship, one-handed, since the crew departed overboard. The sails are set, the wind is stable, and all that is required is to hold the tiller steady until the brigantine clears the headlands at the mouth of the estuary.

"I am in complete agreement," Frost says. "Keep her straight and true."

"No, Willem, we must lower our sails," François says.

"You would give up now, François?" Willem asks. "Within sight of freedom?"

"That is not freedom that awaits you," François says. "It is suicide. Look at the fortress. Look at the size of the guns. A single cannonball would be all it would take to sink this fragile vessel. We must land, and try to find some other way to England."

"I will not turn back," Willem says. "Not now."

"Nor I," Frost says. "And I know I answer for Jack as well."

"No, Willem." François shakes his head. "I cannot let you do this."

"François." Willem walks to him and lays a hand on his shoulder. "You are a true friend, and I know you seek to save me from harm, but I must see this through."

François pushes him away abruptly. "You misunderstand me, Willem." The pistol has somehow appeared in his hand. "I cannot let you escape to England. I cannot let you go against the will of God."

"What are you talking about, François?" Willem asks. "The will of God?"

"What madness is this?" Frost asks.

"God has chosen Napoléon to unite Europe and I cannot let you stand against that."

"François!" Willem cries.

"I am sorry, Willem," François says. "Lieutenant, tell your man to turn toward shore. Willem, you will be imprisoned, but at least you will live. There has been too much killing already."

"I will not," Lieutenant Frost says.

"Then you force me to shoot Willem," François says. "Either way your plans will come to an end."

The conversation is in French, and although Jack cannot understand it, there is no doubt about the meaning of the gun in François's hand. Jack takes his hand from the wheel and starts to move toward François.

"Stay where you are, Jack," Frost says. "Keep the ship on course."

Jack places his hand back on the wheel and corrects the steering slightly.

"There is only one ball in that pistol," Frost says. "If you shoot Willem, broken arm or no, Jack will tear you to shreds."

"I do not doubt it. That is a sacrifice I am prepared to make," François says. "It is just one of many that I must bear."

"François," Willem says sadly, lowering his eyes. "François, when I learned that the Duke of Wellington knew nothing of the dinosaurs, I became suspicious. But I could not believe that you would move against your own cousin. When Thibault called your name it pained my heart, because what I did not want to believe must be true. But still I had to be sure. And that is why I gave you the pistol and sent you off with our shipping papers."

As he is talking he has been moving toward the stern of the ship.

"If you suspected me so, then you should not have trusted me," François says, following him with the pistol. He is well out of the range of Jack's long arms, and Frost, sightless, merely sits on the deck near the mast, powerless to help.

"I did not trust you," Willem says, moving even farther toward the stern.

"Move no farther, Willem," François says. "If you try to escape overboard, I will fire without compunction."

"François," Willem says. "I fear you not. I have already been shot once by a pistol, and survived. Would you see me again produce a musketball from my mouth?"

"God will not help you this time," François says.

"We heard a pistol shot back at the wharf. Was that you?" Frost asks.

"I am afraid so," François says.

"You shot Héloïse!" Willem says.

"At great pain to my heart," François says. "I—" He stops and looks carefully at Willem. "How did you know I shot Héloïse?"

"She told me," Willem says.

François half turns at a sudden noise behind him. Too late he realizes that Willem's movement has been to make him put his back to the open hatch.

He sees Héloïse hurtling over the deck toward him, a deep red stain on her smock the evidence of Willem's subterfuge. He spins around but she is already there, launching herself at him, scratching and biting, thrashing and flailing at him. François, although bigger and stronger, is no match for her ferocity. He stumbles backward toward the stern of the ship, his knees catching on the gunwale. His arms windmill but his balance is gone and then so is he, with barely a splash to mark where he has fallen. He re-emerges, coughing and spluttering, floundering in the water. He tries to catch the dory as it passes him, but it is already out of his reach.

Héloïse snarls at him as the brigantine swiftly leaves him behind.

"Another deserter," Cambronne says, watching through his spyglass.

"Does the boat show any sign of slowing?" Napoléon asks.

"None, sire," Cambronne says.

"Then that is a clear message," Napoléon says. "And they leave us with no choice."

Baston signals the gun captain and they hear his voice clearly in the fresh coastal air. "Aim!" And a moment later, "Fire!"

Twenty guns fire simultaneously, shrouding the fortress with smoke.

The sound is the shrill whistle of wind around a loose shutter on a stormy day, but multiplied many times over. It gets louder but Jack does not flinch, nor leave the wheel. A garden of waterspouts rises into the air not far from the boat.

"Distance?" Frost asks.

"About fifty yards short, sir," Jack says. "Port bow."

The first shots are always short. Jack knows this well. His friend Wacker—who he last saw flying through the air in pieces—explained it all to him. The first shot is to estimate distance and the gunner cannot do that from an overshoot.

Willem speaks rapidly in French to the lieutenant, who nods. Willem hurries down a ladder through one of the open hatches.

"When I give the order, take us closer to shore," Frost says.

"Closer, sir?"

"They will adjust their range for our current position. I would prefer not to still be here when they next fire."

Frost is counting, mouthing numbers to himself, estimating the time of the reloading sequence.

"Now, please, Jack," he says.

Jack spins the wheel and the brigantine heels steeply as it veers to the left, just as the guns sound again. Now Frost is counting off the seconds as the cannonballs approach, with that ghostly, high-pitched whistling noise.

The volley passes over their heads. They can hear the cannonballs above the rigging, but the watery plumes that erupt from the ocean are well off to their starboard side.

"What now, sir?" Jack asks, straightening the wheel to point the bow of the boat back toward the mouth of the estuary.

"They'll expect us to move again," Frost says. "So let's stay here for the moment."

He is right, and the next volley again passes over their heads.

"Note where the splashes are," Frost says. "Imagine that as a line in the water. Head straight toward it."

Jack turns the wheel again and the boat rises up on a slight swell, dropping down as it turns. Frost is still counting under his breath.

"No, back, back now, Jack! Quick as you can," he says.

Jack spins the wheel and the boat turns again.

The crash of the cannon and the whistle of the balls is followed by another series of splashes right where the brigantine would have been, had they not turned back. Even so it is close. The balls hurtle past, just overhead, and one tears a long rip in the mainsail.

"How did you know what they would do?" Jack asks as the sharp salt spray of the water plumes drifts over the boat.

"That is what I would do," Frost says.

"When is Willem going to do . . . whatever he is going to do?" Jack asks.

"Soon, I hope," Frost says.

Jack looks around, realizing that he hasn't seen the girl for a while. To his surprise, he sees her in the dory. She must have shimmied down the towline. She is removing a tarpaulin from a series of boxes and metal troughs.

Confused, he turns back and concentrates on his steering.

"The little brigantine is jigging about like a drunken whore," the gun captain calls. "But don't worry, sir, she will not escape us."

"I will wager your life on it," Baston calls back.

The game of cat and mouse continues, but with each volley the shots are getting closer, and although the estuary mouth is wide, it is not wide enough to hide in.

"Willem," Frost calls from abovedecks.

Willem climbs the short ladder up through the hatch. His work below is finished anyway.

"Whatever you are going to do, do it now," Frost says. "They have our range and our speed. It is only good fortune that we have not yet been sunk."

"I cannot," Willem says back. "We must be clear of the headlands."

"The next volley will destroy us," Frost shouts over the roar of angry water from either side of the brigantine. Seawater rains down on them.

"Stand fast, Lieutenant, until we are clear," Willem shouts back.

Another peal of thunder from the fort and although Jack has jigged the brigantine toward shore, the balls tear great holes in the sails. Shrouds snap and the foremast explodes in a shower of wooden shards.

"Willem!" Frost shouts.

"Five hundred meters more. That's all," Willem shouts.

"We don't have that long," Frost says, but his voice is lost in the roar of more cannon.

These are different though, in both sound and direction.

"What is it? What is that?" Frost asks.

Willem looks out to sea and sees what seems at the moment to be the most beautiful sight in the world. A British ship of the line, in full sail, battle colors flying, wreathed in smoke and leaning backward from the broadside she has just delivered.

Stone shatters above Baston's head. Cannonballs ricochet off the stone floor of the fort and into the side of the observation tower. One of the great cannon is hit, smashing its carriage. Screams sound from the gunners who lie injured amid the wreckage.

Baston has flung himself over the emperor to protect him, dragging him down below the parapet, but Napoléon now pushes him away and stands back up.

"Sire!" Baston calls, but Napoléon waves him away.

"They reload, Baston. There is no danger yet," he says, raising his spyglass to his eye.

"What ship is it, sire?" Cambronne asks. His own spyglass lies shattered on the ground at his feet, dropped when the fragmented stone sprayed around the tower.

"I cannot read the name," Napoléon says. "But if my captains were as daring as hers, then it would be the French navy, not the British, that rules the channel. Look how close he brings her. Into the very mouth of the wolf."

Around them the gunners have run to the seaward-facing guns. They load and aim to meet this unexpected threat.

Still the man-o'-war sails parallel to the coast. She turns slightly toward shore to bring her guns back to bear, and again thunder and lightning ripple along her side.

Napoléon crouches, taking shelter behind the heavy stone parapet wall.

Baston ducks down also. The second broadside is a mixture of solid iron balls and explosive shells, for the impact on the walls of the fortress is not as great, but there comes a series of explosions, above, against, and in the fortress as the shells detonate. Shrapnel gouges chips out of the stone floor of the observation platform.

There is no third broadside. A glance over the parapet shows that the ship is retreating, not waiting for the return fire. She heels over, her full set of sails catching the sun. She presents only her narrow stern to the fortress, and races for the open sea.

Now the cannon of the fortress sound and a bracket of shots fall about the audacious British ship, raising plumes of water on either side of it.

"Forget the man-o'-war," Napoléon shouts. "Sink the brigantine!"

"Explosive shells!" the gun captain calls, taking his lead from the British.

The attack by the man-o'-war has bought some time for the little brigantine and she has used it well, darting out from the estuary mouth to the open sea beyond, but still within range.

Sponges dip into water buckets. Powder cartridges are rammed and spherical case shot quickly follows. Within seconds the guns lurch back on their carriages, filling the air with smoke and noise. Explosions bracket the brigantine, tearing her sails to shreds and showering her deck with hot fragments of metal.

She slows, drifting to a halt in the water, her sails and rigging in tatters.

"Now we have her," Napoléon murmurs. Already the gun crews are reloading their weapons with solid shot.

"Aim," the gun captain calls.

"The boy put up a good fight," Baston says.

"Not good enough," Cambronne says.

"Ready," comes the shout from below.

But before the guns can fire there is a sharp retort from out on the water. The dory, trailing behind the brigantine, has exploded, and a thick plume of white smoke bursts upward into a mushroom-shaped cloud. There must have been fireworks on board also, as the yellow trails of rockets are streaking up into the air.

The explosion, the plume of smoke, the rocket trails, it all happens in an instant, but in that instant the impossible happens.

The brigantine disappears.

One moment it is there, drifting slowly on the tide, without sails or rigging, then, seemingly in the blink of an eye, it is gone, vanished as if it never existed.

"Fire," comes the call from the battlements below, but the gun captain's voice holds only uncertainty.

"This is not possible," Cambronne says.

The cannonballs cut grooves in the air and make dents in the surface of the ocean where the boat had been, but air and water are their only victims. The ocean lies empty. No brigantine, no wreckage, no sign that a ship ever existed in that place.

All that remains is the low, drifting hulk of the still-burning dory, settling into the water and sinking as it drifts away on the seaward breeze.

Napoléon calls down to the gun captain. "Did you hit it?"

"I don't know, sire," comes the answer.

"Did you sink it?"

"I do not believe so, sire. There is no wreckage."

The brigantine has vanished in a waft of smoke. Dissolved into thin air before their eyes.

The silence on the battlements is matched by the silence on the observation platform.

It is finally broken by the emperor of France.

"The child is a greater conjurer than the father," Napoléon says.

SHIP OF THE LINE

The dory, now smoldering, and somehow still afloat, drifts unnoticed by the officers and soldiers on the fortress.

Nor, at that distance, can they hear the shouts that come from the figures that cling to ropes on the seaward side of the dory, out of sight of the shore.

The British sailors can hear them, however, and with impeccable seamanship the man-o'war maneuvers itself between the dory and the shore, shielding it from view. Rope netting tumbles down the seaward side of the ship and Jack grips a rung tightly with one hand, while his broken arm in its wooden splint is latched around Willem's shoulders. Lieutenant Frost also has an arm entwined in the rope ladder and a firm grip on Willem's collar.

Willem is unconscious, but breathing. For now that is all they know. He was slower than the others to dive from the brigantine and when the barrels of gunpowder exploded inside the hull, he was caught in the blast and tossed into the water.

If it was not for Jack, diving below the waves and hauling him back to the surface, he would have been lost to the currents of the ocean.

The explosives that rendered Willem unconscious also rent great holes throughout the bottom of the hull. That by itself would not have been enough. The real secret was the iron bars that filled the hold, and the hatches that were deliberately left open on the deck.

From the crack of the explosion to the top of her mast slipping below the waves, the gallant *Épaulard* took no more than two seconds to sink out of sight.

The sound of the explosions was heard clearly on the fortress, but was assumed to come from the dory, as the barrel of magicians' powder exploded simultaneously, creating the sudden and short-lived smoke cloud, that, along with the fireworks, distracted the eye just long enough for the brigantine to vanish.

On board the dory, oil in metal troughs burned fiercely, creating the impression that the dory was on fire and sinking as it drifted slowly out on the tide.

There are shouts from the deck of the warship, and the end of a rope splashes into the water, just a yard away. Frost feels for the rope and ties it around Willem's body, under his shoulders. He tugs on the rope when he is finished, and Willem quickly slides upward out of Jack's arms.

"It has been an honor to serve with you, Lieutenant, sir, if you don't mind me saying so, sir," Jack says. "We wasn't sure you'd be much chop, sir, when we first saw you arrive. You being so young and all. But you're all right, sir."

"The honor was mine, Private Sullivan," Frost says.

"Thank you, sir," Jack says. He waits for Frost to find his footing, then makes his own way up the netting as best he can with one broken arm. It is an arduous climb. Even in the light swell the ship rolls considerably from side to side. He stays below Frost, in case the young lieutenant should lose his grip and fall.

Jack climbs past gun ports, now shut, blackened around the edges by the smoke from the cannon. One gun deck is followed by another, and then a third, until finally he is at the gunwales and hands are helping him clamber over onto the deck.

Héloïse is already on board, hissing like a cat at two red-coated marines who are trying to approach her.

Willem lies on the deck, where a sailor is listening to his breathing.

The deck is wide, the boards unpolished, the masts so broad that two men could not join arms around them. This is a British ship of the line and the crew are neat in their striped uniforms.

A detail of marines approach Lieutenant Frost, muskets presented, followed by the ship's captain, in a very fine uniform, and a midshipman in a black coat and top hat.

"Good morning, sir, and welcome to the HMS *Impregnable*," the captain says.

"State your name and your rank, or risk being shot as spies," the midshipman says.

"Go easy, Evans," the captain says. "Do you not recognize a British soldier when you see one?"

"In the future, I will know one when I smell one," the midshipman says with a screw of his nose. Jack doesn't blame him. A thorough rinse in the ocean has not expunged the stench of Antwerp's sewers.

"I am Lieutenant Hunter Frost, G troop, Royal Horse Artillery, in the service of His Grace the Duke of Wellington," Frost says, saluting. "I was present at the battle near Waterloo."

"Captain Cameron Henderson, at your service," the captain says, returning the salute. "I know about the battle. The fleet evacuated the duke and much of the army yesterday."

"We have heard some shocking tales," the midshipman says. "One hopes they are greatly exaggerated."

"Unfortunately, they are probably not," Frost says.

"If they are true, then there are difficult times ahead," Captain Henderson says.

"Indeed," Frost says. "Captain, was it your ship that sailed under the guns of the fortress to engage them whilst we escaped?"

"I fear I must take the blame for that particular moment of lunacy," the captain says.

"A brave action, Captain," Frost says.

"Foolhardy, but we were lucky," the captain says, with a glance at the midshipman, and they both look up at a spar, smashed and splintered by cannon shot.

"Captain, it is a deed that will make history," Frost says. "They may well raise a statue to you in Charing Cross."

"I do not think so." The captain laughs. "It was but a minor exploit in what will be a long and bitter war."

"It may well be remembered as the action that helped us win the war," Frost says.

"You speak in riddles," the captain says. "I do not understand."

"You will," Frost says. "But for now can I ask that you put your ship in no further danger, and proceed immediately for the nearest British port."

"It is a big request from an officer of little rank," the midshipman says.

"True," Frost says. "But we have precious cargo on board."

"The girl? Or do you mean the boy we just hauled out of the sea?" the midshipman asks.

"I mean the young man who lies unconscious on your deck. Please have your ship's surgeon see to him, and pray for his continued good health," Frost says.

"He is important to you?" Captain Henderson asks.

"Captain," Frost says, "he is important to all of us."

LE PRISONNIER
DE SOIGNES

The right-side wheels of the carriage dip into a rut, throwing Cosette across into Marie Verheyen's lap. Cosette straightens herself with as much dignity as she can. Her hands are tied together, as are Willem's mother's, and she is unable to grasp the side of the carriage. Keeping her balance on the rough dirt track has been a constant battle since they entered the forest.

The entrance to the track is well concealed, and well protected by armed men standing in the shadows of the trees. The carriage traveled north from Brussels, then looped around south into the forest.

The reason for the secret route becomes clearer as they approach the remains of an old abbey, standing proud on a small hill in the deepest heart of the forest.

A wagon, loaded with supplies, is just entering the courtyard through a gate in an old, crumbling wall. They follow it through, and the gates shut behind them. Inside, the abbey is a bustling anthill of activity. Soldiers are everywhere, disguised in their gray peasant smocks.

Others in full uniform march in tight squads, or practice bayonet drills with wooden dummies.

All of the narrow stone windows of the abbey buildings are awash in laundry.

The carriage comes to a halt and an officer politely helps them down from it with a hand to their elbows, then unties the ropes that bind their wrists.

"I do not like this place," Cosette says.

"Nor I," Marie says. "But we are alive, and for that we will be thankful."

She has not yet told the girl what she saw as they left the village, nor the reason for the tolling of the church bells. There will be a time when that will have to be said, but for now it can wait.

Gaillemarde. It was a pretty little village. A happy village, despite the bickering and daily dramas that were a part of the fabric of life there. The thought of what remains there now is best pushed out of mind, lest it be too much to bear.

They are led to an arched doorway in the side of a building, and then along a corridor where a heavy wooden door is attended by two guards.

Behind the door is a bare, stone-walled room with nothing in it but two sackcloth beds and a pail for toileting. Perhaps once this was accommodation for the monks.

A square hole in the wall on either side is the only ventilation. It is too small to crawl through, should she even think of trying to escape.

"I am glad the general is not here," Cosette says. "I do not like the way he looks at me."

"Cosette, listen to me. This ordeal will end," Marie says. "Until it does, you do whatever you have to do, to survive."

"But, madame," Cosette says.

"Whatever it takes," Marie says.

The sound of movement comes from an adjacent room and a moment later a voice sounds close to the window. Another prisoner.

"Who is there?" a deep male voice asks, in accented French.

"I am the widow Verheyen, and with me is Mademoiselle

Delvaux, both of Gaillemarde," Madame Verheyen says. "Whom do I address?"

"Marie?" The voice sounds suddenly hushed.

"Maarten?" Marie collapses on the edge of the rough bed, her legs unsteady beneath her.

"It is someone you know?" Cosette asks.

In a voice no longer her own, Marie hears herself say, "It is my husband."

AUTHOR'S NOTE

My apologies to paleontologists and dinosaur enthusiasts, who will take great delight in telling me that dinosaurs could not actually survive on the modern Earth. The climate, the atmosphere, and the plant life are so vastly different now from when dinosaurs roamed the planet.

They will also tell me that the word *dinosaur* was not even coined until 1842, well after this story is set.

My apologies also to historians, who will point out that the absence of the United States of America would have had a huge effect on European affairs. In a world without America, it is unlikely that events on the other side of the world would have unfolded exactly as they did.

Putting these issues aside, I tried to make this book as historically accurate as possible. The locations, events, and many of the characters are real, and depicted as accurately as I could do within the scope of the story.

I am greatly indebted to the excellent book *The Waterloo Companion: The Complete Guide to History's Most Famous Land Battle* by Mark Adkin, which was one of my primary historical sources.

Readers who want to know more about the real history of Napoléon and Waterloo can visit the *Battlesaurus* page on my Web site: www.brianfalkner.com/battlesaurus. On this page I have listed many of the real historical figures and events, with links to information about them. I have also outlined some of the differences between *Battlesaurus* and reality and have put up some of the notes and images that I uncovered during my research.

Thanks to Adam Paylor from Crafty Fox Productions for the reenactment footage in the book trailer.

Not all of my characters are based on real people; some are purely fictional. But some of those fictional characters have the names of real people. These are the grand-prize winners of my school competitions. Congratulations to:

- Nikolas Bishop, Beaconhills College, Pakenham, Australia
- Hunter Frost, Brundrett Middle School, Port Aransas, Texas, U.S.A.
- Lachlan Grace, Remuera Intermediate, Auckland, New Zealand
- Cam Henderson, Rangiora New Life School, Rangiora, New Zealand
- Mathan Mogansondram, Onslow College, Wellington, New Zealand
- Douglas Richardson, Bowen State High School, Bowen, Australia
- Sam Roberts, Kimberley College, Brisbane, Australia
- Blake Sinclair, A. B. Paterson College, Gold Coast, Australia
- Jack Sullivan, Brisbane Grammar School, Brisbane, Australia
- Dylan Townshend, Albany Junior High School, Auckland, New Zealand
- Harry Wacker, Nudgee Junior College, Brisbane, Australia

- Dylan Wenzel-Halls, Silkstone State School, Ipswich, Australia
- Ben Wood, Brisbane Grammar School, Brisbane, Australia
- Lewis Wood, St. Peters School, Cambridge, New Zealand

And a special thanks to:

Sofie Thielemans, Somerset College, Gold Coast, Australia